RAVES FOR DENNIS HENSLEY

"How hip can you get? *Misadventures in the (213)* is packed with the obscure, commercial-quoting brand of humor pop culture buffs will adore and usurp for themselves. This is a hilarious, celebrity-skewering romp through L.A."—*The St. Petersburg Times*

"Truly outstanding . . . A wild, witty, name-dropping, sexy romp through the streets of Los Angeles, *Misadventures* takes aim at a lot of targets—and hits the bull's-eye with almost every one. This is one of the best, insightful Hollywood coming-of-age novels ever penned . . . Hensley knows L.A. like the back of Angelyne's hand . . . Don't miss *Misadventures in the (213)*."

—barnesandnoble.com

"Very sharp, very funny . . . The great pleasure of this book comes from its superior comic writing." —*The Advocate*

"A worthy fix for beach-bound television junkies."—*New York Post*

"Caviar for those who soak up glitterprint." —*Kirkus Reviews*

"Hensley's enthusiasm is a welcome relief from the downer pose that often passes for Gen-X profundity." —*San Francisco Chronicle*

"*Misadventures in the (213)* paints a picture of life in L.A. that is both bizarre and true to life, thanks to Hensley's unique insider perspective. It's a fluffy, sugar-dusted, chocolate-dipped dessert of a novel with a cherry on the top, and if you have a sense of humor and an open mind, its charms are irresistible."

—Amazon.com

"The perfect Hollywood novel." —*Lambda Book Report*

"The dizzingly fast-paced farce is a pop culture panacea."

—*Paper Magazine*

"*Tales of the City of Angels* meets *Entertainment Tonight* on ecstasy."

—*H/X Magazine*

MISADVENTURES

IN THE (213)

DENNIS HENSLEY

ROB WEISBACH BOOKS
WILLIAM MORROW AND COMPANY, INC. • NEW YORK

Published by Rob Weisbach Books
An Imprint of William Morrow and Company, Inc.
1350 Avenue of the Americas, New York, N.Y. 10019

www.robweisbachbooks.com

The Library of Congress has cataloged a previous edition of this title.

Library of Congress Cataloging-in-Publication Data
Hensley, Dennis.
Misadventures in the (213) / Dennis Hensley.—1st ed.
p. cm.
ISBN 0-688-15452-2 (alk. paper)
I. Title.
PS3558.E543M5 1998
813'.54—dc21 98-4990
CIP

Paperback ISBN 0-688-17128-1

Printed in the United States of America

First Paperback Edition

1 2 3 4 5 6 7 8 9 10

BOOK DESIGN BY FRITZ

www.misadventures.com

MISADVENTURES IN THE (213)

1

My biggest fear has always been that if my life were to pass before my eyes during a moment of life-threatening duress, it would be rated PG. Now that it's happening—with a furious sixtyish redhead in a floral jumpsuit named Loretta aiming a shotgun at my palpitating chest—I decide I might as well go for a PG-13 and swear a little.

"Oh fuck," I gasp.

"It's all your fault!" Loretta hisses. "And now you're going to pay."

A part of me always knew this day might come. I've been an assistant cruise director for Empress Cruise Lines for nearly five years and, as such, part of my job is to hand a loaded trapshooting shotgun to passengers who can't even control their own bladders. An accident seemed inevitable. But this is no accident. This woman wants me *dead*.

I catch the eye of my fellow assistant cruise director, Mitch, who gives me an I'm-going-for-help look, then disappears inside.

"What's my fault?" I stammer, trying to stall for time.

"Don't play dumb with me," Loretta growls, as she circles the gun around, causing everyone here on the Aloha Deck to do what might best be described as the opposite of the Wave. When she finishes, she returns the business end of the shotgun back to me. I watch in frozen horror as her wrinkled trigger finger starts to contract and I entertain my last hope: that after I'm gone, Valerie Bertinelli might be willing to cut her hair and play me in the TV movie.

"Prepare to die," Loretta says.

"No . . . no . . . no . . ." I cry.

"Well, then we also have nice tortellini."

I slam open my eyes to see the perplexed face of a redheaded woman, but this one's young and not nearly so unfoxy. And she's *not* wielding a gun.

"That's fine," I say.

The flight attendant slides over my pasta dinner and moves on to the next row.

"Are you okay?" asks the blond housewife type sitting next to me. "I think you were having a nightmare."

"Yeah, I was," I respond, in regards to what in the last four months has become my version of a recurring Vietnam flashback. "But I'm fine."

"Are you from Phoenix?" she says, referring to our destination.

"No, but I went to college at Arizona State," I say between bites. I'm actually from a small town in northern Arizona called Holbrook. Though geographically qualified, Holbrook was left out of the song "Route 66," a fact that I've always resented. Perhaps there were just no kicks to be gotten there.

"Wow! I work at ASU," says the woman excitedly. "My name's Rhonda Whiting."

"Craig Clybourn," I say with a smile so forced that I might just as well be back on the Lido Deck emceeing a limbo contest to Buster Poindexter's "Hot Hot Hot."

After our dinner trays are cleared Rhonda decides she wants to show me pictures of her adorable spawn. I ooh and aah politely, then start digging in the seat pocket in front of me, hoping to find something to read or inject.

"What did you study at ASU?" she asks.

"Broadcasting," I say as unenthusiastically as whenever someone asked me that question at the time. It wasn't that I didn't have any interest in broadcasting. Quite the contrary. But at the time, planning for my future took a backseat to going to movies, hanging around with my friends from the theater department and playing bass in my roommate Ulysses's garage band.

"Where do you live?" Rhonda asks as I thumb through a left-behind copy of *Star* magazine I was lucky enough to find behind the barf bag.

"Phoenix now, I guess, but I'm moving to L.A.," I say before glancing down to the tabloid and noticing a familiar face. *With this woman here,* I nearly add.

There, under the headline "Would You Be Caught Dead in This Outfit?" is my best friend since college, Dandy Rio. Sporting plaid bellbottoms, a crochet top that even on the page reeks of thrift store, and a big fuck-you smile, Dandy seems to be replying, "You're damn right I would."

I smile when I recall the day Dandy and I met back at ASU. It was at the first rehearsal for the theater department's spring '88 production of that old toe-tapper *Anything Goes,* in which Dandy and I were partnered together in the chorus. Looking like a brunette Ann-Margret circa *Viva Las Vegas* in black tights and a clingy fuchsia sweater, Dandy burst into the room with such panache that I could practically see the cartoon thought bubble that appeared over the threatened lead actress's head, which read, "Who does this bitch think she is?"

"Do my tits look big in this sweater?" was the first thing Dandy ever said to me.

"Do you want them to?" I replied.

"Of course," she answered.

After rehearsal, we went to 7-Eleven for a Slurpee and while we were checking out, Dandy picked up the *Star,* opened it to the "Would You Be Caught Dead" spread and said, without a trace of irony, "Someday, Craig, that's going to be me."

Since then, Dandy's been caught dead more times than I can count.

"She's on my show," Rhonda says, imbedding a Lee Press-On nail into Dandy's forehead. "I can't stand her."

"Rhonda's show" must be *Lifestream,* the daytime drama that Dandy's been on for nearly six years doing double duty as twins Nola and Manohla Hughes. Dandy's big break came via Milt Greene, a smarmy New York agent whom Dandy endeared herself to on one of his annual talent scouting visits to ASU. Perhaps *endeared* is the wrong word. A better word might be, um, *blackmailed,* since Milt had nothing but malice for the would-be starlet until the moment when, in a last ditch attempt to get him to give Dandy's monologue a listen, we caught the Star Searcher banging some blond business major in the bathroom at Sky Harbor Airport. Dandy agreed that she wouldn't tell Milt's actress wife about the indiscretion if Milt would represent her in New York for six months. Five and half months later, Dandy landed the gig on *Lifestream.* The day after that, she changed agents.

The last time I saw Dandy was nearly four months ago. She and a handful of her photogenic cast mates had come on board the *Regal Empress* to shoot a few scenes and sign a few autographs as part of a special *Lifestream Takes to the Ocean* cruise. It was on the day she arrived, while strolling down a cobblestone street in Old San Juan, that Dandy announced she was leaving *Lifestream* to move to L.A. and star in her own sitcom.

"The network guys like it when I do funny stuff on the show," she chirped. "They want the sitcom to be ready in time to be a midseason replacement. You have to come out there with me, Craig." Dandy flashed me a mischievous smile, then shouted, "Cocksucker!" before disappearing into a gift shop.

It wasn't until a few seconds later that I realized Dandy wasn't calling into question my murky sexuality, but giving the appalled tourist couple videotaping a few feet away a nice audio souvenir. It was a pastime we'd indulge in repeatedly over the next ten days.

"Do you have a girlfriend?" wonders Rhonda.

"Not anymore," I shrug, as though the only girlfriend I ever had didn't dump me my sophomore year at ASU.

After two semesters of cohabitative bliss, would-be ballerina Michelle Lee (not the one from *Knots Landing,* the one from hell), ran off with the hirsute hoofer who played Rum Tum Tugger in the touring company of *Cats*. Hence Dandy's nickname for her, "The Catfucker."

"Single, huh?" says Rhonda. "I should introduce you to some of the gals I work with."

I beat a hasty retreat to the can and when I return, Rhonda's fast asleep and drooling onto the *Star*. She doesn't come to again until we're on the ground. As we file off the plane, she offers to give me a ride to my aunt's house in Tempe, in lieu of the Supershuttle I had originally planned to take.

"I may not need a ride after all," I say delightedly, as we clear the gate and I notice a sign poking up from the awaiting crowd that reads VANILLA ICE.

"What are you doing here?" I say to the bearer of the sign.

"I wanted to make sure you didn't chicken out about coming to L.A.," says Dandy, before slapping me on the forehead with the sign and giving me a hug.

We're about to make our way to baggage claim when I notice Rhonda shuffling by with her brood. Recalling my row partner's distaste for the two-dimensional Dandy, I'm curious to see how she'll react to her in 3-D.

"Rhonda," I call. "I want you to meet my best friend."

"Oh my God," she says, dumping her two-year-old onto the ground. "I watch your show every day."

I smile as Dandy scrawls Rhonda an autograph, knowing that she's recently taken to writing, "If you don't love me, I'm sorry," a salutation she ripped off from the porn star Savannah, confident (perhaps erroneously) that the pair have no fans in common.

While we wait for my bags to tumble out, Dandy grabs the *Star* from my carry-on and regards the cover photo of Pamela Anderson and Tommy Lee walking through an airport and grimacing.

"It looks like she just farted and he's smelling it," I observe.

"Smelt it," Dandy says flicking her middle finger at Tommy. "Dealt it," she adds, flicking Pam.

On the way to Dandy's hotel, we stop at the Dairy Queen on Mill Avenue.

"Look who's here," says a voice from behind us.

Dandy and I turn around to discover Troy Mendell. Troy was the director's kiss-ass assistant when Dandy and I were in *Anything Goes*. He wore T-shirts with slogans like TRIPLE THREAT and GOTTA DANCE on them and had the major hots for Dandy. When she failed to return his affections, Troy proceeded to boss us around like we were some kind of troublemakers or something.

"How's the Big Apple treating you?" Troy asks.

"Actually, I'm moving to L.A.," says Dandy. "I'm going to be starring on my own sitcom."

"And I'm going to be starring on my own couch," I say before excusing myself to go phone my aunt to tell her I won't be staying there tonight after all. When I return and report that the pay phone is broken, Troy invites me to use the one at his computer showroom across the street.

"You can't bring that in here," he says as we approach the door to Mendell's Megabytes. "It'll drip all over the place."

"Okay, Dandy, I guess I'll call you later," I say.

"I meant the *ice cream,*" Troy clarifies, as unamused as I've ever seen him, and I've seen him plenty unamused.

Later, Dandy and I are sprawled on her hotel bed watching scrambled soft-porn movies and making fun of Troy when Dandy pulls a photo out of my organizer and says, "Who's this cute stuff?"

"His name is Sergio," I say of the curly-headed Italian posing with me in front of a waterfall in Martinique. "He's from Italy and he worked in the galley. He joined the ship the cruise after you got off. Nice guy. Greenest eyes you've ever seen."

"Is he seeing anybody?"

"Sort of," I say before steeling myself for the big bomb. "Me."

I don't know how I expect Dandy to react to this news—tears, a high five followed by a declaration of "It's about time," the vapors—all of the above seem possible.

"Can I watch sometime?" she asks.

Though that wasn't on my list of predictions I think I like it best of all.

"Well, I doubt I'll ever see him again," I say. "But if I do, you're welcome to hide in the closet."

"*Somebody's* got to, apparently," she laughs.

I spend the next three and a half hours giving Dandy every juicy detail of my first consummated crush since the Catfucker.

"So you're officially into men now?" Dandy asks with as much matter-of-factness as she can muster.

"I guess," I say, before killing the light. "Should I send out a press release or something?"

"Nah," she mutters into her pillow. "Just get a few T-shirts printed."

"HOMO," I say as though I'm reading it off a marquee.

"And an I'M WITH HOMO for me."

The next morning, we hop in our rented Blazer and drive to my aunt's house to retrieve the few belongings she's been nice enough to store for the last five years. A half hour later, we're on our way to Los Angeles, with me behind the wheel and Dandy fingering my bass guitar in the passenger seat.

"So how's the screenplay going?" she asks.

"It's going," I say before letting out a yawn.

"It better be."

I hand the driving duties off to Dandy after we pass the state line, then lean back and close my eyes.

"*What's* my fault?" I scream as Loretta waves the shotgun in front of me in a devil-may-care figure eight.

"Manohla's leaving Willow Springs," she screams, "and it's all your fault."

Manohla is Dandy's good-girl character on *Lifestream,* which Loretta apparently has a problem differentiating from reality. Though Dandy's exodus from the show hasn't been officially announced, rumors of it have been circulating on the ship for days. Granted, most die-hard fans would hate to see Nola and Manohla get written out, but Loretta's the only one who thinks pulling a gun on Dandy's best friend might keep it from happening.

"No . . . no . . . you don't want to do this," I say.

"Oh, yes I do," she says caressing the trigger.

I'm sweating through my polo shirt and preparing to meet my maker, when suddenly I hear the voice of my best friend booming over the ship's loudspeaker.

"This is Nola Hughes," Dandy says firmly. "Put down the gun. . . ."

Loretta gasps as though she's seen a ghost. Without lowering the gun, she tilts her face up to the speaker like an *X-Files* extra being beckoned by her mother ship. Dandy, in what could be the best acting of her life, conjures the kittenish Southern drawl she employs as Nola, the baddest girl in Willow Springs, and says, "Put down the gun or I'll come to your house and poison you in your sleep, just like I did to Sonny. . . ."

As Dandy continues to threaten her, Loretta becomes more and more confused and distracted. I can see the gun lowering one centimeter at a time. Just as it bows enough to avoid hitting me, should it go off, a blur in a white tank top tackles the polyester-clad terrorist from the back, sending the gun hurling into the air and over the side of the ship.

With Dandy still going for the daytime Emmy, I look down and see her cute but nerdy costar, Andrew Ormiston, untangling himself from the deranged redhead.

"What a *wacko*," I say to no one in particular.

"What are you talking about?" says Dandy.

I open my eyes and discover that Dandy's voice is coming not from a ship intercom but from the driver's seat across from me.

"I had that dream again about your crazy fan," I sigh.

"Forget it," Dandy says. "You'll be having lots of exciting new dreams soon enough."

I look outside and notice that it's evening. Our vehicle is one of a gazillion parked in rows of four and winding like polka-dot serpentines into the distance. The skyscrapers from *L.A. Law* loom on the horizon.

"We're not moving," I say.

"Welcome to Los Angeles," says Dandy.

2

EXT. LIDO DECK VERANDA - NIGHT

KESSLER, bloody and dying, stumbles out of the cabin onto his private veranda and collapses onto a deck chair. MIRANDA follows. She hurls the smoking gun over the ship's side.

CUT TO:

EXT. ATLANTIC OCEAN - CONT.

From underwater, we see the gun enter the water and descend leaving a trail of bubbles. Then KESSLER's dead body splashes into the frame and bobs there, his eyes open in catatonic terror.

CUT TO:

EXT. LIDO DECK VERANDA - CONT.

MIRANDA reclines on the deck chair, spent but satisfied. She notices a tiny drop of blood on the deck, scowls, then opens up the silver briefcase and dabs it up with a hundred-dollar bill. That's better.

FADE OUT.

Have there ever been two words more delicious to type than *Fade Out*? I suppose *The End* could reap a similar euphoria, or maybe *Fin,* if you were French or something. For my money, it doesn't get much better than *Fade Out,* primarily because I never thought I'd live to type it at all—at least not deservedly—two thirds of the way down the 117th page of my first screenplay.

So it's official. I'm a Hollywood cliché: the new kid on the cul-de-sac with a script to schmooze. I hit ctrl-S, and *Deck Games,* a Craig Clybourn masterpiece, becomes a magnetically recorded reality.

Fed up with hearing me drone on about how I was going to become Hollywood's next literary boy wonder if only I could find a decent pencil, Dandy presented me with a laptop computer as she disembarked the *Regal Empress* four months ago. On the outside cover in red Sharpee, she had written, "Write the fucker and shut up," a salutation I've had to explain to countless fellow coffee-house customers. What I can't seem to stop smiling about is the fact that I did. Sure, my attempt at film noir on water may not shine quite as brightly as Merrill Stubing's chrome dome, but the fact is, *Deck Games* exists, and it didn't a few months ago.

Since I arrived in Los Angeles two weeks ago, I've been crashing at Dandy's rented Beachwood Canyon house, a hillside sixties affair with enough avocado Formica to choke both Nanny *and* the Professor. Her back balcony offers a spectacular view of Hollywood, with the Capitol Building ("The Steel Tampon," as Dandy calls it) as its centerpiece. From her front porch, you can look up and see Madonna's red-and-gold striped Castillo del Lago. One of these days, while Dandy's at work, I want to go out on her white roof with a bucket of red paint and write, "Sean Never Loved You." Just for laughs.

I've been putting off finding my own place until the first draft of *Deck Games* was finished, and it's worked out fine because Dandy is usually at the studio working on *That's Just Dandy*. Though the executive producer, Len Field, likes to take credit for the title, it's an expression that everyone from Dandy's parents to the editors at *Soap Opera Weekly* have worked into the ground. The scenario, last I checked, revolves around a mischief-making but basically good-hearted Brooklyn high school senior (Dandy), who moves in with her uptight suburban aunt and uncle and their three uptight kids in Denver after her hipster single mother buys the farm. Mayhem ensues, lessons are learned, and hugs exchanged all around: your basic mouthy-babe-out-of-water story. I consider the fact that, at twenty-six, Dandy still passes for a teenager is a good sign: proof positive that anything is possible in this kooky town.

Dandy figures that once the show hits its stride, she can get me a job as a staff writer provided I deliver some spiffy spec scripts from which the producers can discern my abilities. I'd pledged to get to it after I finished *Deck Games,* but now that that time has arrived, I can't seem to muster much enthusiasm for the project, or for the sitcom form in general. The one spec idea I do have, for a *Frasier* episode in which the two Crane brothers get drunk and measure their dicks, seems too cutting edge for the family hour, though everyone I've run it by said they'd tune in to see it.

Still reeling from the completion of *DG,* I decide to start the apartment hunt while I'm on a roll. I hop in my '91 aquamarine pearl Celica, the car I bought used the first week I moved here, and head to 7-Eleven to pick up a *Recycler*. Then I return home to call the only person I know in L.A. besides Dandy, Miles Tujunga.

I met Miles on the *Regal Empress*. He was the Hollywood publicist sent to cater to every unreasonable need of the *Lifestream* contingent during that special cruise a few months ago, and one of the first people I told about my possible move to L.A.

"Oh, I love L.A.," the twenty-seven-year-old flack gushed over lunch at the Lido Buffet. "You've got the mountains, you've got the ocean, you've got the desert. Not that I ever go to any of these places, but it's nice to know they're there."

"What about the people?" I asked. "I mean, I'm sort of used to a small-town mentality."

"There are some jerks," he said coolly, "like my boss. But there are a lot of nice people too." He took a swig of iced tea and then added, "You know, I'm pretty small-town myself, but with an edge."

Miles was the first person I'd ever heard assign himself an edge.

The best Miles moment to date occurred the next afternoon while I was officiating at a session of trapshooting on the Aloha Deck. I had just handed the shotgun to Andrew Ormiston, Dandy's babilicious love interest on *Lifestream,* stepped back, and like everyone else in a two-block radius, covered my ears. As Andrew growled, "Pull!" to my coworker Mitch, I noticed that Miles was completely engrossed in his clipboard and had neglected to cover his ears. When the gun went off with a deafening blam, my new friend not only jumped out of his skin, but for all intents and purposes, he jumped out of his skin *and* did a number from *Gypsy*. Though his unmistakable queen-out lasted barely two seconds, its magnitude on the sissy meter provided me with something to hold over him for the rest of his life. Actually, though, it made me like Miles even more. We both knew then that no matter how much of a Jag-drivin', Cannes-goin', personal-trainer-havin' player he became, one unanticipated bang and he'd be right back on the junior high playground unable to catch a ball.

"Where's Sepulveda?" I say to Miles over the phone as I run my finger over the various listings.

"It's on the west side," he says dismissively before correcting my pronunciation of Sepulveda. "You want to stay in the 213, right?"

"Well, both you and Dandy are in the 213, so yeah. Where's Los Feliz?"

"About ten minutes from Dandy's," he says before correcting my pronunciation of Los Feliz. "It's kind of like my neighborhood"—Miles lives off Beverly by CBS—"but with less of an edge."

As I drive to the first of the apartments I've arranged to visit, my trusty new Thomas Guide riding shotgun, I decide to behave as though finding an apartment is as easy a proposition as mailing a letter or scoring some smack. It's only going to be a nightmare if I *make* it a nightmare. I breeze cheerfully through two apartments—both complete dumps—before arriving at a ground-floor single in an old-fashioned building on Cumberland.

With a stagnant swimming pool and ivy-covered stucco walls, the place reminds me of a low-rent Melrose Place, a definite plus. The only things missing, I think, as I stick my finger in the jaundiced pool for a temperature reading, are the ill-advised affairs and bad line readings.

"Of course I love you, baby," I hear a man's voice say gruffly from a second-floor window. "Would I be here if I didn't?"

Take back what I said about the affairs and the line readings.

I'm knocking on the landlord's door when a tall, hangdoggedly handsome guy in his late twenties bounds down the stairs with a Rice Krispies Treat in his mouth, reminding me that I haven't eaten today.

"You have to pound really hard," he says, in the same groggy voice I just heard coming from upstairs. "She's practically deaf."

After thudding on the door loudly enough to wake Sunny Von Bulow, the guy darts off, leaving me to take the rap for the door abuse (assuming it did the trick). After about a minute, the door opens a crack and a lone bifocal peers out.

"I'm Craig," I say. "I understand you have an apartment for rent."

"Are you a smoker? Pet owner? Dope fiend?" an older woman's voice snaps.

"No, no, and no," I say.

The woman opens the door and smiles warmly, as though the dope fiend question left her fresh out of malice. She tells me her name is Viola McGowan, then leads me next door to the available unit. Employing the gestures and theatricality of a geriatric Carol Merrill, Viola shows off the pad. It's cleanish and has a certain charm, what with its 1940s moldings, hardwood floors, and a patio off the kitchen where I can imagine myself typing away and enjoying a nice beverage. I'm one positive omen away from starting the paperwork when a plate of Rice Krispies Treats passes through the front door carried by a woman I assume to be their maker.

"Treat, anyone?" says a bottom-heavy, thirty-something woman with Elayne Boosler hair. There's my last omen.

As I sit by the pool filling out my application, the treat maker, who introduces herself as Claudia Newton, takes a seat across from me and begins telling me about herself. My Hollywood Cliché Quotient increases threefold when I learn that she's an aspiring actress who makes just enough money waiting tables to keep her in headshots and mini-marshmallows.

"My big goal is to mount my own one-woman show by the time I'm forty," she says emphatically.

"How old are you now?" I ask.

"Thirty-two," she says, "so I have time."

I come to learn that the gruff-voiced door batterer I met earlier is Cliff, Claudia's boyfriend of "two years and eleven and a half months." They met in acting class, she explains, and ended up making love for the first time when a scene study they were doing from *A Streetcar Named Desire* went a little too far.

"It was amazing how much it informed the work, Craig," Claudia gushes. "I really had a breakthrough that night."

"I'm sure you did," I say.

Later that night, I'm at Dandy's when I get the call from Viola that her son, Ernie, who lives in the Valley but checks out all potential renters, was dubious about my current state of employment. Though I had arranged for a friend at Empress Cruises to confirm I worked there, Ernie apparently got through to the wrong person and was told that I left the company a few weeks ago. I have enough money saved to last a few months, so the chances of me being a deadbeat tenant are slim, but Viola is still concerned.

"Let's go down there," Dandy says when I express my anxiety. "I'll tell them you work on my show."

We jump in the Celica, head down to Viola's, and explain to Ernie that I am, in fact, gainfully employed on Dandy's TV show.

"What show?" says Ernie after letting us in. "I don't watch TV and neither does Ma."

I look at Dandy just in time to catch the last half of her eye-roll. Ever since *Lifestream,* Dandy is constantly running into people who, in order to come off as nonplused, say they don't watch TV.

Ernie shrugs and says, "There's nothing I can do. You lied on your application. I don't want my ma living next to a liar."

"That's because I'm kind of shy about working in television," I counter. "When people find out I'm the star writer on *That's Just Dandy,* why, they just never leave me alone."

I can't believe I just used the word *why* in the middle of a sentence like that. It's the kind of phony affectation that makes a lie detector pen leap off the paper.

"I don't care what show you're on," Ernie says. "We don't watch TV."

"We *got* that," snaps Dandy, grabbing Viola's suspiciously well-worn remote and aiming it at the twenty-seven-inch screen they never watch.

"That's you!" chirps Viola, pointing to the tube while the opening credits of *That's Just Dandy* unfurl. Talk about perfect timing.

Viola sits in her chair and stares at the screen, riveted. I get the feeling Ernie's about to ask us to leave when his mother hisses, "Son, shhh!" so he takes a seat on the couch and settles in.

After about ten minutes, it becomes obvious that whether or not I get this apartment is going to be determined by how much Viola and Ernie enjoy tonight's installment of *That's Just Dandy*. My trepidation doubles when I realize that this week's show is the "very special" date-rape episode, wherein Dandy's wrestling-star prom date wants to go further than Dandy does. Now *there's* a first. Luckily, the B-story—Dandy's bratty eight-year-old cousin loses the class salamander in the house—isn't such a downer.

During what must be the longest half hour of my life, I only look at Dandy twice because her frozen expression of mortification and boredom—as she fingers an afghan that looks like a reject from the *Roseanne* set—is just too much to bear.

By the time the salamander's discovered in the one place Dandy wouldn't allow her beau to go (her pants), Viola's out cold. Remarkably, not only is Ernie awake but, unless I'm hallucinating, he actually seems to be dabbing at his eyes. Without saying a word, he walks to the kitchen and returns with the keys to my new apartment.

"Thanks," I say. "You won't regret it."

Ernie sniffles and chokes out the words, "You wrote that?"

"Well, yeah," I say. "I just sort of knocked it out."

"That was beautiful, man."

3

It seems somehow perfect that the first piece of mail I get at my swingin' new bachelor pad is a letter from Sergio. Though its contents are for the most part mundane—not surprising since he had to get a friend to translate—I find myself reading it over and over. I'm surprised at how much I miss the guy. I kind of thought I'd get to Los Angeles and get so tangled up in the tinsel that my tryst with the Sardinian, tender as it was, would reassign itself to a less prominent place in my memory. Hasn't happened yet.

The second piece of mail is from Miles, who's throwing a 1980s party to celebrate his twenty-eighth birthday. The invitation features his over-tanned head computer-manipulated onto Jennifer Beals's nubile bod from the *Flashdance* poster. Although he looks as if at any moment he might happily reach into his off-the-shoulder sweatshirt and remove his own bra, does he really expect the rest of us to dress up? As Claudia puts it when I run up to show her, "If you dress eighties, people won't know whether you're adhering to the theme or just have really bad taste. It's just too soon." I have a feeling she's right.

Claudia claims she'd love nothing more than to squeeze into her old Gloria Vanderbilts and live out her Sue-Ellen-Ewing-on-a-nymphomaniacal-booze-bender fantasy, but unfortunately for Linda Gray lovers everywhere, Claudia's already spoken for on the night in question. Cliff has promised to whisk her off to Big Bear to celebrate their third anniversary.

"There's going to be a bearskin rug, Craig," she brags. "Like from a real bear."

"I hope the three of you have a wonderful time," I say, smarting a bit from my lack of romantic entanglements.

The next day, I call Miles from the office of Jupiter Filmworks, the production company I've been sent to on my first day as a temp.

"It's only twelve-thirty," I whisper excitedly into the pay phone, "and I've already managed to Xerox thirteen copies of *Deck Games*."

"That's always how it starts," Miles sighs. "First it's free Xeroxing, and before you know it you're smuggling out a three-hole punch in your ass."

"So, are there going to be industry people at this party?" I ask.

"Tons," Miles replies. "And if you're lucky, that decadent eighties spirit might fool people into thinking they have money to blow on a fresh, up-and-coming—oh, why don't I just say it—*genius* like yourself."

"Miles, you haven't even read it yet."

"I haven't?" he says sounding distracted. "I thought I had. Well, I'm sure it's amazing."

The night of the party arrives and I'm still bankrupt in the costume-idea department. I'm thinking of telling people I'm the lead singer of Men Without Hats, knowing that no one will be able to prove otherwise, when Dandy arrives with two white T-shirts.

"Put this on, Craig," she says, tossing one my way. The white cotton unfurls in the air, revealing giant black letters that read CHOOSE LIFE. "We're going as the Whams!"

We both get hysterical as we recall a videotape I own in which Phyllis George concludes her interview with the duo by saying, "Ladies and gentlemen, the Whams." That moment in 1985 was when I first began to distrust the media.

While we synchronize our "I'm Your Man" finger snaps in the mirror, Dandy announces that she wants to be Andrew Ridgeley because it'll give her a chance to reexperience anonymity. "It's fitting I go as George Michael," I say as we hop in Dandy's red Miata, "because all I've really done in the last five years is take chances with my hair and complain."

Since Dandy's terrorized at the prospect of being a celebrity who shows up too early to a Hollywood soiree, we've planned to get there just past fashionably late. Dandy's particularly paranoid going into this event because in a recent interview with *TV Guide*, she told the reporter she was twenty. As in two, zero. In reality, Dandy's twenty-six, two years younger than me, and remembers far more about the eighties than she'll admit tonight.

Once inside, we head straight for the libations, sideswiping two hardbodies with blond shags and headbands who appear to be fighting over a jump rope.

"What every party needs," Dandy whispers. "Dueling Olivia Newton-Johns."

Just then, Miles, in full Stevie Nicks regalia, rushes up and shouts out, "You guys are just in time. We're going to have fun tonight! We're going to Wang Chung tonight!"

"I don't have to Wang Chung if I don't want to," Dandy announces, stomping her foot.

"Can't Wang Chunging be optional?" I beg.

"Fine, fine," Miles drones. "Amazing shirts, you two. And Dandy, kudos on that date-rape episode. I smell Emmy."

I smell mothballs. Must be the Stevie shawl.

"Hey!" Miles continues. "You two are just in time for eighties Name That Tune."

"Only if you spin for us," I insist.

Miles obliges, whirling his fringe and chanting, "Stand back, stand back," then turns on one platform-heeled boot and leads us to the dance floor. Dandy and I join a semicircle of party guests as a floppy-tressed stud in black parachute pants and Miles's hairdresser, Irene—in head-to-toe acid wash—compete for a Nagel print.

"Miles says that guy was a *Playgirl* centerfold," Dandy whispers.

"Really?" I say. "I would have thought rocket science was more his bag."

Our chatter is interrupted when the unmistakable intro to Hall and Oates's "Maneater" starts to play. Dandy grabs my hand as though it's all she can do not to straddle the clueless centerfold and answer for him. The moment is particularly poignant because I've always told Dandy that "Maneater" should be her anthem, the song they'd have to play during her *Star Search* video photo session.

With Irene one point away from victory, Miles cues the next song. Dandy lets out a frustrated groan, then cranks up the juice of her hand squeeze considerably.

" 'Turn Around Bright Eyes'?" the model guesses.

" 'Total Eclipse of the Heart,' you idiot!" Dandy screams. Everyone in the room turns to look at us. There's an interminable silence, which is finally broken when Miles says, "Dandy, I thought Bonnie Tyler was before your time."

Dandy squeezes my hand even harder and then, in a pathetic attempt to cover her ass, says, "She's my grandmother."

"I hope that grandmother comment doesn't come back to haunt you," I say to her an hour later when we meet up back by the bathrooms.

"No one cares, Craig," she says dismissively before handing me her keys. "You can take my car home. I'm going home with Darren."

"The guy in the parachute pants that you called an idiot?"

"Geronimo!" says Dandy.

With the keys to her Miata in my pocket, and Dandy off giving Derwood a ride in her *other* Little Red Love Machine, I don't know whether to hang at the party or go home and return to the nineties. Before I can decide, I'm cajoled into taking part in a game of Pin the Dexatrim in Lisa Welchel's Mouth, which nets me a fetching backpack from *Breakin' 2: Electric Boogaloo*. I take that as a sign to quit while I'm ahead, and head off in search of Miles.

"Happy birthday, Stevie," I say, before giving my host a hug and making like a white-winged dove.

I get home to find a red-wigged Claudia passed out drunk on the steps between our apartments, bedecked in a half-assed, last minute attempt at Cyndi Lauper drag. Her breath is practically toxic and her face streaked with tears, proving that just because girls wanna have fun doesn't mean they always get to.

"I went to the Dresden," she says after I revive her, "but you weren't there."

"It was *across* from the Dresden," I say.

"Just my luck," says Claudia sadly.

She goes on to blubber through the woeful tale of how Cliff stood her up without so much as a phone call. Not wanting her to be alone in her misery, I invite her to crash on my couch.

"Are you sure?" she says. "You don't really know me that well."

"What are you going to do, steal my laptop?"

"I can't type," she says pathetically, then laughs for the first time in hours.

"Doesn't seeing me like this make you glad you're single?" she asks as we make up the couch.

"No," I say. "If you need anything, wake me up."

"Before I go-go," Claudia says with a tear-stained smile.

Given the periodic sobbing coming from the front room, it takes me awhile to fall asleep. When I finally do, I dream that Huey Lewis is burying me in the sand and Laura Branigan is laughing about it.

I'm awakened the next morning by Dandy, calling to report from Derwood's Pacific Palisades guest house.

"Did you pull the ripcord?" I ask, as if there's any question.

"Not exactly," Dandy sighs. "We didn't have any protection and didn't feel like going to get any. He made waffles and we looked through his telescope."

"Oh, so he's a peeping Tom too?"

"No, he's a rocket scientist," Dandy says warmly, as though he's entangled in her limbs as we speak. "And he makes a mean blueberry waffle."

4

Not surprisingly, Dandy's interaction with the rocket scientist fails to really blast off. She figures it's probably for the best, however, considering that her growing infatuation with one of the writers on her show—a certain Houston transplant named Kyle McKeever—is reaching fever pitch. Why else would she insist on dragging me to Lloyd's Cantina and Boot Shine in outermost Burbank to try and bone up on Kyle's favorite pastime, country line dancing?

"This is the kind of dive," I say as we scuffle across the sawdust-covered floor, "where a Jodie Foster character would get sexually harassed."

"Why do you think we're here?" Dandy replies.

"I don't get why you're so crazy about this guy," I say as we saddle on up to the bar. "He looks like someone who's seen all *The Gambler* movies."

"He wrote the last two, F.Y.I.," she retorts. "I just think he's dreamy, like the way his Wranglers are faded in all the right places. Plus, he wrote my favorite episode."

"The one where you get sent to detention for bad grades?" I ask.

"*D Is Not for Dandy,*" she says, practically swooning. In her just-bought red satin cowgirl shirt, baggy 501s, and motorcycle boots, Dandy looks like Shannen Doherty if she had been born a Mandrell. "I mean, the guy's been putting words in my mouth for the past two months . . ."

"So why should he stop there?" I say.

"Exactly."

"Because he's engaged maybe?" I suggest, knowing full well that a ring on a man's finger has never served as anything but an aphrodisiac to Dandy "Always the Homewrecker, Never the Bride" Rio.

I spend the next hour and a half trying to boot-scoot in my Hush Puppies while avoiding the "Who the hell are you, city boy?" glares of the Lloyd's regulars. Finally, I throw in the bandanna, opting instead to down a few complimentary hot dogs and listen in wonderment as Reba McEntire invents an entire alphabet of new vowels in the course of one chorus.

Of course, it beats staying home and starting the much-needed rewrite of *Deck Games,* or worse yet, dealing with the continuing saga of Claudia and Cliff. The swaggering Lothario claimed that the reason he didn't show for the Big Bear trip was that there was a hostage situation at the high school where he sometimes works as a bus driver. Cliff swears he went into the school to use the can and ended up spending from seventh period until four A.M. holed up with a bunch of stressed-out sophomores saying things like, "Everything is going to be okay." Ever wary of Cliff, I insisted that while he caught up on his sleep, Claudia come down to my place and watch the TV news. My suspicions were tempered somewhat when we learned that, sure enough, a delusional high school counselor went bonkers in Burbank, holding over one hundred students hostage. What I found odd was the fact that the egomaniacal Cliff was not interviewed by a single news crew in the aftermath. This was a guy who could find a video crew in Amish country, after all.

"Did you ask him why there were no sound bites of him?" I ask Claudia when I return home from the hoedown.

"Yes," she says defensively. "For your information, he said he avoided the media so he could get home to me."

"Right," I mutter.

"And he didn't like the way his hair was looking."

"Now *that* I believe."

The next day, despite a post-Lloyd's headache of Judd-like proportions, I decide to further ward off the cabin fever and call my temp agency in the hopes of picking up some much-needed rent money.

"They need someone to do data entry over at Jupiter Filmworks," Clarice, my mistress of all things clerical, says.

"Is that all you got?" I ask.

"You can sound a bit more excited than that," she replies. "Besides, Carolyn loves you over there."

Despite the fact that I'd rather enter data on the planet of the same name, I am on my way back to Jupiter Filmworks. The problem with Jupiter is not the virtually nonexistent workload. The problem with Jupiter is Carolyn.

"It's so good to see you, Craig," she gushes looking down over me and rubbing my shoulders from the back. Carolyn's dressed in a tight navy skirt and a white blouse with one of those frilly collar knots that looks as though if you tugged on it correctly, it would render her buck naked in a matter of seconds. Her long red hair hangs halfway down her back and swings like Jan Brady's when she walks to the water cooler.

"Good to see you too," I say, not taking my eyes off the monitor.

"So, is that girlfriend of yours still giving it to you twice a day?" she asks, not beating around the proverbial bush for a second.

"Uh-huh," I say as I reach down to my shoe, never once making eye contact. "Sawdust," I explain as I flick out a chunk. "We went country dancing last night."

"I bet you're a great dancer," she says.

The first time I temped at Jupiter was a few weeks ago and for reasons unknown, Carolyn, the office manager, took a shine to my ten-dollar-an-hour ass from the get-go. She expressed her intentions that first week in the copy room, where for some insane reason, I claimed to already be involved with someone, instead of simply telling her she wasn't the right sex.

"What's her name?" Carolyn wanted to know.

"Kelly," I said, literally reading from the stack of Kelly Paper boxes across the room. "Kelly Goldenrod."

"Goldenrod?" she cooed. "That sounds like it should be your name."

Since then, every time I splash down on Jupiter, Carolyn has to have an update on Kelly and me. "She's a Leo," I said one time, "and you know how *they* can be." Inexplicably, the last time I was in, I really felt like talking. "Well, we have our ups and downs," I said employing that ambivalent whine people use when they talk about their relationships, "and the communication could be better, and we're both really busy—she's a stockbroker—so we don't see each other as much as we should, but overall, it's great. She's great. And the sex is phenomenal. Sometimes twice a day." I have no idea why I had to throw that last bit in.

"You know what's depressing?" I say to Dandy via telephone during my lunch break. "Kelly Goldenrod is the second longest romantic relationship I've ever had and she's made up."

"Speaking of relationships," Dandy says, "Kyle's taking me to Lloyd's tonight after we tape. The fiancée's in New York."

"Yippee-ay-kay-yay," I mutter.

"And if that wasn't enough good news," she adds, "they want me to be on *Circus of the Stars*."

"Are you going to do it?"

"Of course not. I want to do features," she snaps. "But here's the funny part. You have to *audition,* which I guess means they might not pick you. Could you imagine anything worse than being rejected by *Circus of the Stars?*"

Unable to come up with something, I sadly mumble, "Kelly loves circuses," and hang up.

• •

Two weeks later I'm still at Jupiter. I haven't seen much of Dandy lately as she's been lighting the fire of a certain screenwriting Marlboro Man. She seems to be as emotionally involved with this particular love slave as I've ever seen her. During the few times we've hooked up since the affair began, I couldn't help but notice that her entire aura appeared to be glowing, as though she'd been *Xanadu*'d in postproduction. At one point, when Dandy was describing the way she and Kyle liked to take long walks with their hands in each other's back pockets, I was certain that if I had stuck out my finger, one of the animated birds that were swarming around her would have perched there and tweeted on endlessly about the power of love.

"Are you in love with him?" I asked her a few days ago.

"I've lost seven pounds, Craig," she cooed. "You do the math."

Carolyn, meanwhile, hasn't let up in the relentless barrage of on-the-job woo-pitching that's just this side of *Disclosure*. I'm about to illustrate for her on a Post-it note the way Kelly and I like to fall asleep spooning when Dandy calls, hysterical.

"Trouble on the ranch?" I ask.

"The cowboy called it off," she fumes. "He said that I was too much of a *spectacle* for him, that he couldn't live in the shadow of my rising star, or some bullshit. That he wants a simpler life, with a wife and kids and all that shit, so he's going to marry that other bitch right away. They're on their way to Vegas as we speak."

"I'm sorry," I say.

"I'll show him spectacle," Dandy hisses. "I'm going to go on *Circus of the Stars* and hang myself with the trapeze or dive off the tightrope or sit on an elephant."

"Don't you mean get sat on by an elephant?" I ask.

"Whatever," Dandy says angrily. I can tell she's crying, though she's trying to act like she's not. "Will you go to the audition with me?"

"Of course," I say.

I hang up and feed Carolyn some line about Kelly getting trampled by fellow stockbrokers during a particularly busy day of trading and having to be hospitalized.

"What was that part about the elephants?" Carolyn asks, concerned.

"Some of them were pretty big," I say, before convincing her to give me the rest of the afternoon off.

When a puffy-faced Dandy picks me up at home a half hour later, she's dressed not in the fashionable grunge-chic she's known for, but in the same satin shirt she wore to Lloyd's tucked into a black thigh-length skirt by Danskin. I've never seen her more disturbingly "What I Did for Love" than this.

"But look how pretty it is when I spin," she says demonstrating.

Due to the last-minute nature of her *Circus of the Stars* change of heart, Dandy is forced to audition with several of the cast of *Mighty Morphin Power Rangers*. Though none of them can hold a candle to Dandy in terms of TVQ, their circus skills outshine hers considerably. Who knew that long-haired pretty boy had such a way with poodles?

When it's Dandy's turn to dazzle, I look on in sympathetic horror as she nearly pokes the trainer's eye out with the tightrope pole, refers to Petey the Wonder Chimp as a little fucker (as in "Get that little fucker away from me") and tumbles off the trapeze immediately after being perched on it. Apparently there's only one thing Dandy can ride for more than a few seconds, and they ain't going to show it on *Circus of the Stars*.

When I overhear the producer say to his assistant, "Get her out of here, she's spooking the caribou," I know it's time for us to leave. The producer vows to come up with something for her to do, then bids us farewell.

When I get home, Carolyn's standing in front of my door with a bag from In 'n' Out Burger.

"Is Kelly okay?" she pleads. "I brought you a Double Double."

I'm not sure if it's the post-trapeze trauma or the realization that Carolyn now *knows where I live,* but I decide that the truth must come out.

"There is no Kelly," I confess after polishing off my burger. "I made her up. The fact is"—I wipe the grease from my hands, then place them in hers—"I'm not seeing anyone at this point, and if I were, it would be a guy."

"I knew it!" Carolyn screams like that annoying party guest who invariably repeats the Trivial Pursuit answer the split second after it's revealed. "That explains *everything*."

I go on to embellish this new truth with some lie about being afraid to tell her because I had heard that Carolyn's boss was notorious for humiliating homos, particularly homos he catches using the office Xerox for their own deviant purposes. "By the time I realized that wasn't the case," I say pathetically, "the tales of Craig and Kelly were already the stuff of legend."

After answering the typical when-did-you-know, who-was-your-first, and the Bryan Adams–inspired have-you-ever-really-really-really-ever-loved-a-woman questions, I send Carolyn on her way. As she lopes back to her car, her hair seems to waft back and forth with a tad more world-weariness than before and I can't help but feel somewhat responsible.

I'm about to go inside when I hear a door crash open and someone in pain grunt out the words *son of a bitch*. I look up toward the clatter only to be rained down upon by at least thirty pounds of dirty clothes.

"What are you doing?" I scream from beneath the downpour.

"Getting rid of everything that reminds me of Asshole," Claudia says determinedly. "It's over, Craig."

"Well, you can't just throw all his stuff on my porch," I say scoldingly. "Especially when there's a stagnant yellow pool only a few feet away."

While Claudia and I gleefully toss Cliff's personal effects in the pool, topping our dumpage off with a layer of embarrassingly dated head shots, my scorned neighbress recounts the episode that was to become the final straw. True to my hunch, Cliff wasn't, in fact, one of the Burbank High hostages the other night. If the Polaroid Claudia discovered in his organizer can be believed, he did however, spend the evening holed up with high-schoolers. Two of them, to be exact.

"Brandi and Tami," Claudia says waving the photograph in the air.

"You know their names?"

"They're printed on their cheerleading uniforms," she snaps before handing me the photo. "Their *hiked-up* cheerleading uniforms."

"Isn't that like statutory rape?" I ask.

"Asshole probably figured if you added their ages together they'd equal an adult," she says. She's about to toss the snapshot into the pool, then reconsiders. "I'm keeping this," she says.

I stay up with Claudia most of the night, fall asleep on her couch, and wake up a scant thirteen minutes before I'm supposed to be at Jupiter. Carolyn, God bless her, is cool when I arrive a few minutes late. It turns out she makes a much better fag hag than she does a stalker. In fact, it's Carolyn who comes over to watch Dandy on *Circus of the Stars* with me.

She clutches my knee platonically as Dandy, in Evel Knievel garb, makes a cryptic on-air dedication to her suburban cowboy, and then gets fired out of a cannon.

"So, Dandy, how do you feel?" the ringmaster asks afterwards. Dandy just sort of shakes her head dazedly, unable to speak. "Like a superhero, maybe?" he coaxes, "Like a rocket?"

"Like a sperm," she says finally.

5

Growing up, my family had one of the two nonmotel swimming pools in our small Arizona town. As a result, the kids in my neighborhood would do just about anything to get into it.

My favorite preplunge bribery booty was tame by modern casting couch standards. It was this simple: If you wanted to swim, you had to agree to join me in playing the home version of some TV game show. I had them all: *Hollywood Squares, Family Feud, $20,000 Pyramid, Password Plus*. If Milton Bradley made it, I owned it. And if they didn't, I improvised.

I'm recalling this childhood obsession to Claudia as we stand in line to see *The Price Is Right*, which was my very favorite as a child, despite the fact that, at age nine, the only things I ever actually priced were gum and home versions of TV game shows.

"That is so fucking cool," Claudia says when I tell her about how I once cobbled a Showcase Showdown wheel out of Legos. "Shit, I hope they didn't hear me say *fuck*."

Claudia's paranoid about her bad language because, as potential contestants, the congeniality that we demonstrate here in line is what's going to get us onstage. Though Claudia seems to be coming up with the goods, personality-wise, I feel like I'm back in high school, being told by the president of the Pep Club that I lack spirit. Of course, the fact that it's 7:38 in the fucking morning may have something to do with it.

Claudia's spunk is particularly remarkable considering it was only a week ago that she and I threw our own little Boston Tea Party with everything we could find that belonged to Asshole. Since then, she's had to deal with Viola threatening eviction for the misuse of the pool, hourly visits or phone calls from Cliff—in which he either threatens her or begs forgiveness—and a junk food craving that knows no bounds.

It looks like her karma is going to get put back in balance by Bob Barker, of all people, for Claudia Newton has just been told to go on down. After bidding within $40 on a trash compactor, Claudia soon finds herself on stage getting tight with Bob in front of the miniature-golf-inspired "Hole in One" game. If she sinks her putt, Claudia is told, she could win a *Brand! New! Jeep!*

In order to determine her putting distance, my friend is asked to speculate on the prices of several household products, most of them cleaning items she's never laid eyes on, let alone purchased. Not surprisingly, she chokes, making the putt she has to sink as difficult a prospect as sitting through *Caddyshack II*.

My neighbor rears back and connects. The ball flies across the soundstage, as though it were struck by a 9 iron, and disappears into the wings, where it's only a matter of time before Janice trips on it and sues. After pointing out that Claudia's misfire is the most errant shot in the history of the show, Bob snatches back the putter, presumably before she can kill again. Then Claudia skulks off the stage to a tape that I'm sure must be labeled LOSER MUSIC.

"I don't think Bob liked me much," she says on the ride home.

"I know," I agree. "He looked like he was about to cane you when you didn't get the big wheel all the way around."

"I mean, if I wanted a man to make me feel lousy," she says, "I'd just date him." She takes her hand off the steering wheel and painfully inspects the callus she claims to have gotten from the golf club. "Why couldn't I have been born a lesbian?" she wonders. "Not only would I not have to deal with guys like Asshole, but I would have sunk that putt."

Claudia returns her hand to the wheel, visibly winces, then says, "Jack in the Box okay?"

Claudia's been doing the fast food tour of L.A. ever since she kicked Cliff out and I've taken it upon myself to dab away her tears, usually with a wet nap from KFC. It's just as well, as Dandy's been overseas, kicking off her hiatus by appearing in a commercial for Japanese television. Like Brad Pitt, Jodie Foster, Mel Gibson and scores of other famous faces, my greedy friend couldn't say no to the obscene number of yen a famous face can make doing the kind of ads they'd never stoop to in the United States.

Unfortunately, the item Dandy is stumping for isn't as glamorous as Demi Moore's department store, or Naomi Campbell's yogurt, or even Ringo Starr's apple juice. As Dandy put it, "When you're competing with Oscar winners and Beatles you can't afford to be too choosy." Hence, Dandy's about to become Japan's first-ever pitchwoman for a revolutionary new home pregnancy test. At least it's a product that she knows something about. Not, say, like Ethan Hawke pushing shampoo.

Claudia and I are polishing off our Jumbo Jacks in front of my TV when Dandy calls to let me know how it went.

"It was so easy Craig," she says. "All I had to do was walk in the bathroom and close the door and then walk out later and hug my husband. And the director and everybody were so nice to me. They called me *debu-chan*. Isn't that sweet?"

"What does it mean?" I ask.

"I forgot to ask, but it was really sweet the way they'd say it."

I tell Dandy about the *Price Is Right* fiasco and though she says the appropriate, sympathetic things, there's a detachment in her voice I attribute to a fear that Claudia, some big-assed nobody who doesn't even have her own show, is somehow infringing on her turf. The two leading ladies in my life have yet to officially meet, and frankly it's not a powwow I'm looking forward to.

"Craig, if you wanted to be on a game show, you should have told me," Dandy says. "I used to boff the contestant coordinator at *Razzle*. Get a pencil, I'll give you the number to call."

Two days later, I find myself auditioning to be on "Cable's Most Exciting New Game Show," *Razzle*. All those years of Goodson and Toddman fanaticism must have paid off, for Kurt, the contestant coordinator, tells me that my word unscrambling skills, coupled with my colorful cruise ship history, make me an ideal contestant. Just when I think things can't get any better, he gets a call saying one of tomorrow's contestants was snowed in back east and can't make the show. He hangs up and asks if I can fill in.

The second I get home I call Dandy, who just got back from Japan, to tell her the good news. "By the way," I add. "I think Kurt's still carrying a little torch for you."

"Little torch is right," Dandy says. "Why do you think I'm not seeing him anymore?"

"Can you hold on a second?" I say as my other line clicks, then switch over to the incoming call.

"So, what happened?" Claudia asks.

"I'm going on tomorrow. Can I call you back? I'm on the other line."

"Dandy?" she asks.

Why do I feel like lying? "Yeah. I wanted to thank her for getting me the audition. I'll call you in a few."

"Whatever," Claudia says.

"I'm back," I say to Dandy.

"Was that that Claudia girl?"

"Yeah," I admit. "She wanted to hear about my audition."

"Whatever," Dandy says.

How depressing is it that these two women are destined to be more proprietary with my affections than any love interest I will ever know?

• •

My TV debut less than twenty-four hours away, I ask Claudia to help me cram. She agrees, provided I accompany her to Der Wienerschnitzel for a predinner snack. I hop in the passenger seat of her white Dodge Neon and slap my Post-it note–cum–study aid to the dashboard.

"Is that a coupon?" Claudia asks hopefully.

"No," I say. "For some reason that only the geniuses behind *Razzle* understand, you have to spell out your answers on a telephone keypad, and it's all about how fast you can do it, so I made this to practice with."

"Doesn't that give an unfair advantage to people who make a lot of 976 calls?" she wonders.

"Let's hope so," I say.

While Claudia considers what comes with the various DW Combo Meals, I start punching in everything I see—car, stoplight, hustler, Angelyne. Despite my improving facility with the mock keypad, it takes me forever to enter Der Wienerschnitzel and by the time I finish, we're back on the road.

"Where are we going?" I ask when Claudia turns onto an unfamiliar street.

"Cheerleading practice," she says purposefully.

"That can't be healthy," I say.

"I'm about to eat two chili cheese dogs and a large fries for a snack, Craig," she says bitterly. "Do you think I give a shit about healthy?"

We park across the street from the Burbank High baseball field. While I continue to punch in words, Claudia glares at Cliff, who's leaning on the chain-link fence like an overgrown Outsider looking on as an octet of spirit-pushers in bra tops spell out victory, which, for your information, is 842-8679 on the telephone keypad. Though I'm unable to offer Claudia much comfort or convince her to start the car and drive away, I am able to use the stalking for *Razzle* practice. If *pencil dick, flat ass, textbook narcissist,* or *lying sack of shit* are part of my contest tomorrow, my competitors will be lunching on my dust.

The next day, I turn up at the *Razzle* studio in my Structure best and after a bumpy first round, I hit my stride and start kicking some ass. By the final commercial, I've already wiped the floor with two of my so-called competitors and have one to go. I'm psyching myself up for the kill when Bink Darlington, the show's dashing salt-and-pepper-haired host, saunters over and puts his hand on my shoulder.

"So you used to work on cruise ships?" he asks.

"I was a cruise director for a couple of years," I say.

"Like Julie on *The Love Boat*?" he asks.

"Yeah," I say, trotting out my stock one-liner and doubting he'll get it, "but without the disposable income."

Bink laughs his robust game-show-host laugh, then grabs my hand again and says, "Maybe you'd like to go for a ride on my boat sometime." Before I can say, "Are you out of your mind?" the stage manager breaks in and gives Bink the ten-second warning. He turns to me and looks as far into my soul as one can with fake blue contact lenses. Then he whispers, "Pull my finger," and lets one fly.

Though I proceed into the final round in both a literal and figurative fog, my fingers are more nimble than ever. At the end of thirty seconds, I'm told I've won not only a leather sofa but a pair of diamond earrings—"For the lady in your life," Bink says with a wink.

I call both Claudia and Dandy from the green room to tell them my good news and that each was the first to hear it. Then I pick up my earrings and the certificate for my sofa and, thankfully, leave the studio without having to deal with Bink. I arrive home to find Claudia, a stuffed Taco Bell bag in tow, raring to help me celebrate.

"I'm sure he was just being nice," she says when I tell her about Bink's proposition. "Remember on *Family Feud*? Richard Dawson used to practically French everything in a skirt."

I glance at my watch, remembering I'd planned to go to dinner with Dandy in five minutes. Just then the phone rings. Claudia picks it up and says, "Hello," but whoever is on the other end doesn't speak.

"Leave me the fuck alone!" she screams and hangs up. "It's Cliff, Craig, I know it is." Claudia shoves the phone across the floor and tries not to cry but fails.

When her chain of sobs is interrupted by Dandy honking downstairs, I give Claudia a sad smile, then look closer and notice that her lobes are indeed of the pierced variety. I stand up, reach into my pocket, and present Claudia with the only two studs I know won't disappoint her.

"I'll come by later," I promise.

"Please," says Claudia.

On the opposite end of the emotional spectrum is Dandy, who euphorically announces that her commercial arrived from Japan via FedEx and she couldn't be happier with the way it turned out.

"They put in this really great music and graphics and stuff," she says. "And I look so happy that I'm pregnant. It really has me thinking about kids, Craig."

Dandy says she's already watched it a few times at the house, but since she doesn't speak Japanese, she insists that we go to Terisushi so she can ask her favorite waiter, Shinji, whom she usually terrorizes, to interpret the spot for her.

We all look up at the TV over the bar while Shinji presses play on the VCR. The commercial begins when Dandy, looking uneasy in her tasteful living room, looks down at her stomach, then back to the camera.

"What's he saying?" Dandy asks, in reference to the Japanese announcer's voice-over.

"He says, 'This woman is five months pregnant and doesn't even know it,' " Shinji says before being distracted by a customer with doggie bag needs.

The commercial ends and Dandy looks over at me. "Is it possible to be five months pregnant and not even know it?" she asks, the agitation brimming in her voice. "How dumb do you have to be? Now all the fucking Third World is going to think I'm a dumb ass."

"Anyone who picks up as much money as you did for one day's work isn't a dumb ass," I say charitably, ignoring the fact that Dandy thinks Japan is part of the Third World.

"True," she says as Shinji drops off the check. "Let me get this."

Dandy puts her arm around me as we start to walk out, then realizes she forgot something and rushes back to Shinji.

"Tell me something, Shinji," she says, batting her eyes coquettishly. "What does it mean when someone says *debu-chan*?"

I'm thinking *foreigner with jugs* but say nothing.

Shinji smiles warmly at the woman who gave him the biggest tip of the night, then says, "It means *my little fat friend*."

6

Dandy and I are splayed out in my living room indulging in one of our favorite rituals, Softcore Saturday, wherein we imbibe as many El Pollo Loco products as possible while watching erotic B-movies like today's choice, *Two Moon Junction,* when the phone rings. Not wanting to miss a glorious second of Sherilyn Fenn's deflowering, I opt to screen.

"Craig, this is Bink Darlington," says the unmistakable voice. "Bink Darlington from *Razzle,*" he adds as though there's a chance I might think he's the *other* Bink Darlington. "I just wanted to apologize for my behavior . . ." In one fluid movement, Dandy discards her churro, grabs the remote, hits Pause, and shoves the receiver to my ear.

"Hello," I say.

"Craig, you're home," Bink says.

"Yeah, sorry," I say. "I was just watching a movie."

"What movie?" asks Bink.

I consider saying something like *Schindler's List* when I realize who I'm talking to. "*Two Moon Junction,*" I say proudly.

"Oh yeah," Bink says. "Pretty hot, huh? Have you gotten to the shower scene yet?"

"Just once. We're about to rewind and watch it again." The longer I speak, the more contorted in curiosity Dandy becomes. When I see my friend fall to one knee atop the half-eaten churro, I decide to put her out of her misery and start tapping on the phone with my fingernails. "Bink, my receiver's screwed up," I say, causing Dandy to tremble and arch with Fenn-like ecstasy. "I'm putting you on speaker."

"Craig, I'm sorry about my behavior yesterday at the studio," Bink announces to the room.

"Human beings fart, Bink," I say, trying, for the sake of Dandy's entertainment, to be particularly tactless—though it seems all I really have to do to amuse her is say the word Bink as much as possible. "It's no big deal, Bink."

"Not that. The part where I . . . well, where it may have appeared that I was, you know, propositioning you. Well, I assure you, I'm a red-blooded 100 percent heterosexual man. . . ."

"I'm sure you are, Bink," I say.

"My son, however, is not," Bink continues, causing Dandy and me to drop our jaws in stereo, ". . . and, unless you're already spoken for or my gaydar is completely off, I think you might get along."

While Dandy convulses on the floor, flapping her legs like a displaced mermaid, Bink explains that he's hoping to fix me up with his son, Damon. Damon, a "song-and-dance man just like his dad," just returned from his first tour of duty as a cruise ship chorine, and when I explained on *Razzle* that I had been employed in the same field, a lightbulb went off over Bink's head. No word whether the bulb was connected to the finger pulling or if they were separate phenomena.

"He look anything like you, Bink?" I say flirtatiously, displaying the kind of cojones I can only muster when a paused Richard Tyson is naked and quivering on my TV screen.

"Actually, he's even handsomer, if you can believe it," Bink says with a self-deprecating chuckle. "To give you an idea of what he looks like, he plays Aladdin in the live show that Disney has running before that new *Pocahontas* movie."

"Are you telling me your son has no nipples, Bink?" I say.

"No, my son has nipples," Bink laughs. "In fact, he's got his dad's nipples."

At the risk of inviting other anatomical comparisons, I take down Bink's number and tell him I have to think about it as "I've recently gotten out of something pretty intense." I leave out the fact that that something was Dandy's Jacuzzi. Just last night, in fact.

I decide I have to see Damon Darlington as Aladdin that night. Since Dandy's got a rendezvous scheduled with the young buck from Circuit City who installed her stereo, I call Claudia and beg her to let me treat her to *Pocahontas,* assuring her that she was, in fact, my first choice.

"God, I hate animation, Craig," Claudia groans. "If I wanted to see a teapot sing, I'd just drop acid like a normal person."

"Please, Claudia," I plead. "I'll buy the snacks."

"What time do we leave?"

Two hours later, Claudia and I arrive at the El Capitan Theater in Hollywood, where my lovesick neighbor's concessional needs set me back $11.75. I figure it's a small price to pay to have a second opinion on whether or not I should attempt to venture into the "whole new world" awaiting inside those genie pants.

"He looks like he's about seven, Craig," Claudia whispers when Damon makes his entrance atop a flying carpet.

"If that," I gasp back as I watch as the dimple-faced Damon and his child bride, Jasmine, glide their way from one balcony to the other. "I forgot to ask Bink how old he was."

Between his big brown eyes and peerless teeth, Damon's facial features seem to be engaged in a gleaming contest which will surely end in a draw. In keeping with the tradition of Softcore Saturday, the satin pirate-style shirt he wears is low-cut and reveals a nice slice of cleavage but nary a trace of hair.

"He looks like if you asked his age, he'd hold up a few fingers and say 'I'm this many,' " remarks Claudia.

"Don't look now," I say when I notice the carpet stop moving and the smiles of its riders become strained. "It looks like This Many's stuck."

"Boy, I bet he's wishing he bought Triple-A," Claudia says.

When the live show ends and the film starts, Aladdin and Jasmine are still marooned on their lemon of a carpet and appear to have given up waving in favor of soiling their pants. Their predicament doesn't go unnoticed by the crowd of rugrats, particularly those who will be crushed, emotionally and literally, if the Disney duo were to fall from the rug. The kids' ear-busting cries of concern not only prompt the projectionist to stop the film until the twosome can be rescued, but cause Claudia and me to come up with the same brilliant idea simultaneously.

"Let's go," we say.

"Are you sure you don't want to wait until they get him down?" Claudia adds charitably. "I mean, you'll feel pretty silly if you call Bink to say you're into it and then find out the guy plummeted to his death two nights before."

"Who said I was into it?" I say as we get up to leave.

In order to get the most from our six-dollar parking fee, Claudia and I decide to share a banana split at the ice cream parlor next door and discuss my reasons for passing on what's in the turban behind door number one. Apart from the This Many factor, Damon Darlington looks to be a card-carrying member of the Cute Club, a theoretical fraternity I've concocted that includes persons whose JC Penney catalog–worthy looks are pretty much universally undeniable. Persons whose physical attractiveness is always mentioned in the first breath when they are discussed by others out of their presence. Persons whose destinies, careers, love lives, rapport with waiters, and traffic ticket history have been significantly influenced by the fact that they're easy on the eyes.

"Give me an example of a Cute Club member," Claudia says.

"Scott Wolf on *Party of Five,*" I say. "Try describing him to somebody without mentioning how adorable he is. You can't."

"But he's talented," says Claudia.

"You can be both," I say.

"So what's the problem? I thought the idea was to go out with people you're attracted to."

"It is," I say. "But the whole point of my theory is that Cute Club members tend to stick with their own. And I'm not saying this to put myself down but, historically speaking, Cute Club members don't tend to go for me."

"Craig?" says a voice to the right of our table. I look up and see a young man in sweats and full Aladdin makeup.

"Yeah," I say, feigning ignorance. "Do we know each other?"

"Not really," he says. "I saw you on *Razzle*. Bink Darlington's my dad."

"Your show aired and you didn't tell me?" barks Claudia.

"No," I say.

"We have a tape of it at the house," Damon says before returning to the counter to retrieve his smoothie. While he's gone, I advise Claudia not to let on that we just saw his spectacular but ducked out the second the going got rough.

No sooner has Damon dragged a chair over and settled in at the end of our table than Claudia opens her yap and says, "So did you get down off the carpet okay?"

Either Claudia suffers from a rare disease where your short-term memory malfunctions in the presence of hot fudge or she's doing this for my own good. Either way, she's going to pay.

"You saw that?" Damon says, his perfect face briefly registering the realization that since we obviously have no interest in Pocahontas or the colors of her wind, we must have come solely to inspect him. "That's the second time this week we got stuck. The girl who plays Jasmine is still in tears backstage. As you can see," he continues, stopping to take a swig of smoothie, "I really go out of my way to ease her pain."

By the time our conversation reaches the ten-minute mark, I've confessed to getting the call from his dad and he's confessed to listening to it on the other phone. I also come to learn that he's twenty, his parents are divorced and since he got off the ship he was working on, he's been living with Bink in Beverly Hills. Though his mom, in New York, has known for years that he's gay, he came out to his dad all of two weeks ago. Bink, seeing a chance to latch onto a kind of subversiveness he, as Wonder-WASP, had never known, has been beyond supportive ever since.

"In two weeks, he's become like the poster dad for P-FLAG," Damon laughs. "I can't open a cabinet in our house without finding a rainbow sticker. I'm like, 'Dad, I don't think anyone cares that our coffee mugs are gay.' Get this, he called Cher. He wants to get together for lunch to discuss me and Chastity and how it feels to be famous and have a gay child. I think he wishes I'd become a star so we could be on the cover of *The Advocate*."

"You must be going crazy," I say.

"Thank you," Damon says as though I'm the first to acknowledge the downside of such support, "but every time I feel like complaining I figure he could just as easily have kicked me out on the street."

I excuse myself briefly to run to the men's room, giving Claudia the opportunity to say lots of nice things about me in my absence. When I return Damon says, "Well, I've got a rug to catch," then scrawls his number on a napkin and asks me to do the same.

"You gonna call him?" Claudia says as we walk to the car. "Because if you don't, I will, just for the makeup tips alone. Did you see that eyeliner?"

"I saw it all," I sigh.

"He's adorable, Craig. Charming, and funny and bright and animated."

"I thought you hated animation," I say.

I decide to let Damon call me, which is always the strategy to take where a member of the Cute Club is concerned. That night I fall asleep and dream that I'm on a date with Damon on some Caribbean island.

He's dressed as Aladdin and he keeps stealing fruit and getting caught by cranky vendors, all of whom prove forgiving once the CC factor registers. Damon is about to snatch the most beautiful banana either of us has ever seen when an alarm starts to blare.

"Hello," I growl into the phone, intentionally playing up the grogginess in my voice to make the caller feel bad about waking me up.

"Craig," a woman's voice says. "It's Michelle."

My eyes slam open painfully. I lean up on one elbow and say, "What time is it?"

"Well, it's ten o' clock here in New York. I don't know what time it is there."

Of course, she doesn't. As a Broadway baby committed wholeheartedly to her craft, Michelle has no time for such things as time differences and the feelings of others.

"It's seven, Michelle," I say.

"Oh, sorry."

When Michelle explains the reason for her call—that she's coming to L.A. to dance in the chorus of *Beauty and the Beast* and would love to get together—I feel like a novice warlock who said a complicated incantation that would cause Damon to call, but fucked up and wound up with the wrong Disnoid. As my college sweetheart, who's abandoned the last name Lee in favor of the painfully ironic D'Amore, drones on about her glamorous life, I pad, cordless in hand, to the bathroom and start to relieve myself as loudly as possible. When she gets to the part about how she and Rum Tum Tugger have just bought a loft, I take that as my cue to flush.

"So you're going to come see my show, right?" she whines.

"Can I bring a date?" I say.

"Sure," she says after a beat. "Anyone I know?"

"It's a surprise," I say.

I try to fall back asleep, but that familiar combination of nostalgia and nausea I feel whenever I think about my Michelle era makes it impossible. I decide I might as well work on *Deck Games* so I grab my latest draft, a red marker, and a towel and head out to the pool. By page ten, I'm out cold.

When I wake up and go back inside, sometime after noon, there are four messages on my machine. Dandy wants to know if she should wait for me to watch the ending of *Two Moon*. Miles wants to complain that his Nazi boss is making him work on the weekend. Michelle wants to know if there are any movie people I could bring to her show. The fourth message is the pick of the litter and so far I've replayed it five times.

"Hey, Craig," it begins. "It's Aladdin. My bitch Jasmine is out of town and I was wondering what you were doing this weekend . . ."

7

"Here's what you gotta do, Craig," Claudia says, while shaving my neck in preparation for my first so-called date with Damon Darlington. "Take the cute out of the equation. Try closing your eyes at some point and see if anything interesting is coming out of his mouth. If it is, then great, but you can't just like him because he doesn't have a single bad angle."

"Wanna bet?" I say, before painfully removing the world's longest nose hair. "And let's let the record reflect that *he* called *me*."

When I arrive at the Darlington mansion in Beverly Hills, Bink explains that Damon will be back momentarily.

"He's just gone to the travel agent to pick up some tickets," the *Razzle*-master says, his voice and manner so delightfully "as seen on TV" that I'm excited to be marooned here with him for a while.

He pours me a drink and sits across from me in the breakfast nook. "So Craig," he says, "I've been reading up on all this gay stuff and I was wondering if you were, you know, a pitcher or a catcher."

"You know," I say, trying to cover my shock, "I was wondering the same damn thing."

"Sorry, I'm late," Damon says, bursting through the front door in the nick of fucking time.

"Sorry if my dad was getting too personal," he says a few minutes later as we head for Santa Monica in his restored 1967 Mustang convertible.

"He was fine," I say. "It's just so wild to see a game-show host out of context."

"You should see him on Christmas morning," Damon says.

"He said you were picking up some tickets. Are you going somewhere?"

"Yeah, Colorado for a few days. Every year, my dad and I volunteer at this camp called Dreamtown."

While Damon explains that Dreamtown is a retreat where terminally ill children go for a respite from their lives of sick beds and IVs, I decide that now would be as good a time as any to do Claudia's shallowness check. I close my eyes as Damon waxes on about "giving something back" and "seeing those little faces light up." Not surprisingly, the only shallowness I come across is my own. I decide I'll let him retake the test later, when he's not going on about dying kids.

Five flirtatious, fun-filled hours later, we're at the top of the Ferris wheel on the Santa Monica pier. I close my eyes again.

"Okay," says Damon, patting my leg excitedly. "If this evening were a movie"—he pauses here for effect—"what moments would be in the trailer?"

It's all I can do not to audibly sigh.

Damon and I alternate taking part in the kind of purposeless hypothetical musing I *live* for: Bink asking me what position I played, Damon cranking the radio when "All I Want" by Toad the Wet Sprocket came on, the two of us making the obligatory goofy faces in the photo booth, me turning green on the Tilt-a-Whirl, the waitress at Louisa's who served us nothing but attitude.

"I know a moment we forgot," Damon says before kissing me for the first time.

• •

"It was so much *fun,*" I say to Dandy the next morning. "You'd think we'd never seen cotton candy before."

Just then, the other line clicks. It's Damon calling from LAX just to say hi before he heads off to Colorado.

"He's so excited to go do his Aladdin shtick for these sick kids," I say, when I return to Dandy. "I feel so self-involved by comparison, like I don't care about anything or anyone but myself."

"You do so care about other people, Craig," Dandy says. "What about all those autographed pictures you forged for me? I know at least half of those went to, like, boat children. *That's* something."

"Dandy, I did those in front of the television," I confess. "Meredith Baxter was on in *My Breast*, remember? Signing those pictures was just busy work to keep myself from bursting into tears. Maybe I could be like a Big Brother, you know, get some troubled inner-city kid to come in twice a week."

"Craig, there are far sexier ways to help your fellow men than inviting them into your home," she asserts.

"Like what?" I say.

"I don't know," she says. "But my publicist will. I'll call you back."

The next night finds us at the Hollywood Athletic Club rubbing cues with the likes of David Spade, Joely Fisher and the chick from *Punky Brewster* as participants in the AIDS Project Los Angeles fund-raiser Pool Aid. One of the hosts, Stephen Baldwin, gives Dandy a hug upon our arrival, before describing the green felt minidress she picked up for the occasion as "phenomenal."

"Just wait till I bend over to sink a bank shot," she coos.

Dandy and I make our way over to the players' check-in and are introduced to the third member of our team, a hyper-zealous, thirty-fiveish talent agent named Norbert Gunderson.

"I hope you guys have been practicing," he says. "Because I've got a side bet going with my brother. If you blow it for me, I'm never going to watch your show again, not that I watch it now."

With twenty minutes to spare before our first match, we leave Norbert chalking his cue and head to the bar for what Dandy calls "some booze and cruise."

"Diet Coke," I order.

"Put some rum in it," Dandy tells the bartender.

"No way," I say. "You know what a lightweight I am. I'm going to suck enough as it is."

"You know," Dandy muses as we compare the back view of Dean Cain with that of Cuba Gooding Jr., "the hardest thing about these Help the Homeless benefits is deciding who to go home with."

I'm about to point out that tonight is not a homeless benefit and that Dandy should get her charities straight in case someone wants a sound bite, when I come face to face with my favorite underdog ever, Tonya Harding, surrounded by a handful of supporters in black "Tonya" hats.

"It's *you,*" I gasp.

I turn to grab Dandy, for moral support, but she's disappeared. Noticing my flustered state, Tonya attempts to ease the tension with a little Pool Aid small talk. I explain that I'm yet to play my first match, while she says hers was canceled because some of the members of the other team didn't show.

"I bet they're running scared," I say. "They probably knew you could kick their ass."

It's not until five minutes later when I track down Dandy that I realize I've made a giant faux pas.

"I can't believe I brought up ass kicking," I lament, before asking the bartender to forget what I said earlier about the rum. "I mean, didn't Tonya say she was going to kick Nancy Kerrigan's ass? Aren't those the words she used? I just ruined her night."

"It could have been worse," figures Dandy. "You could have said break a leg."

"Oh God," I say. "Can I have another?" I ask the bartender.

As we fight our way back through the crowd, Norbert rushes up and says, "Come on, you guys, we've got just enough time to do some visualization exercises before the match. Wait a minute, Craig. Is that a cocktail?"

I take a final swig and say, "Not anymore."

"Unbelievable," he mutters under his breath. "I would have been better off with Yasmine Bleeth."

We let Norbert break, which he does with aplomb. Though Dandy can't sink a shot to save her life, the spectacle of her riding the pool table side saddle is more than making up for her lack of pool prowess. It seems the only one who's not bringing anything to the proceedings is me. The only ball I can seem to hit into a pocket is the white one, and I'm pretty sure that's not good. I also seem to have trouble remembering whether we're solids or stripes. As the play continues, Norbert gets more and more angry. By the time we get down to the last few balls, the sweat is pouring off him like lava.

"Blow this one and I might have to hit you," he says menacingly as I look down to a table with only two balls, the white one and the black one. I tap the corner that I intend to aim for as I've seen Norbert do, and line up what, even in my tipsy state, seems like an easy shot. I'm about to let rip when I feel the heat of television lights on my back and hear Dandy's voice somewhere in the distance.

". . . Well, Kennedy, I think homelessness is a really important cause," she says. "I mean, if things had gone differently for me, I could easily see myself living in a cardboard box. Of course, I'd make it really cute and homey . . ."

I close my eyes in a futile attempt to disappear into one of the room's many pockets, then follow through with my shot. When I open my eyes, the eight ball is gone. Unfortunately, judging by the livid look on Norbert's face, it didn't go out the way I intended.

"Prepare to die, you stupid fuck," he growls.

Norbert literally starts chasing me around the table. In my attempt to thwart him, I spill a drink on MTV's Daisy Fuentes, give *Baywatch*'s David Charvet's left loafer a flat tire, and somehow get tangled up in Melissa Rivers's purse. Norbert finally catches up to me and throws me against a pillar.

Just as I think he's going to take a shot at me, Stephen Baldwin gets on the mike and says the party's being closed down because we're violating the fire code. During the confusion, I make a dash for the back door, leaving my by-now-homicidal teammate to wallow in his defeat alone. In the confusion, I lose track of Dandy. Terrified to go back inside, I leave a note on her car telling her I'm going to walk home.

I'm staggering down Sunset when a fire truck speeds by. Dandy waves at me from the back of it and convinces the hunky fireman she's dangling from to do the same. A minute or so later, a limo follows. As it slowly approaches, a hand emerges from the window and whips a small black object at my shin.

"Tonya," I say, reading aloud from the hat.

I'm about to reverently slip it on when a Grizzly Adams type wanders up and asks for coffee money. I pull $1.37 from my pocket and hand it over in the hat.

"It's the least I can do," I say.

8

I have often considered hiring a hustler. Not to have sex with, mind you, but to act out Amy Grant videos with. We'd giggle and touch and "Baby, Baby" our way through a series of impeccably art directed sets: the Laundromat, the car wash, the gorgeous loft apartment that the viewer will assume is mine and not his. We'd take lots of hand-in-hand walks. We'd suck spaghetti off each other's forks, race outside to get the Sunday paper in our underwear, and roll an orange back and forth on my gorgeous hardwood floors. We'd share a rowboat and not even worry about our contact lenses when the intensity of our goo-goo eyes causes the darn thing to tip over. It would be like the Robert Redford–Michelle Pfeiffer falling-in-the-water montage from *Up Close and Personal*, only my love interest would be roughly my age. I'm paying, after all.

I dare say these last two weeks have been the closest thing to an Amy Grant video I've ever known. Damon Darlington and I have seen each other a good twelve times since he got back from Colorado. And I mean good. We've skated, bladed, and waded. Wined, dined and *Chorus Line*d. We even sailed to Catalina with Bink and his current squeeze, Lisa, who, in the spirit of *Up Close and Personal,* is two months younger than This Many.

About the only thing Damon and I haven't done is mess around, our frequent above-the-waist make-outs notwithstanding. This isn't because I'm protecting his virtue, for Damon has had far more hands-on nookie experience than I. He grew up in one of those neighborhoods where treehouse circle jerks and garage rendezvous were as common as a game of Kick the Can. Apparently this sort of thing was going on in every neighborhood in the world except mine. While every other adolescent on the planet was playing doctor, I was playing Operation by Milton Bradley.

The way I see it, Damon and I are abstaining because we can. Besides, who wants to start stressing about safety and linens and histories and performance when there's green pin bowling going on just down the block. I figure it'll happen when it happens. I don't remember seeing Michelle Pfeiffer getting up to go find a towel.

The Courtship of Bink's Son will have to endure a hiatus of sorts this weekend because a month ago I promised my undivided attention to my former college roommate, Ulysses. The reformed party animal figures a few days of L.A. depravity is just what he needs to make him appreciate the mellow life he leads in the comparatively comatose Santa Cruz. Though we've managed to stay in touch since college, our correspondence since I left the ship has consisted primarily of answering machine messages. Lately, his droppings always seem to come when someone famous dies. See, last year, Ulysses joined one of those celebrity death pools wherein you try to predict which stars are going to croak in the upcoming year. Some cyber-geek with a sick mind and a lot of time on his hands has even concocted odds that figure into it all. Obvious candidates like geriatrics, druggie actors and rap stars are worth fewer points than, say, athletes, children and the Osmonds.

I get a kick out of this morbid obsession because it's completely at odds with the rest of Ulysses's personality. He's even mellower now than he was in college, having forsaken, with the help of trained rehab professionals, drug and drink in favor of lots of chicken breasts and various sprouts.

The messages he leaves always consist of only three words, four if the star had a middle name "Craig . . ." he'll say somberly. "Dinah Shore." Beep. Or, "Craig . . . Martha Raye." Beep. I've come to look forward to these long-distance mortality checks and, depending on the star that expires, I often find myself smiling at the news of their passing, confident that I'll soon be hearing from one of my favorite people in the world. Color me twisted, but I just love the thought of Ulysses cutting short one of the yoga classes he teaches so he can run home and find out whether Christopher Reeve pulled through or not.

"I know I won't die young," boasts Dandy who is at my place when I play back the Elizabeth Montgomery message. "I still don't have a good head shot for them to show over the sad music on *Entertainment Tonight*."

"Is that a requirement?" I wonder.

"Absolutely," she asserts. "Did you see Selena's?"

"Breathtaking," I admit.

"I ought to ask her who did hers," Dandy continues, oblivious to the fact that her suggestion would require a Ouija board. "Speaking of pictures, show me This Many."

Dandy has yet to meet Damon, as she's been in New York plugging her show for the last week and a half and just returned today. I grab the head shot of him I keep conveniently on the refrigerator to remind myself to never eat again, and shove it under Dandy's nose.

"You didn't tell me he was Cute Club," she says.

"I was hoping you wouldn't notice," I say.

Since Dandy wants to hear all about Damon, I agree to run a few errands with her. On the way to the first stop, our neighborhood car wash, I explain how despite his age and his looks, Damon is as bright and funny and decent as anyone I've ever gone out with. I even tell her about our game of turning our evenings together into movie trailers.

Dandy seems impressed as we pull up to the car wash attendant. "But be honest, Craig. Have you had to buy him beer?"

"Only once," I confess. "He doesn't really like it. Which is yet another glorious thing we have in common. C'mon, Dandy. I don't give you a hard time about your stereo installers and firemen."

"Yes, but I don't look like I'm about to burst into song," she says before punctuating the comment with the slam of her door.

While Dandy pays the cashier, I stare up at the two solitary head shots on the wall, improbably enough magician David Copperfield and former Carson sidekick Ed McMahon.

Thankfully, in all the times I've gone out with Dandy, she's only given one person a head shot—her current boy toy, Jason, at Circuit City—and that's just because she needed something to write her phone number on. Claudia, meanwhile, has pictures up all over town despite the fact that, to my knowledge, she's never been paid to act.

There's actually a picture of Claudia up at Light Bulbs Unlimited, the store Dandy and I head to after the car wash. Even though they've never met, Dandy doesn't seem too keen on Claudia so I don't comment when Dandy points to Claudia's eight-by-ten, oblivious to who it is, and says, "Oooh, honey, do the words hot oil treatment mean anything to you?" In the hopes of abating more neighbor bashing I switch the focus to the adjacent Cher head shot and make a joke about how the line between halogen and collagen must be even finer than we thought, which no one seems to get.

When Dandy drops me off, we run into Claudia coming out of the laundry room, and the dreaded moment of introduction that I've always known would come is upon me. Their disdain for each other is so obvious as they shake hands weakly and say things like, "Craig's told me so much about you" that I want to shout, "And you call yourselves actresses?"

The minute Dandy leaves, Claudia bounds up with an armful of clothes, explaining she's getting new head shots taken this week and she wants me to go with her. I would sooner have my lungs scraped.

"I can't," I explain. "Ulysses is coming to town and I'm playing cruise director."

"But I need you, Craig," she pleads while holding up various head shot wardrobe options for my opinion. "You're the only friend I have with any taste whatsoever."

"That is so not true," I say as she climbs into a Levis jacket from the late eighties. "I'd ditch the denim if you want to go in for young mom roles."

"See," she says. Suddenly she puts down the outdated duds and turns serious. "Can I ask you something, Craig? Not about clothes."

"Sure," I say.

"Promise you won't get mad," she says.

"I promise," I say. Maybe.

"Why do you hang out with Dandy? Apart from the sort of superficial glamour, what is it that makes you like her?"

No one's ever really asked me that before, though I'm sure plenty of people have thought it. I think about Claudia's question for a moment, then answer it the best way I can.

"When I was in college," I say, "there was a semester right after Michelle dumped me where I didn't have any friends and I was really lonely and depressed all the time. I was taking all these film classes so I would just watch movies all the time, old, new, it didn't matter. And I wondered what it would be like to have what I called Movie Moments in your life, you know, where the people and the places and what was being said and all the elements came together in a way that made you feel like you were alive. Well, the next semester I met Dandy and I started having them."

"But isn't it just her being melodramatic?"

"No," I say thoughtfully. "Some of it is, but it's not all selfish. Dandy's fearless, and she's not jaded and above everything. She hasn't already made up her rules. Anything's possible with her."

"You get to be reckless by association," Claudia says.

"Yeah, basically," I say. "And she believes in me. And we make each other laugh. And she shows up. I think 90 percent of life is just showing up, you know."

"All right," says Claudia, having heard more than she bargained for. "I get it. If I stuffed a sock in your mouth, would that be a Movie Moment?"

"Depends on the sock," I say.

I pick Ulysses up at the airport and barely recognize him. Gone are the beer belly, the dreadlocks, and the pot perfume; here instead is a clear-eyed and trim young man with a buzz cut and a crystal around his neck, but that same easygoing guyness I remember so fondly is present and accounted for. As we embrace in the terminal, I feel like I'm hugging a chunk of home.

"This traffic would make me insane," Ulysses says as we pull onto the 405.

"You get used to it," I say, then notice a hand-printed sign affixed to a light post that someone's printed FADED GLORY on and then drawn an arrow. "See that sign?" I say, pointing. "It means they're shooting a film over there someplace and the sign is so the crew can find the location. It'll probably be a movie we never hear of again, but I still love when I see those signs, especially if they sprung for the neon-colored cardboard."

"So this town is working for you?" he asks.

"You know what I like about it," I say, mentally double-clicking on the imaginary pro column of my Life in L.A. checklist. "There's this sense of possibility all around you, you know? Like, Phoenix doesn't have that. At any given moment, *somebody's* movie's getting made, *somebody's* dream is coming true. It just so happens that right now, it's, you know, Courteney Cox's turn."

"I thought she already had a turn," says Ulysses.

"Some people get two turns," I say.

Wanting to further impress my friend with how quickly I've taken to Tinseltown, I decide to swing by Dandy's studio on the way back to my place.

"Name?" says Clyde, the guard at the gate.

"Craig," I sigh. "Craig Clybourn. Same as it was the last hundred times I've been here."

"I don't have a pass for you," Clyde says.

"Dandy Rio's expecting me," I say. Nothing. "She's on *That's Just Dandy*."

Unable to take one more second of Clyde's blank expression, I turn around in my seat and point to the giant mural of the *That's Just Dandy* cast painted on the side of Studio 6 and say, "That girl in the culottes!"

Clyde shakes his head, goes back in his booth and picks up the phone.

"I should get Dandy to fire his ass," I say. "She could probably do it."

"You know where you're going?" Clyde says.

"Yes," I say as the gate lifts open. I exhale as I drive into the studio, confident that my act as Hollywood insider is back on track.

"God, I love coming onto the lot," I say, just as the gate slams down on my trunk.

It's all for naught because we arrive at Dandy's trailer only to discover that she's not there. "She had to go to some sudden creative meeting," explains Jason, the Circuit City slicker, kicking back like the spawn of Hugh Hefner in a smoking jacket and socks.

We tire of waiting after about fifteen minutes and decide to go to Koo Koo Roo. I'm telling my old friend about my Ed Begley Jr. stalking scare—when I saw the blond actor in three different places over the course of four days—when Ulysses abruptly waves his hand in my face and changes the subject.

"Craig, I know you're trying to give me the whole positive spin on your new life here, but I'm not buying it. Are you really happy?"

"Yeah," I say, then stare into my water glass. "I guess. I mean, you know what it is? It's, like, that thing with the guard gate is the perfect metaphor for my life. As if they don't want to let anyone in. You may be on the list or totally qualified to do something but they're still just not having it. I swear, the day Clyde goes, 'Oh, hi, Craig, how are you today, come on through,' I'm going to drop my dentures."

"Maybe it just takes time," Ulysses says.

When we get back home, I take Ulysses up to meet Claudia and after gushing over his crystal and reading his tarot cards, she convinces my old friend to forgo our planned pilgrimage to Joshua Tree in favor of accompanying her to get new head shots taken. It's the least he can do, considering her reading all but guaranteed that a "big, exciting change" is just around the corner and that he will meet the love of his life sometime next year.

At the behest of a certain agent—with whom she was allowed to schmooze at a recent acting workshop on which she blew half of last month's waitressing earnings, and who showed no interest in ever representing her—Claudia has enlisted a certain pricey photographer, Mr. Pietro Ruiz, to capture her stunning likeness on film. A barefoot and muttonchopped Ruiz opens the door and ushers us into his Laurel Canyon studio. As I set down Claudia's hopelessly dated sweater options, I notice she's crying.

"It's just my allergies," she insists. "He's wearing that awful CK shit. I swear, if I ever run into Kate Moss, I'm going to kick her skinny ass across the room."

Claudia's aversion to CK is a new development, for Cliff used to practically bathe in the stuff without incident. I figure she's crying because of her lingering feelings for him, driven home in the form of a "sense-memory" (a phenomenon that seems to elude her in acting class).

Unable to deal with the clashing colors of her wardrobe and her psyche, I sneak off to call Dandy, leaving Claudia to whiff woefully at Ulysses's battle-scarred bottle of aromatherapy.

"I can't talk long," Dandy snaps. "I have to go to Circuit City before work. Remember that kid Jason?"

"The one who left his tool belt on?" I ask.

"Right," Dandy says. "Well, yesterday an extra on my show told me he was telling everyone at Fairfax High I have cellulite. They're calling me Cottage Cheese Ass, Craig."

"So, you gonna lay him off?" I ask.

"Yeah," she says, "and hopefully get that head shot back, because I'm out and my agent says we have to send one to Tarantino like today."

By the time I finish hearing about how Dandy would do anything to work with Q, as she calls him, and return to the studio, Claudia's already finished her "commercial happy" look and is halfway through her "theatrical sexy" sitting. Ulysses, God bless him, was able to dry her tears and happily took on the role of model stroker, even going so far as to say stuff like, "You seem really centered," and "You go, girl."

Two days and six too many healthy meals later, I drop Ulysses off at LAX and return home to find Claudia at my doorstep, a large white envelope under her arm. It's now been almost fifty-two hours since I've seen This Many, and since we're due to get together tonight, the last person I want to deal with is the one banging on my door.

"Do you know what that agent bitch said?" Claudia screams. "She said my eyes looked puffy, like I had allergies, and I would have to retake them. Can you believe it?"

Before I can think of anything to say but yes, the phone rings. I fumble with my keys and rush in to get it but the machine beats me.

"Craig," says Ulysses from the plane. "Leeza Gibbons."

I yank the phone from its cradle. *"Leeza Gibbons is dead?"* I scream.

"No," he gasps. "She's sitting across from me."

From somewhere over Fresno, Ulysses stage-whispers his way down Claudia's Celebrity-Sighting Checklist, a guide for star encounters my neighbor laid out for him his first night in L.A. What's the star wearing? Are there sweat stains? How large are their pores? Do they have the greasies? What do they smell of? Are their pupils dilated? Any cosmetic surgery scars? And so on. Ulysses is in the middle of describing the faces Leeza's making as she flips through *People* magazine's 50 Most Beautiful People issue when Claudia grabs the phone.

"Can you do me a favor, Ulysses?" she says. "Can you ask who did her head shots?" There's a pause. "Get me a pencil, Craig."

The Leeza sighting properly logged, I explain to Claudia that I'm due at Damon's in less than an hour and will help her deal with her head shot dilemma after the lovin'.

"Bink's out of town," I say, raising my eyebrows, "so we're just going to house-sit and watch videos."

"Uh-huh," says Claudia.

While my neighbor takes to tormenting me with the chorus of Rod Stewart's "Tonight's the Night," I toss my contact stuff, toothbrush, and deodorant into a Ziploc bag—just in case—put on some clothes that I think will look good on the floor and hit the trail.

I greet Damon as though I've just returned from Normandy. Then we go outside to enjoy the setting sun and the company of Bink's golden retriever, Paycheck. We ask the dog what we should order to eat, then disagree about his answer because that's the kind of corny shit people do when they're in a love montage.

The food comes and we settle on the Bink's giant leather couch to watch *Broadcast News*, one of my favorites, which Damon missed when it was in theaters, most likely because he was in the womb at the time.

It doesn't even get past the FBI warning before Damon hits stop.

"I was hoping we could talk," he says.

I've learned to dread sentences like that because they're always followed by, well, they're followed by the words Damon's using now.

"I don't know how to say this," he says. What follows sounds like lines from a soap opera that he's trying to memorize while I hold the script. "Blah blah past two weeks blah blah blah blah amazing," he says. "Blah blah blah incredible person. Blah blah blah think of you more as a friend . . ."

Not yet, I think as I feel my chest compress and every ounce of employable oxygen leave my body. I take a deep breath to try and replenish what's gone missing inside me but I can't. As my heart pounds its way into my throat, I can't help but feel completely defined by this moment. This is who I am, right here.

"Blah blah blah blah not you, it's me," he continues. "Blah blah blah never wanted to hurt blah. Blah blah blah blah be friends. Blah, Craig."

The whole exchange is so civilized and undramatic that a part of me wants to stand up and hurl Bink's daytime Emmy through the big-screen TV just so that when I tell people about how disappointed I am there will be physical evidence. Of course, I don't. That's not the sort of thing an incredible person like me does.

"I got dumped," I call and tell Dandy when I get home.

"Already?" says the mistress of empathy before catching herself. "I'm sorry, Craig. Do you want to come over?"

"Nah," I say, still unable to breathe like a normal person. "I'll be okay."

After hanging up, I find the disposable camera with the pictures of the Catalina trip still inside and take it at its word, tossing it into the trash can across the room for two points. I go to remove my contacts, but realize that my toiletries are in a Ziploc bag in my glove compartment, so I pad barefoot out to get them.

I climb into bed a few minutes later with a stomach full of quicksand and wonder if I'll ever be able to sleep again.

The next day, I take Claudia to Leeza Gibbons's photographer in Beverly Hills. After what we both agree was a better session, we stop at Mulberry Street Pizza, where I'm going to pretend to eat. I'm splashing cold water on my face in the men's room when I look up and see one lone eight-by-ten glossy bolted to the wall next to the sink. Its subject:

Joey Buttafuoco, looking out at me as if to say, "You think you've got love life problems?" I guess the lesson here is if you plan to have an affair with a mentally unbalanced slice of Long Island jailbait who may or may not decide to shoot your wife in the head, make sure you have a good head shot. You're going to need it.

9

"Remind me to never get fixed up by a game-show host again," I say emphatically, as I drive Miles to the dentist to get his wisdom teeth pulled.

"So if Alex Trebek calls and says he has a hot cousin . . ." Miles suggests.

"Not interested," I say.

"If Chuck Woolery says he knows a really great guy . . ."

"Fuck Chuck," I say as we pull up to the clinic.

"Okay," Miles says, pulling himself together. "If this goes well, Craig, I'm going to get that lipo I've always dreamed of."

"Miles, you need liposuction like I need . . ."

"A call from Pat Sajak."

"Exactly."

It's been four days since the Darlington Dump and I've abandoned my scheme to jury-rig his carpet, if only for Jasmine's sake. Still, I can't ditch that dead feeling in my stomach, the one that you think will go away if you can just get a good night's sleep, but before you even open your eyes in the morning, it's upon you again. That's why it's nice to have someone like a dentist-phobic Miles to focus on, someone who at least appears to be worse off than I am. So what if I can't listen to *Love Songs on the Coast* without choking up, at least I'm not about to go under the drill.

Miles is completely out of it when I pick him up a few hours later and falls asleep the second I get him home. He wakes up just in time to join me in watching an encore presentation of the series finale of *Blossom*. Miles has learned over the years that watching the final episode of anything, even a show he's never seen before like *Blossom,* is something he shouldn't do alone. Between that and the drugs, it looks like we've got a prime-time blubberfest on our hands.

"Joey Lawrence is going to be fine," I say assuringly, handing my outpatient friend another Kleenex. "Let's not forget he's got that music career to fall back on."

"Oh, that's right," Miles sobs. "Thank God you're here."

When Miles nods off during the last commercial, I call to check my messages and learn from Claudia that her new head shots are "fantastic." The other message is from Michelle, saying she's "looking forward to seeing me and this mystery date person," and that our tickets for Sunday's matinee of *Beauty and the Beast* will be at the box office.

"I don't know why Michelle gets under my skin so much," I say to Dandy as we head to the Rose Bowl Swap Meet the subsequent Sunday morning. "I still care so much what she thinks of me."

"Was she the biggest love of your life?" Dandy asks.

"So far," I mutter. "That's so pathetic."

"What about Aladdin?" she says.

"Too soon to tell."

"What about that chef guy from the ship?" She thinks for a moment. "Rug."

"His name was Sergio," I say. "And that was his real hair. Luigi wore the rug and we were just friends."

"No. I meant add 'rug' to my swapping list. If I don't find a rug for the front room today, I'm just going to fucking move and start over."

Hauling my depressed ass to Pasadena at seven o'clock on a Sunday morning to watch Dandy fight over knickknacks with Janet Charlton from *Star* magazine is not normally my idea of fun. It's the least I could do, however, considering Dandy's agreed to be my "surprise date" at this afternoon's matinee of *Beauty and the Beast*.

"Why did we have to get here so early?" I ask as we approach the front gate. "Look, it's cheaper to get in after nine o' clock."

"It's worth it to come early and pay the extra five bucks," insists Dandy, "because if you don't, Diane Keaton would have already been here and bought all the good stuff for a song."

Once inside, it takes Dandy all of eight seconds to make her first purchase, a vintage leopard-skin coat with matching earmuffs. She's able to barter the starstruck vendor down to half the original asking price and seals the deal when she agrees to wear the coat on *That's Just Dandy*.

"It's amazing," Dandy says as we walk away. "Since I've been famous, I get better deals on everything. It's so ironic. When you can finally afford to buy shit, they give you everything for free. After my show's been on a few years, I want to go on *Lifestyles of the Rich and Famous* and see if I can go a week without having to open my wallet."

After her second purchase, a Spanish-style lamp Dandy describes as "very 'Take a Bow' video," I allow my famous scavenger friend to set her own pace while I wander the aisles alone and worry about what this afternoon's reunion with the Catfucker will hold.

Two hours and several star sightings later—Cher looking for items to rip off for her Sanctuary catalog, Luke Perry pretending not to notice that his 90210 doll has been marked down twice—I realize it's time to locate Dandy and head out. By the time I find her, rifling through the vintage Adidas booth, we've only got an hour to make it to the theater.

"But Craig," she pleads, "I haven't found my rug yet."

"If we don't leave now, we'll never make it," I argue. "And we still have to change."

"Can't we go like this?" Dandy asks. "I mean, it's Disney for God's sake."

"I don't want Michelle to think I can't afford long pants," I beg.

In return for thirty more minutes of rug shopping time, Dandy buys us both new outfits from a booth specializing in wide-wale corduroy.

"We look like a bag of Ruffles," I say as we high-tail it back from Pasadena, despite our best intentions, sans rug.

We make it to the theater with forty-five seconds to spare and attempt to pull ourselves together in the parking structure elevator.

"Tucked or untucked," I say, holding out my shirttails.

"Untucked," says Dandy, before whipping the leopard-skin ear muffs out of her purse. "Muffs or no muffs."

"No muffs," I say pleadingly.

"I better just in case," she says. "Disney songs drive me crazy."

Muffs in place, Dandy puts her arm in mine and leads me to the box office. We follow a remarkably tall family of four—bedecked in Disney logowear from head to toe—into the auditorium and end up sitting behind them.

"If they put on mouse ears," Dandy says, "I'm calling the usher."

When Dandy opens her program to get a gander at the woman she's come to intimidate, a small slip of paper falls out.

"Goddammit, Craig!" she says disgustedly and, judging by the miffed reaction of the logowear mom, quite audibly. Dandy shoves the paper under my nose. Under the *Beauty and the Beast* logo are printed the words, "In this performance the role of Cheesegrater will be played by Jeffrey Howe."

"I didn't come all this way to see some second-string Cheesegrater," she huffs.

"An outrage," I say, joining in her horrified disgust. "At least the real Spatula showed up."

"If these tickets weren't already free, I'd be up there at the box office right now making a scene," Dandy says.

"As opposed to making one down here," says the logowear dad, apparently unconcerned by the Cheesegrater switcheroo.

The lights go down and the show begins. I spot Michelle for the first time as a peasant in the opening number and point her out to Dandy, who clasps her hands together like a gun and pretends to spray my ex's corset with bullet holes. When Michelle changes costumes for the "Be Our Guest" number, Dandy draws her gun again, but can't seem to figure out which piece of cutlery she is.

"She's the first salad fork on the left," I whisper.

"Nice tines," observes Dandy before taking aim at the Cheesegrater. "See, Craig, this Jeffrey guy can't grate for shit. What a rip-off."

Just then, an area rug with a gymnast inside it flip-flops across the stage.

"That's my rug!" shrieks Dandy, her right hand pointing to the stage, her left trembling on her cheek.

My date gets shushed by the logowear mom and the next time I look over, Dandy's out cold, her leopard-skin earmuffs shielding her from the impossible-to-sleep-through screams of Tom Bosley, who's putting around the stage in a decorated golf cart bellowing "I'm lost! I'm lost!"

"No, you're not, Tom," I want to shout. "You're upstage left."

Backstage after the show, Dandy picks the sleep from the corner of her eyes and rubs it voodoo-style into the photo of Michelle in the program. Then, without my needing to tell her, she grabs my arm like the touchy-feely famous girlfriend she's agreed to be for the afternoon, causing me to wonder if I shouldn't be giving out little slips of paper that read, "In this performance the role of Craig's Love Slave will be played by Dandy Rio."

I can't help but shiver when Michelle, in her postshow kimono, emerges from the dressing room and slinks down the hall to greet us, seemingly in slow motion. Dandy and Michelle shake claws, then there's an awkward moment when I think Dandy might lose her cool, brought on by Michelle's confession that she has no idea who Dandy is.

"I'm sorry," she says. "I just don't watch television. So, what did you think of the show?"

"I was a little disappointed," says Dandy, yawning. "I thought it was going to be on ice."

"I'm curious," I say. "Is there a whole other troupe of dancing silverware back here for special occasions? You know, does the stage manager ever say, 'Eisner's coming today. Let's get out the good china'?"

Dandy and Michelle fake-laugh in stereo and then Michelle asks, "How long have you two been together? I mean, I haven't seen anything about it in the press."

"Couple months," I say.

"I thought you didn't know who I was," says Dandy.

"I know who you are," Michelle backtracks, "I just haven't seen the show."

There's an awkward silence, which Michelle finally breaks by saying, "I assume the writing's going well, Craig. I mean, you look like you spend a lot of time at the typewriter."

As I rile under Michelle's reference to my fleshy and pale appearance, Dandy asks if there's a ladies' room she can use. "I would have gone in the lobby," she adds, "but I hate signing autographs on the can."

"You wouldn't believe the kinds of things people give her to sign," I say as though Dandy's being so famous as to be asked to sign a tampon wrapper will somehow make Michelle kick herself even harder.

Michelle points Dandy to the dressing room, then takes me out to the curb where she can smoke.

"I like your outfit," Michelle says, straightening my collar maternally. "It's so retro geek."

"Dandy bought it for me," I say. It's the first thing that I've said to Michelle that wasn't a lie. "She buys me stuff constantly." And the last.

"Speak of the devil," Michelle says as Dandy screeches up in her Miata.

"We gotta go, Craig," Dandy says nervously, her eyes gesturing suspiciously to a Hefty bag on the floorboard. "I need you *now*."

"You know how love is when it's all fresh and new," I say before pecking the Catfucker on the cheek and peeling out with Dandy.

Two nights later, Dandy invites Miles and me over to watch the final episode of *Full House*. Dandy's auditioning to be in some stalker TV movie opposite John Stamos and figures watching tonight would be good for her karma.

"I love how you've decorated," Miles gushes as we enter the front room. "And this rug is sensational. Where'd you get it?"

"Some place in Century City," says Dandy matter-of-factly.

"The colors are so rich, so vibrant," he continues.

"It practically dances," I add.

"I might have to use it to dry my eyes," Miles jokes as the *Full House* theme plays for the final presyndication time. "You know how I get."

"Be my guest," says Dandy.

10

I'm temping again at Jupiter Filmworks when I get the call. Seems This Many is going to be in the neighborhood and would like to get together for lunch as he's leaving for Japan to sing in some Chippendale's knockoff at the end of the week.

"I got fired from the Aladdin gig," he explains. "I'll tell you the whole story over lunch."

We meet at the Spielberg/Katzenberg-owned, submarine-themed eatery Dive in the Century City mall. By the time Damon arrives—twenty minutes late—the obnoxious underwater milieu, coupled with my mixed feelings about seeing him again, have me suffering from a major case of the bends.

"So how did you get fired?" I ask, once we're seated.

"Okay," says Damon, as though he's told the story a thousand times already. "Remember how I'm not in the last number of the show?"

"Vaguely," I say.

"Well, just for funzies," he continues, "I used to stand in the back where the carpet drops us off and try to think of funny things to do to make the rest of the cast laugh. The audience, of course, couldn't see us, just the people onstage. So it started out with just making funny faces but then it got bigger and bigger. Like one time, I put on the usher's uniform and pretended to vacuum, then I covered myself in Christmas lights. One time Jasmine pretended to blow me."

"I am so scared of where this is going," I say.

"So the other day I couldn't think of anything, so at the last second, I took off all my clothes and stood there with a leaf over my privates that I would occasionally lift up."

The realization that Mowgli and Mary Poppins and God knows how many other furry creatures have had an audience with Damon Darlington's periscope and I, who have actually spent time and money wooing the brat, couldn't pick it out of a lineup, hits me like a torpedo from an enemy sub.

"So long story short," Damon continues, obviously enjoying his newfound status as Magic Kingdom iconoclast, "it got back to the director what I did and then it went all the way to Eisner's office. And they canned me. It was this huge scandal. My dad is totally freaking out. He figures that I just blew his chance to be the voice of *The Lion King* 2 or something. That's another reason why I'm leaving town."

Damon claims that, as "featured vocalist," he won't be taking off his clothes in his new job in Japan—for a change—although everyone else in the cast of vaudevillian steroid-heads will. I make him promise to send video, then, noticing the time, suggest we leave.

As we walk out into the mall, I am surprised to realize that Damon's "blah blah blah be friends" proposition might actually come to pass. We hug good-bye and are about to go our separate ways when he asks about the Catalina pictures.

"They're still in the camera," I say truthfully, leaving out the fact that the camera proper is probably in some landfill by now. "I'll send them to you."

As Damon disappears down the escalator, the notion that we're not even remotely a good match enters my mind. He is just not the one. But that doesn't mean I can't make him regret his decision to give me the boot. The next time I see him, I decide, I'm going to be represented, muscled and, if seasonably appropriate, tan. Not wanting to let my newfound resolve wither under the fluorescent pall of Jupiter, I call Carolyn and tell her I'd need the rest of the afternoon off to deal with the chipped bicuspid I purport to have suffered at Dive.

Practically skipping back to my car, I head straight for Samuel French and purchase a listing of literary agents. It's time for *Deck Games* to see the world, and hopefully vice versa. While I'm at the register, I notice a stack of flyers advertising classes in creating your own one-person show and take one for Claudia, even though she has a good seven years to go on her self-imposed deadline. No sense hoarding this burst of ambition for myself.

When I get home, I decide that first, I should reward myself for my newfound gumption and call my local cable company. I've done without my favorite channels long enough. Enough of the depressing local news, whose top story always seems to be, "Innocent person dies senselessly just down the street from you." Enough of Jay and Dave and Conan. Give me E! or give me death.

The next morning, Bud, the cable guy, has me channel surfing within an hour and I spend the rest of the day spread out all over the front room, labeling envelopes, printing out letters to agents and catching up on my *Real Worlds*. Puck is such an asshole.

Three days later, I'm positioned in front of *The Gossip Show*, a program full of faces that need to have drinks thrown in them, when the phone rings. A literary agent, albeit one located in the outback of Encino, read my script and wants to meet for lunch to discuss representing me. I'm feeling so triumphant, I decide to treat myself to a month of HBO. Hell, I'm worth it.

"So, *Deck Sports*," gushes Rose Stubach, the aforementioned agent, over lunch at Stanley's in Sherman Oaks. "I stayed on the Lifecycle an extra twelve minutes just so I could finish it. I can't wait to start sending it out."

"That's great," I say, "but it's *Deck Games*."

"Even better," the sixtyish agent chirps. "Don't change it. Oh, look who's here, it's my daughter, Elise."

A breathless and overly made-up Elise plops herself down at our table and explains that she's been dress shopping for a cousin's upcoming wedding. It's tough to find the proper frock, she explains, because she needs something she can move in. Apparently Elise has been known to cut quite a rug at cousins' wedding receptions.

"Craig," says Rose, "did you do any dancing when you worked on the cruise ship?"

"Oh God," I sigh, "as assistant cruise director, 'Drag-a-Bag' was a big part of my job."

"What?" says Rose.

"I mean, dancing with the passengers."

While I ponder whether or not I just in some way referred to the only person on earth who's shown an interest in my writing career as a *bag,* Elise asks what dances I know.

"Oh, you know, the basics—Lindy, foxtrot, waltz, Safety . . ."

For some reason, shaking my groove thang is something I've always had a natural knack for, though I've never studied. I feel about dancing the way really well-hung guys must feel in the locker room, like I was blessed with a freebie and I might as well work it.

"Hustle?" Elise asks.

"Of course," I say, practically pshawing her. "Latin *and* regular."

"It's so rare to meet a man who's bi-hustle," Elise coos.

Given our shared enthusiasm for tripping the light fantastic it's only a matter of minutes before Rose suggests that I escort her daughter to the wedding. The fact that she does so while literally salivating over my script makes it virtually impossible for me to tell them the truth—that I'd rather get a Fresca enema while watching Kevin Costner in *Wyatt Earp*—so it looks like it's a date.

• •

"It's only one night," I say to Claudia, who's popped down to test-drive my new array of channels. "How bad can it be?"

"Kool and the Gang?" Claudia says distantly.

"I know," I sigh. "They always play bad music at weddings. But I can deal with it."

"No, on the TV," she shouts. "Come quick!"

I got cable in the nick of time, for it seems that VH1, bless their identity-crisis-having hearts, have started running original episodes of *American Bandstand*. Claudia and I have been lucky enough to tune in at the outset of an eight-hour marathon.

"I can't believe I used to think these people were sexy," says Claudia while watching a black man the size of a Fotomat booth slide his head back and forth Egyptian style to some forgotten track by DeBarge. "Not one of these people could get past security at MTV's beach house."

Though any unexpected exposure to DeBarge can send one reeling, my biggest shock comes during the fifth hour when Dick asks a young gal in a tube top and Sergio Valente jeans and her obviously gay Puerto Rican "boyfriend" to assess the danceability of Matthew Wilder's "Break My Stride" during the show's Rate-a-Record segment.

"I can't fucking believe it," I say.

"I know," says Claudia. "I would never have given that song an 89."

"No, not that," I gasp. "Guess who's got a date with the chick in the tube top."

"Oh my God, Craig. I'm so sorry."

We spend the remainder of the marathon combing the crowd for shots of Elise, which are not at all hard to find. Given the number of close-ups she gets and how blatantly unworthy she is of them, I can't help but suspect that the camera operator had also written a script that Rose Stubach had expressed interest in representing.

The second the marathon ends, I get on the phone to Dandy, who's just the person to call when a situation requires that you think only of yourself and you need help rationalizing.

"You're overreacting, Craig," says Dandy. "What, besides the tube top, was so bad about her?"

"Well, first of all, she lied about her age. She told me she was twenty-six, but if she was nineteen when Matthew Wilder was all the rage, you do the math. Plus, she's had breasts and I think a chin installed and the way she dances, I mean, she makes Whitney Houston look like a fly girl."

"She's a maniac on the floor?" says Dandy, still not taking me seriously.

"Exactly," I rant. "I know I should be stronger but I just can't go there."

With Dandy's invaluable input, I concoct a plan. The day before the wedding, I call Elise and tearfully explain about the sudden death of my brother-in-law in a freak backhoe accident. Though I can sense her disappointment, the depth of my sorrow eclipses it enough to get me off the hook.

The day of the wedding arrives, and instead of staying home and channel surfing my guilt away, I let Dandy talk me into tagging along to the AIDS dance-a-thon at Universal Studios, where she's serving as one of the celebrity emcees.

Though getting down with my bad self is about the last thing I feeling like doing, how can I resist when Rosie Perez, one of Dandy's cohosts, grabs me in the wings and drags me out on top of a speaker with her? As I attempt to keep up with the queen of grind, the crowd erupts. I now know what it must have felt like to have been featured in the spotlight dance on *AB*. I'm about to ask Rosie if she would mind if I went to my knees and tossed my head hither and yon in front of her Oscar-nominated crotch when I feel something grab my ankle.

"You lying sack of shit!"

"Elise," I say, looking down into the sweaty, irate face of my erstwhile wedding date. "What about the wedding?"

"The bride got cold feet," she shouts. "What about the backhoe death?"

"False alarm," I stammer. "They checked the dental records and it wasn't him."

During my ludicrous alibi-giving, Rosie slips away, leaving a vacancy on the speaker that Elise wastes no time in assuming, ensuring that whatever transpires between us does so in front of hundreds of perspiring, charitable onlookers.

"Look, loser," she spits, grabbing my collar. "You dance nice with me like you did with that little tart and I won't tell my mother what a two-faced prick you are."

Pilfering what moves I recall from the oeuvre of *Dance Fever*'s Deney Terrio and Motion, I spin, lift, head-roll, and shimmy as if my career depends on it, but it's still not enough to keep up with Elise, who with hundreds of eyes on her has turned into a one-woman disco inferno.

"We're doing an over-the-shoulder lift combination fish dip!" she shouts. "Whether you want to or not."

"No fucking way!" I shout, but it's to no avail, my partner is already leaping into position. A second later, Elise is spinning over my head in a fuchsia blur.

A tiny part of me, shocked at the finesse at which we executed the difficult move, wants to shout, "I still got it!" into the crowd of revelers. The rest of me, however, is wishing there were no such thing as AIDS so I wouldn't have to be here, disco-ing atop a speaker, with the scene-making Elise Stubach whirling overhead like a taffeta propeller.

"Craig!" someone yells. "Down here."

It's Dandy, standing under us with one of the event's photographers.

"Say cheese!" she shouts.

Realizing that this is her big chance to be immortalized as the disco diva she is, Elise whips around to offer the shutterbug her good end, which she contends is the one with the eyes. What happens next might best be described as a camera flash, followed by a scream, followed by another fuchsia blur, followed by a call to 911.

• •

A sobbing Rose Stubach meets us at Cedars Sinai Medical Center, where I've come with Elise to have her broken legs tended to. My would-be agent follows her daughter into surgery dotingly, but not before telling me to fuck off and die, in that order.

When I get home *Dirty Dancing* is on HBO. I watch for a few minutes and decide that Patrick Swayze would never have allowed Elise Stubach to tumble ten feet to the pavement and break both her legs. He would have caught her, kissed her, married her, impregnated her, all of it.

"I'm glad somebody's having the time of their life," I mumble, before calling the cable company and begging them to make it go away. Nobody should have to pay *extra* to be reminded that they're not Patrick Swayze.

11

Given that I'm the only one in my calling circle who couldn't care less about *Melrose Place*, it's oddly fitting that my first day as a paid extra is being spent on the nighttime soap's Valencia soundstage. Burnt out on temping, I signed up yesterday to do extra work with Nice Atmosphere, the agency that handles the background actors on *That's Just Dandy*.

Though contributing to the net worth of Aaron Spelling by mouthing "peas and carrots" to geeky strangers has never been high on my list of career goals, at least it doesn't involve diving into a temperamental Xerox machine for misfeeds. And I'm hoping that I can slip *Deck Games* to Josie Bissett, who, now that I think of it, would be perfect as the bodacious newlywed who dumps her husband to become an exotic dancer in Barbados.

We're halfway done with the first scene, which is set at a cocktail reception at the office where Heather Locklear's character works, when the stage manager announces it's time for lunch.

"Be back here in an hour," she says before pulling out a list and reading. "And if we catch any of you doing the following: wading, bathing, having sex, urinating, or defecating in the pool, we will not hesitate to press charges." Noticing the mortified looks on all of our faces, she sheepishly adds, "We've had some problems in the past."

Since taking a dump in the pool's out, I head to the phone to give the *Melrose*-obsessed Miles an update.

"Andrew Shue's bone!" he shrieks when I report that I was able to snag for him a half-eaten chicken wing from the actor's plate following a scene set at the local hangout, Shooters. "I always *figured* him for a dark meat eater," Miles continues. "Courtney Thorne-Smith notwithstanding."

Not surprisingly, Miles wants to know every little detail, from who I have and haven't rubbed elbows with to how warm the pool is. Fifteen minutes later, he's still riveted and I'm grasping at trivia.

"You might be interested to know that Shooters shares a common wall with Heather Locklear's office at D & D," I drone on. "That way, if she gets thirsty at work, she can just punch a hole through the wall and grab herself a cold one."

"Tell me more!" Miles pleads.

"Um, I wanted to tell you about this in person," I say covertly, building the suspense. "But what the hell. In my backpack, as we speak, leftover from a party scene in which I toasted the promising future of D & D, is a champagne glass with Heather Locklear's lipstick marks on it."

I hear what sounds like a publicist's head hitting a desk blotter. I try halfheartedly to revive him, fail, then hang up and make a beeline for craft services.

That night I arrive home to ten phone messages: nine from Miles and one from Dandy, asking if she can crash at my place because her house is getting painted and she can't deal with the fumes.

I've sort of been avoiding Dandy of late as her moods have been swinging like saloon doors. It seems *That's Just Dandy,* like the vinyl LP and that poor whale from *Free Willy,* is just this side of extinction. Though her recent ratings were no worse than say, *Walker: Texas Ranger*'s, the buzz is that the network's had it up to their pie charts with Dandy's diva shenanigans, and would just as soon amputate.

"If I kiss the right asses at the affiliate convention this weekend," Dandy says while attempting to find the makings of hot tea in my ill-equipped kitchen, "I just know they'll renew me. Jesus, Craig, don't you have any spoons?"

"They're all in the dishwasher," I say, "which has been broken since a week after I moved in."

Dandy disappears into the appliance for two spoons and comes out dry heaving. As if the stench weren't enough, she swears she saw a family of roaches doing the Electric Slide atop an encrusted piece of Tupperware.

"That does it," she snaps, "I'm calling Kathryn. I don't care. I'll pay for it."

Kathryn is Dandy's born-again housekeeper. She drives a Toyota truck packed to the gills with cleaning products and the spirit of the Lord. I met her once at Dandy's and remember asking her about her GOD IS MY PILOT bumper sticker.

"I though the expression was 'God Is My Copilot,' " I said.

"I promoted him," she said, eyeing me judgmentally, "and you should too."

The next morning I'm awakened by the disturbingly alien sound of someone vacuuming. I wrap a towel around my waist and wander out to find Kathryn behind the Eureka.

"Dandy let me in before she left," she explains.

I'm about to ask her if she can't find a more quiet chore to start with, like sandblasting, when the phone rings.

"Why haven't you returned my calls?" Miles hollers. "I didn't sleep at all last night thinking about Andrew Shue's bone."

"You and the rest of America," I say.

"Well, Craig, here's the deal. I must have it in my hand today or I'll lose it. Oh, and about the champagne glass, I need it too . . ."

I look to the kitchen table where I left my *Melrose* souvenirs and neither are there. Panicked, I turn suddenly to see Kathryn standing at the sink, caressing Heather's glass flute with a soapy sponge.

"Goddammit, Kathryn, no!" I scream.

When I lunge toward the erring domestic, my towel falls away, giving the already mortified zealot an audience with my most private of popes. She crunches her eyes shut in the way one does during the bloody parts of *ER*, sets the glass on the counter and starts to collect her belongings.

"I'm sorry, Kathryn," I say. "Please stay."

"Look, I don't have to take this," she says heading for the door. "I am a child of God and I've had a really long week."

"What was that about?" Miles asks when I return to the phone.

"Um . . ." I stammer. "You know . . . the Heather glass . . ."

"Right," he says, "I'm donating it to PAPT."

While Miles explains that PAPT stands for Plants Are People Too, a group of philanthropic green thumbs who tend to the shrubbery of the terminally ill, I examine the glass and discover that the outside lip print is history but the inside print is still intact.

"They're having an auction tonight," he continues, "A day-old Heather glass could bring in big bucks. And besides, I'd still have the bone to keep me warm at night."

While Miles rambles on about all the people in his office who can't wait to see the second hand *Melrose* merchandise, I dig in the garbage and find the bone, thank God. When Miles insists that I bring the booty and meet him for lunch, I agree, deciding that I'll just fudge the lower lip print. I mean, the plants won't know the difference, right?

I wrap the delicate vessel in a sheet of bubble pack I've been keeping for just such an occasion and head to the Beverly Center in search of the matching lipstick. I realize, of course, that I could just get any old lipstick and replace the entire print and no one would be the wiser, but some part of me, the part that cares about dying people and their bougainvillea, wants it to be as authentic as possible.

Three and a half hours later, I've gone to every makeup counter in the mall without coming up with a match. Oh sure, some shades are close, but at this point, I'm on a mission from God.

"This stuff is pretty waxy," says the fourteenth salesperson I visit. "Maybe you should try Sav-On."

With fifteen minutes to go before my lunch date with Miles, I screech up to Dandy's studio and, after enduring the usual "who are you?" song and dance with Clyde the security guard, I'm given passage onto the lot. Fortuitously, Dandy's on lunch break and has time to recreate the bottom lip. I know I could do it myself, but what if the lipstick won't come off and Miles busts me at lunch? Besides, I want it to be a woman's lips—a famous woman's lips at that.

"Wet and Wild?" Dandy says in disbelief, dumping out the lipstick from the Sav-On bag.

"Ninety-nine cents," I say. "Who knew?"

"I'm so glad I don't work for Fox."

I'd heard tell of Dandy's oral finesse but never gotten to witness it for myself until this moment. Raptly, I watch as she bears down on the glass with Zen-like precision, maintaining lower lip contact for a good ten seconds. Then she pulls away from the goblet, tosses her hair triumphantly and presents me with a lower lip smack so Locklear-esque it could fool Richie Sambora.

I'm fifteen minutes late for lunch with Miles, but considering my cargo, he's more than forgiving. The next day he calls to tell me that two rival dignitaries from countries he's never heard of got into a bidding war over the Heather glass and the more handsome of the two finally won out with a bid of $2,800 and a threat of war. The pathetic irony—that a silly champagne flute I was thoughtful enough to steal and then donate brought in more money than I made in the last two months—is not lost on me.

"That prince guy better not be planning to do something gross with it," Miles laments.

I'm about to remind him that a person who's slept the previous night with a half-eaten chicken bone on his nightstand shouldn't play the gross card, when the other line beeps.

"Get your ass in a suit, Craig," screams Dandy. "I'm picking you up in fifteen minutes."

"Where are we going?" I ask.

"You're going to be my date for the affiliates luncheon," she rants.

"Thanks to you and that bitch Heather Locklear I now have a fucking cold sore the size of a small child on my upper lip. So it's going to be *your* job to make sure the two pounds of Clinique I've got covering it are doing *their* job while I try to save *my* job. Got it? Good."

Had she not hung up in my ear, I might have pointed out that Dandy's had a good dozen holidays in Herpetia since I've known her and that to lay the rap on an innocent prime-time soap vixen is downright unfair, perhaps even slanderous. After some consideration, I decide to let Heather remain the scapegoat, for Dandy's going to need her wits about her if she's going to be schmoozing the network brass.

On the way to the luncheon we develop a hand signal for "Get thee to the powder room," which, thankfully, we only have to use once. Dandy's black rubber minidress, chosen specifically for its ability to keep people's eyes *off* her face, does its job beautifully. By the time we make our exit, hundreds of air and ass kisses later, Dandy's been given an assurance from the network president himself that *That's Just Dandy* would be around for at least thirteen more episodes.

"Oh, Craig," she hollers while changing into sweats back at my filthier-than-ever pad. "I told Kathryn why you freaked and she said if it's God's will, she'd like to come back and finish cleaning."

"Who is she, Maria Von Trapp?" I say.

"She also said dressing, for you, is optional," Dandy adds, laughing.

"Good God," I say.

12

After months of telling me how "totally toxic" L.A. is every time we talk, Ulysses calls from Santa Cruz to tell me he's decided to move here.

"I can't deny my musical dreams any longer," he proclaims. "I'm coming to L.A. and starting a band. I mean, if Keanu can do it, how hard can it be?"

"Well, you got me there," I say.

Three days later, we're moving my old friend into the apartment building across the street from mine. I'm sifting through his record collection reclaiming the LPs that belong to me—even though I don't know a single soul with a turntable—when Dandy shows up to bitch about the uninspiring state of affairs on *That's Just Dandy*.

"I mean, I'm an *artist*," she whines. "The only creative thing I ever do on that show is change my hair."

"Well, it looks incredible," Ulysses says.

"You think so?" she says, her voice cracking with vulnerability. "Thanks."

While Ulysses hooks up his synthesizer, Dandy lies on the floor and stares up at the ceiling. "You know, my only regret from college is that I never got to see you guys play. What was the name of your band again?"

Ulysses and I utter "Kaleidoscope Eyes" simultaneously, with wildly divergent levels of enthusiasm.

"I bet you were hysterical," Dandy continues. "You were all into that eighties thing."

"It *was* the eighties," I say defensively.

With his keyboard now operational, Ulysses starts to tinkle away, causing Dandy to break into the kind of stream-of-consciousness oohing and aahing I suspect Chynna Phillips does in the shower. Unable to stomach the musical marriage unfolding before me, I disappear into the kitchen, return with a Snapple fruit punch and get the news.

"We're forming a band, Craig," says Ulysses, shortly before watching his security deposit disappear in a sticky ocean of Snapple.

"What?" I gasp, wishing I had taken a swig so I could at least punctuate my horror with a spit take.

"I can't deny my musical dreams any longer," pleads Dandy.

"You don't *have* any musical dreams," I point out.

"That's because I've been denying them."

I spend the next two hours listing the twenty-seven reasons why I can't join my friends in their musical crusade. I even reveal the embarrassing fact that I had to sell my bass two months ago to pay the phone bill, but they're having none of it.

"I came to L.A. to be a screenwriter, not a rock star," I plead.

"C'mon, Craig," begs Dandy.

"You know the rules, one impossible dream per person," I say finally, before disappearing across the street.

The next day on the set of *Murder, She Wrote,* where I'm doing extra work as a waiter in a pool-party scene, I get my first gander of my fellow extra, Godfrey Scott. With his tousled INXS hair, hazel eyes, and wiry but attractive bod, Godfrey is what Miles would lustfully refer to as a "snack." Snacks are different than Cute Club members in that they have a certain rough-around-the-edges quality that means they're not everyone's cup of tea. This particular one, however, happens to be mine.

In my experience, snacks aren't renowned for their conversational skills so much as for their ability to speak volumes with a single simmering glance. Godfrey seems to be the exception to this rule.

"Next take," he says, squinting up at me from his lawn chair, "I'm going to pretend my drink's poisoned, seize up and crash dead in the pool just to keep Jessica Fletcher on her toes."

We spend the rest of the day cracking wise and making fun of Angela Lansbury, who I'm sure is very nice. We manage to kill one entire forty-five-minute break in shooting by coming up with alternate titles for the show. *Emmy, She Lost,* I suggest. *Freedent, She Chewed,* Godfrey counters.

I'm still chuckling to myself about *Stone, She Passed,* when I arrive home to find that Dandy, Ulysses and Miles have let themselves in.

"What's going on?" I ask.

"Blast from the past, Craig," says Ulysses, waving the VCR remote. "Kaleidoscope Eyes live at the Sig Ep house, 1989."

When the doorbell rings, Dandy jumps up, assuming it's the pizza she ordered, but, alas, it's Claudia, whose way of showing up at the wrong time is so uncannily Lenny and Squiggy–esque, I'm surprised she doesn't let out a nasally "Hel-lo" with every entrance.

"Having a party?" she asks.

"More like a college reunion," Ulysses bluffs.

"I didn't know you went to college with these three, Miles," Claudia says.

"I didn't," says Miles.

After an awkward pause, Ulysses hits play. There in two dimensions, recorded via the half-inch video technology of the day, are Ulysses, me and the two other members of Kaleidoscope Eyes in all our Chess King glory.

"Craig, your ass was way better in college," Dandy observes.

"You're more than welcome to kiss it," I retort.

"This is my favorite part!" says Ulysses. "Craig unzips his parachute pants and he has *another* pair underneath."

Unable to endure both the audio and video portions of the excavation simultaneously, I drop my face into my hands and try to think about more pleasant subjects, like gum disease and that Long Island high-schooler who got sucked into a Jacuzzi on prom night and died.

"We knew three songs," I groan. "Why is this taking so long?"

The band on the TV finish their set to a smattering of drunken applause. I peek through my fingers and see the camera zoom in on a sweaty but ebullient Ulysses.

"Thank you, Tempe!" he shouts before the screen turns to static.

"Bravo, Craig," Miles says. "I mean, Mr. Headbanger."

"I had the hair," I say defensively as Miles imitates my rock 'n' roll posturing. "What was I supposed to do, stand there? No, I had to work it."

"See, Craig, you did love it," says Ulysses.

"Oh, so that's what tonight's about," I say, finally catching a clue. "Let's remind Craig how much fun he had and then he'll join our new band."

"Which we're calling *Rio Grande*!" chirps Dandy.

When an expression of abject horror appears on my face, Ulysses explains that they figured incorporating Dandy's name into the band's moniker would attract Dandy's TV fans. The fact that Dandy's TV fans can't even drive, let alone get into a rock club, was apparently not a consideration.

"You worry about the music," Miles says when I broach the subject. "And let me worry about the fans."

"Who are you," I say incredulously, "Reuben Kinkaid?"

"I'm your manager," he says, "and I'm going to make Rio Grande a household name."

The room gangs up on me but I hold my ground, explaining that it's going to take a lot more than a grainy six-year-old video to get my ass—this not-so-great-as-it-used-to-be ass—back in parachute pants.

"We thought you might say that," says Dandy before pulling a brand-new bass guitar with a big red bow on it out from behind the sofa.

"I hope you kept the receipt," I mutter.

"Craig, get over it," she says adamantly. "This isn't about you. It's bigger than you. It's bigger than all of us."

"It's downright grande," says Miles.

The next day I'm back on the set of *Gazillionaire, She Is,* cutting up with Godfrey, who's become so snackable by this point, I'm surprised the craft services people don't complain about the competition.

"What's in the notebook?" I ask, in reference to the pad I've seen him scribbling on in between takes.

"Lyrics," he replies. "I'm in a band."

"Really?" I remark. "So am I."

"We knew you'd come around," says Ulysses when I arrive that night, tail between legs, at our first official band meeting. Miles and Claudia, in full groupie mode, are already on hand. "You've got the music in you."

Just then a leather-clad Dandy bursts in carrying one of those rain sticks percussionists use.

"All right, motherfuckers," she bellows, shaking the stick violently. "Let's rock! This is going to be my instrument," she continues, tipping the rod to and fro. "Doesn't it sound beautiful? And I can totally hump it, too."

While Dandy and her new rain stick get to know each other better, we take turns relating bits of band business. Ulysses reckons he can track down a drummer and a guitar player through the ads in *Music Connection*. Miles passes around the first draft of a press release he plans to send to everyone on earth. Dandy makes the none-too-surprising announcement that she knows someone from the Viper Room whom she's willing to abuse to get us a gig. Then I report on the Los Angeles Songwriters Showcase I've been invited to attend with my new friend Godfrey.

"You get to pitch your demos to A-and-R people," I say. "Some bands get signed on the spot."

"Rock 'n' roll," says Dandy, before lighting some incense and reading down her roster of song ideas, a list which includes such never-to-be-written titles as "Bitch Box," "I Got to Hate You to Love You" and "Pussy Willow." When she comes to the only palatable title of the lot, "Temporary Insanity"—a concept I find particularly apropos—Ulysses and I simultaneously give the thumbs-up sign. Two hours later, we have ourselves a tune.

"I also want to do a song that says, 'This ain't the same old Dandy you see on TV,' " says Dandy, getting her second wind. "Something that says there's a new girl in town."

"Sounds like the theme from *Alice,*" I yawn.

"Craig, you're a genius!" Ulysses crows. "Let's do the theme from fucking *Alice*!"

As I'm the only one who knows the words to the Theme from Fucking *Alice,* I'm relegated to singing them into Ulysses' portable tape recorder. He vows to turn my warblings into an arrangement by our next meeting.

"I had forgotten how fun it is to make music," I gush to Claudia two days later. "Oh, my God. Look, there's the Snack."

Claudia has allowed me to drag her along to FM Station, a rocker hangout in the Valley, to see Godfrey's band, the Godmakers, work their magic.

"He keeps looking over here," says Claudia as Godfrey sings "Driven to Distraction," a Godmakers original about "endless nights of passion," while tossing those perfectly imperfect locks hither and yon.

"No, he doesn't," I snap. "He hasn't opened his eyes in twenty minutes."

"That's because he's *thinking* about looking over here."

A few days later, Rio Grande, which now features a drummer and guitar player who haven't played a note since their last band lost to Sawyer Brown on the first season of *Star Search,* cuts its first demo. "Temporary Insanity" turns out remarkably well considering Dandy's range is all of four notes. I pick up the final mix from Ulysses as Godfrey pulls up in his black Jeep to pick me up.

We arrive at the showcase, check in our tapes and sit nervously as Don Delmondo, a fortyish A & R guy with a widow's peak and an attitude, mercilessly trashes tune after tune. Finally, he hears one he likes. It's "Driven to Distraction." The Godmakers' endless-nights-of-passion song. Mine and Godfrey's song, I can't help thinking.

"This is a keeper," Delmondo announces before inserting the next tape and saying, "Number 51." My number. There's an amateurishly long leader on the tape, causing Delmondo to groan scoldingly, then, finally, an unaccompanied voice. But it's not Dandy's. It's mine.

"There's a new girl in town and she's feeling GOOD! There's a fresh, freckled face . . ."

"Is that you, Craig?" Godfrey whispers, my already unbearable mortification quadrupling with the realization that I had grabbed the wrong tape and that a room full of strangers is now listening to me croon the Theme from Fucking *Alice.*

Delmondo, smoke billowing from his ears, literally shoves the tape player off the table and rants, "What the hell is this? Some kind of joke? I don't have time to waste on this TV jingle bullshit!"

While Godfrey looks into his lap and tries not to laugh, I huff disgustedly and, like O.J., comb the scene for the real killers.

"Well, you're no Linda Lavin," is about the only thing Godfrey says to me on the way home.

• •

It's two weeks after *Alice*-gate, as it has come to be known, and I haven't seen hide or glorious hair of the Snack, despite leaving several messages on his machine. Meanwhile Dandy has pulled a few strings (among other things), and landed us a gig at the Viper Room.

"I just got off the phone with Miles," Dandy says excitedly when she calls to tell me about the booking, "and it looks like *E.T.*'s coming down to see us play."

"Please tell me it's the alien and not the TV show. We are *not* ready for prime time."

"Don't be such a downer, Craig. Rio Grande is going to knock the Sunset Strip on its ass."

"That's a mighty lofty goal for a band with two songs," I point out. "One of which is the theme from *Alice*."

"Well, if the Grateful Dead can drag out a song for forty minutes, dammit, so can Rio Grande."

The night of the gig arrives and I wait backstage with the rest of the band, unable to sneak a peek at the crowd for fear of what I'll see. Miles or Dandy, or some combination thereof, trotted out their charms on the bouncer, who vowed to be lenient on those Dandy fans who are underage, just plain geeky or both. Though I can sense that a good-sized crowd is forming, my hunch is that they are all Sharpee-clutching, autograph-seeking, eleven-year-old Dandy-ophiles, which is not the sight you want to see when you're preparing to rock the house, or la casa, as the case may be.

I'm in the dressing room zipping up the pink waitress uniform Dandy pilfered from the studio when I notice it says VERA on the inside tag.

"Oh my God," I say happily, wanting to call attention to the first good omen of the night. "This is really Beth Howland's uniform."

"I know," says Dandy cockily. "Wardrobe rocks."

Once zipped, Dandy turns around so she can scrutinize the crotch of my borrowed leather jeans.

"Which way are you hanging, Craig?" she asks, her face smushed up in confusion.

"Just kind of down," I say. "Middle."

"This is rock 'n' roll, Craig. Do you have any socks?"

"On my feet," I scoff.

Dandy lets out an exasperated sigh then reaches under her skirt, removes her panties, rolls them into a sprightly cylinder and hands them over. "Here, meet your basket."

I install my package, then get Miles to snap a group shot of all of us, knowing that the chances of us being in the mood to smile and touch each other after the gig are slim.

We take to the stage and start into "Temporary Insanity." The stage lights make it nearly impossible to see the crowd, but I do notice a metallic glare coming from the front row, which I'm choosing to think is a hardcore rocker's dog collar and not some preteen's retainer. Dandy prances out with her rain stick in one hand and a martini in the other. She knocks back the cocktail, taking the olive in her mouth, then looks around for something to do with it. As the crowd chants, "Dandy . . . Dandy . . . Dandy . . . ," she struts over, grabs me by the back of the head and bestows our first, and probably last, mouth-to-mouth exchange ever, sending the olive skidding bitterly over my taste buds and down my throat. Then Dandy struts to the mike and starts singing.

"Insanity" comes to a clumsy but well-received finish, and though the audience probably has about thirty pubic hairs between them, it still feels incredible when they go bananas.

"Thank you, L.A.," growls Dandy once the applause dies down. "See if you remember this one."

We kick into our newfangled version of the *Alice* theme. To give extra spice to the first chorus, Dandy poses with one of her sensibly shod feet on the monitor, giving the first few rows a panties-free view of both London and France. By the time we launch into the instrumental break, the spectators are reaching their adolescent limbs skyward, beckoning Dandy to mosh. She tosses the microphone to the ground and turns to face me.

"I'm diving, Craig," she says. "It's my destiny."

Just then, out of nowhere, someone near the stage grabs the mike and hollers, "Look, everybody, it's Kelly Bundy!"

Dandy hurls herself into the throng just as everyone turns to see Christina Applegate, who has just sauntered in wearing fishnets. I watch in horror as my most famous friend does a belly flop onto the averted heads of her so-called fans. After calling the cocktail waitress, who would have caught her had her hands not been full, a useless c-word, Dandy tumbles to the floor as the Applegate hysteria continues.

I jump off the stage and help my friend up. Once on her feet, Dandy pushes past me, climbs awkwardly back on the stage, giving everyone who missed the first tour a second chance to view London and France, then scurries to the dressing room in a tearful pink flurry.

I make my way backstage and find Dandy crying into her own reflection.

"There's a lot of fans out there, Dandy," I say, "and they want to hear our other song."

"I'm leaving the band, Craig," she says pulling a bloody piece of shot glass from her quivering upper lip. "My rock 'n' roll heart has been broken."

She sputters something about how she wants to return to the relatively tranquil world of sitcom acting where it's "safe," then disappears under the fluorescent exit sign.

Ulysses and I are about to go find her when the burly manager of the Viper Room says, "Hey, you owe us twenty more minutes."

Thinking fast, Ulysses and I return to the stage and commence an impromptu auction of Dandy paraphernalia that not only takes up the bulk of our twenty minutes but nets us a startling $165 for the rain stick alone. When Miles, who's standing offstage with the Viper Room owner, motions for us to stretch, I do the only thing I can think of. I reach into my pants.

"Okay, everybody," I say, grabbing the mike and dangling Dandy's panties tantalizingly, "we have one more item left to auction."

Though the crowd goes wilder over Dandy's yellowing underpants than it did for "Temporary Insanity," the one song that we actually finished, I'm pleased to have at least ended on a high note.

"I'll take care of the equipment, Craig," says Ulysses. "You go find Dandy."

A few minutes later, I'm heading to my car when I hear footsteps behind me.

"I said it before, and I'll say it again," a voice says, "you're no Linda Lavin."

"Godfrey!" I gasp excitedly, before remembering how over him I am. "I don't have time now. I've got to go find my friend."

"I'll help you look," he offers.

We hop in his Jeep and ride for a while.

"Your opener ruled," he says finally.

"Everything was going fine until fucking Christina Applegate showed up," I sigh.

"That wasn't even her," he says. "Just some girl that looks like her."

"Turn left on Beachwood," I say, and he does. "By the way," I say bitterly as we pull up to Dandy's, "where the fuck have *you* been?"

Godfrey pushes his hair out of the way, looks into my eyes and smiles. "Breaking up with somebody," he says.

13

Though it feels like an eternity, I actually only spend fourteen minutes comforting Dandy about the self-destruction of Rio Grande. The second she heads to the shower to "wash that band right out of her hair," I bid a tender farewell and beat it back outside where I pray Godfrey's still waiting.

"Good, you didn't leave," I sigh as I bound, as ruggedly as possible, into the open-air vehicle.

"Why would I leave?" he says.

Because you can pretty much have anyone you want? Because making Craig Clybourn weak in the knees holds all the challenge and mystery of a game of Candyland? Because you can tell how much I like you and isn't that always the kiss of death? Because you noticed how I ran like a girl into Dandy's house and suddenly you're reviled? Because because because because because.

"I don't know," I say. "Where are we going?"

"I'm starving," Godfrey says. "Do you mind if we stop at McDonald's?"

If I wasn't already writhing naked in the palm of his guitar-callused hand, Godfrey's matter-of-fact propensity for committing nutritional suicide in the middle of the night would have put me there. I've always said any friend of the Hamburglar is friend of mine.

"I'll try the Arch Deluxe," I tell the order taker, Samuel, then look to Godfrey. "I'm feeling very grown-up tonight."

"Well, I'm not," says Godfrey before ordering the two-cheeseburger combo meal and asking them to Supersize it. (Please, God, don't let size be important.)

Around the time that Samuel should be telling us our total and heading off to the fry area, I notice his brow furrow in frustration. He's pushing way more buttons than necessary and pushing them repeatedly. At one point our total reads $97.55, which would be understandable if he were throwing in a full-body massage, but I don't recall Godfrey ordering one.

A good ten minutes later, Samuel finally presents us with our order as though it were a house of cards he spent days on. With a half hour left to closing, Godfrey and I have the dining room to ourselves. We carry our trays to a corner table and settle in. I steal a stare as Godfrey negotiates his ketchup, hoping that somehow my infatuation with him will become manageable under the unforgiving fluorescent lighting. Alas, he even looks hot in a halo.

"I still don't get what's so Adults Only about this sandwich," I say between bites of my Arch Deluxe. "I'd understand it if there were a picture of Elizabeth Berkley's beaver embroidered into the patty, but no such luck."

"You have to order that special," says Godfrey. "This is what I wonder: Say if your kid wanted to have an Arch Deluxe, would you be concerned? Would you be like, 'No, Timmy, you're just *too young*. Wait until you're sixteen'?" Or would you be *proud*? Like, 'Our Timmy, he's so grown-up for his age'?"

God, I think I'm in love.

"So, this person you broke up with . . ." I say casually after a few fries.

"Terry," says Godfrey.

Good Lord. What sort of *It's Pat* nightmare is this, anyway?

"Do you still talk?" I ask.

"I don't know. We'll see."

"So what does Terry do?"

"What does Terry do?" echoes Godfrey. "Snore. Practice law. Sleep around. Lie about it."

"What does Terry not do?"

"Seem to care," Godfrey says. "Get my jokes."

Temporarily wordless, I glance down at my place mat and wish that I had a pencil so I could draw a dick on Ronald McDonald and scream, "Terry doesn't have one of *these,* by any chance?"

"Terry's a guy, F.Y.I.," he says, finally breaking the silence.

(*It's so amazing, Dandy,* I can hear myself saying later. *It's like he knows exactly what I'm thinking at all times.*)

"How long were you seeing him?" I say.

"Five, six months," he says. "Only the second guy I've ever been with. I was engaged for a year before that."

I listen intently as Godfrey tells the tale of Holly, the high school sweetheart he broke it off with when he drunkenly realized that he wished that whoever organized the entertainment for his bachelor party had thought of a circle jerk. Holly didn't take the news too well and made sure that Godfrey's fine upstanding family got wind of their son's curiosity about the wonderful world of mansex. Only one of Godfrey's immediate family, a sister, has spoken much to him since.

"So that's pretty much my story," he says while I ponder whether the design he was absently stroking into the ketchup with his third-to-last French fry was, in fact, heart-shaped, and if so, if I was meant to see it. "So, what's yours?"

I take a final swig of my diet Coke, using the time to strategize, but I slurp for so long that I make that embarrassing gurgling noise on the bottom of the cup. Please let Godfrey find that endearing, I think, like something a free-spirited Meg Ryan character would do on a first date to demonstrate not only how beguilingly childlike she is, but also the fact that she swallows.

Godfrey slides his barren tray out of the way and rests his angular jaw on one hand, creating a pose so come-hither that I decide to remember it for when he's posing for his band's first album cover. I'll be standing by dutifully like Brooke Shields at Wimbledon, giving my opinion only when it's asked for and "being cool" so as not to embarrass him in front of his liberated, yet nonetheless straight, bandmates.

Godfrey listens intently as I go on about my pockmarked past. I relate the saga of Michelle with particular gusto, hoping to underscore the fact that both he and I have had relatively long relationships with members of the opposite sex that ended in disaster as just one more glorious thing we have in common. The stories of my ship days bring with them a surprising sense of nostalgia and I realize that I'll probably never go anywhere fun again. As for the tryst with This Many, I talk it up as though it were a common cold that took me a month to shake and decide to let Godfrey believe it was my idea to call it off, not Damon's.

Satisfied that we've both divulged and, I imagine, omitted an equivalent amount of information, Godfrey smiles slyly then leaps out of the booth.

"Follow me," he says.

Godfrey bounds out the front door and into the psychedelic world of the PlayPlace, McDonald's attempt to give the kiddie element something fun to do after spending their parents' money on Happy Meals. Before getting up, I steal a glance back to the counter, where Samuel is being coached on his soft-serve technique, which not surprisingly is sorely lacking. I then look outside and see that Godfrey's going to the considerable trouble of removing his Timberland boots.

"You have to take off your shoes and put them in the Sneaker Keeper," Godfrey says, taking on the tone of my second-grade teacher.

"Shucks," I say, pointing to a sign with a height restriction. "We're too tall."

"Fuck that," he says before diving down to untie my shoes. "It's just another example of how ageist this evil place is. Like that damn Arch Deluxe."

“*‘Leave toys, food and other stuff back at the tables,’* ” Godfrey reads aloud from the sign listing the PlayPlace rules. “I wonder what they mean by other stuff. Like emotional baggage?”

“I guess,” I say. “Maybe I should have left my fear of intimacy back at the table.”

“Maybe you should have,” he says, causing my recently filled stomach to do a small somersault.

With our footwear safely ensconced in the Sneaker Keeper, I let Godfrey lead the way into the first of many brightly colored crawl tubes.

“This is like a Habitrail for humans,” he says.

“If we end up in Richard Gere’s ass, I’m never speaking to you again.”

When we arrive at the top of the twisty slide, Godfrey raises his eyebrows and says, “You’re going first.” Then he grabs my shoulders tightly, positions me at the mouth of the slide, leans his entire weight into me and shoves forward. I only slide for a couple of seconds before getting stuck. Eventually, I have to scooch myself with my hands to the end of the slide. I finish my sluggish dismount, strike a gymnast’s pose, then lay back on the ground so that I can watch my playmate’s arrival, positioning myself in such a way that if he were athletic enough to actually gain some momentum, unlike say, myself, he might accidentally mount me.

This almost happens when Godfrey, apparently an experienced twisty slider from way back, opts to tackle the apparatus on his back like a break-dancer. He drops his stockinged feet to the ground just as he clears the end of the slide then lets the momentum carry him forward onto the left half of my frame. Don’t you dare move, Craig, I think to myself.

“Last one in the Crawl Ball’s a rotten egg,” Godfrey says, rising. He gropes me as he stands as though he needs the leverage to help him up but I choose to think it’s groping for the sake of groping.

“I wonder if a toddler’s ever gotten buried in here and suffocated to death,” I say as I take my first steps atop the ocean of rubber balls.

"Stop it," he says. "You're making me hot."

He shoves me onto my back, looks down at me and smirks as though this moment has always been part of the plan. I say nothing, knowing there's not a word or sentence in my vocabulary that won't fuck everything up. Instead, I spontaneously reach forward, scooping up as many balls as I can and start burying myself alive. Godfrey, apparently keen on this idea, starts contributing to my spherical grave. When only my neck and head are visible he straddles the mound where my torso is, leans his face into mine and says, "Maybe I just ought to leave you here to die."

Godfrey cracks a long and broad smile, then struggles to his feet and starts to head for the portal we came in from. Cock tease, I think as I unbury myself, but before I can get up, my dinner date turns and throws himself on top of me, mouth first. His kiss is hard and considerably warmer than room temperature and I want to crawl into it head first and slide.

Our faces twist back and forth, our noses snapping against each other so much that I'm surprised it doesn't make a noise. I grab Godfrey's shoulders, flip him onto his back and prepare to kiss him again. The view from above is so incredible I have to savor it for a moment: the gleeful colors of the jungle gym reflected in his eyes, his lips fuller than ever, as though they've actually gotten more robust through usage.

Then suddenly Godfrey pulls me back and wraps his lips around my tongue, holding it there. It's the most static moment of the evening that doesn't involve Samuel, and it allows for a truly errant thought to crash the party. What if I'm a lousy kisser? What if I'm flat-out bad at it and nobody ever bothered to tell me?

"Nice," Godfrey says, withdrawing his face for a moment, then dives back in.

The scope of my relief is of such a magnitude that I could literally kiss him. Oh, that's right, I'm already doing that. Godfrey removes his hands from the small of my back, then grabs a ball in each hand and starts shoving them down the back of my shirt like ice at a frat party.

I decide that two can play at the stuffing game and flip Godfrey over. I grab a yellow ball, then dump it for a green one, hoping that the M&M's rule will apply here as well, and shove it down the front of his jeans. I'm about to pull my hand out and grab another when I feel something warm and bright hit my face. I look up and see Samuel standing outside of the Crawl Ball with a flashlight. On his left is his lady manager, looking on like Kathie Lee and Cody at a leather bar. On his right is some kind of security guard person wearing a uniform and a scowl.

"Put your hands up," Samuel shouts firmly, *"and come out of the Crawl Ball!"*

When we first encountered him, Samuel didn't seem to know his ass from a Quarter Pounder with Cheese, but now that he's no longer encumbered by that cash register, the trainee proves himself to be quite a can-do guy by busting up the best foreplay I've had in years.

Godfrey laughs, of course, because that's just the kind of couldn't-give-a-shit attitude he has, an attitude I both covet and dread. As we crawl out of the ball I hear the manager mutter, "You know, these guys are the third couple this month. They should really put something about this in the training video."

When I bend down to the Sneaker Keeper to retrieve my shoes, I feel the guard slap my back and pray that someone's outside video-taping in case things get brutal. Turns out the guy's just trying to retrieve the two balls that are still trapped in my shirt. Like a third-grader who just got busted stealing Now and Laters from 7-Eleven, I stand up, pull out my shirttail, and watch as the balls fall to the floor and bounce sadly. Samuel bends down to get them, then tosses them back into the Crawl Ball, sighing as if it's the most work he's done in months.

"You can put your shoes on outside," the guard scoffs. "Right now we just want you guys out of here."

I'm all the way out in the parking lot when I realize that I'm alone. I look back and see Godfrey, sitting in the same position I left him in, lacing up his boots methodically and smiling up at his evictors as if to say, "I will exit your fine establishment when I've completed lacing up my boots and not a moment sooner." It's the kind of youthful defiance that I, as a complete confrontation-phobe, find impossible to resist.

I'm trembling a bit when we get back in the Jeep. Neither of us feel the need to speak, so we ride in silence. I use the time to steady my breathing and sort through the details of the adventure so that when I talk about this, and I will, I'll be not only kind, but accurate. I look in the rearview mirror and see the manager and the guard shaking their heads and congratulating Samuel on a blue ribbon banishing.

Finally, Godfrey says something—"My place all right?"—then grabs my hand, turns it facedown and deliberately places it in his lap, where it connects with something big and hard and round.

"Ball," he says.

14

I wake up first. Godfrey's still out cold, tangled up in the sheets like Houdini, looking so magically delicious that someone should take a picture of him. Remembering I still have my camera in my jacket pocket from last night, I decide it might as well be me.

Tiptoeing like Elmer Fudd to my pile of clothes, I retrieve the camera, point and shoot. The shutter lets out a much louder click than I anticipated, but Godfrey doesn't so much as grunt. I'm smiling triumphantly and sneaking back to my clothes when the gadget in my hand betrays me, loudly rewinding its contents with all the delicacy of Fran Drescher hailing a cab. Damn, that was the last picture.

"What," Godfrey mutters dazedly, his eyes still closed.

Panicking, I shove the camera behind my back and start to speak in a tone so annoyingly perky that I want to take a hammer to my own head even as it's happening.

"Good morning, sleepyhead," I chirp, trying to outdrone the still rewinding Nikon.

"Morning," he says.

Just as his eyes open for the first time, the clock radio clicks on behind him, thankfully contributing to the room's confusing cacophony of sounds. Howard Stern burps and farts his way through a commercial for car insurance, and Godfrey stands, kisses me on the forehead and pads into the bathroom. The second he steps into the shower, I grab the phone from the nightstand and call Miles.

"Craig, it's seven o'clock in the morning," he grunts.

"I know," I whisper, "and guess where I am?"

"Gee, um, at the top of my shit list?"

"No," I say looking around the foreign bedroom ecstatically. "Godfrey's."

"The Snack's?" he exclaims. "Did you do it?"

"No," I say. "He said he didn't want me to be some rebound guy and I just sort of nodded. Look, I gotta go. I just wanted to call someone so if it turns out I dreamt the whole thing, we can check the phone records."

"Does Dandy know?"

"She's next," I say. "Now, go back to sleep."

Figuring I have a few more minutes calling time before Godfrey emerges from the shower all dewy and new, I call Dandy.

"Where are you?" she says groggily.

"Here's a hint," I say. "My contacts are in two paper cups by the sink and the hairs on the next pillow are really long."

"What are you talking about?"

"I spent the night with the singer guy," I say, annoyed that my best friend's not up for my early morning riddling. "After I left your place we went to McDonald's and starting making out and then we came here."

"Where is he now?" she asks.

"In the shower," I say. "I'm trying to get in as many calls as I can before he comes out. It's like Beat the Cock. I mean, clock."

"Did you do it?"

"Not yet," I say, before enduring that familiar scoff Dandy lets out whenever she's had enough of my sexual tentativeness. "He said he didn't want me to be some rebound guy. We're going to wait until the right time."

"There's no such thing," says Dandy. "Bang the guy."

"The shower just cut off," I say. "I gotta go."

"When do I meet him?" she asks.

"Soon," I say before hanging up. "Real soon."

I collapse back onto Godfrey's bed and stare up at the framed poster hanging over it, a huge blowup of the bright green slide that appears before movie trailers that says, "This trailer has been approved for all audiences by the MPAA. The film advertised has been rated R." As I pull Godfrey's pillow to my nose, I can only hope that, at some point, something goes on in this bed that a thirteen-year-old shouldn't be allowed to watch without a parent or guardian.

As I wait for Godfrey to pad out and hopefully pop my ass with the towel, I realize I just lied. I'm not excited for Dandy to meet him. It's not that I don't think that the two will get along. On the contrary, I'm afraid the sexually charged pair will get along *too* well. I'm looking for my pants and imagining a worst-case scenario in which Dandy and the Snack run off to Cancun together leaving me jilted and alone (like Sharon Stone in *Intersection*), bad hair and all, when I feel the wet terry cloth connect with my left cheek.

"Good morning, sunshine," Godfrey says before casually wrapping the towel around his waist and securing it. "Sleep okay?"

"Never better," I say.

I wait almost a week before introducing the Snack to Dandy. In that time, I've spent a good—but not excessive—amount of time with him and things seem to be proceeding smoothly. While hanging out with This Many sometimes felt like I was a Valley Big Brother taking my charge on various exhausting field trips to places with names like Toontown, time with Godfrey is more grown-up, mellower, more still. He's the kind of person who could fit right into that mutual artist fantasy I've always had wherein my beloved and I spend hours pouring ourselves into our respective art forms in different parts of the house, occasionally looking in on each other to bring liquid refreshment or have sex on the piano. He'd flip through my latest short story and say things like, "I find the third paragraph a tad pedantic, but other than that, it's aces," and I'd start to cry and say, "Oh my God, you painted me?" when I realize that that mystery canvas he's been slaving away on for weeks is actually a portrait of me playing hopscotch on the Spanish Steps. Naked.

Though my irrational fear that the two will be attracted to each other has abated somewhat in the last week, I'm happy to see that Dandy couldn't be looking worse when we pull up to her place on the night before Thanksgiving,

Dressed in OshKosh B'Gosh overalls and covered in mud, Dandy waves at us with the spade she's apparently been wielding for the last two hours, judging by the size of the hole she's standing in.

"It's my koi pond," she says proudly, after being introduced to Godfrey and biting her mud-stained knuckle to me behind his back. "You're nobody in this town unless you have a koi pond."

Dandy explains she's been digging since about six this evening, when she returned from a party at Tina Louise's, where she claims she spent the entire time gazing into Tina's magnificent body of water.

"It was like the Sea of Tranquillity," explains Dandy serenely. "You know, after the band breakup and everything, I really needed to clear my head. Being around the fish was almost cleansing in a way."

"Let's face it, the woman knows from lagoons," I say while Dandy strategically places the rocks she bought from Home Base around the hole. As she lays a plastic tarp inside and starts filling the thing with water, Dandy laments the fact that she'll have to wait until morning to buy her new pets.

"That's if you can find a fish place that's open on Thanksgiving," Godfrey points out before sticking a flyer for his band's next gig in the front pocket of Dandy's overalls.

"No way," Dandy whines. "I want my koi *now*. I'll lose it if I have to wait another two days."

Hoping to change the subject, I inform Dandy that Godfrey's written a song that would be a perfect new theme for her show.

"It's kind of like that *Friends* song, but edgier," I say, prompting Godfrey to return to the Jeep to retrieve the demo tape.

"Friends, Friends, Friends," rants Dandy. "I'm so sick of hearing about the Friends. The other day I saw that one guy at the Beachwood Market. I said 'Hi' to him and he just sort of groaned at me. I was like, 'Look, jerk, I'm on TV, too. I'm not some *fucking fan*!' "

With Dandy this close to dripping crocodile tears into her new pond, Godfrey saunters back from his Jeep, playfully swinging a beat-up Igloo Playmate ice chest in front of him.

"I know something that'll make you happy," he says tauntingly. "Where does Tina Louise live?"

"No way," I say.

"Come on, Craig," Godfrey whispers, with a come-hither tilt of his head. "It'll be fun."

If the next hour and a half of my life were going to be developed as a movie—not that it should be—the perfect pitch would be *Free Willy* meets *The Living End*. Conveniently dressed in all black, my playmate with the Playmate and I make our way to Miss Louise's digs, which Dandy swears are Doberman-free to the best of her knowledge. Godfrey plants one on me just before we shimmy over the voluptuous redhead's back fence, then pulls out the "map to pond" Dandy drew for us on the back of one of the Godmakers flyers.

"We should have brought a net," I gasp as we crawl up to the pond.

"Annette who?" Godfrey quips, then cops a feel.

"Shut up and start grabbing," I say, opening the Playmate. "The *fish*, I mean."

Thirty minutes later, neither of us have so much as brushed against one fucking fish. As anyone who's tried to steal koi with their bare hands can tell you, it's virtually impossible to get those pesky varmints to hold still. Dejected and sweating buckets, Godfrey leans back on his elbows on the lawn. Suddenly paranoid that his next words are going to be, "I think we should stop seeing each other," I continue to swipe my hands through the cold grimy water, perversely believing that if I can just capture one measly koi, the closest thing I've come to a real, grown-up, land-locked romantic relationship since the Catfucker won't implode in an ill-advised evening of trespassing and larceny.

"This isn't working," Godfrey says grimly.

I'm about to cry, "Please, please don't dump me!" at the top of my lungs—Ginger be damned—when a seemingly bionic member of the koi commune flies out of his watery home and starts flopping about on the grass in front of me. Thinking fast, I grab the scaly orange creature with both hands, deposit it in the ice chest, and look to Godfrey with a wide-eyed mixture of shock, squeamishness and pride.

"You're my hero," he says.

We hightail it back to Godfrey's Jeep, then flee the scene of the crime. As we drive, Godfrey suggests we name our captive the Professor, then inexplicably pulls off Mulholland and parks.

"What are we stopping for?" I ask, taking in the spectacular view of the Valley below us.

"What do you think?" he answers, leaning over and opening the glove compartment.

Forty-five minutes later we return to Dandy's to find my famous friend meditating cross-legged in the aptly named shallow end of her new pond.

"What took you so long?" she asks, grateful as ever.

I say nothing, letting my flushed face answer for my whereabouts. Dandy, no stranger to roadside rendezvous, raises her eyebrows and does a little happy dance, which, thankfully, Godfrey misses as he's bent over sliding the Professor into his new home.

"Oh my God, Craig," says Claudia the next day. "You have a sex life."

"Don't you have to do it more than once to have a sex life?" I ask.

"Normally, yes," says Miles. "But because of the Jeep factor, I think we can count it."

Having all of one kitchen skill between us, Claudia, Miles and I have ventured to the Hollywood Roosevelt Hotel to hunker down on their Thanksgiving buffet. Dandy was invited but had previously agreed to add her debatable star quotient to a charity dinner that's being thrown by the network. Ulysses, bless his heart, is downtown somewhere slopping out stuffing to the homeless. As for the Snack, he had previously agreed to spend the day with his sister in San Diego, leaving me free to talk about him incessantly.

"So, was it good?" asks Miles after we quiet down long enough to say grace by association with the people at the next table.

"I liked it," I say quietly, hoping to spare the adjacent family of four the sordid details of my brand-spanking-new sex life. "I don't know how he felt about it. I mean, you know how I am. I wish there was a Special Olympics for sex so you could get a hug at the end no matter what."

"How's his bod?" asks Miles.

"Nice," I say, "though he says he never works out. It's like he did fifteen push-ups when he was a sophomore in high school and they just took."

"Fucker," Miles says.

"Was there music?" wonders Claudia.

"Just the crickets," I say, "and the nervous knocking of my knees."

"The next time I have sex, I want it to be to Luther Vandross," Claudia declares as though she's been thinking about such a prospect for some time.

"At the rate I'm going," Miles says sadly, "the next time I have sex, it's going to be *with* Luther Vandross."

"Oh, please, Miles," I scoff. "What has it been? A week?"

"And a *half,*" Miles says.

After practically licking her first plate clean, Claudia pulls two giant Ziploc bags out of her purse, explaining that her favorite thing about Thanksgiving is leftovers and she wants us to help her smuggle some out.

"I don't know," I say. "Is that right?"

"Craig, you just kidnapped one of Tina Louise's pets," Claudia says, "and probably smashed some flowers in the process. Is that right?"

"White meat or dark?" I say, heading to the buffet.

The next time I see Dandy is four days later at "Cookin' with Gas," a comedy improvisation show at the Groundlings Theater. Each week, the regular team of fast-on-their-feet thespians invites a special guest star to join in their theater games. Dandy's this week's guest and Godfrey and I have come to lend our support.

"There's nothing I love more than getting to stretch as an actress," Dandy gushes to a group of fans before the show, before whipping out Polaroids of the Professor and the four other fish she bought over the weekend to keep him company. "Except maybe my new koi pond."

The audience and the more experienced Groundlings go easy on Dandy in the first act, allowing her to take on such close-to-home personas as a girl scout, a prostitute, a bench, and a Twinkie.

"Piece of cake," Dandy chirps after receiving the Twinkie suggestion.

"Where's a good gong when you need one?" someone behind us mutters.

Things start to go downhill in the second act when Dandy walks downstage center and says to the audience, "Okay, I need an occupation."

A woman in dark glasses and a hat who must have come in at intermission stands up, points at Dandy and shouts out, "Fish thief!"

"Okay," Dandy repeats. "I'm a fish thief. Now I need an emotion."

"Coy!" the same woman hollers.

Dandy's confused face washes over with horrified realization, but, being the show biz trouper that she is, she plays it cool.

"Okay," she reiterates for the audience. "I'm a coy fish thief."

Dandy exits the stage just as we've seen many of tonight's actors do before reentering in their new characterizations, but I have a feeling that, like the Von Trapp Family Singers fleeing the Nazis at the end of *The Sound of Music,* Dandy ain't coming back on.

The woman in the glasses leaves dramatically and the next time we see her, in the parking lot, she's lying on top of Dandy's Miata, refusing to let my friend drive away without her. The woman's hat has fallen to the ground and her red hair blows in the cool fall breeze.

"Check it out," says a looky-loo. "It's Ginger."

Dandy calls the next day from Palm Desert, where's she's gone to get her head together, and tearfully explains how Tina Louise busted us. Seems Godfrey, in what I choose to believe was a fit of lust and not stupidity, left the "map to pond" at the crime scene. The ever-resourceful Tina then showed up at Godfrey's Saturday gig, which was advertised on the back of the map, saw the *That's Just Dandy* theme tape on the seat of Godfrey's Jeep, remembered how infatuated Dandy had been with her pond just days before and put two and two and two together.

"Is she pressing charges?" I ask.

"No," says Dandy.

"What does she want then, money?"

"Not exactly."

Remarkably, Godfrey and I are still together when the first episode of *That's Just Dandy* "with Tina Louise as Principal Hinton" airs the week before Christmas.

"She looks amazing," I say.

"Goldfish cracker?" he offers.

"No thanks," I say.

15

I spend Christmas weekend in Arizona with my family. My four primary activities while there seem to be feeding my face, missing Godfrey, dreading the dump that I'm predicting will come by New Year's and enduring patronizing comments and questions about my "L.A. friends," as if they were of a lesser caliber than regular people. You know, shallow, disloyal, only out for themselves, L.A. friends. Of particular interest was Dandy. People seem to think that if you have a friend on television, they can say things to you like, "That show sucks," "Your friend could stand to lose a few pounds," or simply, "Gag," and you won't be offended.

During the train ride back to L.A., I repeatedly envision my reunion with the Snack as being just like that scene in *Grease* where Olivia Newton-John and John Travolta are surprisingly reunited at Rydell High after enjoying the summer love affair of their dreams. The second he realizes his fellow T-birds are watching, John starts to act like a macho shithead and blows her off. If Godfrey does that to me, I think as I pull up to his apartment, I'll just learn to smoke and become a big Spandex whore like Olivia and then watch him come crawling back.

My fears are quelled somewhat when Godfrey opens the door and greets me with a big, sloppy, beer-breath-laden kiss. Inside, I discover the rest of the Godmakers drunkenly strewn about the living room engrossed in one of their favorite postgig pastimes, "The Tom Snyder Drinking Game." I'd heard tell of such a ritual but was hoping I could date Godfrey without having to be party to it. Nothing against Tom, really, I'm just not much of a boozer.

"You're just in time, Craig," he says cracking open a Bud Light and handing it to me. "Okay, if it's your turn and Tom guffaws, you have to take a swig."

"Oh God," I moan.

"No, it gets better," Godfrey says excitedly. "If Tom calls a person or a movie or a show or whatever the wrong name, which he does at least three times a show, you have to finish off whatever's in your bottle."

The *Late Late Show* host goes easy on my lightweight ass, giving up simple guffaws whenever it's my turn. My beloved, however, doesn't get off so easy. In fact, it doesn't look like he'll be getting off at all tonight, thanks to Tom Snyder, that fucking enabler. Godfrey was a few sheets to the wind when I arrived and, now, every time it's his turn, our genial interviewer seems to deliver a major type-O, like referring to guest Cynthia Stevenson's sitcom *Hope & Gloria* as *Hope & Girl*. Repeatedly.

When the credits finally roll, Godfrey kills the sound on the TV and struggles to stand.

"I've got a surprise for you," he slurs before sliding a tape into the stereo and then curling up on the couch next to me. I stroke his hair and smile as I listen to "Playground" for the first time, a song that was obviously inspired by a certain Big Mac attack we were both party to.

"Welcome home," he says before passing out on my shoulder and drooling.

• •

A week later finds Godfrey splayed naked atop the sheets of my bed when Dandy's Christmas present, in the form of a bimonthly visit from Kathryn, the born-again maid, arrives to give my hovel the once-over. I'm in the shower at the time so I don't get to see the mortified look on her face when she catches sight of my favorite male vocalist, dead to the world, with one obvious exception. Something tells me, though, that it's not unlike the appalled face I pull nine hours later when I return from a torturous day of temping to find my modest digs just as dirty as I left them.

"Kathryn didn't have time to do much," explains Godfrey. "We spent the whole day talking about sin. She was hoping you wouldn't mind if she skipped some stuff."

Apparently, Kathryn would much rather save Godfrey and me from eternal damnation than waxy yellow build-up, for the next morning she drops by with a stack of "literature" intended to facilitate the "spring cleaning of our souls." Among the many pamphlets is one entitled "They Don't Call It Sodomy for Nothin' " that immediately gets magneted to the fridge next to Joey Lawrence's workout regimen as printed in the *L.A. Times* Life and Style section.

Unfortunately, Godfrey and I will have to wait until later to dive into the literature, as he's in the studio today and I've reluctantly agreed to accompany Ulysses to the Inkslinger's Ball, an annual festival of tattoos, piercings and the like held at the Hollywood Palladium.

At the last minute, Dandy decides she wants to come along, so I end up riding in Ulysses's back seat with the latest issue of *Playboy* to keep me company.

"This is what I've always imagined the hot button in the White House looks like," I say in regards to cover girl Farrah Fawcett's undeniably surreal nipples.

"Aren't they amazing?" enthuses Ulysses. "And here I thought those giant nubs had finished changing my life in the seventies."

"Oh, please," dismisses Dandy. "It looks like Ryan O'Neal hung her from them in the basement or something."

It's always dodgy to discuss *Playboy* in front of Dandy, for not long ago she was offered a nice chunk of change to pose for the magazine and was ready to go for it when the network got wind of it and threatened to cancel her show if she followed through.

"I'm curious, Ulysses," Dandy says, tossing the magazine to the floor. "When was the last time you went out with someone? I mean, you're cute enough. You shouldn't have to get off on some fifty-year-old with Tater Tot nipples."

"Well, if they're Ore-Ida—" I say.

"—They're all righta!" says Ulysses.

As we pull into the Palladium, Ulysses says, "It's been almost a year, if you must know. I don't get these L.A. women. Or maybe I should say, they don't get me. But I have a feeling something good's just around the corner."

"What about that model chick you met at the DMV?" Dandy asks.

"Okay," says Ulysses, recalling for Dandy a story I've heard before. "We're on our first date, and we're driving down the street and there she is on a billboard on Santa Monica Boulevard, wearing a negligee, humping a giant beeper. I never called her after that."

"Good call," I say.

We pay the $15 entry fee and make our way inside where tattoos of every shape, size and color compete for our curiosity with piercings of body parts that I didn't even know I had. Topless women with serpents disappearing into their cleavage abound while men whip out their accessorized penises at the drop of a leather cap. The only place you're likely to see more dick is at a Harvey Keitel film festival.

Though initially somewhat shocked, our threesome warms rapidly to the goings-on.

"This feels like the prom I never had," jokes Dandy, while posing for a picture with a harness-clad *That's Just Dandy* fan who's sporting an ear-to-ear smile in spite of the two miniature barbells hanging from his testicles.

After an hour or so, the only thing I still find surprising is the large number of children on the premises. Apparently, wearing testicle weights doesn't, in fact, render one sterile.

"If one more biker brat steps on my foot," rants Dandy, "I'm going to lose it."

"No wonder no one went to see *A Little Princess,*" I say. "They were all getting pierced."

The reason we're here today, aside from having our horizons broadened and visiting the snack bar, is to cheer on Ulysses, who's come to compete for Best Native American tattoo. Despite the fact that he's as milky white as a bottle of Liquid Paper, Ulysses, during a particularly heady peyote trip five years back, consented to having a portrait of Lewis and Clark's guide, Sacajawea, tattooed on his lower back. Coming away with a trophy today will allow him to feel, momentarily at least, a little less self-conscious about it.

The competitions begin with Best Portrait, which goes to a court reporter with a Mona Lisa on her ass that smiles when she does a leg lift. Though the truck driver with the Charles Manson on his skull had her licked in terms of likeness, there seemed to be a real backlash in the room against the glorification of mass murderers.

The Native-American competition is next and I know things aren't going well for Ulysses when he has to explain to the crowd who Sacajawea was. Despite the fact that when he flexes his lower back muscles, Saca points the way to the Pacific, my friend ends up losing to a buxom Scandinavian babe with Lou Diamond Phillips on her stomach.

"I was robbed," Ulysses says afterwards. "Ever since *Pocahontas,* I think people are really burnt out on Indian maidens who point."

"Well, you got the kids' vote," I offer.

While Ulysses mingles with the tattoo press and the other contenders backstage, I follow Dandy upstairs to the piercing floor where, out of nowhere, she decides to get a ring put through her navel.

"Don't you have enough problems with the holes you already have?" I offer, to no avail.

• •

Dandy's new navel ring is on display the next time we get together, at an impromptu hot tub party at her place. Dandy's invited Ulysses, Godfrey and myself over to celebrate the fact that the ratings for *That's Just Dandy* hit a record high last week.

"What caused the jump?" wonders Godfrey.

"Well, the only thing I can figure is this," Dandy says grabbing an issue of *Star* from a nearby lawn chair. There, on the rag's cover, competing for elbow room with a bald Liz Taylor, is Dandy, in the arms of a man they're calling her "phantom lover." Though the tattoo-covered gentleman's private parts have been covered with a thin strip of black, the weights that dangle from them haven't.

"Oh my God, it's her," gasps Ulysses.

"Of course, it's me," says Dandy. "You were there when they took the picture."

"No, not you," Ulysses says breathlessly, while pointing through the sliding glass door to Dandy's living room. "Inside. It's her."

"That's the maid that's been trying to get Craig and me to see the light," mutters Godfrey in reference to Kathryn, who's busy dusting Dandy's living room and humming something by the Winans.

"She was at the Inkslinger's Ball," Ulysses says. "She has nipples like Farrah Fawcett's and a labyrinth on her back that looks like a Chuck E. Cheese place mat. I swear to God. She won for Best Interactive Tattoo."

"Impossible," Godfrey and I say in stereo.

"It's her," insists Ulysses. "I know because I've been thinking about her ever since."

In a conniving attempt to settle the matter, Dandy invites the domestic out to take a load off and join the bubbling festivities. When Kathryn refuses, citing a sink full of dirty dishes, a head cold and a church meeting among her reasons, Dandy decides to play dirty.

"Shove her in, Craig," she says.

I choose to think Dandy picked me because I'm standing right behind Kathryn and have the best shoving opportunity and not because I'm completely pussy-whipped by my famous friend. Whatever the reason, I do it. I shove Kathryn into the Jacuzzi.

I half expect lightning to come from the sky or the voice of God himself to boom down, "Why can't you just play nice?" Instead I hear Ulysses say, "See, I told you. Farrah city."

Before Kathryn has time to get the water out of her nose and damn us all to Hades, Ulysses explains that he saw her at the Palladium and that none of us would believe him. More relieved than upset, Kathryn borrows a bathing suit from Dandy, hops back in and comes clean to us about her double life as an Inkslinger/Bible thumper, a situation she can completely reconcile but fears others won't be able to.

"Guess I missed my meeting," she says while allowing Ulysses to navigate her labyrinth tattoo with his index finger.

"Guess so," says Ulysses.

Three weeks later, my college crony is still completely smitten with her, in spite of the brick wall she's erected at third base until marriage. Kathryn seems quite keen on him as well. As for my kitchen floor, it's never been cleaner.

16

"He looks eleven," says Godfrey, pointing at the television. "Geez, Craig, you are such a chicken hawk."

Back when Damon Darlington dumped me, if you had told me that he was going to make good on his promise to "blah blah blah be friends," I would have been mildly flabbergasted. If you had told me that I would be enjoying the contents of one of the friendly parcels he would eventually send from Japan in the company of someone as splendifcrous as the Snack, I would have been *really, really* flabbergasted. But here we are, Godfrey and I tangled up on his bed, watching in hysterical horror the home video Damon sent of the creepily tacky strip show he's doing in Tokyo.

"I found out the night I got here that I would, in fact, have to wear a G-string," I say, reading aloud from the letter This Many sent along with the tape. *"I was like, 'There's no way. I think it's totally degrading and tacky,' and they're like, 'Well, you won't get the $300 a night in tips then,' and I was like, 'Do you think blue would be a good color on me?' So now I'm working out all the time . . ."*

"Wait, Craig," says Godfrey, hitting the pause. "You have to watch what this stripper does."

I look up and see an over-tan, long-haired Chippendale type, apparently on some kind of 'roid rage, yank a fragile female fan from her chair and hurl her across the stage onto a prop bed, then proceed to dry-hump her to within an inch of her young bespectacled life.

"Ah, romance," says Godfrey.

"Listen to this," I say, going back to the letter. *"The strippers have this little competition going to see who can be the roughest with the fans. And these women come back again and again and again just to have these guys throw them around and grind their dicks into their foreheads. Even though the money's great, I feel like I'll be haunted by this for the rest of my life. . . ."*

Godfrey and I take turns embellishing on my fantasy that This Many will be tormented by his stint with Tokyo Men like a disenfranchised ex-marine flashing back to his raping and pillaging days in 'Nam. Later, we're one verse into the finale, "Don't Stop 'Til You Get Enough"—something we have no intention of doing—when the phone rings.

"You're kidding," says Godfrey, after listening for a few minutes, his face a mixture of shock and excitement.

He hangs up and literally bounces me off of the bed, explaining as he bounds that "Driven to Distraction"—which, thanks to A & R whiz Don Delmondo, is currently being featured in a Japanese car commercial—has become so popular with viewers that Sony Japan wants to get a Godmakers album in stores as soon as possible. Since the band has already recorded a whole slew of demos, bumping the whole production up a notch will not be that difficult.

"So this is what a big break feels like," I say, once he's calmed down.

"I guess," he says, trembling boyishly with excitement. "I can't feel anything."

I leave Godfrey to start making plans with his bandmates. I turn on the computer when I get home, hoping that some of his good fortune will rub off on *Deck Games*. After staring at the screen saver for twenty minutes, I remember that I still haven't finished reading Damon's letter, then proceed to do so.

"Lately, I've been spending my spare time teaching my Japanese fans English," he writes. *"So far they've mastered "Kiss my ass" and "Bite me,*

baby." My dream is to one day teach them to answer the phone by saying "Suck my dick."

Well, that's all for now. I think about you often, Craig, and can't wait to see you again. In closing, I'd like to quote my favorite fan, Miyo. "Eat my titties."

Love, D.D.

P.S. Has Dandy popped out that kid yet? Her commercial is on constantly.

A week to the day after he got the big-break phone call, I'm dropping Godfrey off at LAX, where he and his cohorts will jet off to conquer Asia.

On the ride there, we talk about everything except what really matters, namely what the fuck is going on with *us*. I promise to keep an eye on his apartment. Godfrey promises to call. I joke about being the bimbo who does the splits across car hoods in their first video. Godfrey jokes about emulating This Many's strip video and flogging the screaming fans across the face with his leather-clad basket.

As we walk through the airport, Godfrey swings his guitar case merrily, obliviously providing me with yet another image for my Creative Genius Couple fantasy. While he checks in, I putter around like a fidgety zombie and try to remind myself that what is transpiring here is a good thing, and that when one shops for love in the dream factory, such logistical hiccups are bound to occur.

As we wait at the gate, I want desperately for us to fill the time with a little good old-fashioned gut spilling, but with every soul-bearing declaration that forms in my mind comes a rebuttal from Godfrey that I don't want to hear. Finally, when they call his seat number and he gets up to go, I force myself to say something moderately significant.

"I'm not going to see anyone else," I say.

"Okay," says Godfrey tenderly, not reciprocating, yet not *not* reciprocating. "Okay," he says again, glancing toward the door to Japan. "There's something I want to do before I'm too famous."

He laughs for a moment, then leans in and gives me a kiss, the duration of which is such that three different people are told to pick up a white paging phone before we separate.

"Good-bye," he says. "Thanks for the ride."

"Exactly," I say.

To say I spend the next few days depressed as a dog would be an insult to dogs. Whatever I'm doing at any given moment is accompanied by the gnawing act of missing him. I feel like an overachiever, except that I don't get anything done. Three days have passed and I've only heard from Godfrey once, when he first arrived in Tokyo. I'm starting to wonder if the Santa Ana winds that are sweeping through the Southland, causing brush fires in Malibu and mussing hairdos in Beverly Hills, are really just me getting blown off from the other side of the planet. My despondent state leaves me particularly vulnerable to Miles's invitation to attend some afternoon tea party he believes could be a real "breaking through" for me.

"This better not be another Marianne Williamson mixer," I say before sliding into Miles's beat-up Suzuki Samurai, "because if I hear so much as one pretty boy go on about how learning to love himself helped him land a role on *Silk Stalkings* I'm out of there."

"Just keep an open mind, Craig," Miles says as we pull up in front of a five-story West Hollywood town house. Once inside, I head straight for the bar, and learn from the strapping, goateed bartender that my choices are limited to waters and soft drinks as this particular soiree is booze-free.

"They want everyone to be sober at these parties," he explains. "With all the money flying around, you can't really afford not to be."

I'm about to say "What money?" when Leon Mosley, a fortyish casting director with a tan so phony it makes his nose look real, gets on the microphone and says, "Good afternoon, friends, and welcome to the Money Tree Gift Exchange."

I dash across the room, grab Miles by the shoulders and gasp, "You brought me to a *pyramid* scheme party? That's even worse than Marianne."

"It's not a pyramid," snaps Miles in harmony with at least six nearby

Money Tree members. Apparently, using the word *pyramid* around these folks is akin to raving about the new Mariah album in front of Whitney.

"No one's going to force you to do something you don't want to do," Miles continues under his breath. "We like to think of it as Friends helping Friends."

"Then why the hell isn't David Schwimmer here?" I wonder aloud.

I listen skeptically while Leon explains how the Money Tree "blossoms." Each member puts in $2,000 in cash. Then you try to convince others to do the same. As more and more people join, you work your way up the pyramid—I mean, *tree*—and are ultimately presented with $16,000, which you then employ to get all you deserve out of life.

"The 'Counting Out' is my favorite part," enthuses Miles when, at one point, two lucky, not to mention gorgeous, "Chairmen," one of whom I'm told has a recurring role on *The Bold and the Beautiful,* receive their sixteen grand.

"Twelve . . . thirteen . . . fourteen . . ." the room chants maniacally as though a cure for male pattern baldness will be unveiled at sixteen.

The two Chairmen flash their blinding smiles for a minute, then Leon wraps up his speech with a plea to us newcomers to "come to terms with our own prosperity." Once he's done, Miles drags me over to where Mr. Bold and Beautiful is allowing fellow guests to fondle his wad in ten-second intervals. After Miles takes his turn, I wipe the drool from his chin and drag him to the food table.

"All this moolah flying around," I groan, looking down at a worse-for-wear six-foot hoagie, "and all they could spring for is Subway?"

"Don't look now," Miles says nonchalantly, "but I think Goatee Man behind the bar is cruising me."

When he's not busy loathing the way he looks, Miles, God bless him, goes through these periods where he thinks that the entire free world wants to vacation in his pants. Waiters, valets, American Gladiators, chorus boys, women, you name it. Once, during a play, Miles leaned over to me and whispered, "Willy Loman wants me." What's most annoying about this tendency is that he's usually right.

• •

"So enough about this bartender," rants Dandy when we meet her later for dinner. "I want to know more about the pyramid thing."

"It's not a pyramid," says Miles.

"You gonna do it, Craig?" asks Dandy.

"No way," I say. "I mean, do the math. Somebody's got to get screwed."

"It sounds to me like you have unresolved money issues," says Miles smugly.

"How can I have money issues when I don't have any money?" I ask.

"Think what you could do with 16 Gs," oozes Miles, his eyes practically morphing into dollar signs like a cartoon character's. "You could fly to Japan and see Godfrey or, even better, you could quit doing shitty temp jobs and just work on your screenplay. I mean, you said it yourself, how are you supposed to make your mark in Hollywood when you can't even make the rent?"

I'm about to point out how irrelevant Miles's whole argument is because I don't have the $2,000 to begin with, when Dandy shoves a check for just that amount into my open mouth and says, "Just pay me back when you cash out."

At the next party, this one at a gaudy mansion in Laurel Canyon, I sign on under Miles's branch of the tree. My next task is to find people to come in under me. The normally game Dandy passes because she prefers people to think she already has more money than she knows what to do with. Claudia would love to join, but she's even more broke than me and besides, she wants to lose at least twenty pounds before she goes to a party with that many industry people. I decide to try Ulysses.

"No way, Craig," he says. "It's just wrong."

"But how much different is this than that celebrity death pool you do?" I ask.

"It's a lot different," he says. "No one gets screwed in my game.

It's not I like I bumped off Jerry Garcia just to score points. Someone's gonna get screwed, Craig. You're committing karmic suicide. And for what? Some stupid pyramid scheme."

"It's not a pyramid," I say.

Two weeks, six parties and countless solicitations go by and I still have no one to come in under me. If I don't come up with a sucker soon, I'm going to be booted out faster than a Menudo member with a five o'clock shadow. To make matters worse, I've only heard from Godfrey four times since he left, and two of those were messages. He says he's been insanely busy and he can't figure out the time difference, but that he thinks of me often, presumably in between ruminations on his long-deserved fame and fortune.

"I had better luck getting a date for my senior prom," I whine to Leon, the Money Tree guru, at my ninth party.

"Okay, Craig," Leon says impatiently. "Who do you know who really needs something good to happen in their life? Think low self-esteem."

Two minutes later I'm on the phone to Carolyn, the office administrator from Jupiter Filmworks. After all, we hung out as friends for a while last year, but it was a tricky friendship to maintain because I had this pesky habit of never calling her back.

"It's so perfect that you called," she says happily, "because I was about to join the investment group that the office is all into, but I'd much rather join *yours*."

With Carolyn on board, things are looking up, although I have to admit I'm getting sick of "networking" with a bunch of shallow losers over stale Subway when I just want to get my fucking money and go home. Between the phone calls, the parties and the daydreaming, this investment plan is becoming a full-time job, something to which we all know I have an aversion to begin with. What's more, other branches of the tree are doing what's called "poaching"—or stealing people from our branch and delaying our payday. For some reason, everyone wants to be on the same branch with the people from the recently canceled *Models, Inc.*

"God knows why," I carp to Dandy before my tenth party. "It's not like any of them have jobs."

"Okay, Craig, you can stop dropping hints," Dandy says. "I'll come to your party."

With Dandy hovering around our branch in latex booty shorts, the starstruck commoners come from miles around to give their $2,000 to the cause. She's such a hit, in fact, that Miles is able to cash out at this party and it looks like I'm going to cash out at the next one.

"I can't wait to have that cashola in my hand," I say on the drive to my payday party in the brand-new midnight blue BMW Miles was able to put a down payment on with his loot from the tree.

"Well, I can't wait to see Goatee Man," Miles sighs. "He's going to be all over me when he sees me pull up in this."

After what seems like years of celebrating the windfall of others, I'm finally having my day in the sun. As I walk up to the podium, I catch myself in one of the room's many mirrors and am taken aback, not so much at what an opportunistic phony I've become, but at the miraculous coincidence that my hair's having as good a day as my wallet. Leon places his hand on my shoulder, the glare of his new Rolex practically blinding me, then the chanting begins. I enjoy the delightfully weighty feeling of the stack of bills in my hand for a moment, then embrace Leon as if he were Betty White and we'd just gone to town in the bonus round of the *$20,000 You Know What*.

Miles starts singing "Sukiyaki" on the way to the car, I presume to commemorate the fact that a romantic getaway to the Orient is now a distinct possibility.

"I'm numb," I say breathlessly. "I cannot believe I have $16,000 in my pocket."

"Believe it, fucker," says a voice from behind me, shortly before I feel the cold steel of a .38 press into my back. "Now, hand it over."

"Goatee Man!" says Miles to the bartender-turned-Reservoir Dog who, at the moment, seems far more interested in what's in my pants than my friend's. "Now lay down on the ground, both of you, and count to a hundred. I know you can count, because I've seen you do it."

"One . . . two . . . three . . . four . . ."

Rebel-rousers that we are, Miles and I only count into the mid-sixties before staggering shell-shocked back to his BMW and driving back to my place. Instead of going inside, we walk across the street to Ulysses's, where he and Kathryn are busy cutting pictures of themselves from the Inkslingers Ball out of tattoo periodicals. Miles and I join them at the kitchen table and tremble through the telling of our true-crime drama.

"Why am I not surprised?" Ulysses says with loving superiority, like a skinhead version of Mike Brady.

"Are you going to call the police?" asks Kathryn.

"I guess," I say.

"You can't go to the police, Craig," Ulysses says, "because what you were doing is illegal. Pyramid schemes are illegal."

"It's not a pyramid," I say. Ulysses and Kathryn just stare at me. "Miles, tell them it's not a pyramid."

"Of course it's a pyramid, Craig," Miles says. "What did you think?"

The fact that Miles says this while twirling the keys to his new Beemer makes my urge to perform an emergency tracheotomy on him with Ulysses's kitchen scissors nearly impossible to resist, but I do.

"So what should I do?" I ask.

"Chalk it up and move on," says Ulysses.

"And be glad he didn't shoot you," adds Kathryn. "It sounds like you were very lucky."

The four of us, Miles, myself, and Mike and Carol Brady, sit for a moment in silence, allowing this week's moral to fully infiltrate my thick, self-serving skull.

"Maybe you should go back and warn the others," says Kathryn finally.

"Maybe *you* should," I say to Miles. "I'm out of outfits."

17

I have always thought of my next-door neighbor and landlady Viola McGowan as little more than the grumpier old woman who cripples my bank account once a month and who called the cops when Claudia and I dumped Asshole's stuff in the pool. It isn't until the UPS man has me sign for a package for her from Paramount that I discover Viola's glamorous little secret.

"Why is Paramount sending you stuff?" I ask when I drop off the box.

"Oh, they all send me stuff this time of year," she says wearily. "Tapes mostly."

"So," I say casually, as though I'm not about to leap from my skin, "are you an Academy member?"

"Does this answer your question?" she says then steps back from the door and gestures to a coffee table overflowing with screening tapes.

Without waiting for an invitation, I rush past Viola and fall to my knees in front of the tapes like Jane Fonda at the Fountain of Youth. As Viola adds the elaborately boxed Paramount offerings to the already overpopulated table, I tenderly run my fingers over such freebies as the Disney tote bag, the *Dead Man Walking* pine box, and the videos of such Oscar shoo-ins as *Waterworld, Losing Isaiah,* and *Roommates.*

"I just want to take off my clothes," I mumble to myself, "and have someone lay all these tapes on top of me."

"That can be arranged," Viola says with a wink.

Instead, she pops in *The Scarlet Letter* starring Demi Moore—"something we can talk over"—pours me an iced tea and starts relating anecdotes from Oscar campaigns past, like the year a delivery man presented her with a single long-stemmed rose.

"I thought I had me a secret admirer," she says disgustedly. "But it was just Diane Ladd trying to get us to vote for that *Rambling Rose* picture."

Not long into the film, Viola's head falls to one side and it looks as if my landlady, like most people who saw *The Scarlet Letter* in the theater, is going to sleep through most of it. I, on the other hand, manage to stay conscious clear through Demi and Gary Oldman's final round of tonsil hockey, then cover my neighbor with her *Roseanne* afghan and let myself out.

The next night Viola invites me over to watch *Summer Solstice,* the film for which she was nominated for Best Supporting Actress in 1946. She's wonderful in it, playing an alcoholic heiress whose uptight world is rocked when a sexy blond drifter comes to town.

"Who's that guy?" I ask.

"His name was Ty Walker," says Viola. "Nicest actor I ever worked with."

"Please tell me you had a torrid affair with him," I say practically salivating.

"No," Viola laughs. "I didn't have a torrid affair with Ty Walker. You would have had been more likely to turn his head than I was."

"Whatever happened to him?" I ask.

"Ty took an overdose of pills right before the movie came out and died," Viola says sadly. "He had a hard time dealing with himself and Hollywood and all of that stuff. It was terribly sad."

We watch in silence until the final scene, when I just have to compliment my landlady on how undeniably hot she looks in the strapless red evening gown Ty's lowlife character bought for her before breaking her heart and skipping town.

"They're real too," she says proudly, grabbing a seventy-eight-year-old breast in each hand and yanking. "Not like actresses today."

My bonding with Viola couldn't have happened at a better time. Ever since my Money Tree was so brutally uprooted, I've had a little trouble coming up with money for things like food and rent and cable. Viola's stockpile of free movies will come in handy too, because the last thing I can afford to do at this point is shell out $7.50 to see how Greg Kinnear fares in *Sabrina*. And with Godfrey off becoming Asia's answer to Evan Dando, there's nothing I'd rather do than sit on my ass, eat a bunch of crap, and watch first-run movies for free.

"This isn't bad for a movie named after a Styx song," says Ulysses in regards to the talking-pig opus *Babe,* the film we watch at my first Academy screening party.

Charmed by my interest in all that is Oscar, Viola's not only giving me an extension on my rent, but she's letting me borrow some of the screening tapes, provided they don't leave the apartment complex. That way, if she has a burning need to see, say, *Jumanji,* she can just throw a shoe against the wall.

"I still can't believe I write a rent check every month to an Oscar nominee," says Claudia as *Babe* nears its triumphant conclusion.

"Shhhhh," says Miles. "This is my favorite part."

We all look on with watery eyes as the proud farmer looks down at Babe and delivers the film's final line, "That'll do, pig."

"Reminds me of the last time I had sex," says Claudia.

The movie-watching frenzy continues as the weeks go by. One night, Viola decides she wants me to be her guest at a glamorous screening at the Academy Theater. We get dolled up and go watch *Heat,* a film that loses me completely when it asks us to believe that Amy Brenaman's book clerk character, who makes about as much as I do, can afford a sumptuous bachelorette pad over Sunset Plaza.

After the screening, Viola tells me that she needs the *Sense and Sensibility* tape back because she wants to watch it tomorrow.

"I'll bring it over in the morning," I say, my stomach tightening. "I'll finish it tonight."

The truth is, I broke the rule about not letting the tapes leave the complex and lent *Sense* to Dandy. Of course, I would have lent her my esophagus if it would keep her from bringing up the two grand I owe her from the pyramid fiasco.

The second I'm back in my apartment, I make a frantic call to Dandy, who claims she left the corset fest in the limo of a certain British rock star.

"It could be playing on some Virgin Atlantic airplane even as we speak," she admits. "Sorry, Craig."

Stuck between a rocker and a hard place, I'm forced to improvise. I whip open the TV listings and sigh with relief when I see *The Remains of the Day* (another period piece about repressed Brits starring Emma Thompson) is playing on HBO in twenty minutes. With no time to go buy a new videotape, I grab the first tape I can find, my overplayed copy of VH1's Janet Jackson–athon, and head to Dandy's. Unlike myself, who irrationally dumped my HBO during that particularly low moment last fall, Dandy still welcomes the premium channel into her home.

While *Remains* is taping, I scurry to Kinko's and do my best to create a reasonably believable label and video box. I return to Dandy's just as the film is ending, rewind the tape, slide it into its new home, and then drop it off at Viola's.

My sneaky substitution must have passed muster, for my landlady says nothing about it the next night when I go next door to help her fill out her ballot. I'm genuinely touched when I discover that Viola's prepared a candlelight dinner for two to commemorate our first Academy nominating season together. If the smell of mothballs is any indication, I'd venture to guess that the sexy red dress she's squeezed into is the same one she wore in *Summer Solstice*. Though it was obviously designed for a woman in her twenties, it's oddly flattering on the geriatric sitting across from me, or maybe I just want it to be.

"I know I'm going to see less of you after tonight," Viola says tenderly while pouring her fourth glass of red wine.

"That's not true," I say, even though I know it is.

"I've grown so fond of you, Craig," she laughs, "that I don't even care that you lost *Sense and Sensibility* and tried to hoodwink me with a phony tape."

Unable to speak, I stare into my glass and ponder both the error of my ways and the origins of the word *hoodwink*.

"Next time you would do better to substitute a woman who is at least the same race as Emma Thompson," Viola continues. "Although I did enjoy the 'Escapade' video."

I want to have a full-on, Oscar-worthy emotional meltdown and bellow, *"When am I going to learn how to use a fucking VCR?"* at the top of my lungs. Instead, I sit idly by and watch Viola's back-combed head plummet into her pasta.

"Good, you're home," I say to Dandy over the phone.

"Craig, I think you broke my VCR," says Dandy.

"Put it on my tab," I say. "Listen, I need your help. Viola's passed out drunk and this ballot's due at the Academy tomorrow."

"I'll be right over," Dandy says.

Viola's still out cold when Dandy arrives—Ulysses and his Ouija board in tow. Together we prop Viola up on the couch facing us in case she decides she has anything to add.

"Who would she put as her top choice for best actor?" I wonder.

"Nicolas Cage in *Leaving Las Vegas,*" says Dandy as though it's a foregone conclusion. "The drunks gotta stick together."

"Perfect," I say, and write Nic in. "Okay, actress?"

"The Ouija pointer keeps drifting off the board," says a confused Ulysses.

"It's pointing toward her feet," Dandy says knowingly.

"Elisabeth Shue!" I say and start scribbling.

We put John Leguizamo as our top choice for Best Supporting Actress for *To Wong Foo* because Viola actually thought he was female until she saw him on *Extra* three days after she saw the movie. Dandy insists that the guy who made Elizabeth Berkley put ice on her nipples in *Showgirls* be our number one choice for Best Supporting Actor and Ulysses and I couldn't agree more. Viola even lets out a snort as if to say, "I'm so glad you reminded me of him."

Using every means but eeny-meeny-miny-moe—I can't help but think Marisa Tomei has stooges like us to thank—we come up with four more names to list in each of the acting categories. Which brings us to best picture.

"*Babe!*" Ulysses hollers.

"No way," I say. "Viola hates it when farm animals take jobs from real actors."

"Look," says Dandy jutting her chin at my inebriated landlady. "She's drooling onto *The Scarlet Letter* box. It makes it look like Demi's crying."

"It's a sign!" Ulysses gasps.

"That *was* the first film Viola and I watched together," I say, my voice suddenly brimming with nostalgia. I smile at Viola and write it in.

The morning the nominations are to be announced, my landlady wakes me up by hurling a shoe against the wall. I throw on my robe, grab some Pop-Tarts and head next door.

"They egregiously overlooked our movie," I say sadly when *The Scarlet Letter* fails to make the cut.

"I'm not surprised," Viola says, rubbing my forearm tenderly. "Some people just don't understand forbidden love."

18

I'm in Dandy's trailer, converting her messy address book to computer—part of my penance for the pyramid fiasco—when Colleen, Dandy's beleaguered publicist, pops by to have her Jennifer Aniston-shaped head handed to her on a plate.

"I haven't been on a single talk show in six months," rants Dandy. "What the hell gives?"

"They're waiting to see if your show gets picked up for next season," Colleen stammers. "The hosts all love you, Dandy, really. I promise you, in a couple of months, you're going to have sofa burn from sitting on so many couches."

"Like I believe that," grumbles Dandy.

Colleen shoots me a look of helplessness and shrugs.

"Maybe I should be shopping for another publicist," Dandy adds.

"Well, *Politically Incorrect* has expressed interest," says Colleen, grasping at straws. "But I really don't think it's the right kind of showcase for you."

"Book me," Dandy demands.

The next day, Colleen calls and begs me to talk Dandy out of doing the show.

"They'll eat her alive on there," Colleen whines. "I mean, the woman thinks Whitewater is a rafting movie with Meryl Streep."

"Isn't it?" I say.

"You have to stop her, Craig."

"But she's got her heart set on doing it," I say. "We watched it together last night and the whole idea of a spontaneous, open forum of ideas really appeals to her."

"Are you serious?" Colleen asks.

"Okay, she wants to fuck Bill Maher."

Since we both know resistance is futile, I tell Colleen I'll coach her client on current events and such if she, in return, will agree to pass *Deck Games* onto her William Morris agent husband. Colleen goes for it, provided that come taping day, Dandy resembles a person who has at least once picked up a newspaper.

"To me, Bill Maher is like a cuddly Dennis Miller," gushes Dandy at the outset of our first alleged tutoring session. "My fantasy is to lie in bed with him and massage his temples, so that he can think even better."

"That's a nice dream, Dandy," says Ulysses. "But it's never going to happen if you don't buckle down."

I've invited Ulysses over in the hopes of exploiting his *Meet the Press* frame of reference. Despite the fact that my illustrations of Hillary Clinton's haircuts were all the rage at Claudia's recent Pictionary party, my knowledge of things political seems to have stalled at "I'm just a bill, yes I'm only a bill . . ."

"Now Dandy, with the campaign going on, Bob Dole is sure to come up," Ulysses says firmly. "What's your take on him? And no Dole banana jokes."

"I just think he needs a good lay," Dandy says. "Is that a banana joke?"

Ulysses frowns and says, "You'll impress Bill Maher more if you say something like, 'You know, instead of focusing on all of us corrupt Hollywood heathens, Dole should be worrying about the real problems in this country, like what are we going to do about the deficit?' "

"Oh, that's *good,* Ulysses," enthuses Dandy. "Now, what's a deficit?"

"Please God," I say to Ulysses while Dandy takes a potty break. "Let her be on with Kato and the Olsen twins."

Subsequent attempts to educate the TV diva prove equally exasperating. With six hours to go before taping, Ulysses is still in coach mode, reciting a diatribe on the possibility of a gay gene to Dandy who writes down his every word on Post-it notes that will later be placed God knows where.

"Wait, go back," says Dandy, laughing. "How do you spell Liberace?"

"Joke all you want," Ulysses barks, finally running out of patience. "It's your ass on the line. It's not like I'm going to be hiding behind a potted plant like Cyrano feeding you profound things to say."

"That's it!" I shout. "Ulysses, you're good with gadgets, can't we get her one of those earpieces like Marlon Brando uses and feed her things to say?"

"Craig, you're a genius," hollers Dandy before adding that the problem drinker who plays her TV uncle uses just such a device on *That's Just Dandy*. "God knows why," she continues. "The only line he ever has is 'Dandy, come sit on your uncle's lap.' "

We pick up the earpiece and wireless mike on the way to the studio, then finalize our game plan. Ulysses will be in charge of feeding her sociopolitical insights, I'll try to come up with a one-liner or two, and Dandy will simply try to look pretty and keep her wits (or our wits, as the case seems to be) about her.

After testing the earpiece in the parking lot, we drop Dandy off at her dressing room, where we learn who her copanelists will be: Camille Paglia, Dick Clark and Daryl Gates.

"Is that the guy from the Captain and Tennille?" wonders Dandy.

"He's L.A.'s former chief of police," I say. "Just relate to him as if he were a cop that pulled you over for speeding."

"Got it," Dandy chirps while adjusting her breasts in her leather bustier, then topping it off with a tasteful Richard Tyler jacket for that well-read hooker look.

Ulysses and I wish Dandy luck, then find a place in the back of the studio where we can whisper into our mike without anyone seeing us.

"I'm worried about Camille Paglia," says Ulysses, whose palms are only slightly less sweaty than my own.

"I'm not," I say. "She loves a brazen, unapologetic woman with a nice rack. I'm worried about Gates. Dick Clark seems harmless enough."

With a few minutes to go before the taping begins, Colleen rushes up to fidget with her hair and wish us well.

"If you get us through this, Craig," pledges Dandy's stressed-out flack, "your script will be the talk of William Morris by the end of the week."

Like the stakes weren't high enough already.

I get my first indication that trouble's afoot when Dandy makes her entrance dressed, not in the well-read hooker get-up, but in a skimpy white toga ensemble with a wreath of grapes around her head.

"What's with the sheet?" I spit into the mike.

"I wanted to match the set, Bill," Dandy says, gesturing grandly to the Roman pillars that surround the stage.

"I feel overdressed," quips Camille Paglia when she makes her entrance.

Once the shock over Dandy's attire blows over, the first half of the show proceeds relatively smoothly with Ulysses feeding her astute comments about campaign finance reform and me chiming in with a one-liner in response to Daryl Gates's comment about a flat tax.

"I think it's so unfair," Dandy says playfully. "I mean, flat people have enough problems as it is."

Even Dick Clark laughs at this one. We're going to pull it off, I think, as we head into the final commercial. When we come back the topic turns to sex and violence in movies and TV, something our heroine has at least some grasp of.

"I think there's a double standard," says Dandy, echoing Ulysses in her earpiece. "You blow someone's head off and get a PG-13 but show a nice little artistic lap dance, and boom! You're branded NC-17."

"Lap-dance Dick Clark!" I gasp into the microphone.

Before Dandy even gets up from her chair, I'm wondering what could have possessed me to say such a thing. I got caught up in the spectacle unfolding before me and now we're all gonna pay.

I look on in horror as Dandy walks barefoot over the coffee table and perches herself atop Dick Clark's eternally young lap.

"I mean, what's so bad about this?" she says between gyrations. "I mean, is anyone here truly offended?"

"Well, I am," groans Dick. "I just had this suit pressed."

Dick hoists her onto the coffee table and in her wake, she leaves a Post-it note with her musings on gun control on the former *American Bandstand* host's lap. Then Dandy returns to her seat with a chastised plop the force of which causes the earpiece to come loose and fly skittering across the stage. Ulysses and I look at each other like a pair of football coaches who just lost the Super Bowl in the last quarter.

Back onstage, Maher wisely changes the topic completely, to gun control, of all things.

"I can tell you what Lolita here thinks about it," says Dick Clark while wagging the Post-it in the air. Then Dandy, sans her trusty earpiece, finally voices a thought that's hers and hers alone.

"Would anyone like a grape?" she says with desperate coquettishness. "Dick?"

"No thanks," grumbles Dick.

"For Christ's sake," says Camille Paglia, "have a grape, Dick."

"Don't mind if I do," says Daryl Gates before indulging.

Maher helps himself, too, then thanks his guests and wraps things up.

When Ulysses and I catch up with Dandy backstage, she's even more upset that I feared she'd be, but not because, as Ulysses so delicately put it, she "may have made an ass of herself on national TV."

"Please, I do that every week on a show called *That's Just Dandy,* perhaps you've heard of it?" Dandy carps dejectedly. "I'm pissed because Bill Maher took off before I had a chance to throw myself at him. Goddammit."

Fuming and ferociously sexed-up, Dandy does what any self-respecting starlet would do after being rejected by the talk-show host of her dreams: She fires her publicist. So much for my in at William Morris.

I haven't been able to bring myself to watch *Politically Incorrect* since the Grapes of Wrath episode, although a commercial for the show turned up on something I was taping. In the ad there's a snippet of Dandy lap-dancing Dick Clark then returning to her seat, followed by Bill Maher—different suit, different day—burying his face in his hands in disbelief. The best part is, if you play it back in slow motion, you can see something fly out of the side of Dandy's head: her senses taking leave of her, as it were.

Strange, it's usually the other way around.

19

Until recently, I thought having my screenplay, *Deck Games,* reviled or ignored by virtually everyone who'd laid a hand on it had me about as low as I could get on the ladder of self-esteem. Of course, that was before I started whiling away the hours asking hundreds of strangers if they'd be willing to sit through a hot new film starring Rhea Perlman as a high school basketball coach in the 'hood.

"It's supposed to be really funny," I say to one potential victim, a friendly-looking woman in nurse's garb, even though I'm not even sure if the movie's a comedy.

"No thanks," she says. "The last time one of you guys told me that, I ended up at *Nine Months.*"

"You got me there," I agree.

Before I can add, "It'll be different this time, I promise," the woman's already disappeared into Lady Foot Locker and started a conversation with the referee. It's been the same story all day. Either there's a real Rhea backlash afoot or I'm just not a good salesman, and as a "recruiter" for United Research Group, a market research company that tests movies and their marketing, salesmanship is the name of the game.

Having had my fill of temping and extra work, I've taken on this particular odd job because (a) I thought it'd be fun to see movies before everyone else, (b) it will give me some insight into the testing process so when *Deck Games* ultimately gets made I'll be hip to it all, and (c) I have all of $31.74 in my bank account. So for the past four days, I've been the guy with the clipboard and the farmer tan who stands outside your gym or in the mall and tries to cajole you into attending a hot new film starring Rhea Perlman as a high school basketball coach in the 'hood. That's entertainment.

"I see why they call this recruiting," I say to Gordon, my uptight superior and, I'm guessing, a recent soul-donor, who's taken time out of his busy day to come out to the Glendale Galleria to see how I'm doing. "Most people would rather air-drop into Bosnia than see this movie."

"And your attitude is really helping," Gordon says before wandering over to the food court. I let a good dozen potential seat-fillers stroll by as I watch Gordon salivate over the Hot Dog on a Stick girl who's committing her entire young body to the making-of-the-lemonade ritual.

When Gordon returns, I've just given my spiel to a potential victim in a Planet Hollywood shirt and the guy, believe it or not, actually says he'd love nothing more than to drive to Van Nuys and stand in line for an hour and a half to see a hot new film starring Rhea Perlman as a high school basketball coach in the 'hood. As the guy snatches a flyer from me, then practically skips down the mall, I turn to Gordon with a self-satisfied smile.

"Craig, that was Todd Bridges from *Diff'rent Strokes,*" Gordon chides.

"I know," I say. "Doesn't he look great?"

"You're not supposed to give fliers to people who are in the entertainment industry."

"Oops," I say, as the wind drifts out of my sails. "I didn't realize he was."

Two hours and as many hundred rejections later, I leave the Galleria and take refuge at Chevy's, my favorite Mexican restaurant, with Dandy.

"What really sucks," I lament between bites of fajita, "is that I'm getting paid on commission, so because nobody wants to see Carla from *Cheers* try to fit in the same frame as a bunch of tall black guys, I go hungry. It's so fucking unfair."

"So, can't you lie," Dandy suggests, "and say it's like a Jim Carrey fart comedy or something, just to get people in the seats?"

"Believe me, I would," I say, before digging out of my bag a flyer for *The Curator,* the sure-to-suck flick we're testing after the Rhea flick, "but the cast and a synopsis are listed on the sheet you give them. I mean, you can mislead people, like Gordon was telling me that to get people to see *Driving Miss Daisy,* they were billing it as an uproarious Dan Aykroyd comedy."

"Oh my God, Craig," she gasps, staring at the *Curator* flyer. "I'm *in* this."

"Oh, I remember now!" I exclaim. "That director guy with the ponytail."

"Richard Rand," Dandy groans.

When I was still on the ship and Dandy was in New York, she wrote me about an affair she was having with a music video director turned feature film auteur, Richard Rand. Though the fling was lamentably brief, it was well timed, and garnered my thespian friend a small role in what was at the time a supernatural thriller called *Dance of the Mummies* about a museum curator who becomes intimate with a quartet of female cadavers that mysteriously come to life. Last I heard, the film was so godawful it was going straight to video, but in the last few months, the formerly unknown hunk who plays the title role has risen to doctor-series stardom, so it looks like they're going to release it in theaters, as, according to the flyer, "a comedy in the tradition of *Beetlejuice.*"

"Watch it turn out to be a huge hit," says Dandy, who plays Lucinda, an industrious janitor with her own designs on the hunky curator and a mighty fine rack. "And I bet that jackass is going to leave me on the cutting room floor."

"Didn't you guys do it one time on the cutting room floor?" I say.

"Did I tell you about that?" she asks momentarily surprised by her absolute lack of discretion.

I just nod.

"Do I tell you *everything*?" she continues.

I nod again.

With that, Dandy dashes to the pay phone to see if she can find out from the grip she used to party with on the set if Lucinda's still in the film.

"Guess who's making the transition to the big screen," she boasts upon her return. My mouth full, I gesture to her with a tortilla chip. "Now guess who's going to help me." When I shove the chip into my mouth, indicating myself, it goes down the wrong pipe and I wind up having to have the Heimlich maneuver performed on me by a wandering mariachi.

In the days leading up to the screening, Dandy and I get on the horn to coerce our nearest and dearest to attend *The Curator* and throw a few superlatives Lucinda's way. Convinced that that alone isn't enough to deliver her from cinematic amputation, Dandy asks if there isn't some way we can doctor the comment cards.

"I don't know, man," I hedge. "Gordon's like Price Waterhouse with those things."

"What if you were to sneak into his office," she says, practically twirling her mustache in delicious premeditation, "grab one of the forms, and then Xerox a bunch of them?"

"Who do I look like," I say, "one of Charlie's Angels?"

"No, you look like that one ax murderer guy," she replies, "but you hate when I tell you that."

A few hours later, against my better judgment, I arrive at Gordon's office. The plan is for me to say I was in the neighborhood, thought I'd just say hi, come up with a reason to get him out of the office, then, assuming I can find one, pilfer one of the forms. Piece of cake.

"I was just in the neighborhood and I thought I'd say hi," I say to the man who I've done nothing but revile ever since that day in the Galleria.

"Craig," Gordon says, surprised to see me. "We need to talk sometime, attitude type things, but I'm a bit busy now."

Now, this is the part where I'm supposed to come up with something to get him out of the office, but I neglected to do so in advance, thinking something would just come to me if I stayed in the moment, as though this were improv comedy and not larceny.

I'm about to stick my head in the pencil sharpener and end it all when I notice his celestial-themed mouse pad and decide to take a shot in the dark.

"I almost couldn't park," I say with feigned exasperation. "They're shooting a scene for *Star Trek: Voyager* across the street and it's a madhouse out there."

Gordon looks me dead in the eye, then tears off like the Road Runner, leaving the door to his office wide open with me inside. Calling upon my powers of TV transformation, I morph into Tanya Roberts, aka Julie Rogers (in my opinion, the best snooper of all the Angels because you got the feeling that given her streetwise background, she'd do anything—and I mean *anything*—to find that secret microfiche).

With Gordon gone, I turn to the stack of stationery boxes on his desk and get lucky on my first try. I shove a couple of blank *Curator* comment cards in my notebook and disappear before my boss can beam back up and bust me. From there, I haul ass to Kinko's and reproduce the form on exactly the same shade and grade of card stock, shrewdly employing the "auto-contrast" button to insure that the pink paper doesn't copy gray. If there's one thing all those hours of temping taught me, it's that the Xerox machine is my friend.

I leave Kinko's, grab some takeout from Chin-Chin, then head home to cohost, with Dandy, the first, and hopefully last, unofficial Save Lucinda Pledge Drive.

"What do you want us to put?" asks Claudia, one of the several different handwriting stylists we were able to gather on such short notice.

"Okay," says Dandy between golf pencil sharpenings, "Where it says, 'How would you rate the following characters?' go down to where it says, 'Lucinda, the Janitor' and check 'Excellent.' I don't care what you put for the rest."

"Aren't they going to get suspicious if everyone puts 'Excellent'?" asks Ulysses, ever the voice of reason. "We should do some that say Lucinda's 'good,' but that everybody else is 'average.' As long as that curve is consistent."

"Good idea," agrees Miles. "By the way, I don't think I should come to the screening tomorrow night because too many people in the business know who I am."

"Okay, everybody," I announce, holding up a form. "Where it says, 'Other comments on the plot or characters,' come up with complimentary, but vague, things to say about Dandy. Don't say, 'She was funny,' or 'She was scary,' because we have no idea what kind of movie they've made out of it."

"Can I say, 'Lucinda has a nice rack?' " jokes Ulysses.

"No," says Dandy indignantly. "Because I've already put that on a bunch. But you *can* say something nice about my ass."

The next night, I show up to work with a stack of 121 pro-Lucinda comment forms tucked into my hot little pocket. The plan is for me to disappear into the men's room after I collect the cards from the audience and switch ours with theirs. Lucinda will be saved and nobody, least of all that dipshit Gordon, will be the wiser.

"Good evening, Craig," says Gordon slyly as he greets me outside the theater. "You know, I was all ready to strangle you yesterday and then I realized it was April Fool's. Very funny, Mr. Clybourn."

It was? I think as Gordon slaps me on the back.

"Just remember," he says before limping away, no doubt due to an injury he suffered yesterday on the wild-goose chase I sent him on, "revenge is sweet."

The realization that I inadvertently pulled the *Voyager* stunt on the one day out of 365 that it would be excusable leaves me feeling a bit delirious, as though our scheme to save Lucinda is charmed in some way. My confidence is shot to hell, however, when a white-trash garbed Ulysses and Claudia show up, as planned, with an incognito Dandy, who, for everyone's sake, had agreed to stay the hell away tonight.

"What are you doing here?" I growl under my breath as she passes. In a long auburn wig, dark brown foundation, Coke bottle glasses and a business suit, Dandy looks like a cross between Marcia Clark and Maria Conchita Alonso.

"I couldn't just sit home and do nada," she whispers in a Charo-by-way-of-Carol-Burnett accent that goes great with the wig. "You gusto a bite of mi churro?"

"No," I bark. "I gusto a bite of your head."

"Craig," says a voice from behind me. "Help me pass these forms out."

I turn around to see Gordon standing at the top of the aisle cradling a stack of pale green comment forms.

"But they're green!" I practically scream. Catching myself, I add in a sort of "how peculiar?" tone, "We don't usually have green forms, do we?"

"I know," Gordon sighs, handing me a stack. "I had to recopy them because the lead actress—Penelope Mary Elizabeth Louise Anderson—whatever her three names are—I spelled one of them wrong and if the studio saw it, we'd probably lose the contract, especially since she's engaged to the director."

My first thought is to send Ulysses or Claudia to go copy more forms, but before I can even find them, the lights go down and the film begins. I'm considering abandoning my position as "bathroom pointer" and going myself when Gordon saunters up and suggests we have that little attitude talk now.

For the next forty-five minutes, my superior officer and I sit on a bench across from a poster for the latest Chris Farley vehicle and discuss such concepts as positivity, confidentiality and the company good. At one point, I have to smile at how ironic it would be if I were to be fired for my attitude when there are 121 better reasons making a dent in my pocket as we speak. By the time my boss wraps it up, asking me to repeat aloud a pledge that I will buck up and become a team player, I'm wishing Chris Farley would just step out of the poster, sit on me and get it over with.

When I return to the screening, with twenty minutes to go, it looks like I've missed all of Dandy's scenes, so now I have no idea what I'm even crusading for. My spirits lift slightly when the lights come up and the suburbanites applaud, indicating that something in this celluloid travesty might actually have its finger on the pulse of middle America.

Team player that I am, I start collecting the comment forms while Gordon thanks the guinea pigs for coming, then tells anyone who would like to stay and be in a focus group for $20 to remain seated and he'll come around and choose you. When both Dandy and Claudia are chosen, I make a beeline to the back of the theater, where I can cringe in peace while avoiding the stray wigs and expletives that are sure to start flying.

"My favorite character was the janitor," gushes Claudia, whose closest thing to a paid acting job is unfolding before my eyes. "She was pretty and nice and I really related to her." As mortifying as this whole charade is, I can't help but be slightly touched by the sight of Claudia and Dandy, who have always resented each other, uniting against a common foe.

"Me too also," adds Senorita Rio. "She is very, how you say, likable and sympathetic."

If she starts to hoochie coochie, I'm going to open a vein, I think, before burying my face in my hands.

"The whole film should have been about her," says a third voice, one I don't recognize. Dammit if some horny teenager in a Lakers cap didn't stick up for Lucinda completely of his own accord.

"I missed her when she wasn't on the screen," says yet another stranger, this one a middle-aged black woman. Oh my God, I think,

Dandy's crossing over. With just a little prompting from Dandy and Claudia, this so-called focus group has turned into a veritable Lucinda Love-In.

"She was much prettier than the wife," says a smart-looking fortyish man in a suit and tie who looks like he came straight from the office. "I thought the wife looked *old*."

"She has to go," I hear a voice whisper behind me. I slowly turn and steal a glance at Penelope Mary Elizabeth Louise Anderson—whatever her three names are—looking on indignantly. Next to her, shaking his ponytail to and fro in frustration, is *The Curator*'s creator, Richard Rand. "I'm not going to be upstaged by a no-talent sitcom slut," the actress continues, seething.

"Well," sighs Richard, "the film's too long anyway. Something has to go. It may just as well be the no-talent sitcom slut."

I decide not to tell the no-talent sitcom slut about what I overheard. I think it's better for all of us—Dandy, Claudia, Ulysses, Miles and myself—to think that we were triumphant tonight, that we beat the system at its own game. After everyone leaves the theater, I even invite my four favorite recruits over to my place to swap war stories and eat Domino's. Who said I wasn't a team player?

So don't be surprised if some unfortunate night at three in the morning, you happen upon *The Curator* on cable and Dandy Rio's not in it. She'll be surprised enough for all of us.

20

Ask me for my definition of happiness and I'd have to say, "a Pizza Hut coupon, the right friends and a beauty pageant on TV." Though I've never launched a formal study, I figure that if you looked back on my life and charted the high years and the low, there would be a direct correlation between my sentiments about our reigning Misses—America, USA and Universe—and my general level of happiness. Case in point: I've seldom felt more betrayed than the year that that Carolyn Sapp was Miss America. Oh, you remember her, she was that big-boned opportunist from Hawaii who made her acting debut in an autobiographical TV movie about her abusive Polynesian boyfriend *during* her reign. Hold on a second, I remember thinking at the time. Aren't you supposed to wait until *after* your year is over to start taking Hollywood by storm? I can just imagine the pageant organizers going, "Carolyn, you're scheduled to cuddle crack babies today at noon," and the Sappster going, "Sorry, I have looping." To this day it makes my blood boil.

The reason I have pageant on the brain is that Dandy's just been asked to serve as a judge for the Miss Teen America pageant and we couldn't be happier about it. Actually, she could be a lot happier about it but with her series about to go on hiatus and the network waffling about whether or not to renew it, she can use all the publicity she can get. Though she hasn't actually come out and said it, I think she also sees this getaway as a chance to get me out of my Missing the Snack doldrums and give me something to believe in, even if it is a brain-dead fourteen-year-old from Roanoke, Virginia, with the cutest dimples you ever did see. So off we go to San Diego, where this year's cavalcade of cuties is being held.

"Ricardo is the only reason I'm doing this," Dandy says as she slips the latest CD by Ricardo De Leon, Latin America's answer to Jon Bon Jovi and a fellow judge, into her car stereo. "I could give two shits about those flat-chested teeny bopper virgins. They should just call it 'Cherries Jubilee.' "

Given Dandy's vehement disregard for the whole bedazzled affair, I suggest we use the rest of the car ride to hatch a plan wherein I'll assume the judging responsibilities—covertly, of course—leaving Dandy free to concentrate on seducing the Brazilian balladeer. No reason why we can't both have lifelong dreams realized this weekend.

By the end of the first day of the preliminaries, I already have a few faves. Though most would deem it pageant suicide, Miss New York won big points with me during the interviews when she said that condoms should be available in schools. This caused an audible gasp to emit from my least favorite lass, Miss Kentucky, who, at fifteen, has been in so many pageants that she can't say "Thank you" in ordinary conversation without holding her hands out in gratitude to the imaginary judges that, like God and her lucky Care Bear, travel everywhere with her.

During each break, I meet Dandy in the lobby for the preplanned Evian swap wherein she takes my bottle—with a list of my favorites written in code on the label—and I take hers. We nearly get busted when one of her fellow judges, a dehydrated Dr. Joyce Brothers, appears out of nowhere, but all she says is, "You were smart to bring your own water. I had no idea these pageant people were so cheap."

That night in our hotel room, I spread out my umpteen pages of notes on the bed and attempt to run some strategies past Dandy, but she's having none of it.

"Ricardo didn't say so much as 'Hola' to me all day," she says. "His eyes were glued on those fucking contestants, especially the blondes. He's got a thing for blondes, Craig. I want to go home."

"We can't," I say. "You signed a contract. Besides, we owe it to the underdogs to stick it out. What if we were to leave and Miss Kentucky were to win? Would you be able to forgive yourself?"

"Please, I already have," Dandy retorts. "Ricardo likes Miss Kentucky," she continues with a sigh. "Every time she comes out, he starts chewing his pencil. I want her dead."

"Well, at least we agree on something," I say.

Our water-swapping plan gets us through Day 2 without incident. I find another keeper during the bathing suit competition—Miss Hawaii. Not only does she manage to not make a complete ass out of herself with the potentially disastrous sarong choreography, but, if I'm not mistaken, she actually tells a story with her sarong, something about her first plane ride to the mainland. Take that, Miss Kentucky.

Meanwhile, continuing to be ignored by Ricardo while simultaneously having to evaluate an endless parade of nubile-beyond-their-years bims in their Jantzen best seems to be taking a toll on Dandy. By the end of Day 2, when we adjourn to the hotel bar for a drink, she's practically on the verge of tears.

"I didn't expect them to be so stacked, Craig," she says sadly. "I thought they'd just have little nubbins like Kerry Strug."

"Miss Vermont has nubbins," I point out.

"That's one out of fifty," Dandy retorts before ordering another drink. "I'm fat, Craig. That's why Ricardo doesn't like me. I have a fat ass and huge love handles. No, they're too big to be handles. They're like love cantilever shelves. I hate my body *so much*."

Her fifth rum and coke and the tears arrive at roughly the same time. I look on helplessly as she dribbles into the peanut dish.

"I couldn't help overhearing," says a voice from the next table. "I think I can help you."

I leave Dandy in the famously capable hands of Dr. Joyce Brothers and head up to the room. I'm still up—preparing our interview questions for the big night—when Dandy stumbles in six hours later. Her eyes are puffy and it looks like she puked on her shoes but she's wearing a smile.

"That lady is so amazing," Dandy says. "She knows so much, Craig, and not just about psychology, about everything."

"Well, how could you put in that much time on *Hollywood Squares* and not?" I say before helping my drunk friend into bed and killing the light.

The next day, Dandy wakes up a new woman with a take-it-or-leave-it attitude toward Señor De Leon. As the pageant proper is tonight, we have the day free to hang out by the pool and finalize our game plan.

"You'll keep this on vibrate in your lap," I say to Dandy, holding up a pager I picked up especially for tonight. "I'll page you from the cellular at the end of each round and tell you, by number, who to rank first, second and in the case of Miss Kentucky, last. Then you'll enter it on that little keypad."

"Seriously, Craig?" Dandy sighs. "You remember what happened the last time we used a gadget. I ended up not getting to have sex with Bill Maher."

"This is much less complicated," I say. "You don't even have to speak."

"Why don't I just vote for Miss Hawaii?" Dandy asks, still feeling a bit hungover from last night. "She's your favorite."

"Yes, but that could all *change,*" I say. "I mean, I just saw Miss Arizona in the elevator and the Muzak version of "A Little More Love" by Olivia Newton-John was playing and *her lips were moving*. She knew the *words,* Dandy. I might have to go with her."

Any modicum of attention that Dandy may have been giving my instructions is instantly obliterated when a Speedo-clad Ricardo De Leon emerges from the pool and saunters over to chat. Maybe Dandy's new hard-to-get attitude is working. Either that or Ricardo realizes that going after the nookie he really wants is, in this country, anyway, a felony.

At Dr. Bro's urging, Dandy decides on a gown for the pageant that is so low-cut that I worry the satellite feeds will be impaired. Still, she looks stellar when she's introduced and gives her wave. And Ricardo can't seem to take his eyes off her.

Based on the fact that of the five girls who make the finals, four are my personal faves, it looks like our paging system is working. That the fifth is Miss Kentucky is, frankly, terrifying, but it does add to the suspense. Ironically, it's Miss Kentucky who draws Dandy's name during the final round of questions.

"My question is two parts," Dandy says, making me break into instant bum-clenches because none of the questions I prepared for her had two parts. "First, what woman do you most admire and why, and second, where did you get your shoes? They are so cute."

Once Miss Kentucky finishes yammering on about Mother Teresa, Hillary Rodham Clinton, her cancer-ridden grandmother, the Wild Pair, and, of course, God, the competition is officially over. I put in my final call to Dandy's pager, ranking Arizona first, then stew in my own raw nerves until the envelope is opened.

" . . . *And the first runner-up,*" reads the evening's host, Alan Thicke, over the din of my beating heart, "is *Miss Arizona*. Miss Kentucky, *you are the new Miss Teen America*!"

This can't be happening, I think. Though stunned, I try and count the number of times Miss Kunt-Lucky mouths "Thank you" during her victory stroll, but lose track at sixteen when my eyes become too watery to see.

Backstage after the show, I grab my most famous friend by the shoulders, shove her against the green room door and shriek, "What the fuck happened?" in a vocal register that's higher than any of the contestants and most of their dogs.

"I don't know," Dandy cries. "I voted just like you said. Maybe we were just outnumbered. Or maybe I messed up in the final round because I was using my left hand."

"Why were you using your left hand?" I ask, my blood vessels threatening to explode out of my temples. "What was your right hand doing?"

"Um . . . international relations," says Dandy.

Dandy ends up riding back to L.A. with Ricardo, which is definitely for the best as I have nothing to say to her. As dejected as I feel about all that's gone on down here in San Diego, I feel even worse about the heaping helping of same old same old that waits for me back in the 213. Wanting to put off the inevitable for as long as possible, I decide to loiter at the pool for a few hours before driving Dandy's Miata back to L.A.

After devouring the new issue of *Movieline,* I strike up a conversation with a beautiful young lass on the next deck chair. She not only turns out to be quite personable, but she also happens to be Miss Arizona's big sister, Helene. After telling her how robbed I think her sibling was, we start to exchange pageant gossip. When she expresses a deep-seated hatred of Miss Kentucky that rivals my own, it's all I can do not to hold her and tell her that everything's going to be okay.

"I don't get it," I say. "Apart from how completely phony she was, I didn't even think she was pretty."

"I know," says Helene. "You know who else I thought looked like a cow?"

"Miss Minnesota," I venture to guess.

"No, that judge, Dandy what's-her-name. What a pig."

The second the word Dandy leaves her mouth I reach for my empty can of diet Coke and pretend to drink so I won't have to comment.

"You're getting really red, Craig," she says. "You want me to rub some suntan lotion on your back?"

"That'd be great," I say.

While Helene applies the Hawaiian Tropic to my skin, I wonder if Dandy really did look like a cow and if so, should I have said something? I thought she looked hot. Am I losing perspective? Am I really no better than the supposed FOPAs (Friends of Paula Abdul) who, back in the early nineties, allowed the singer to perform "Vibeology" on the MTV Awards dressed as a fireplug in fishnets? These concerns soon vanish as the delicious smell of coconut hits my nostrils like a tranquilizer. All at once, I feel Helene's hands stop moving and rest on my back. Then I feel her remove them completely.

Having long suspected that the nerve endings in my back were inadvertently hardwired directly to my brain's pleasure center, I'm tempted to offer Helene money if she'll just not stop touching me. Fortunately, before I can make such an offer, she returns to my back with a newfound vigor. I'm about to drift into a blissful sleep when I detect something foreign and yet somehow familiar about the feel of her hands on my skin. Calluses, maybe?

It can't be, I tell myself. All the same, I turn my head to the other side to check out the reflection in the hotel windows. Godfrey's illustrious hair bounces with his every stroke and he smiles goofily at Miss Arizona's sister in a way that says, "How long before this idiot figures it out?" I say nothing, preferring to concentrate on what it feels like to have my heart pound out of my chest, not to mention the ramifications of my aforementioned misplaced back-to-crotch nerve endings.

When I can no longer endure not being able to touch him back, I flip over and hope like hell that he'll lead the way so I won't have to worry about what kind of affection he's expecting.

After a good long hug, I introduce Godfrey to my new friend. He thanks her for playing along and then asks me if there's somewhere we can go to catch up. I throw on my shoes and a shirt and since Godfrey's hungry, we head to the outdoor bar for lunch. While he settles in at a table, I excuse myself to go to the bathroom, but instead head to the front desk to ask if it would be possible to keep Dandy's room for one more night. They assure me it would, for $160. I say, "Fine," even though I don't have that kind of money to spend, then return to the table.

"You look tired," I say as we look over the menu.

"I didn't sleep much on the plane," he says. "Plus, the schedule they've had us on is just insane."

Godfrey explains that the record company flew the Godmakers back to the States to knock out a video, which they'll start tomorrow, then it's back to Japan for more touring and promotion. After that, there's talk of a U.S. release and possible tour, though nothing's carved in stone. When I ask how he found me, he explains that he called Miles the second he got home from the airport.

"You didn't want to wait until I got home?" I say.

"Well, I knew starting tomorrow I'd be busy with the video and everything," he says. "And after all the time in Japan, the idea of getting in my car and driving someplace sounded really good and I got to see my sister who lives here. Plus, I wanted to talk to you."

Not see you, I think. Not hold you. Not kiss you. Not bang you. Talk.

"I wanted to talk to you too," I say.

Why does my body suddenly feel three times heavier than it is? "Um, I don't really know how to say this." In fact, I know exactly how to say it, I just don't want to. I have to say it first, I think. "I don't know if this is going to work," I say.

"I don't know either," Godfrey says after a long pause. *No shit*. "I mean, with all that's happening to me now, I don't think I can keep it going. I can't balance it all." I look down at the table for this part.

"I understand," I say. "I feel the same way. This incredible thing is happening to you. This giant balloon is taking off for you and I don't want to be the guy back home who makes you feel like you're tied to something on the ground."

"Maybe I want to be tied to something on the ground," he says.

"If you wanted to be tied to something on the ground," I say, "we'd be up in that hotel room right now."

Godfrey and I spend the remainder of the afternoon sitting in the same two chairs, talking alternately about things that matter and things that don't. What those two months meant to each of us. The exchange rate for Japan. The pressure he's feeling by the record company to play it really straight. The fact that Miss Kentucky is flying home with a crown in her carry-on. The mutually agreed upon notion that it is not out of the question that the two of us could end up together when the stardust settles. The price of a Big Mac in Hiroshima.

"Do they have Play Places in Japan?" I wonder as we get up to leave.

"I didn't see any," says Godfrey, with a yawn.

"Their loss," I say.

We hug each other good-bye out by his Jeep and for the first time that I can remember, Godfrey looks both ways before giving me a peck as though if the coast weren't clear, his locking lips with another man in a San Diego resort parking lot might keep the Godmakers from attaining their destined status as household names.

I make it a point not to watch his Jeep disappear into the distance. Instead, the second he pulls away, I turn and walk back into the hotel, and tell the front desk I won't be needing the room tonight after all.

I don't discuss Godfrey with Dandy when I get back to L.A., preferring to pore over those details with Ulysses, who, heterosexuality notwithstanding, possesses the most discerning view of the big picture of anyone I know. In fact, I don't hear from Dandy until a week later, when she calls to tell me that, after enjoying a good dozen sessions of love deluxe with Ricardo, she caught him in a clinch with California's representative to Miss Teen America, whom he apparently bumped into while shopping for a present for Dandy in the Westside Pavilion.

"I don't even remember Miss California," I say. "Was she the half-breed?"

"I don't know, Craig," Dandy barks, "and I don't care. I just know that it's really fucked me up."

"Maybe you should call Dr. Bro to talk about it," I offer.

"I tried," cries Dandy, "but she's out of the office shooting a *Friends* episode. It always comes back to the fucking Friends, Craig."

While Dandy sobs on, I catch Miss Kentucky, I mean Miss Teen America, sidling up to Conan out of the corner of my eye and want to heave. It's not going to be a good year.

21

Damon Darlington's latest care package has just arrived from Japan and I don't know whether to laugh, cry or play with myself. There on top, under a single errant Styrofoam peanut, staring up at me through the shrink-wrap, is Godfrey on the cover of the Godmakers cassette.

Damon, who I never told about Godfrey, writes in his letter about how the Godmakers are currently making it big in Japan. He goes into great detail about his fantasy of throwing himself at the leather-panted lead singer at their upcoming Tokyo concert. I don't see it happening, frankly, because Godfrey, God bless him, has always seemed to be immune to the charms of the Cute Club. Be that as it may, the only thing I can imagine that would be worse than a carnal union occurring between This Many and the Snack would be me having to hear about it. Still, it's nice to get the tape. Godfrey was supposed to send a CD over the second they were pressed, but never did. But that's fine. I only *inspired* the fucking thing.

The silver lining in this particular cloud comes in the form of a cassette This Many sent along with the Godmakers. Damon shares my insatiable passion for silly girl groups and was generous enough to send his new discovery, five bodacious British street babes who chirp peppy songs about friendship and boys, my two all-time favorite themes.

"I'm borrowing this," says Dandy the second I start playing it for her in the car.

"Okay, but copy it and give it back, because that's my only copy, and they're way too spicy and fun to ever come out here," I say. "Where are we going?"

"On a secret mission," says Dandy. "Relax, Craig, there's food involved."

Now, I've been on more secret missions with Dandy than I can count. But I think this may be the only time I wasn't let in on the secret in advance. Dandy's seriousness, not to mention the fact that she's actually wearing a bra, leads me to believe this particular sojourn is professionally motivated rather than romantically, which makes sense because though *That's Just Dandy* has been renewed for next season, the network made it very clear that if it doesn't bring in the numbers when it returns in the fall, the ax will drop.

Our destination turns out to be Swingers diner on Beverly, home of the sexiest hash slingers in town. Our server, Mike, a pointy-sideburned hunk with sinister eyes and a smoky voice is, in my opinion, the hottest of the hot. But then, I've always been attracted to people who might actually kill me.

"There's going to be a third person," Dandy tells him.

"Who's this third person?" I ask.

Just then a tall, pale man with a shaved head and tattoos on each of his well-toned biceps approaches the table and gives Dandy a big, familiar hug. He looks me in the eye as he sits down and cracks a smile so satanic I'm surprised he doesn't work here.

"Remember when I first moved to New York," Dandy says, after introducing the mystery man as Keith, "and there was that photographer guy in my building that I went out with . . ."

"Well, I don't know that we ever actually went *out*," Keith says with a leer.

Dandy gives Keith a playful slap, then says, "Anyway, this is him.

We bumped into each other at a club last week when I was out with Ricardo. Keith's going to help us save my show."

After we order, Dandy cases the joint for eavesdroppers and members of the Gossip Posse, then leans in, bears down and commences with the plan-hatching.

"Remember when that picture of me and the tattoo guy with the weights hanging from his nuts was all over the place and my ratings went up?" Dandy asks.

I nod. I'd like to say I'm terrified of where this is going, but I've actually come to *enjoy* these shenanigans that are the Dandy Rio experience, even *crave* them. I know I should know better, but I just don't want to. I mean, if all the Dandy-related schemes and machinations were removed from my life, would what's left be any fun at all?

"Well, if that stupid picture helped my ratings," Dandy continues, the cogs of her brain outgrinding the nearby blender, "just imagine what a nice *Playboy* spread could do."

"But we've been through this," I say, disappointed in the anticlimacticness of it all. "Hasn't the network forbidden it?"

"Of course," gripes Dandy before lowering her voice to a scarcely audible purr. "But what if the pictures were taken *before* I was famous and then surfaced, like Vanessa Williams."

"Do you have pictures like that?" I ask, knowing full well that I would know if she did.

"Not yet," says Dandy.

"That's where I come in," says Keith.

"I'm sure it is," I say.

Over a mammoth plate of French fries that are nearly as scrumptious as the ex-con who delivered them, Dandy continues to spew forth the details of what I'm choosing to call Operation Beavershot. She and Keith will go to great pains this weekend to "recreate" the kind of pictures she would have gullibly allowed to be taken during her "experimental college days." Every detail of the photos will be orchestrated to scream 1988. Keith will develop and print them himself in his own darkroom, then sell the pics to *Playboy*, or if they balk, *Pent-*

house, and split the money with Dandy. When the shots hit the stands, Dandy will have a very public meltdown, then go on the highest-rated TV show she can get and open up about the shutterbug college boyfriend who coerced her into dropping trou.

"Then all we have to do is sit back and count the ratings points," Dandy concludes.

The words "Where do I come in?" seem to fall out of my mouth of their own volition.

"Moral support mostly," says Dandy.

"And to be like a P.A. on the shoot," adds Keith.

"And also to run interference between me and Keith," interjects Dandy, "because after the photos are taken, we shouldn't be seen together. We probably shouldn't even be here now."

Keith says good-bye, explaining he's expected at the Palace, where he works as a bouncer, then Dandy asks Mike for the check.

"Just promise me one thing," I say, turning serious. "Promise me you won't show pink."

"Duh," says Dandy, while writing her phone number on a napkin for Mike. "What kind of a whore do you think I am?"

When I get home that night, I make a list of things to remember for Operation Beavershot and title it Operation BS List, for secrecy's sake. Among its items are "Hide Dandy's navel piercing" and "Find Donna Mills's *The Eyes Have It* makeup video." I half-seriously write myself a reminder to "Take leave of senses" at the top of the page, as if I hadn't already done so.

Saturday arrives and, having told Miles, Claudia and Ulysses that I'm attending a workshop called "Sell That Screenplay," I drive to the predetermined location on the campus of USC. Keith was able to convince a friend who was out of town to let us use his dorm room. Though the plan is for the photos to only show Dandy against a plain background or at the most sprawled atop some generic college twin bed, I have to appreciate Keith's sense of verisimilitude.

As I amble down the dormitory hallway checking the room numbers for 217, a tall, thin guy in overalls and no shirt strides by with a U2 *Joshua Tree* poster. I take this as a good omen—that the spirit of the late eighties will indeed be with us today—until I see the man disappear into room 217. Soon after he goes in, I hear the voices of at least four separate people emit from the room and I stop dead in my tracks. As I'd understood it, Operation BS was to involve three people: Dandy (the model), Keith (the photographer), and me (the lost soul). If at least four people are in room 217 and one of them isn't me, then the cast and crew of Operation BS has practically doubled, something that it cannot be allowed to do if the confidentiality of our undertaking is to be preserved.

I can feel my simmering blood come to a full boil when I walk in and see that the entire room has been art-directed to within an inch of its life. Overall Guy is hanging Bono and the gang over one of the beds, while two other strangers stand at the desk and peruse a box of old magazines. There's a giant eighties ghetto blaster on the nightstand and a number of different outfit options being spread out on the bed by a person resembling an androgynous Munster.

"Where's Dandy?" I say angrily, realizing that Operation BS now numbers six.

"She's in with the hair and makeup people," says Keith. Make that eight.

I stomp across the room and throw open the bathroom door but instead of finding Dandy, I come upon a very small man taking a leak.

"Hey, somebody's in here," the little guy says. "Can't a guy take a piss in private?"

I finally find Dandy in the dorm room next door being primped and groomed by a hair person, a makeup person and, I kid you not, a manicurist. So now we're up to ten, eleven if you count the midget, though I don't know if he's involved or just passing through.

"Hi Craig," Dandy chirps as though everything's hunky-dory. Even though I'm livid I can't help but admire the bang-up job the trio of beauty pros have done on her. With a long, dark, tousled wig and the kind of makeup one might wear to a *Falcon Crest* cast party, she looks like a long-lost member of Heart—the one who complains backstage because Ann and Nancy have devoured the hospitality spread before she could even pick up a plate.

"Can I talk to you in private, please?" I say.

Dandy nods, then follows me into the hall, all the while blowing on her wet nails.

"What the fuck is going on here?" I hiss.

"What are you talking about?" she says.

"What are all these people doing here? I thought we all understood how important it is that no one know about this but you, me and Keith."

"Well, Keith and I got to talking about how we could really do something cool if we had the right people so he brought in some friends of his. Most of them are from Paris and they're going back tomorrow so they won't spill the beans."

"*Some* friends," I scream. "There's like ten people now."

"It's mostly just for hair and makeup, which you must admit is crucial," says Dandy. "Then there's the wardrobe stylist and Keith's assistant."

"What, no caterer?" I grumble.

"No, but we have a midget."

"I saw him peeing," I scream. "What's his job, best boy?"

"No, he's going to be in the pictures with me."

I stare dumbfoundedly at Dandy for a moment, then turn on my heel and start to stalk away. Dandy skitters after me, shaking her nails as she runs.

"Wait, Craig," she says, placing her splayed hands on my shoulders and looking me dead in the eye. "I know we planned to do it another way, but Keith and I decided yesterday that if the pictures don't rock, it's not going to matter how secretive we are because nobody will ever see them. I know we're taking a chance and I'm sorry I didn't consult you, but it's my ass on the line."

"Among other things," I mutter.

"Please don't be mad," she says. Dandy puts her arm around me and starts herding me back to 217. "Look, I really appreciate everything you're doing for me," she continues. "I have to say I really feel good about this, Craig. I found the best eighties ghetto blaster at the swap meet and Keith's going to make the room look perfect. And, you have to admit, I look pretty classic."

I look her in the eye and shake my head resignedly. "Dandy, a midget?" I say.

"Remember Toby, the R.A. at my dorm at ASU that we used to hang out with?" she asks. "Well, we're not going to show this guy's face so I'm going to say it's Toby. It's genius, because I always tell Toby stories in interviews so it'll make perfect sense."

"I'm sure Toby will be thrilled by your sensitivity," I say.

"Toby's dead, Craig," she reminds me. "We went to his funeral together."

"Oh, that's right."

Later on, I watch as Dandy poses for Keith and am amazed at the transformation she undergoes in front of the camera. Gone from her eyes is the paranoid desperation of a woman clinging to the tattered corner of some imaginary Hollywood picnic blanket and in its place is the sexy naiveté of an ASU ingenue who'd never even laid eyes on a casting couch, let alone traveled with one. Some of Dandy's finest acting is unfolding in this dorm room and if all goes according to plan, and the attending throng keep their yaps shut, the world will never know it. Though I can't say that things are not going well, a churning uneasy feeling invades my stomach as I watch my friend, looking pretty much how she looked when I met her, make tender teenage love to the camera. Should I be allowing this to happen, I wonder. Probably not. Could I do anything to stop it? Hell, no.

I nearly leave when a sweat-dripping Keith complains that there are too many people in the room for him to concentrate, but decide to ride it out until the end.

"Bring in the midget," says Dandy.

On second thought . . .

As I walk back to my car—Dandy and the Toby Proxy getting up to God knows what in my absence—I recall the many evenings Dandy and I spent shooting the shit with Toby back at the front desk of Manzanita Hall. Toby liked us because we treated him like we did everyone else, which is not to say particularly well, but over time, a nice rapport developed among the three of us. Toby was the only one back then who thought something sexual was going on between Dandy and myself. Either that or he understood that I wouldn't mind being perceived that way. He used to say the raunchiest things to me in the mornings as I would leave and I would respond in kind.

I start to laugh as I pull onto the freeway, remembering the sophomoric pranks and rude comments Toby used to inflict on the innocent residents who approached his counter. There was one rich bitch named Bianca that he insisted on calling Binaca no matter how many times she corrected him. Another, a stuck-up cheerleader named Terese or Theresa, who we suspected had an eating disorder and used to anonymously order pizzas for. Fucked up, I know, but it was college.

I shudder to think what's going on in Room 217 as we speak, but I do know one thing. Toby would have totally dug it.

22

"So how did that screenplay workshop go?" asks Miles over dinner at the Beverly Connection Souplantation, a buffet-style scarfathon that we try to do only once a month in order to give them time to restock.

"Workshop?" I say, my mind temporarily lost under some crouton or other.

" 'Sell That Screenplay,' " says Claudia.

"Oh, um, it was pretty cool," I say. "I learned a lot."

"Like?" says Miles.

"Just um, stuff about agents and unions and like what size of gold brads to get at Staples, that kind of thing."

"What size?" asks Claudia.

"Well," I say, reluctantly dropping my fork in order to use my hand as a visual aid. "The instructor told us to get the ones that are about as long as your thumb."

What a load of horseshit, I think, as I watch Miles and Claudia refrain from chowing long enough to scrutinize the size of their own thumbs.

The latest on OBS is that the pictures turned out great and now we're waiting for the right time to pitch them to *Playboy*. In a perfect world, they'd run just as *That's Just Dandy* is about to make its season premiere. This means we hold out a month or two before sending Keith out to peddle the wares and hope we're not done in by some bigmouthed midget or materialistic manicurist.

I saw the photos for the first time last night at Dandy's and I still can't believe how oddly beautiful they are. Seriously. There's something wonderfully hazy and nostalgic about them: the afternoon sun beating through the dorm room window on one of those days when you needed to be studying but would rather look at your own nipples in a hand mirror. They hearken back to a time when dancing around naked in front of a U2 poster or having a pillow fight with your favorite dwarf seemed like an expression of hope and love. The eroticism is just the icing on the cake. Well, actually, the icing on the cake—a chocolate confection that was strategically placed atop the Toby Proxy's head to keep the camera from getting *too* intimate—is the icing on the cake.

"So did they say anything about the benefits of having a reading at this workshop?" Miles says.

"Yeah," says Claudia. "Did they?"

Miles and Claudia have been trying for ages to convince me to throw a reading of *Deck Games*—the new and improved third draft of which has been done for almost two months—but my garden variety fear of failure has always led me to resist them.

"No," I mutter. "They didn't say anything about it."

"What are you so afraid of?" asks Miles. "It doesn't have to be a big production, Craig. Just something to give you an idea of what works and what doesn't."

Nothing and everything, respectively, I think.

"I'll make my Rice Krispies Treats," offers Claudia as if she's the only person on earth with the recipe.

"I want to make one more pass at it before I have a reading," I say.

"Cop out," Miles says before stealing the last chocolate minimuffin from Claudia's fourth plate. "Okay, whoever's the biggest pussy at the table has to go get more muffins."

"I'll be right back," I sigh, then head away to muffin-land, thankful, at least, that Claudia's outgrown her Ziploc doggy bag stage.

Two days later, Miles calls from his office.

"What are you doing next Saturday?" he asks.

"I don't know," I grunt. "Nothing."

"Good, because you're hosting a reading of *Deck Games*. And don't try to argue with me, Craig. It's time for some tough love."

"It is?" I say.

"Yes, and you'll never guess who I got to read Luther," he continues, referring to the story's young cruise director hero, who's basically just like me except better looking, good with gadgets and sexually active. "Are you sitting down?"

"Pretty much," I say, sitting down.

"Andrew Ormiston," he says.

"*My* Andrew Ormiston?" I say, remembering Dandy's cute costar whom I bonded with after that trapshooting nightmare during the *Lifestream Takes to the Ocean* cruise.

"The very same," says Miles. "He left the soap a few months ago and moved to L.A. He's trying to get into films and he's crazy about your script. He wants you to meet him at Insomnia at two o'clock to discuss it."

Insomnia turns out to be an appropriate venue, because Andy is sporting bags under his eyes so large they wouldn't fit in the overhead bin and would have to be checked.

"I almost didn't recognize you," I say, taking in his grungy visage. As a ne'er-do-wrong preppie on *Lifestream,* Andy was always clean-cut in khaki. Today, looking thinner than I remember him in vinyl jeans and a long-sleeved disco shirt, I can't decide which he resembles more: hell warmed over or a Calvin Klein model.

"Just tryin' to change my image," Andy says, lighting up the Grand Marshal of the forthcoming Parade of Marlboros. When I offer to buy him a dessert, Andy accepts gleefully, claiming he's been ravenous for sweets lately. What do you know? A Cute Club member who knows the word ravenous.

We hang together at Insomnia for nearly three hours, but only talk for about two, because Andy keeps taking these lengthy trips to the can. Before we go to leave, I make my own such trip and when I return he's passed out on the couch. I watch him sleep for a while, still unable to get over how much he's changed, then rouse him and say good-bye.

"Andrew Ormiston was such a square when I worked with him," Dandy says when I call later to tell her who I hooked up with. "I had to do a love scene with him one time and he wore sweatpants under the sheets and cried for two days afterwards."

"What's that sound?" I ask, referring to the loud rat-tat-tat-tat-ing I hear in the background.

"Do the words *white shorts* mean anything to you?" Dandy says teasingly.

Indeed they do. The other night when we were checking out the OBS pictures and channel surfing, I watched Dandy nearly choke on a SnackWell when Jay Leno brought out the flannel-wearing, sweat-dripping, all-male tap troupe from down under called the Tap Dogs. As the testosterone literally dripped from the screen onto her *Beauty and the Beast* rug, Dandy made herself a challenge to take in their show at UCLA, saunter backstage half-clad, and, in no short order, land herself a Dog, preferably the bare-chested one in the white shorts. After Mike the Swingers waiter failed to ring her bell, Dandy wanted to prove that she still had it, whatever *it* is. That she was able to do so in no less than forty-eight hours is remarkable, even for Dandy.

"You should hear what he can do with the bed frame," she coos. "It's like a symphony."

I call Dandy again later that night, no doubt interrupting some headboard cantata or other, to report on the confusing evening I just spent with Andrew, who called a few hours after I left him just wanting to hang.

"Did he hit on you?" she asks.

"No, nothing like that," I sigh. "Besides he couldn't stay awake long enough to hit on me. We went to the movies, he fell asleep. In the car, asleep." I pause for effect, then drop my bomb. "I think he's dropping smack, Dandy."

"You don't *drop* smack, Craig," she says smugly. "You *shoot* it."

"Thank you, Courtney Love," I retort. "The point is, I'm worried about him."

"Did you see any track marks?"

"Long sleeves," I say. "Both times I've seen him. And he goes to the bathroom *constantly*. And these are the tapes he has in his car: everything Nirvana, Smashing Pumpkins, Blind Melon, Color Me Badd . . ."

"Color Me Badd don't use, do they?"

"No, but if you were going to listen to them, wouldn't you want to be high?" I plead. "There's just too many signs to ignore. What should I do?"

"Do that thing with your heels on the nightstand again," she says. "I love that."

"What?" I say.

"Sorry, I wasn't talking to you."

Over the next week, Andy and I get together so often I have to wonder if he has any other friends. At one point, between naps, he actually refers to me as his "best friend" and I literally have to dab my eyes. Miles claims Andy's known to be quite a fixture in the Young Hollywood scene and has tons of young, beautiful playmates, but opts to hang with me instead.

"Is it so hard to imagine that Andy's tired of the clubs and the starlets and finds your company a refreshing change?" Miles asks.

"Um, yeah," I say. "It is."

Claudia meanwhile has a different theory about my friendship with Andy, a theory she has no problem whatsoever sharing.

"You want him, don't you?" she says one night after watching Andy leave my place at three A.M.

"We're just friends," I say. "We were watching videos together and he fell asleep. No big deal."

"Craig, why are you always going after these guys you can't possibly have?" she says. "Some rock singer, this soap guy, Aladdin. You should just find a nice, like, accountant or something and settle down."

"Oh, that's right," I say. "I keep forgetting how little I have to offer."

"That's not what I mean," she says. "It's just, you go for these sort of star guys who have all kinds of star crap to deal with. And you can never be as into them as they are into themselves, so it's doomed to fail."

"This may come as a surprise to you," I say emphatically, "but I'm not romantically attracted to Andrew Ormiston. I just think he really needs a friend right now."

"Why?" Claudia asks pointedly. "What's wrong?"

"Nothing," I say, bluffing. "He just moved here and he doesn't know anyone."

I don't bring up my heroin hunch to Claudia because she'd have me booked on an "I Love My Junkie Friend" episode of *Jerry Springer* before I knew what hit me. I don't tell Miles either because I don't want to jeopardize Andy's publicist/client relationship when I'm not completely certain. Still, the signs persist. The other night at the Good Earth I could swear he was foaming at the mouth, but maybe he's just a messy eater. And I do seem to pick up the check a lot. Could all that *Lifestream* money have gone right into his bloodstream?

"Good news, Craig," says Miles, calling from his office one morning. "I've got a literary agent from Writers and Artists coming."

"I didn't even know you were dating one," I say.

"No, coming to your *reading,*" Miles says perturbedly.

Oh, that's *right*. What with all the smack speculation, I've nearly forgotten about the *Deck Games* exhibition that's to take place in less than forty-eight hours. What could turn out to be my big break is about to happen, and yet I've spent more time fantasizing about the intervention I've been planning to mount for Andy (after the reading, of course) in which I would drag the young rebel into rehab by his perfectly gelled hair while he screams, *"I am not your problem to solve!"* like Meg Ryan in *When a Hag Wants an Oscar*.

The afternoon of the reading arrives and all systems (including Andy's nervous one) appear to be go. The venue Miles lined up, The All-Star Cafe in the prehistoric Hotel Knickerbocker, with its old-Hollywood speakeasy charm, seems the perfect place for someone's Tinseltown dream to come true. While we wait for Andy to come out of the bathroom—big surprise—so we can start, the club's genial proprietor, Max, keeps everyone entertained with stories about the ghosts of Frances Farmer and Rudolph Valentino that supposedly haunt the joint.

"I thought I felt something weird on my leg," says the easily spooked Claudia while going over the twenty-seven "beats" she's broken down for her twelve-line role as a boozy travel agent.

"Let's get the show on the road," shouts Dandy while cuddling with her hot diggity Dog on one of the coffeehouse's many comfy sofas. "We've got places to go, people to see, sounds to make."

"Exactly," agrees the disenchanted guy from Writers and Artists between bites of Rice Krispies Treat.

Just then Andy strolls out from the bathroom raving about the *Sid and Nancy* poster Max has over the toilet. Dandy, picking up on the Sid Vicious drug connection, gives me a knowing look. I walk behind her, lean in and whisper, "I'm going to get this horse off Andy's back if it *kills* me." Then Miles stands up, thanks everyone for coming and gives me the go-ahead.

"Exterior, cruise ship, evening," I read from the script that's shaking in my lap. *"The ship is docked in San Juan and passengers are filing on. Cut to: interior, Miranda's stateroom, evening. The door opens and Miranda, a beautiful, sophisticated young woman in travel clothes, enters, followed by her submissive husband, Walter. She gives the room a disapproving once-over, then speaks."*

Dandy clears her throat, then reads the first line of dialogue.

"Well, the closet's okay," she gripes. *"Now, where's the damn room?"*

Just then, every light in the place goes off. Claudia, who I assume must figure this is all part of Valentino's ghost's plan to get in her pants, lets out a scream that could curdle even the most heroin-laced blood.

"Nobody panic!" shouts the ever level-headed Ulysses.

"I've got a flashlight," says Max.

We sit in the dark for a moment while Max, using a cigarette lighter supplied by White Shorts, searches for the flashlight. He comes across a radio first—which when turned on reports that the blackout is affecting several Western states—but still no flashlight.

"Maybe Frances Farmer took it," Ulysses jokes, "and hocked it to buy a new brain."

"That's not funny," shrieks Claudia.

While Max continues to hunt for the light, White Shorts keeps us all entertained with an impromptu in-the-dark tap dance atop the glass coffee table. The sounds made by his Doc Martens on the plate of Rice Krispies Treats are particularly intriguing but, alas, they're cut short by Max's joyful announcement that he's found some candles.

We get the room illuminated and discover, not surprisingly, that the agent is long gone and the Rice Krispies Treats are inedible. A third discovery, Andrew Ormiston sprawled out on the floor like a *Diagnosis Murder* day player, comes a few seconds later and gives us all a bit of a start.

"Relax, everyone," I say. "He's probably just asleep. He falls asleep all the time."

"Who are you, Marcus Welby?" snaps a nearly hysterical Claudia.

"No," I say, staring her down. "I'm his *best friend*."

We try to revive Andy the way one would any sleeping person, but he's having none of it, so it's off to Cedars Hospital we go. When Andy comes to briefly in the car, I tell him the junk jig is up.

"What are you talking about?" he mumbles.

"You saved my life back on the ship," I remind him. "Now I'm going to save yours."

"I want a Whopper with Cheese," he says dazedly.

"What did he say?" says a confused Ulysses from the driver's seat.

"Nothing," I say. "That's just the smack talking. Just drive."

We screech up to the ER, carry Andy in and wait. Ulysses offers to bring me back a Whopper with Cheese—the normally healthy eater's been craving one since the car ride—but I tell him I'm too worried about my friend to eat.

After what seems like hours, a lady doctor takes me aside and says, "Your friend's going to be fine. Based on what Andy's told us—when he's conscious enough to talk—and some tests that we ran, it looks like he started a special diet some time recently and his system just couldn't take it."

"You mean he's not on heroin?" I say.

"No," she says.

"No smack or acid or Special K or anything?"

"No, nothing like that."

"What about pot?"

Head shake. No.

"So he's not a drug addict?" I say pleadingly.

"Not unless you consider tofu a drug."

When I call Dandy from the hospital to tell her the upshot, she says, "You mean he's a fucking *vegan*?"

"Something like that," I say sadly.

"I told you he was square."

"At least it looks like he's going to be okay," I say.

"Is there any press there?" she asks.

"No," I say.

"Good," says Dandy.

• •

I've seen Andy only once in the two weeks since the blackout. I mean, he calls me constantly but I either don't pick up or I come up with an excuse as to why we can't hang out. Andrew Ormiston's just boring. There, I said it. I guess the good part is, if I ever do befriend a drug addict, not that I want to or anything, I'll know exactly what to look for. And I'll kick that monkey's ass.

23

It had to happen eventually. Ever since she found out Amanda Bearse was getting to direct episodes of *Married . . . With Children,* Dandy's been talking about how she wants to get behind the camera. I just never thought anyone would let her.

"Guess what, Craig," she says breathlessly, calling at four in the morning a few weeks after the *DG* un-reading. "I'm going to spend part of my hiatus directing the new Hi-D-Ho video."

"Where are you?" I growl, still half asleep.

"I'm at a party at some A-and-R guy's house in the hills," she shouts over the thumping beat of rap music.

Dandy continues to barrel on excitedly, about what, I have no idea, and I nod off. I wake up the next morning to a phone call from Miles. Miles has agreed to act as my wake-up caller until I can get started on a second script. Fed up with *Deck Games* and my rash of failed attempts to drum up some interest in it, I've decided to start a new script, *The Last Prom,* a period piece about what happens to a small-town high school when a film crew comes in to shoot one of those gruesome drivers' training movies from the sixties. As charmed as I am by the premise, I've yet to type so much as *Fade In,* which is where Miles' cheerful, get-your-ass-out-of-bed calls come in. I realize an alarm clock could serve the same purpose, but I can't seem to find one that's nearly as annoying as Miles.

"I had the weirdest dream last night," I say. "I dreamed Dandy called me from some crazy party and said that she was going to be directing a rap video."

"That's hilarious," he says. "Dandy doesn't even like rap."

"I know," I say. "She freaked out the other day at the studio commissary because she thought Queen Latifah was looking at her funny."

Just then, our conversation gets interrupted by a series of car honks coming from outside. I look out the window and see Dandy's Miata pulled up on the grass in front of my building. In the passenger seat is a large black guy in sunglasses. Perched atop the driver's-side door and thrashing about to the car stereo is Dandy. It's now eight A.M.

"What are you doing?" I ask after throwing on some clothes and stumbling out to the car.

"Just coolin' in my ride," she says, sliding down into the car seat. "Craig, this is Hi-D-Ho. Hi-D, this is one of my most dope peeps, Craig."

I haven't needed subtitles this badly since *Trainspotting*. I guess I wasn't dreaming after all. It seems that last night, at some record company party in the hills, Dandy made such an impression on Hi-D-Ho and the execs from his label that they offered to let her direct the music video for his next single, "Drive-By Lover." That all this dealmaking went down in an overcrowded Jacuzzi is not at all surprising.

"It'll be a great chance for me to get my directing feet wet," says Dandy, "and it'll get my mind off Operation BS until it's time for us to make our move. Play him the song, Hi-D."

Roughly three seconds after Hi-D cranks the stereo, Viola comes running out of her apartment yelling at us to "turn that shit off." Frustrated with Viola's lack of tolerance, Dandy invites me to come along with her and Hi-D to scout possible locations. Since Dandy's car is a two-seater, I offer to drive mine, but since I don't have a stereo, that idea is swiftly aborted and I end up riding on Hi-D's lap.

"It's perfect!" Dandy shouts as we pull up to a rundown Los Feliz liquor store. "This store is da bomb."

While Dandy goes inside to exploit her TVQ and whatever other charms she can come up with to try and procure use of the location, I get better acquainted with Hi-D. After he pays a compliment to my shoes, which I inexplicably respond to by saying, "Thanks, I think they're pretty fresh," we get to talking about college. Turns out Hi-D, who's real name is Dietrich Waters, has a degree in English from Morehouse.

"Don't tell anyone, okay?" he says.

"Chill," I say reassuringly. "I'll be cool."

Dandy, who, believe it or not, has a hell of a work ethic once she sets her mind to something, spends the next week in preproduction for "Drive-By Lover." She lucks out when Nigel Swope, one of the most respected cinematographers around, comes on board to pick up a couple extra days' work between features so he can pay off his teenage girlfriend's American Express bill. Insomuch as I can understand her—Dandy now talks as though she's stage-managing *Def Comedy Jam*—the concept of the video is to juxtapose shots of Hi-D performing in an empty swimming pool (an idea ripped off from Spandau Ballet's "True" video, though Dandy will deny it to her death) with footage of Hi-D holding up the liquor store.

On the first day of shooting, Miles and I stop by the house where the pool footage is being shot. Our first clue that things aren't exactly going swimmingly comes when the wardrobe stylist asks Hi-D to remove the gun from his front pocket because it's affecting the line of the pants. Hi-D cooperates, handing the piece off to his homey, T-Spoon, then returns to his mark. As Dandy starts to boss people around, I can't help but fret with the knowledge that there is a loaded weapon on the same set that my power-hungry friend is barking out orders on. By the end of the day, I have a feeling the entire crew is going to be standing in line to use it.

In the front of that line, it seems, would be Nigel, the DP. From what I can tell, every instruction Dandy gives to him is self-contradictory. When asked by the fifty-six-year-old Brit, who appears to have rented every light in town for the shoot, whether she wants the image to look matte or glossy, Dandy replies, "Matte, definitely, but I want it to be really slick."

Miraculously, the day comes to a close without a single bullet being fired. Hi-D-Ho seems pleased with Dandy's work and bids her farewell with a chipper, "Five thousand!" which she reciprocates.

The next day, I know disaster is imminent when I show up at the liquor store location *before* Dandy. A very testy Hi-D and the film crew are standing about wondering where she is, when a low rider, belonging to T-Spoon, pulls up and deposits Dandy headfirst onto the pavement. When an empty forty-ounce bottle of Olde English 800 comes tumbling after her I know we're fucked. Remarkably, all Nigel does is laugh.

"Where the fuck have you been?" snaps Hi-D.

"Just chillin' in my crib," Dandy says with a belch. "Now, let's shoot this fucker."

"Anything you say, boss," says Nigel with mock subservience.

I have a feeling the disgruntled DP's going to let Dandy hang herself. After watching the first few takes, I can see he's following her inexperienced—and O.E.-addled—instructions to the letter, as opposed to yesterday, when he paid lip service to Dandy's orders, then did what he knew would look best. After a couple of hours of this, I can't bear to watch anymore so I bid a half-assed "Five thousand!" then head home.

Dandy calls me two days later in tears. My fears about Nigel were right. Every inch of the liquor store footage was underexposed and is unusable, and she's supposed to turn in her cut to the record company by the end of the week. Worse, there's not one person on that set who would work with her again and to top it all off, she's out of money.

"My directing career's over before it began," she sobs. "Why did everyone gang up on me?"

"Because you were mean and drunk, maybe?" I suggest, impressed that I'm actually challenging her on something.

"No, because I'm a woman!" she barks. "Barbra Streisand is so right about all that stuff. Remind me to never make fun of her again. Hold on a second."

Dandy clicks over to the other line and by the time she comes back, I've come up with an idea that may save "Drive-By Lover."

"For the liquor store shots," I suggest, "shoot new footage using the store's surveillance camera. Not only is it cheap and easy, but I think it could really turn out to be da bomb."

"Great idea, Craig," Dandy mutters, "but that was the record company on the other line. Hi-D's just been arrested for carrying a concealed weapon. He's locked up."

"Damn," I say, then think for a moment. "What if you use somebody else? Call that one black friend of yours and put a ski mask on him. Those cameras are so grainy, no one will know the difference."

"My black friend's out of town," Dandy sighs, "Can't we use yours?"

"Mitch?" I say. "He's still on the ship."

"Figures," Dandy says. There's a pause on the other end, then Dandy casually says, "How tall are you, Craig?"

"I'm *white,* Dandy."

"So I'll push the film. We have to get this done tonight or we're screwed."

That night after the liquor store closes, Dandy, myself, the liquor store owner, and the man who hooked up the liquor store's camera system—I can only imagine how she convinced them to cooperate—return to the location. Wouldn't you know it, nobody remembered to bring a gun, so we make do with a toy one, which, of course, I'm forced to pay for, since Dandy left her wallet in T-Spoon's car.

Using her hands to form a mock frame, Dandy fastidiously lines up her shot. Just because the camera is mounted to the wall and Dandy's composition is pretty much determined for her doesn't mean she shouldn't be allowed to use hacky director's gestures.

"Okay, Craig, now put these panty hose on your head," she barks, "and run from the Slurpee machine to the cash register. Action!"

I'm halfway to the counter when Dandy yells, "Cut! You're running like a girl, Craig. Butch it up."

The liquor store owner and his camera-installing buddy are laughing their asses off. Perhaps they've agreed to cooperate for the sheer entertainment value. I know that was my motivation, but that was before Dandy started in on the way I run.

In spite of the mutual testiness, Dandy and I manage to get the shots that we need. By the time we finish editing the video later that week, word of Hi-D-Ho's run-in with the law is everywhere. "Drive-By Lover" is getting tons of airplay and the world is clamoring for a video. Dandy and I drop the edited clip off at the record label, and on the way home, Dandy notices a familiar-looking house off Wilshire and stops the car abruptly.

"I'm pretty sure that's T-Spoon's place," she says scratching her head. "Craig, go in and get my wallet."

"Are you kidding?"

"Okay, then come with me."

We tentatively push open the front door which is already ajar and find not T-Spoon, but Hi-D-Ho stretched out on the sofa. His shirt is lifted and his stomach is bandaged with what looks like the aftermath of lipsocution surgery.

"I thought you were locked up," Dandy says.

"Publicity stunt," Hi-D says, then shoots me a wicked look. "Keep your mouth shut about it, white boy, and I won't have to ice you." Then he starts to laugh and offers us both an O.E.

Two days later, we're back at T-Spoon's crib—just chillin'—when "Drive-By Lover" makes its debut as the most requested video on *Yo! MTV Raps*. When Hi-D gets his first gander of the liquor store footage, he scratches his head and says, "Daaamn, I look fat."

I'm not sure if he means F-A-T or P-H-A-T, and I don't ask.

24

I've just learned that the reason I haven't seen much of Miles lately is because he's knee-deep in what he refers to as "love, love, love."

"Whatever, whatever, whatever," I say upon getting the news via one of his good-morning calls.

"Seriously, Craig," he spews. "This time I know it's for real."

"Did you mean to quote Donna Summer just now or was that an accident?" I ask.

"An accident," he says, guffawing maniacally. "It's what we in the biz call a happy accident."

"Is that so?" I groan.

I should be happier for Miles, for his romantic dry spell has lasted about as long as my own, though I suspect he's been indulging in the odd meaningless physical encounter. He stopped telling me about these bumps in the night months ago because I wouldn't stop teasing him about the flight attendant he hooked up with at the gym who complained that the "body butter" Miles picked up for the occasion wasn't fat free.

My reluctance to board his love train probably has less to do with

Miles specifically than with the fact that everyone I know seems to be happily hooked up as of late. Having finished his U.S. tour, White Shorts is due back in town tomorrow to enjoy a few weeks of percussive passion with Dandy before going back to Australia. Ulysses and Kathryn are so happy together it's scary. He not only seems okay with her vow to not put out until the honeymoon but says he kind of digs it. Then just yesterday, Carolyn called from Jupiter Filmworks to say she's engaged to some guy she met through the pyramid scheme I roped her into doing and they're opening up a Mail Boxes Etc. franchise with their loot from the Money Tree. Claudia, meanwhile, has been keeping a provocatively low profile and I've repeatedly seen a certain bandanna-wearing gentleman leaving her apartment at all hours. And now Miles is in love, love, love. Though I know that it's just a matter of minutes before at least half of the above unions fizzle, I still feel like I'm stuck in a game of Romantic Musical Chairs in which the calliope music's just gone off and everyone's found a face to sit on but me. To top it off, a new billboard featuring two cigarettes cuddling on a hammock has just gone in down the street and I can see it from my front window. "So, we cause cancer," they seem to be saying to me, "at least we're not *alone*."

I apologize to Miles for my lack of enthusiasm, then get the details on his object of affection, a thirty year old transplanted Floridian named Tom Romano whom he met at gay traffic school.

"We had both made illegal U-turns in the same intersection exactly one day apart," Miles says. "Isn't that amazing?"

"Talk about your happy accidents," I say.

"The only hitch is he used to make adult movies," Miles adds matter-of-factly. Before I can even gasp, my lovestruck friend starts in with what sounds like the first performance of a well-rehearsed disclaimer. ". . . but he hasn't done it in a long time. He wants to put that behind him and open his own Mail Boxes Etc. franchise."

"Who doesn't?" I say.

"Speaking of business," Miles says. "I'm helping out with crowd control on the MTV Movie Awards and they need seat fillers. You interested? It doesn't pay anything but I can get you into the after party."

"Count me in," I say. "I sit down better than just about anyone I know."

Miles gives me the details on the MTV gig, then hangs up to accompany Tom (aka Sterling Rodd) to the Farmer's Market, where the ex-blue movie boy will purchase the makings of a romantic candlelight dinner for two. How nice.

I hang up with Miles and get on the horn to Dandy.

"Are we still on for Softcore Saturday tomorrow?" she asks.

"Yes," I say. "But I think tomorrow should be hardcore."

"It's about time," says Dandy.

Just because Miles doesn't want to see his beloved's body of work ("I prefer live to Memorex," he claims) doesn't mean the rest of us have to remain in the dark. Dandy picks up the El Pollo Loco while I rent a Sterling Rodd triple feature and we meet back at my place.

Sterling is no slouch in the looks department (though I could live without that orange porno star skin tone) but his line readings are so stilted they make Andrew Shue look like, well, Elisabeth Shue. I have to give him credit, though, for tearing up at the end of *This Ol' Bathhouse* when he discovers that the lumberjack he thought he'd truly connected with in the previous scene busted into his locker and stole the St. Christopher's medal that we learned in flashback was bestowed on Sterling by his first drill sergeant.

"Miles *said* he was vulnerable," I recall.

The screen fades to black and I'm about to hit rewind when a lone red door appears on the screen, presumably the door to the title edifice. Then, one by one, the film's performers amble out and *bow* while two or three drug-addled crew members applaud, whoop and whistle offscreen. Any shred of machismo that the cast was able to achieve in the film (particularly by Sterling, who all but curtsies) is obliterated in a poof of poofdom by this display of fey theatricality.

"I'm so glad we made it to the end," says a hysterical Dandy as each skin trader, dressed in his own woefully dated clothes, has his awkward moment in the sun. "I want to do bows like this on *That's Just Dandy.*"

"I just feel bad for the guys who shot their wads hours ago, but had to hang around," I say. "You just know they thought a curtain call was a good idea at the time, but now they just want to go home."

Dandy and I nod off at some point during the second film, *Green Grocer,* and are awakened by the shrieks of Claudia who, as usual, let herself in.

"You both disgust me," she hisses.

Dandy and I rub our eyes and turn to the TV screen to see Sterling and an even more orange stud coupling with what appears to be the world's unluckiest watermelon. The conversation that follows takes place only between Claudia and myself, for it looks like Dandy is going to need a respirator to help her recover from the hysterics she's collapsed into.

"You have to tell him, Craig," Claudia insists.

"What am I supposed to say?" I ask. " 'Hey, Miles, remember that trip to Farmer's Market? I think your boyfriend was trying to pick up a third.' "

"Just tell him the truth," she says. "If it were you, wouldn't you want to know?"

"I guess," I say. "But I've never heard Miles sound happier. Who's to say if it would even make a difference?"

"*He* is," Claudia replies. "That's why you should tell him."

"I'm sure he wouldn't care," I say. "I mean, he already knows the guy did porn, and in L.A., doing porn is like being an Amway representative. It's just an offbeat job that some people have. No one cares."

"If you don't tell him about the watermelon, Craig," Claudia threatens. "I will."

I manage to convince Claudia to give me a week to see if the romance burns out on its own. After all, anyone who's turned to produce for companionship can't have much of an attention span.

• •

By the time the MTV Movie Awards roll around a week later, Miles and Sterling are talking about moving in together, Claudia's practically bursting to spill the beans, and Dandy and White Shorts have come up with a veritable patchful of melon-themed one-liners. "Gee, I wonder if he thumps people's asses before taking them home," is Dandy's favorite to date.

Since she's almost as good at sitting on her ass as I am, Claudia jumps at the chance to fill seats with me on MTV. Dressed in the trendiest togs we own, we head over to the Disney lot where the casino-themed event is being held. I bring along a copy of *Deck Games* in the hopes of getting it to Alicia Silverstone.

"Alicia would be perfect as the ship's aerobics instructor," I remark to Claudia and Sterling, a seat filler from way back, as we receive our instructions from the SF coordinator.

"Speak of the devil," Claudia replies as Miss Silverstone, sporting a beehive the size of, well, a watermelon, saunters by with her handlers. "Just stick your script in her hair, Craig. She won't even notice till she gets home."

Unfortunately, before I can make my move on Alicia, I'm asked to join a group of fellow SFs in front of the stage where we'll form a faux mosh pit for the performance by Garbage. It's a perfect assignment because that slick, grungy sound of "Stupid Girl" always makes me want to brush up against strangers anyway. Unable to handle both my script and my moshing duties, I hand *Deck Games* to Claudia, who soon gets her first seat-filling assignment when David Duchovny gets up, presumably to take a leak and look for aliens.

"It's still warm," Claudia mouths to me while caressing the sides of Duchovny's seat cushion.

After the Garbage gig, I'm sent spent and sweating to occupy a place next to the comparatively chaste Brandy. From there, I look on in horror as Whitney Houston sweats her way through yet another song from *Waiting to Exfoliate*. The woman is perspiring so profusely that

I'm surprised that it looks like she's going to melt away leaving nothing on the floor but a puddle and a weave. I look to Claudia to see if she's as distracted by the dripping diva as I but, alas, she's busy mouthing something to our beheadsetted friend Miles and fanning her face with *Deck Games*.

During the next commercial, both Claudia and I are sent back to the SF's holding area where Claudia returns my script to me along with the information that she just saw Sterling "flirting shamelessly" with a couple of cater waiters near the refreshment tables. Before I have time to ponder this tidbit of gossip, I'm grabbed by the SF coordinator and told to go fill a seat that has just been vacated near the front of the audience, a seat that I'm unable to see from here because it's being blocked by Alicia Silverstone's beehive.

"Bingo!" I whisper to Claudia, and then head out.

I settle in next to Alicia. Play it cool at first, I think, before joining the rest of the planet in staring at Jamie Lee Curtis's rack as she unloads yet another award on *Braveheart*, a movie I'm determined to go to my grave without seeing. Then as Jamie Lee sashays off the stage in her transparent gown, without taking my eyes from her near-poetic ass, I nonchalantly pull *Deck Games* up from my lap and rest it in front of Alicia.

Alicia meets my gaze and half-smiles with that beguilingly naughty-looking mouth of hers. Then we both look down to the script, where I notice for the first time that someone has written something on it.

"Your boyfriend has sex with watermelons," reads the note, written in the unmistakable pen of my former friend Claudia. *"I thought you should know."*

Alicia makes a disgusted face ten times harsher than a *Clueless* "As if!" More like, "As if, you fucking psycho pervert freak!" Before I can retrieve the script and fling myself off the giant slot machine that's serving as the evening's set, Alicia shunts the screenplay off to a woman sitting next to her. During the next break, the woman calls for a headsetted crowd controller and shows him the note.

"I *know* my boyfriend has had sex with watermelons," shouts Miles, "and I don't care! Craig, why are you doing this? It's none of your business! Why don't you just get Ben Stiller and Janeane Garafalo to come back onstage and make a little comedy bit out of it!"

No one around us can seem to speak. Alicia's practically resting her jaw on one of the umpteen awards she's picked up that evening. Miles says something about if he loses his job, it's my head, then makes a beeline for the nearest Porta Potti to cool off.

I say the following things to Alicia Silverstone, then head for my car: "I'm so sorry." "The note wasn't meant for you." "*The Crush* changed my life." "You look *really* thin."

I flee the Disney lot before the awards are finished, allowing the loose-penned Claudia to figure out her own way home. After a few hours of in-bed fretting, I finally fall asleep only to be awakened by a two A.M. phone call from Dandy and White Shorts, who it seems, showed up at the postshow party just in time to see Sterling making out with a trio of cater waiters in the back of some limo. After hearing about the Alicia debacle from a regretful Claudia and knocking back a few cocktails, Dandy decided it was her duty to report the limo sighting to Miles, who was still crowd-controlling.

"They had a big ugly breakup right in front of the blackjack table," says Dandy. "It was just like *Casino,* only watchable. I just wished they had remembered to bow."

It takes Miles, who's still employed—thank God—a few days to stop screening and pick up the phone, but when he does, he seems to be in a forgiving mode, understanding that everything we did, we did because we care about him.

"You know what he said to me when I told him my friends had brought up the watermelon stuff?" Miles asks.

"I shudder to think," I say.

"He said, 'Tell them I'm in much better shape now.' Can you believe it? He had not one ounce of concern for the embarrassment he caused me. It all comes back to him and what he looks like."

"So are you going to miss him?" I ask.

"A little," Miles sighs. "But not as much as I'm going to miss watermelon."

25

Blame Antonio Sabato Jr. If it weren't for him—sprawled out over Sunset Boulevard in nothing but the world's luckiest pair of Calvin Klein underwear—Dandy could have kept her eyes on the road and neither of us would be where we are now: sharing a hospital room at Cedars Sinai Medical Center. Though I'm due to go home tomorrow with a few bruises and a major case of the shakes, Dandy's broken leg and whiplash will keep her Cedars-bound for a few more days.

Dandy's having her cast set when Ulysses and Miles show up, so I'm forced to recount the accident on my own.

"I said, 'Hey, isn't that Antonio Sabato Jr.?' " I recall, "and then she said, 'Junior, my ass,' and then we hit the other car and everything went black. That's all I remember."

"It was already on the news," says Ulysses.

"What did they say?" I ask.

"Just that Dandy Rio, star of the sitcom *That's Just Dandy,* and an unidentified male friend were in an accident on Sunset," Ulysses says. "Then they showed the scene. Her Miata looks like a Coke can. Thank God you guys are okay."

"I was so scared," gushes Miles.

Our brief love-in is interrupted by the arrival of two candy stripers with armfuls of flowers and cards for "Dandy and Friend." Dandy, with a fresh cast on her left leg, rolls in a few minutes later. She gets hoisted onto her bed by a dreamy young intern—the ink from whose phone number is still drying on her cast—then reaches toward the mountain of gifts and says, "Gimme."

"Oh my God," she says her eyes starting to water. "Molly Ringwald sent a telegram from Paris. We've never even *met*."

Dandy's mistiness increases with each card read. The network, her costars and a smattering of ex-lovers' kind words were, for the most part, not surprising, but Ben Vereen? Brooke Shields? The cast of *Living Single*?

"All this for a broken leg," sighs Dandy, before tossing the teddy bear sent by Jonathan Taylor Thomas to Miles so he can smell it.

"Just imagine if it was like a spinal cord injury or something," I say.

"More flowers!" hollers a voice from outside.

"Come on in!" yells Dandy gleefully.

One of the stripers, whose head is completely eclipsed by flora and fauna, enters and scuffs toward the corner of the room Ulysses has dubbed "gift mountain."

"Really, Craig," Miles says scoldingly, "a spinal cord injury."

"Oh my God," Dandy says, sobbing, "Elijah Wood sent muffins. He is so beautiful."

"Tell me about it," agrees Miles. "I wonder if he's seeing anyone."

Just then, the striper, having unloaded the flowers, produces a camera from his pocket and starts snapping photos of the black-and-blue, bed-ridden Dandy.

"Get the fuck out of here," shouts Ulysses before shoving the shutterbug outside and calling hospital security.

"I hope they run the picture under 'Would you be caught dead in this outfit,' " chirps an unfazed Dandy. "I haven't been on that page for a while."

The next day, Ulysses drops me off at home, where Claudia bestows a plate of her famous treats on me along with this morning's *L.A. Times*, the front page of which features the best Smelt It/Dealt It picture I think I've ever seen. Unfortunately, it's of me and Dandy. Dandy is gritting her teeth and squinting and I'm literally covering my nose with one hand and rolling my eyes to heaven.

"Have you seen the *Times*?" I say when I call Dandy at the hospital.

"Yep," says Dandy. "Don't you hate when your own joke comes back and bites you on the ass?"

"You raise them like a child and then this happens," I say. "So how are you feeling?"

"Pretty good," she says. "I had a freaky moment this morning where I thought about what *could* have happened. We were really lucky."

"Tell me about it," I say.

"I can't talk now, Craig," she adds. "I've got to go do my press conference."

"Press conference?" I say, cringing.

"Miles set it up," Dandy says, then starts to hang up. "Oh, wait. Craig, I need you to call Keith and tell him to hold off on Operation BS. I want to see how all this accident stuff plays out before we start shopping around the you-know-whats."

After I hang up, I try to recall what the status of Operation BS is at present. Keith had planned to go to *Playboy* this week with the photos, but now, with Dandy already all over the news, it looks like the world may not have to see the fruits of Operation BS after all.

I leave a cryptic but clear message on Keith's machine to hold off, then turn on the TV just in time to see Dandy meet the press. After thanking everyone for their kind wishes—the list now includes Sandra Bullock, Jennifer Tilly and the U.S. Olympic water polo team—the wheelchair-bound Dandy fields questions from the crowd of reporters.

"Miss Rio," shouts the guy from channel 5. "There's a rumor that in addition to your broken leg, you have a spinal cord injury. Is that true?"

"Let's just say I'm incredibly happy to be alive," says Dandy.

"Do you think this will help your chances for an Emmy nomination for *That's Just Dandy*?" shouts the skunk-headed broad from channel 7.

"That's the least of my concerns," Dandy says. "Right now, I just want to concentrate on healing."

By the time Dandy's released from the hospital a week later, the words *spinal cord injury* are swirling about her like the flying cows in *Twister*. Dandy, whose house still looks like an FTD outlet store, is doing nothing to quell the buzz by publicly using a wheelchair when crutches would suffice.

"I think you should come clean," I whisper while helping her navigate through the Beverly Center. "I just don't think it's right. And my arms are getting tired."

"Just wait until the Emmy nominations come out," she says pleadingly. "After that, I'm planning to go on *Oprah* and walk for the first time and then it'll be over."

"I can't believe this," I say through gritted teeth. "I ought to just leave you here in the fucking Gap."

"Look, Craig," she says pulling my face to her level. "I didn't start it. I mean, how many times has the rumor mill screwed me over? Here's my one chance to make it work in my favor. Besides, it's not like you're not benefiting. What about all those people who want to read your script because you were in the wreck with me?"

She has a point. At least a dozen parties have expressed interest in *Deck Games* since the accident, including a guilt-ridden Antonio Sabato Jr. I decide to play along for now.

"Your courage is so, like, amazing," the Gap girl says to Dandy as we roll out. "Here, help yourself to a mock T. And take one for your friend. You deserve it."

I'm cutting the tags out of my new shirt next morning when Claudia calls.

"I've got someone for you," she says with an exasperated sigh, as though, unbeknownst to me, everyone in California is determined to get me laid so they can get on with their lives. "The guy on my refrigerator."

Claudia has a picture on her refrigerator of a group of her waiter friends that was taken two Halloweens ago at Zach's. The first time I was in her apartment I commented on the attractiveness of the guy dressed as the Jolly Green Giant's apprentice, Sprout, only to learn he was taken.

"I ran into him last night and he's single now," she says. "He wants you to call him."

"He knows who I am?"

"Yeah, he saw the picture of you and Dandy in the *Times*."

"Ugh," I groan. "And he still wants to meet me?"

"I told him that wasn't a very good picture."

"Thanks," I say. "So what's his name? I've always just thought of him as the Sprout Guy."

"Fritz," she says.

"By the way, where have you been? I never see you."

"I've been pulling extra shifts at the restaurant."

"Uh-huh," I say dubiously. "All-nighters? With men who wear bandannas and walk around barefoot?"

"Look, Craig, I promise I'll tell you all about it when it's the right time," she says.

"Just tell me one thing," I say. "Is he married?"

"No," says Claudia. "Okay, here's Fritz's number."

I grab a Post-it and write the name Fritz. Considering the bad fortune I've had with preciously nicknamed beaus in the past, I decide that from this point on, my Fritz will never be referred to as the Sprout Guy.

I decide to call Fritz *after* I've called Viola to ask for a rent extension and after I've called the cable company to complain that they're still charging me for the HBO I got rid of months ago. That way, by the time I get to the date call, I'll be cranky enough to come off as sufficiently detached. Apparently, it works, for Fritz agrees to have dinner with me the next night. He asks me to meet him at the real estate office he started working at after he left Zach's.

Though I tell myself not to, that night as I fall asleep I imagine Fritz and me carrying on in the various luxurious properties he has access to, porch swing picnics off Mulholland, telescope fun in Westwood, Jacuzzi make-outs in Brentwood. As I look to the side and imagine his jolly green form next to me, I can't help but feel bad for the identity crisis I must be causing my poor pillow. I'm surprised it doesn't get fed up with my perpetual state of longing and say, "Okay, Craig, who am I tonight?"

I arrive at the office and as I'm walking down the sidewalk I notice a young man who I assume is Fritz standing with his back to the window and looking down as though he were relieving himself. In front of him are five women of various ages and types looking down as well, as if they were pissing coaches, if there were such a thing.

"It's Dick Day," Fritz blushes, when I ask him about it later at the restaurant. "Every Friday, I show the ladies in the office my dick. I don't remember how it started but we've been doing it for a while. I used to get to see their breasts but that part sort of stopped and now it's just the dick."

"I'll have the fettuccini," I tell the waiter, muzzling my amazement.

As Fritz orders, I take the opportunity to become better acquainted with his visage. Though he has a nice enough face, Fritz looks like one of those men, usually gay, who have made the absolute most of what they have: guys who pulled it together in their late twenties so that when they go to their high school reunions, they're able to bench-press the jocks who used to torment them. The jocks who haven't become fat as houses, that is.

As Fritz talks about his job, I smile with relief when I realize that, unlike past suitors, this one probably doesn't have a head shot. Then somehow we get onto the subject of his last relationships.

"Well, I broke up with my ex about two months ago, so that was the last time I was with anyone," he says. "Well, unless you count this one guy I met driving down the street. He was just jogging and I sort of saw him out the window and slowed down and he waved and I backed up and then we went back to his place and had bone-crushing, furniture-breaking sex."

The second he tells me this, I can feel my entire countenance change. Fritz can't possibly be interested in me, I decide, otherwise he would never have told me that. I don't care how liberated you are, you don't woo somebody with the details of your random shags. Do you?

"Oh yeah, I know all about furniture-breaking sex," I stammer, trying to think of something to say. "One time, during my last relationship, I started crying and threw a chair."

My already unbearable chagrin increases tenfold when Fritz doesn't so much as crack a smile. Taking stock of the situation, I decide that if the concept of Dick Day was a red flag, then the headboard-shattering jogger was Dennis Rodman coming down a spiral staircase in a scarlet dress. I realize it's time to chalk this one up and yet, if Fritz suggested adjourning to some vacant hillside duplex for a nightcap, I'd probably go. What's that about?

We finish dinner and walk back to his office. Oddly, I'm still feeling amorous. Not really for him, just in general. My mood isn't helped much by the music blaring from the club next door, another Garbage ditty which, we've established, I find to be the audio equivalent of Spanish Fly. As Fritz leads me down a thin outdoor corridor to the back door of his office, I rub my hands over the bricks and can feel the vibration of the music. Sometimes, don't you just want to be thrown up against a wall and mauled while Shirley Manson croons on about girlish stupidity? I do, and now is one of those times.

"I have something I want to show you," Fritz says, sounding as excited as I've seen him all night. He leads me into his office and explains, "I'm sending out magnets with my picture on them to try and get more clients. Which shots do you like best?"

He hands me four contact sheets and a loupe, turns the dimmer light all the way up and sits back and waits. I consider putting my grease pencil check marks by the shots he looks the most bloated in, but just return the shirtless contact sheet to the desk without even looking at it. I'd prefer to think that my realtor was spending his time crunching numbers on my dream house and not having his chest waxed.

Fritz, looking perplexed at my indifference to the contact sheets, thanks me anyway then yawns in my face.

"I had a nice time," he says, giving me a chaste peck on the cheek.

"Yeah, thanks," I say, relieved that the chances of hearing from him again are slim.

As I leave him to scrutinize his personal real estate and walk down the vibrating hallway, I can't help but wonder if we'd be making out right now had I reciprocated his jogger story with some truck stop encounter of my own.

"I'm originally from Arizona. I used to work on cruise ships. I'm working on my second screenplay," I say in the car on the ride home, answering all those questions Fritz never asked.

The morning the Emmy nominations are to be released rolls around and Dandy drags me to the television academy for the announcement. After fielding questions about her physical therapy regimen, I roll Dandy to a place near the front row. My bum-footed friend squeezes my hand nervously while the Best Actress in a Comedy Series nominees are announced and when she fails to make the cut, her hand accidentally slips from atop mine and lands on the button that powers her chair. She does two complete 360-degree turns in front of God knows how many camera crews before I can gain control of the vehicle.

Luckily, we're able to make a relatively low-profile exit as everyone there seems to be preoccupied with their cell phones, placing wake-up calls to the likes of Helen Hunt, Julia Louis-Dreyfus and the already Emmy-laden Dime Lady.

Dandy ends up walking later that week, when she gets her cast removed, but not on TV. Seems that wily ersatz candy striper got a hold of her medical records and now, thanks to the *Globe*, everyone knows all she had was a broken leg, which, let's face it, doesn't exactly drip with ratings potential. I've tried following up with the people who wanted to look at my script, but no one will take my calls. One producer even instructed his secretary to "tell the faker's friend to get lost."

Dandy went on the E! channel this morning to claim that she never once said she had a spinal cord injury. Though her assertion is essentially true, Dandy swears she saw Steve Kmetko roll his eyes, and has been crying on and off ever since. She's being comforted by a certain dreamy intern as we speak.

26

This is the closest I've come to having something serendipitous happen in my life since MTV trotted out a *My So-Called Life* marathon the very afternoon the sofa I won on *Razzle* arrived. In the first bit of good fortune to occur since her whirling dervish act at the Emmy nominations, Dandy has been asked to read for a voice-over role in the next animated Disney feature on the very same day that Miles has invited us to accompany him to Gay Day at Disneyland.

"It must be destiny," says Dandy as we say good-bye to our car in Kanga, "and I'm not going to say anything bad about anyone today because I don't want to fuck up my Disney karma."

Dandy's resolution lasts all of four minutes, for we're scarcely in the gate before she starts in on Tigger, who's been nice enough to refrain from tigging long enough to pose for a few pictures.

"Wouldn't this be the worst job in the world, Craig?" Dandy bellows, oblivious of the seething minimum-wager sweating inside the animal head next to her. "I'd rather work at a Burger King managed by Scott Rudin."

Miles, who's manning the Nikon, shoots Dandy a "behave yourself" look, but the damage has been done. Even though they're made of immovable plastic, I could swear Tigger's eyes look sparked with annoyance as he tigs away from us.

"It's so nice to be here and not to have to deal with the negative element," says Miles, who's now literally skipping his way down Main Street, USA.

"You mean homophobes?" I say skipping to keep up.

"No," he replies. "Children."

Miles is right. There are virtually no rugrats to be found anywhere, though there are a good many women with childbearing hips. My favorite image so far, however, is of a leather daddy hollering, "Wait up, son," to his harness-wearing companion outside of Cinderella's castle, before stopping to relace his uncooperative leather pants and muttering, "I shoulda worn the chaps."

In terms of rides, we opt to start with "It's a Small World" because there's no line and I feel sorry for it.

"This poor ride is like the John Tesh of Disneyland," I observe as we jump into our little boat and head to our doom. "It can't catch a break to save its life."

"Miles, take my picture," says Dandy as we sail into the Polynesian section, where she drops her pants and moons the hula puppets. As though there aren't enough incriminating pictures of her in existence already. Miles clicks away, then Dandy sits down triumphantly and pulls out a doobie.

"What the hell is that?" I ask.

"I wasn't going to, Craig," Dandy says before gesturing to the endless displays of singing muppet-wannabes that surround us, "but this is an emergency."

Once outside, Miles hooks up with a guy from his gym whom he's been crushing on forever and, unlike Dandy and myself, is willing to stand in line for an hour and a half to ride Space Mountain. So we agree to meet our boy-crazy friend at closing time at the Matterhorn, then head to New Orleans Square to satisfy Dandy's roarin' case of the munchies. We don't quite make it though, as we're intercepted by a gaggle of *That's Just Dandy* fans in muscle T's who say they want their photo taken with their favorite celebrity. I'm not positive they're referring to her, as Goofy's in the picture too.

"Fucking Goofy!" Dandy shouts over her shoulder as she returns. "That stupid sasquatch kept stepping on my foot."

A few rides and several Dandy vs. Disney run-ins later (she actually taunted Chip 'n' Dale with incest innuendo), I'm sitting on a bench outside the toilet kiosk waiting for Dandy. A strapping young man in costume approaches me and introduces himself as John Smith from *Pocahontas*. When I ask him if he's bumming because his film didn't gross as much as *The Lion King* he emits a robust laugh, then whispers, "Your friend, Dandy Rio, I really want to meet her."

Dandy emerges from the ladies' room a moment later and I introduce the two. Before long John's covertly inviting us to party with him and a few of his equally desirable friends on Tom Sawyer Island after it closes at dusk.

"I promise it'll be cool," enthuses John. "We do it all the time."

"I remember This Many telling me about doing that when he used to work here," I add.

"Well, it has to be more fun than this," Dandy says.

"So, here's what you do," John whispers. "Take the last raft over, then don't come back. We'll meet you in the log cabin at nine, party for a few hours, then bring you back on our company boat before the park closes."

Leave it to Dandy to score a rendezvous with the one straight guy within a ten-mile radius. As per John's instructions, we ride the raft over, then hide out under a fake rock formation like the Von Trapp family while some borderline Nazi park employees with flashlights clear the island. Once the final return raft leaves, Dandy and I go to the log cabin and wait for our new friends.

"I'm so glad we're out here," she says while reapplying her lipstick and pulling out a flask. "Those fucking characters were giving me the creeps. I think they had it in for me."

"That's just the pot talking," I say.

"Thanks for reminding me, Craig," she scoffs. "Now I'm hungry again."

Nine o'clock comes and goes, as does ten, eleven, and twelve. By now, it's become obvious that John Smith is pulling one over on us. We peek out from the fake cabin and see the hordes of happy homos heading toward the exit, the liberation in their walk obvious, even from here. Once they're gone, a small collection of characters, including the previously encountered Tigger, Goofy, and that little grifter John Smith, gather at the bank of the lake in a show of solidarity. They dance merrily and occasionally look our way with a smile and a fist to the sky.

"They set us up," I say, panicked. "We gotta swim for it."

"No way," snaps Dandy. "If this gets back to the people at Disney, they'll never give me a job. We have to stay here."

Dandy promises me half of her paycheck if I'll stay with her here overnight and then discreetly climb on the first return raft when the park reopens in the morning. I accept her offer—there doesn't seem to really be any alternative that doesn't involve large-scale humiliation and wet clothes—then use Dandy's cell phone to call Miles and inform him of our predicament.

"We should get their furry asses fired," pants Miles.

"We can't," I say. "Because then it'll get out about Dandy and she has more to lose than them."

"Okay," he sighs. "Well, I guess I'll be at the gate to meet you when the place opens."

"Great," I say. "So how did it go with the gym guy?"

"Ugh," Miles groans. "Not only is he dumb, Craig. But *stupid*."

"So you didn't make out in the teacups or anything?"

"Well . . ." Miles says.

"You amaze me," I say, before taking on Miles's voice and adding, " 'He was so unappealing that I just had to have him.' "

"It was that or listen to him talk, Craig," Miles claims.

"See you tomorrow," I say, then hang up.

"Craig, what if we get attacked by a bear?" Dandy asks, her teeth chattering in the balmy September air.

"Well, the thing to remember is to not be afraid, because they can smell fear," I say. "And if that doesn't work, go for their batteries."

Realizing that sleeping is going to be impossible, what with the deafening din of Dandy's growling stomach, I take off to do a little spelunking in the man-made caves. Ten minutes later I decide to return to base camp. As I approach, I can see Dandy through the brush, her back to me as she delicately relieves herself in the moonlight. I'm admittedly shocked, but not because Dandy's stooped to take a leak outside. What's surprising is that this is the first time I've seen her do so. You'd think we'd have covered this already.

I leave her to her business and go sit on a distant rock with a beautiful view of Thunder Mountain. Ten or so minutes later I hear Dandy shout, "Craig! Come quick! I found a Whatchamacallit!"

"You mean a secret passage off the island?"

"No, a candy bar."

Dandy and I alternate taking bites of the Whatchamacallit while sitting Indian-style on the bank of Tom Sawyer Island and listening to what I assume to be crickets, though it could just be Peter Pan in the throes of his first wet dream.

"Very nice of you to share your candy bar," I say. "You could have just downed the whole thing while I was off in the cave."

"I know," says Dandy. "But you deserve it for putting up with me."

I say nothing, but lean back on my elbows and look up at the moon.

"You never told me how your date went with the Sprout Guy," she says after a pause.

"Fritz," I say. "The pits." I recount for Dandy the chemistry-free details of the dinner date. "Do you ever feel like it's just not going to happen for you, that you're just never going to hook up?"

"All the time," says Dandy.

"You know, if one more person says, 'When you least expect it . . .' or 'The second you stop looking . . .' I'm going to slug them," I say. "Meanwhile, Miles can score standing in line at the ATM."

"You could do that if you wanted, Craig," Dandy says. "But you've decided to take the high road."

"I just didn't think the high road would be so desolate," I say. "I thought there would be like a Stuckey's or something. Some gas, food and lodging."

"Well, I've got gas if it's any consolation."

She picks up a rock and tosses it across the water. I select one and do the same.

"You know," she says, putting her arm around me. "It kind of feels good to just stop."

A few minutes later Dandy and I manage to fall asleep, our heads side by side looking up into the heavens. I'm awakened at sunrise, but not by the kiss of a strapping prince or even the coast guard. It's by Dandy, dancing about under a fake tree and singing gibberish to the tune of "It's a Small World." One night marooned on a theme park island and suddenly she's Jodie Foster in *Nell*.

When the park opens a few hours later, we manage to sneak onto the first raft without getting busted. We're sailing to our freedom when Miles calls on the cell phone to inform us he'll be at the gate when we emerge. Then he asks to talk to Dandy.

"I feel so in touch with nature," Dandy coos into the phone. "It's like we lived off the fat of the land, you know?"

Dandy's broad grin disintegrates when Miles bestows the news that, according to the *L.A. Times*, her year-and-a-half-old eponymous series, *That's Just Dandy*, has just been canceled by the network. Miles says he didn't want her to get the news from the paper, or worse yet, Dopey and Sneezy on the way out, so he told her himself. Dandy thanks him calmly, hangs up, then gingerly tosses her cell phone into the lagoon, eschewing modern technology and all the pain it brings with it. Nell would be proud.

27

Miles greets us at the gate of Disneyland with food, water and blankets, as though this particular rescue mission were taking place on the hull of the *Poseidon* and not in the parking lot of a theme park. Still, neither Dandy nor myself can resist the urge to hug him.

Dandy reads her show's obituary in the car on the way home and decides she's going to call her show's producer, Len Field, to find out what gives, or actually, what gave.

"Give me my cellular, Craig," she says. "I need to talk to him *now*."

"You threw it in the lagoon," I remind her. "The Little Mermaid is probably swimming around it curiously as we speak."

"That bitch better not run up any charges," Dandy says.

"Here," says Miles, handing her his phone. "Use mine."

Dandy puts in six calls to Len during the remainder of the hourlong car ride but gets his machine each time.

"We have to go find him, Craig," she says as Miles pulls up to my place.

I give Dandy a plaintive look as if to say, "Haven't I been through enough for one lifetime?" which she trumps with, "Who shared their Whatchamacallit with you, Craig?"

On the drive to Field's house in Laurel Canyon, Dandy tries to figure what went wrong. The numbers for this week's season premiere were not Must-See caliber by any means, but were good enough to place her second in her time period after *America's Funniest Animal Attacks.* What more could they want?

"I think it's something personal," says Dandy, as she rings Field's doorbell.

"He's probably out of town for Labor Day," I suggest.

Just then we hear a splash coming from Field's backyard. I boost Dandy up so she can peek over the gate. "Guess who, Len?" she shouts. "Let us in!"

A shirtless and paunchy Field opens the gate for us. An ear-to-ear smile spreads across his dripping face.

"Why aren't you furious?" barks Dandy.

"Life's too short," he says. "There'll be other shows."

"For you maybe," spits Dandy. "They canned our asses after one new episode."

"Well, what did you expect them to do," retorts Len, "given the circumstances?"

"What circumstances?" asks Dandy.

Dandy's former boss gives us both a dubious look, then invites us to join him for some iced tea on the patio.

"Dandy, as you know, our network is owned by a major corporation whose bread and butter is family entertainment," he says, speaking to us not only as though we were children, but children from Mars. "Having the lead actress in one of their sitcoms—a show about a teenager, no less—turn up naked in *Penthouse* licking chocolate frosting off the head of a dwarf, well, it's not the kind of thing they like to see. . . ."

The lightning-quick speed at which Dandy shifts into the clueless ingenue role is astounding, particularly since she's going on virtually zero sleep.

"What are you talking about, *Penthouse*?" she asks with a bewildered tilt of the head.

Gathering that Dandy and I haven't seen the issue in question, Len describes the photographs in vivid detail, leading me to believe that some of the published images were more explicit than the shots Keith allowed Dandy and me to see.

"Do you have a copy?" Dandy asks coolly.

"Of course not," he scoffs, as though he's been too busy rereading *Infinite Jest* and watching *Meet the Press* to bother with such smut.

"Is it out on newsstands?" I ask.

"No, someone at the office got an advance copy. I think the big bosses wanted the show to be history before the thing hits the stands."

"I was always afraid this day would come," says Dandy before dissolving into tears and blubbering through the tall tale about the college boyfriend who talked her into posing for a photography project he was working on for school.

"It happened a long time ago," she pleads at the end of her sob story. "It's not as though they were taken last week. Don't you think they're overreacting?"

"I mean, what kind of a message is it sending out," I say as though I've suddenly taken on the social conscience of a Baldwin brother, "if they cave in to some big conservative outcry that hasn't even happened yet?"

"Yeah," says Dandy.

"Dandy, they don't think you're worth the frustration," Len says dryly, "and frankly neither do I. I mean, if it were Téa Leoni licking cake off the head of a dwarf it might be a different story."

"How many chances does that twig *get*?" Dandy rants.

"Look, Dandy, the network has to pick its battles," Len says. "They just didn't happen to pick yours."

And with that, Len Field dives into the pool and gets back to enjoying his unemployment. Since we're both too tired to wage much more of a fight, Dandy and I get up to leave.

"I'm going to use the can," I say to Dandy, and make my way into Len's house.

After a couple of false turns, I happen upon Len's bathroom. There I discover the probable reason the producer seems so at peace with the cancellation of *That's Just Dandy*. In front of the toilet is a script entitled *Untitled Joey Lawrence Pilot* with a handwritten note on top that reads, "Give it a read, Len. We'd love to have you on board." I pick up the script, curious to know what the future holds for my beloved Joey, and discover underneath it the "Randy Dandy!" issue of *Penthouse,* the one Len purported not to own. I find the idea that Len might be wanking to images of his half-his-age starlet truly unsettling.

"Look what I found," I say, waving the *Penthouse* in the air as I return to the yard. As I watch Len's face contort into an expression of resigned mortification, I'm surprised at my own brazenness. Two years ago, I would have left that magazine where it was and wiped my fingerprints off with a hand towel. Last year, I might have snuck it out in my sock and showed it to Dandy later in the car. Somehow, today, with not a whole hell of a lot to lose, I decide it's best to come out waving the rag like a *Les Misérables* flag.

"I forgot about that," says Len, scratching his head in what Claudia's acting coach would call a textbook example of bad indicative acting. "I guess I do have a copy."

"Whatever," says Dandy, grabbing the magazine from me.

As she flips through the pages of her pictorial, Dandy offers one word assessments of each image. "Nice . . . gross . . . wow . . . yuck . . . fine . . . jugs . . . nice . . . fine . . . double-chin . . . pink." She closes the magazine and shoves it under her arm. "One semi-pink shot, Craig," she summarizes, as though she's using her last ounce of energy to look on the bright side. "That's not too bad."

"No, it's not," I say, doing the same.

"Guess I won't be auditioning for no Disney cartoon," Dandy says.

"Guess not," I say.

"We're taking this with us," says Dandy, patting the magazine. "Hope you were through with it."

From Len's, we drive straight to Keith's apartment, which we find dirty and deserted, the one-bedroom equivalent of *Tombstone*. After learning from a neighbor that Keith loaded his belongings into a brand new Toyota 4Runner and drove off into the sunrise sometime last week, we head home to Dandy's and discover twenty-four messages on her machine. The first is from Keith.

"By now you probably know what I've done," he says, over the din of Tejano music in the background. "I couldn't wait anymore and I really needed the money. I don't expect you to understand this but my mother passed away last week and I have to pay for the funeral . . ."

"What, did they bury the bitch in a brand-new Toyota, you asshole?" Dandy screams.

". . . If it makes any difference," Keith's voice continues, "I kept up our plan to say the pictures were from eight years ago or whatever. No one at *Penthouse* knows the truth. Hope they help your show. Bye."

Keith's electronic swan song is followed by missives from reporters from every news outlet from *Access Hollywood* to *Geraldo*. Conspicuously absent is Miles, who's been acting as Dandy's makeshift publicist since the car accident. The hardest message to listen to is from Benjamin Burton, the talented young actor who landed a gig as the nerdy new friend on *That's Just Dandy* this season after struggling for years as Claudia's favorite waiter at Chin Chin.

"Hi, Dandy," he says, his voice quivering with concern. "This is Ben. I just wanted to see if you were okay . . ."

Unable to bear the thought of all the other people who are going down with her, Dandy walks into the bathroom and splashes water on her face, a precursor of the flood to come.

"I'm such a bad person, Craig," she says, padding back in, the tears beginning to roll.

I put my arms around her and for the next half hour all I say is, "Shhhh."

We decide to spend the next day, Labor Day, coming up with a plan. We both agree that it would probably be good for her to go on some show and talk about how the pictures were taken last decade and how betrayed she feels, etc. Though it probably won't resuscitate *That's Just Dandy,* it could help in her quest to find future employment. Miles, however, our resident media expert, has yet to answer our umpteen calls and pages and we really shouldn't proceed without his schmooze savvy.

When Claudia and I finally go over to his apartment on Labor Day morning, his neighbor Wallace, a fifty-something coffeehouse owner, notices my distress and offers his two cents.

"He left here yesterday afternoon with this really beefy guy," Wallace says with a lascivious lift of his eyebrows. "I think they were going to the circuit party out in Pasadena."

"Why way the hell out there?" I wonder. "There's a Circuit City right down the street."

"Not Circuit City," Claudia says, "circuit party. It's where all the A-list homos go do drugs and dance around half naked. Jesus, Craig, what cave have you been living in?"

"Well, I don't *know*," I retort, before shifting into *Dragnet* mode and turning back to Wallace. "So what did this other guy look like?"

"Like I said, beefy," Wallace says with a mixture of efficiency and lust. "Dark buzzed hair, about five-eight, really tan, no shirt, shaved chest, six-pack abs."

"Any distinguishing marks?" I ask.

"Yes," he says pointedly. "A cobra tattoo around his left ankle."

Wallace tears an ad for the party, complete with a map, from a local gay zine and sends us on our way.

"They're having it at the mansion they used in *Dynasty*," says Claudia, looking up from the clipping as we head to the freeway.

"Like that place wasn't already the catfight capital of the world," I say.

We arrive in Pasadena and have to park in a distant parking lot and be shuttled to the mansion proper. Claudia and I leap into a departing van full of wonder boys and try to crack a few Joan Collins jokes, only to realize that our fellow passengers must have left their bantering skills in a pile next to their shirts.

"Fritz?" I say, recognizing one of the guys as my uninterested realtor date.

"Kirk?" he says vaguely, proving once and for all that for some guys, every day is Dick Day.

"My name's Craig," I say.

"*I'm* Kirk," says the disgruntled guy holding Fritz's hand. Let the catfighting begin.

We arrive at the mansion and after talking Claudia into using half of last night's tip money to pay our $20-a-pop entrance fee, we make our way through the house to the backyard, where the bulk of the partiers are shaking their well-toned booties to a house ditty that sounds just like the one that came before it.

"This is so *Exit to Eden,*" Claudia says, looking on at the poolside carnality.

"Without the laughs," I say.

It only takes us about five minutes to find Miles, staring catatonically out at the goings-on from underneath a cabana. We say his name repeatedly but he doesn't utter a sound. He just continues to stare at the heaving mass of perfect bodies.

"I think he's in a K hole," says a nearby Speedo-clad reveler.

Before I can embarrass myself further by voicing my naïveté out loud, Claudia steps in for clarification.

"It's a drug thing, Craig," she says.

"Is there a doctor around?" I say, the panic starting to creep into my voice.

"There's a bunch of 'em," says Speedo Guy, calmly pointing to the dance floor and laughing, "but they're all fucked up, too."

"Corbin," Miles says dazedly.

"What?" I say.

"That's the guy he came with," says Speedo Guy. "I think he's out dancing."

"Great," I say. "What are we supposed to do?"

"He'll come out of it in a while," the guy says. "They usually do."

"What are you . . . guys . . . doing here?" Miles says, recognizing us for the first time.

"Looking for you," says Claudia.

"Hold, please," he snaps, bringing his hand up to an imaginary headset.

I pull it down, grab him by the shoulders and bore my gaze into his. "We're taking you home *now*."

"I want you to meet my new . . ." Miles looks around and realizes his date is long gone. "Where's, um . . . ?"

"We don't know," I say, pouring water down his throat. "It doesn't matter. We're leaving."

"Not without my car," Miles says firmly, as though it's the first clear thought he's had in days. He may be in a drug fog, but he has his priorities clear.

"Okay, Claudia will drive your car home and you'll ride with me," I say. "Give me the keys."

Miles pats the four pockets of his shorts maniacally as though he were playing a game of Junkie Hambone.

"Corbin has them," he says.

"Okay," I say to Claudia, "You stay here and take care of him and I'll go find Corbin. If he comes back, get the keys."

As I head into the crowd I feel like I'm back in junior high P.E., playing a nightmarishly reversed game of shirts-versus-skins basketball. The only difference is there's no ball and about a million baskets. It takes me about two seconds to realize that Wallace's description could apply to virtually anyone here, except for the two black guys. What were these people like before they became each other, I wonder, as I ask guy after guy, "Are you Corbin?" Frustrated after too many failed attempts to count, I look back to Claudia and shrug. She responds by pointing to her ankle and I remember the tattoo.

While physically precarious, dropping to the ground and looking for a snake in the grass seems like a worthy idea not only because it might work, but because I can rule people out without having to *talk* to them. After about ten minutes I've spotted a couple of roses, a good number of tribal designs, some barbed wire, a tattoo of Fred from *Scooby-Doo*, and on the crowd's lone drag queen, a faux ruby ankle bracelet. But still no cobra. I stand up and shrug at Claudia again before diving back down.

A minute or so later the music stops and I hear Claudia's voice booming through the speakers.

"I've got fifty bucks up here for whoever can find me a guy named Corbin Buckroyd," she says waving the rest of last night's tip money. "This ought to buy someone a little more fun."

An arm shoots up in the back of the crowd—the area I was just about to get to, I swear—and a really tan beefy guy with buzzed hair, no shirt, six-pack abs, and a cobra tattoo on his left ankle gets hoisted up and passed toward the stage mosh style by his buff buddies, providing the crowd, at last, with a practical use for all those steroids.

The second Corbin hits the stage, Claudia snatches Miles's keys out of the pocket of his surf shorts, then slaps the bills into his hot little hand. Claudia, a half-coherent Miles and I regroup at the cabana, then hit the trail as the music pounds on.

"What the hell are you doing?" I ask Miles as we drive back to the city.

"Fuck you, Craig," he says. "I was just having fun."

"It looked like *tons* of fun," I remark. "Right up there with being audited."

"You know, there happens to be something really great about it, but you'll never get it, so why even talk about it?"

"No, go ahead," I demand. "I'm curious."

"It's like making up for all those years when you thought you were a freak because you liked guys," he says. "It's like a bonding thing, you know, with all those gorgeous guys around you and the music pounding and the feeling of the sun on your back. There's something really tribal about it."

"Oh, I get it," I retort, "like *Dances with Drugs*."

"Admit, Craig," Miles sneers. "You're just putting it down because you know you'll never fit in there."

"And I *so* want to," I say.

"I don't want to talk about this anymore," Miles says.

We ride for a while in silence and then I bring up the Dandy situation. I tell him that the pictures were, in fact, taken in college. What he doesn't know can't hurt him.

"We would have gone ahead without you, but we want your input," I explain. "Besides, it could be good exposure for you if it goes well. Dandy wants to go with *Entertainment Tonight* because they have old interview footage of her talking about Toby that she figured they could intercut."

"Fuck *E.T.*" says Miles with newfound sobriety. Nothing like the threat of a Mary Hart encounter to get you out of a K hole, I always say. "This is prime-time news magazine territory."

"You're the expert," I say.

Even strung out, it looks like Miles may be right on about this. The pictures hit the stands the next day and bring with them a rash of tabloid-TV coverage. It seems like everyone who's ever known Dandy is being interviewed, and luckily they're all sold on the idea that the pictures were taken last decade. Some of my favorite endorsements to date have been from the ubiquitous Camille Paglia and Dandy's favorite rapper Hi-D-Ho. Dandy's first agent, Milt Greene, turned up on today's *Hard Copy* to brag about how her star quality knocked him off his seat all those years ago. He neglects to mention that it was a toilet seat and that he was banging some blonde atop it at the time.

The beaver fever reaches its crescendo when Dandy sits down with Barbara Walters on *20/20*. Miles and I watch from the sidelines as Dandy, in what could be her finest performance ever, opens up to Babs about Keith, her college boyfriend and "first real love," who sweet-talked her into posing for the pictures all those years ago.

"I know some people think it's dirty," says Dandy, while the camera cuts to a shot from the magazine of her straddling a ghetto blaster, "but when I look at those pictures, I see a young woman in love. Of course, I would prefer that they weren't being shared with the world, but that was a beautiful time in my life and I'm not going to apologize for it."

The interview gets some much needed comic relief when Barbara brings up Dandy's partner in crime, Toby the R.A. Dandy tells a funny anecdote about how, to save money, her petite pal would wrap himself around her waist and the two would go to the movies together as one very pregnant young woman. A minute later, as the tears start to flow and Dandy recounts where she was when she learned Toby had been killed in a skiing accident, I'm surprised Barbara Walters doesn't send a triumphant fist into the air and scream, "I've still got it." Of course, Dandy has reason to cheer as well, for it seems like the world might just be buying her story. If Barbara were to ask Dandy right now what kind of tree she would be, I dare say the truthful answer would be, "the luckiest fucking tree in the world."

The next morning, I'm at Dandy's sorting through the supportive faxes and gifts when Jane Larson, programming director for one of the non–Big Three networks, I forget which, calls with an offer to put *That's Just Dandy* back on the air. Less than twenty-four hours later, I'm watching as Jane tells the world of her offer at an impromptu press conference.

"We're proud to welcome Dandy Rio and her show to our family," says the power-suited Jane, standing stalwartly with her arm around my flabbergasted friend. "I have complete faith in Dandy Rio as a talent, as a woman and as a new friend."

When asked by a reporter how Dandy's reputation as a molester of ghetto blasters would affect how the show played in Middle America, Jane says, "Honestly, I don't know. I just know that I believe in her. I also believe that if what had happened to her had happened to a man, we wouldn't be having this conversation. If nude pictures turned up tomorrow of Noah Wyle, it wouldn't be 'Oh, what a slut.' It would be more like, 'Wow, what a stud.' "

One must admit, she has a point. If you had told me back when I first set foot in room 217 that our undertaking would spark a national debate about gender roles, celebrities' private lives and skiing safety, I would have laughed you out of the area code. But lo, it's happening.

Over the next week, Jane Larson and Dandy become fast gal pals, going on shopping sprees, taking out their aggressions at the Beverly Hills Gun Club firing range, checking each other for lumps, you know, girl stuff. Jane's seeing to it that Dandy gets whatever she wants for her show, short of a salary increase, and one of Dandy's requests is that I be brought into the writing staff even though I've never actually written a spec script or even so much as a tag. (That's sitcom lingo for the last scene of an episode, btw.)

I'm in a writer's meeting, doing what we in the biz call brainstorming, on my first day of work when one of the writer's assistants bursts into the room and says, "Turn on channel 7."

We get the TV on and the first thing I see is a familiar face, but I don't quite place it until the words, "Troy Mendell: College Boyfriend of Dandy Rio" appear at the bottom of the screen. Neither Dandy nor I have seen or heard from Triple-Threat Troy since the Dairy Queen encounter back in Arizona, except in our nightmares. I have a feeling our biggest one is about to come true.

"I used to date Dandy in college so I was curious to see the pictures," Troy says, sitting on an office chair, a computer with its screen saver going in the background.

"He's lying," I tell the room. "Dandy couldn't stand him."

". . . and since computers are my business," he continues, gesturing to the Mendell's Megabytes logo on his T-shirt, "I thought I'd have some fun, so I scanned in a couple of the photos and when I zoomed in on one particular shot, and played around with the resolution, I discovered something very peculiar. . . ."

The shot of Dandy and the ghetto blaster appears on the screen, her private areas blurred to preserve the innocence of the one person in America who hasn't already seen them. Then the TV cuts to a more concentrated shot of the stereo, followed by an even closer shot of the cassette window. At this magnification, the cassette's title is clearly legible.

"Gee," Troy smirks, then scratches his head. "I don't remember the Spice Girls being around in 1988."

The rest of the staff turns to look at me. Unable to speak, I let out a doubtful huff and leave the writer's bullpen. Forever, as it turns out.

It's been two days since Troy Fucking Mendell cracked the Case of Operation Beavershot and I haven't so much as turned on the television since then for fear of what I'd see. According to Miles, now that the secret's out, everyone from the Toby Proxy to the Parisian makeup artists (and their interpreters) have taken to the airwaves with their recollections of what went on in room 217.

Needless to say, a "wounded and betrayed" Jane Larson rejected Dandy's friendship and sent *That's Just Dandy* back into oblivion before I could even steal any office supplies. Dandy, meanwhile, has decided to take a little chunk of her nest egg and get away for a while. A week after Troy's revelation, she calls me from some spa in the middle of nowhere to check in.

She sounds numb, resolved to endure whatever's coming her way, like she's thrown in the towel and since discovered she never really liked that towel anyway. Either that or she's drugged.

"You wouldn't believe it, Craig," she mumbles, between bites of what she brags is her third carton of Ben & Jerry's today. "Every person that doesn't glare at me wants to give me a hug. It's so weird. How are you?"

"Okay," I say. "Kinda the same."

"Well, don't let this screw up your life," Dandy says. "Do your thing, Craig. I'll be okay. This is all going to be funny in a few months."

"We almost pulled it off," I offer. "We should get something for that, like an honorable mention for scams or something."

"A certificate, at least," says Dandy, before slurping away another mouthful of Cherry Garcia and laughing. "Done in by the fucking Spice Girls. I can't believe it."

28

Ten long months ago, I made two New Year's resolutions for 1996: (1) no parking tickets, and (2) join a gym. For some reason, I forgot to make the third: Don't let your best friend pose nude no matter what. So far I've only managed to keep the first one because I can't decide which gym to join. Well, that and I'm lazy. I'm on my way to go check out a workout club in Silverlake, I swear, when Claudia bounds down with big news. After a decade-plus of pushing redial, she finally got through on the K-Rock contest line and won herself a free sports club membership to Crunch, which just opened in West Hollywood. Since she doesn't want to be the only softbody in the place, she invites me to tag along and if we both like it, we can split the price of one membership.

"See, Craig," she says, "there was a reason you kept putting it off until now."

"I know," I agree. "The fact that I'm a fat pig."

We pick up the certificate, then head to our new palace of perspiration for our introductory workout. A strapping blond named Milk Boy shows us around, starting with the provocative brushed-glass hallway outside the showers where, if one wanted to loiter, one could enjoy backlit silhouettes of fellow members lathering up their most private of areas. Then he takes us to the spinning floor, where a roomful of sweaty stationary bikers faces a giant video screen showing footage from the Tour de France.

"The screen helps keep people pedaling," Milk Boy explains.

"If you really want people to pedal," I suggest, "you should put the screen behind them and turn on *Sister, Sister*."

Once our tour's finished, I tell Claudia I want to check out the step class accompanied by live gospel musicians. Claudia, who's always had a problem with organized religion, opts instead to sit her ass on the nearest Lifecycle and read the new *Dramalogue*.

"Damn," she says, digging in her bag. "I left it at home. Do you have anything to read?"

Before she can argue, I hand Claudia the latest draft of *Deck Games* (perpetually on my person), then head off to the aerobics studio to step for Jesus.

I forget I've even given her the script until the next morning, when Miles wakes me up to tell me he just talked it up to a development exec at New Line who wants to read it ASAP. I roll out of bed and start to head up to Claudia's when I discover that my entire being is throbbing like a cartoon thumb that's just had an anvil dropped on it. Unable to take one more step, I fall painfully back onto the bed and call Claudia.

"Sorry, I didn't get to read very much of it," she says, handing it over. "I started getting carsick so I set it down." A likely story, I think.

"Wait, this isn't my script," I say.

Claudia takes it back from me and after some serious head scratching, which I would be happy to help out with if only I could lift my arms, she explains that there was a certain gregarious gentleman on the next bike who was also reading a script. When they both decided they'd rather watch Johnathon Schaech do abwork than read, they tossed their scripts on the floor. Then, after forty-eight minutes at level whatever, they hopped off the bikes and, obviously delusional from the endorphin rush, accidentally grabbed the wrong scripts.

Of course, the obvious solution to this dilemma would be, as Claudia points out, to simply print out another copy. I turn on my trusty PowerBook, pull up the file, and hit ctrl-P.

"Come on, baby," I say as though I were wooing a race horse. "Don't crash."

About two seconds later, it does exactly that.

"It was the 'baby,' " I say, trying in vain to get the cursor to move from its frozen position. "If only I hadn't called it 'baby.' "

"You have a backup, don't you?" Claudia says nervously.

"Yes, of the draft before this," I say, seething. "The only copy I have with the new and brilliant revisions is now in the hands of your little bike friend, whatever his name is."

"Angel," she says. "It's no big deal, Craig. Angel told me he's teaching aerobics there today at one. Just show up and make the switch."

I get to the club and curse Claudia when I see that the teacher is not her Angel, but a black woman with blond streaks in a hot pink jumpsuit. I hobble to the counter and ask Milk Boy to tell me when Angel teaches.

"He's just finishing," he says.

"But that's a girl," I say.

"I know," he says. "Isn't he amazing? The first time I saw him all dressed up I actually tried to hit on him. Don't tell anyone, okay?"

Wait, I think. That girl was Angel? What sort of *Crying Game*–meets–*Perfect* joint are they running here, anyway? Apparently, I should have had my Angel sighting at the all-too-revealing shower wall.

I go back to the studio only to find out from a man claiming to be her biggest fan that Lady Miss Angel has left the building. I run outside and break into an agonizing sprint when I see a black woman with blond streaks and a gym bag step into the elevator. I make it inside just before the doors close and gasp, "Thank God I finally found you."

"What ya talkin' about, luv?" coos the woman, in the unmistakable voice of *Gossip Show* hostess and Crunch member Julie Brown.

"Oh, I'm just a big fan of your work," I lie. Embarrassed, I bid farewell to Julie with her own oxymoronic catchphrase, "Peace, love and gossip."

When I get home, there's a message from Miles saying that Mr. New Line guy wants the script tomorrow morning because he's leaving for New York that afternoon. So, with the help of two pots of Claudia's wonder-coffee, I stay up all night re-revising *Deck Games,* trying to remember what I changed the last time and adding in what few new bits of inspiration I can come up with. The next morning, having not slept at all, and even sorer than the day before if that's possible, I drive to New Line only to find out from the receptionist that the exec I brought the script for had to catch an earlier flight and I just missed him. I walk sadly back to the car and discover that I had forgotten to feed the meter. So much for resolution number 1.

I've been to Crunch several times since but still haven't run into Angel. I got his number from the front desk and left several messages but he hasn't called me back. Milk Boy says he's out of town at some fitness convention or Wigstock, he forgets which.

A week after the Julie Brown encounter, I'm at home telling Dandy over the phone about the life-changing spinning class I took at Crunch. Though she's back in town, I haven't seen much of her as she's still in her "cocooning" phase. Still, I try to check in a few times a day and serve up as much positivity as an unemployed, undersexed underdog like me can muster.

"There are three reasons to take this class: *Hah-Vee-Air,"* I say, referring to Javier, the Spandex-clad spin instructor. "He is hot as a pistol. There's a moment after the first song where he takes his T-shirt off revealing a tight tank underneath that's not to be missed. And he plays stuff like the Pet Shop Boys and the Spice Girls."

The word *Girls* has scarcely cleared my larynx before I start kicking myself.

"Fucking cunts," Dandy spits.

"Sorry," I say. "I forgot."

"I wanna go next time," she says after a few seconds. It's the first moderately optimistic thing I've heard her say in weeks. "I think it's time I left the house."

"Now, that's the Dandy Rio spirit I know and love," I say. "See, you're like a Weeble. You may wobble but you don't fall down."

"What are you saying? I'm fat?" she snaps.

Before I can answer, the other line beeps.

"Craig Clybourn?" a deep but breathy voice says. "This is Angel from Crunch."

"You have my script," I say.

"Not anymore," he says. "See, I thought it was really great, so I gave it to the producer I work for and now he wants to meet with you. Believe it or not, he's interested in making it."

I pick my chin off of the coffee table, ask Angel to hold for a moment and switch back to Dandy.

"I gotta go," I gasp. "I'll tell you about it later."

"Well, who is it?"

"An angel," I say, with a giddy laugh. "*My* angel."

29

"This doesn't make me a has-been, Craig," snaps Dandy while we peruse the racks of Junk for Joy, one of our favorite vintage clothing shops in Burbank. "I mean, look at Rosie O'Donnell. Look at Brooke Shields."

"I didn't say anything," I say.

Ever since *That's Just Dandy* bit the big one—twice—a few weeks ago, Dandy has been adjusting to a life of empty days and financial insecurity. In other words, a life not unlike mine. Right before we entered the store, my unemployed friend dropped the bomb that she was going to deal with her predicament in the same way many jobless starlets have in the past, by playing the tough and trampy Betty Rizzo in the touring company of *Grease!* Hence the references to Rosie and Brooke.

"The producers think I'd be perfect for the part because of what happened with the pictures and all," she explains. "Besides Craig, it'll give me a chance to get out of L.A. and get back to my musical theater roots." This from a woman who has been in as many musicals as I have—one—and that was back in college.

"Why are you laughing?" she says, noticing the half chuckle I let slip.

"I didn't say anything," I reiterate.

We make our way out of Junk for Joy and across the street to a similar store called It's a Wrap. We're scarcely in the door when Dandy bolts over to one of the racks and yanks out a pair of baby blue vinyl pants.

"We had pants just like these on my show," she says ecstatically, "but they canned me before I had a chance to steal them."

My sister in shopaholism disappears into a fitting room and emerges a few minutes later, her lower half virtually embalmed in baby blue vinyl. Then she baby-steps her way over to the three-way mirror to have a look.

"Fuck, they're too small," she says sadly, trying in vain to coax the reluctant zipper into doing its job. "I must have worn a bigger size on the show."

"Those *are* the pants from the show," shouts the perky salesgirl, who's looking on from behind the register. "We get all our clothes from movies and TV shows. That entire rack is from *That's Just Dandy.* Anything with a TJD on the tag."

Thanks to the three-way mirror I get to see my best friend nearly lose it from six different angles, each more unflattering than the last. Dandy makes it back to the dressing room before the tear dam breaks, then calls me in to help separate her from the pants. By the time we finish, ten sweat-soaked minutes later, I'm wondering if she wouldn't have been better off summoning the Jaws of Life.

"I cannot wait to get the hell out of this town," Dandy blubbers when we're back in the car.

"Do you think that's the best thing to do?" I ask.

"What the hell else am I supposed to do?" she says.

"I don't know," I say.

"I know why you're acting like this, Craig," she says. "You don't want me to leave town."

I start to scoff but then I realize Dandy has a point. As much as I hate to admit it, being in L.A. without Dandy would be like going to Las Vegas and finding out Siegfried and Roy had gone fishing, like they ever would. Just as I'm about to cop to my codependency, she pops the *Grease!* karaoke tape into the car stereo and starts wailing Rizzo's signature tune, "There Are Worse Things I Could Do" and suddenly, life in L.A. without Dandy seems almost inviting. I think of all the writing I could get done.

Two days later Dandy flies out to go into rehearsal so that in a few weeks she can step into Sheena Easton's saddle shoes. I return home from dropping her off at LAX to find Claudia's door ajar and some odd percussive moaning coming from inside. I creep upstairs and lean against the door jamb, hoping against hope that she didn't go out and become sexually active on me.

"Use your diaphragm," a man's voice commands. "That's beautiful."

Unable to endure the audio titillation without the visual, I poke one eye around the door and look inside. The room is bathed in the light of at least a dozen candles. Claudia's furniture has been cleared to the side and she's standing in the middle of the floor with her chin hanging down to her chest. In front of her, on his knees, is the mystery man in the bandanna. He's touching her belly with both hands while she continues to moan. Stunned by the spectacle of this odd intimacy, I stumble and catch myself on the door handle, causing Claudia to lift her head and look directly into my eyes. I dash downstairs to my apartment, pick up a magazine and try not to look busted. A minute later, there's a knock on my door.

"I'm sorry," I say before Claudia can even utter a word. "I was on my way to go get some food and I was going to see if you wanted anything."

"It's not what you think," she says. "We were doing breathing exercises."

"Whatever," I say. "It's none of my business."

I look back down into the magazine, then, unable to contain my curiosity, say, "What do you mean, breathing exercises? Like foreplay?"

"It's not a sexual thing, Craig," explains Claudia. "It's an acting thing."

"Oh. Who's the guy?" I ask.

"He's directing my show," Claudia says, then lets out a resigned sigh. "My one-woman show."

The constipated look on her face as she says "one-woman show" leads me to suspect that this is the first time she's used those words aloud to describe an event that's actually happening and not one that *might* happen some time next millennium.

"You're *doing* it?" I ask.

"In two weeks," she says nervously.

"That's six years ahead of schedule!" I say, giving her a hug.

It turns out that unbeknownst to everyone, Claudia's been sneaking out to a workshop called "Creating Your Own One-Person Show" twice a week for the last nine months. She claims that it was yours truly who turned her on to the class by bringing her a flyer I'd picked up somewhere, and though I only vaguely recollect said good deed, I'm proud of it nonetheless.

I spend the weekend helping Claudia with details for her extravaganza, a humorous and uplifting look at women throughout the ages being done wrong by the men in their lives. Hoping to tap into the power woman movement characterized by the likes of *Set It Off* and *Tank Girl,* Claudia's taken her nightmare experience with Cliff—not to mention the truckload of incriminating letters, photos and answering machine messages she collected during the ordeal—and turned it into what on paper reads like a dishy and fun evening of Theater of Cruelty. Dammit, she's made lemonade.

By Sunday afternoon, I've run Claudia through her lines a good three times, though she refuses to perform the show full-out in front of me. During the process, I suggest a few one-liners, a couple of cuts, and even convince her to add in a bit about how we threw all of Asshole's stuff in the pool. Now when she brings out the first artifact—a giant Pink Panther Cliff won her at Knott's Berry Farm—she literally has to wring it out into a puddle on the stage before continuing with her anecdote.

"Which I can then blame on the dog!" she says enthusiastically.

"Cliff!" I chortle.

"It's perfect," Claudia says.

Sunday night rolls around and Claudia's yet to settle on a title for her tour de force. As I sit at the computer working on my design for the untitled show's flyer, I beg her to stick with her working title, *Asshole 'N' Me*.

"It's too crude," she worries.

"Okay, how 'bout *Me and My Asshole*," I suggest, "or *Touched by an Asshole?*"

"No way. I get enough Della Reese comparisons as it is."

Just then Viola walks by outside. I summon her in and run the idea of *Asshole 'N' Me* by her. When she busts out laughing and drops the crossword puzzle she's been working on, Claudia comes around.

Later that night, I go to Kinko's to copy the flyers while Claudia works her shift at Zach's. I'm on my way out, flyers in hand, when I run headlong into the show's eponymous Asshole.

"How's it going, Craig?" Cliff asks.

"Fine," I say curtly. Claudia instructed me just after the breakup that if I were to ever run into him I should be aloof, if not downright aggressive, and that I'm not to give him any information on Claudia, especially her new unlisted phone number.

"What are you working on?" he asks, gesturing to the stack of flyers.

"My script," I say, though even a nimrod like Cliff probably knows that Astrobright Yellow card stock isn't exactly industry standard for screenplays.

"It's been a while," Cliff says. "I haven't been back in this neighborhood since I tied the knot."

A few months after he split from Claudia, Cliff wormed his way into the well-manicured clutches of the washed-up nighttime-soap diva Carlotta Cavanoff. Though the so-called actress, who doubles Cliff in both age and tonnage, hasn't had a gig in ages, the press gave their seaside nuptials plenty of coverage, and nobody thinks the marriage is anything more than a bit of late-in-life love for sale.

"How's Claudia?" Cliff asks.

"She's fine," I say. "Look, I gotta go."

I report the Cliff sighting to Claudia when she returns home from work that night. Though she claims she's over talking about him, the number of times she feels the need to reiterate that claim leads me to believe otherwise. To make her feel better, I claim that Cliff looked like hell and was having trouble grasping the complexities of Kinko's copy card system, neither of which is true.

I continue to help Claudia with show details over the next two weeks, in between temping and calling Angel to see if there are any new developments on my script, which of course, there aren't. The night of her dress rehearsal arrives and I've yet to really see her perform it, which I find terrifying and exciting all at once. I'm unable to attend final run-through because that's the evening Dandy arrives in town to perform *Grease!* at the Cerritos Center for the Performing Arts, south of L.A. Claudia's none too thrilled with this scheduling glitch, but since I provided her not only with moral support but some of her best lines, she can just deal.

Dandy's only gone on as Rizzo twice so far and tonight will be her third performance. As per her instructions, I show up, with Miles and Ulysses in tow, at the afternoon sound check just in time to see that *T. J. Hooker* refugee, Adrian Zmed, aka Danny Zuko test his body mike.

"He's a total hot-ass for his age," I whisper to Dandy. Dandy simply nods, explaining via pantomime that she's saving her voice for the show.

When Adrian finishes, it's Dandy's turn. She heads out onto the stage, awkwardly adjusting the body mike pack that's strapped to her back and thrusting her famous chest out past the proscenium. When the sound engineer instructs her from the booth to kindly stop fiddling with her equipment, Dandy emits the most audible thing we've heard from her today.

"Look, Radio Shack Boy, it was cutting off my circulation, okay?" she rants. "Do you want me to pass out?"

"It would be a nice start," the sound guy replies.

While Miles chases after Adrian Zmed to see if he's in the market for a new publicist, Dandy and the sound engineer continue their sparring, causing everyone in the zip code to break into spontaneous butt tuck exercises from all the cringing. It becomes obvious to me, based on past experience, that Radio Shack Boy and Dandy must have bonded carnally on some bus or truck or other and it didn't end well. At least, not for him.

"This is nothing," one of the chorus guys whispers to me as the sniping wears on. "You should have been here when the choreographer accidentally called Maureen McCormick 'Marcia.' "

Dandy finishes her sound check, finally, and then the four of us head to an early dinner at a nearby Coco's. With Dandy saving her voice, the rest of us take turns talking about what's new in our lives. It's an odd experience for all concerned, as Dandy, with her TV star needs and peccadilloes, usually controls the floor. Ulysses, Miles and I struggle to try to make what we're up to seem half as interesting as what it must be like to stay in the same hotel night after night as Adrian Zmed. Finally, unable to listen to any more about my new script, Miles's new trainer, and the new Armani tuxedo Ulysses was given for his job playing piano at the Bonaventure Hotel, Dandy comes up with a nonverbal way to upstage us all and kicks her left leg onto the next table, then leans over it in a dancer's stretch. Since when has the hand jive required such flexibility, I wonder.

When we return Dandy to her dressing room, Miles insists I get a photo of him in Dandy's Pink Lady jacket.

"So this is what Sheena Easton smells like," says Ulysses, retrieving the jacket and burying his face in the armpit. "Mmmm, delicious."

"Okay, guys, out," Dandy whispers, gesturing us away. "I have to vocalize now."

On the way out, we pass Sally Struthers, who plays Principal Lynch, comforting a tear-stained Radio Shack Guy, proving once and for all that her compassion doesn't begin and end with Third World children.

We take our seats in the auditorium and endure a preshow sock-hop hosted by Joe Piscopo as Vince Fontaine. Then the show proper begins. Dandy appears and delivers her first few jokes and I have to say, she seems far more at home playing a slutty teen with birth control management problems than she ever did goody-two-shoe-ing it on *That's Just Dandy*. Though I'm surprisingly impressed with her performance, I do notice that she keeps making gestures that don't seem to be part of the choreography and directing more dirty looks to the sound booth than to her onstage nemesis, Patty Simcox.

By the end of the first act, my head is pounding, thanks in part to the set's garish neon color scheme. I won't be surprised if in twenty years we have an Agent Orange type situation on our hands, where former gypsies start croaking left and right from neon poisoning due to overexposure on the set of *Grease!*

I'm in the lobby at intermission, knocking back some Advils I was able to bum from a stranger, when an usher taps me on the shoulder and says Dandy would like a word with me.

"Is my sound all fucked up?" Dandy asks pleadingly when I meet her backstage. "The sound guy is totally dicking me over. I can't hear myself at all."

Despite my assurances that her sound is aces, Dandy gets right on the horn to Radio Shack Guy and claims that I said otherwise. He rants back some kind of promise into the phone to which Dandy says, "It better be!" then hangs up.

By the time the second act starts, Dandy's cheeks are nearly as pink as her jacket. Still, she's doing a fine job, though I can't help but long for the Scottish lilt Sheena would have brought to the role. Then the oddest thing happens. When Dandy leaves Sandy alone onstage to croon her big ballad, we can still hear Dandy's voice.

"Adrian, come here!" Then a pause. "My friend Craig thinks you're a total hot-ass." Then another pause. "Second row, center, with the red shirt on."

Fortunately, when he returns to the stage, Adrian Zmed has the consideration not to glare at me. Unfortunately, a good part of the audience does not. Preteens are pointing me out to their siblings and giggling, while a by-now-livid Sandy does her best singing of the evening to an audience more interested in the Zmedophile in the red shirt.

A few minutes later we hear Dandy's voice again.

"I'm sorry about what happened during the dance contest, Joe," she says. "Midols always give me the farts."

The crowd is practically hysterical when Dandy returns to the stage to do "Worse Things." As she stands center stage and sings poignantly, I try my damnedest to catch her eye and explain with a zipped-lip gesture and a point offstage that we can hear everything she's been saying. But just as I do, our Rizzo closes her eyes, overcome with the poignant realization that, though she may be knocked up, at least she's not a cock tease like *certain* people at Rydell High.

Either Radio Shack Guy figures Dandy's had enough or else Dandy gets wind of what's up, because we hear no more disembodied Rizzo throughout the show. Backstage afterwards, Adrian Zmed says, "You must be Dandy's friend," before introducing me to his lovely wife. When we finally make it to Dandy's dressing room, Dandy's holding a note from the sound guy saying he's off to work for *Sesame Street Live* and thanks for nothing.

Oblivious to what happened with her mike, Dandy invites us to Jacuzzi with her and Sally Struthers back at the hotel.

"Gloria stew," Ulysses pants eagerly.

"It takes me a while to come down after a show," Dandy says between head rolls. "I go through such an emotional journey."

While Dandy's signing autographs by the stage door, one of the mothers whose spawn snickered at me clear through the curtain call rushes up to Dandy and hands her a bag from Thrifty.

"Midol does the same thing to me," she whispers. "Try these."

"I wonder how she knew," Dandy says cluelessly and looks at me for some kind of explanation. All I can do is shrug.

Back at the hotel, Dandy waxes on about how fulfilling it is to be performing in front of an audience, then asks us whether or not we think she should take advantage of the woo that's being pitched her way by the boyishly cute actor who plays Doody.

"I'm not really into him," she says. "I just think it would be cool to be able to say I made Doody in the Jacuzzi."

"Well, you just did," I say, laughing. "So leave the poor boy alone."

The next night as Miles and I arrive at Glaxa Studios, the small Silverlake performance space where *Asshole 'N' Me* is to make its world premiere, I can't help but be grateful for the smaller scale of Claudia's undertaking. No body mikes, no neon, no Doody. What could possibly go wrong?

The lights come up on Claudia and though she's visibly nervous in the beginning, the small crowd seems to warm to her. When she opens a trunk full of Asshole paraphernalia, which she refers to as her "Given Up Hope Chest," the crowd surrenders its biggest laugh of the evening. It's soon topped, however, by the wringing-out-of-the-Pink-Panther gag. The bit goes over so well that Claudia has to actually hold for a laugh. As the stuffed animal continues to relieve himself on the floor, I realize that this is the first time that anything I've written has been received by a real audience, and well received at that.

I'm about to explode with pride from how well it's all going when Miles leans over and whispers, "Don't look now, but I think the guest of honor just showed up."

I steal a glance over my shoulder and see an incognito Cliff, in dark glasses and a baseball cap, settling into a seat in the back row. Oh, fuck.

I say a silent prayer that Claudia won't notice him, that she'll continue on, oblivious in her own little acting bubble, but between the intimacy of the place and the unmistakable stench of Cliff's trademark CK One, it's not long before Claudia's in on the horror. I think it's all over when she catches my eye and looks like she's going to start sobbing. Instead, she keeps trudging on, flubbing a line here, skipping a whole section there, but remarkably never losing the audience.

In fact, the scope of their goodwill is so palpable that, toward the end, Claudia shifts into a confident fuck-you mode and starts aiming her barbs directly at the man who inspired them. When the show ends and she takes her bow in the Pink Panther puddle, the audience applauds vigorously.

The house lights come up and Miles and I make a beeline for the green room, hoping to get there before Asshole in case there's trouble. While I'm embracing Claudia and telling her how well I think it went, a tiny but formidable woman in a man's suit cuts in and starts singing the praises of *Asshole 'N' Me.*

"I own a theater in West Hollywood," says the woman, her New York accent making her come off as more credible than she probably is, "and I'd like you to consider playing there in repertory with a handful of other solo shows I've got coming up."

Claudia takes her card and assures her she'll be in touch. When the woman strides off, Cliff steps in to replace her.

"Wow," he says. "If I'd known you were putting together a show I'd have knocked you around a little."

"You weren't supposed to know about it," Claudia mumbles.

"I found this," he says pulling a white copy of Claudia's flyer out of his pocket. "Craig left it in the copy machine at Kinko's."

"Oops," Miles and I say in unison.

"You look great, by the way," Cliff says.

"Thank you," says Claudia.

"Well, I don't want to rain on your little parade here," Cliff says, "but I won't allow you to keep trotting out my private life for the masses."

"Masses?" says Claudia. "There were forty-five people here."

"I just heard the woman wanting you to do it at some theater," Cliff says.

"So?" says Claudia.

"So that'll happen over my dead body," he says.

"That can happen," says Claudia.

Just then a young pair of female audience members interrupt and ask Claudia to autograph their programs.

"I'm never going to complain about my boyfriend again," the older of the two girls says, oblivious to the fact that the genuine Asshole's standing right next to her.

"I would have killed the guy," the younger one says.

"Better to just move on," says Claudia warmly, as though she's actually been able to do any such thing.

When the girls finally walk away, Cliff lets out an audible huff and says, "See, shit like that can't keep happening."

"Look, Cliff," I say, shifting into wheeler-dealer mode. "You don't want the world to know you're Asshole, right? Especially your wife. Well, neither do we. So don't make a stink. If anyone asks her she'll say it's some guy that moved to Europe, won't you, Claudia?"

"I was thinking South America," says Claudia.

"Whatever," I say. "But if you try to stop her, it'll be news . . ."

"Or we'll *make* it news," adds Miles.

". . . and everyone will wonder what's in that little play that Carlotta Cavanoff's young stud of a husband is so upset about," I say.

Claudia's looking at me as if to say, "When did you sprout nuts?" while Cliff mentally combs my ultimatum for a loophole.

"Wanna protect your precious little living arrangement?" I say, trying to sound as conclusive as possible. "Then walk away."

And then he does.

30

A week after the premiere of *Asshole 'N' Me,* Miles calls from Las Vegas, where he's gone to help with publicity at ShoWest, the annual convention of theater exhibitors.

"Craig, I've got a proposition for you," he says. "How does a Vegas vacation sound?"

"You know how much I hate Chevy Chase," I grumble.

"No, a real Vegas vacation," he says. "My assistant has appendicitis so I have an extra room and I could really use your help."

"I don't have the disposition to do that publicist stuff," I say. "The second Julia Roberts starts complaining about the cream cheese, I'll start crying. I know it."

"Craig, it's basically standing around doing crowd control," he says casually. "Plus, I have two words for you: Gift. Bags."

"When's my flight?" I say.

Of all the excesses of Hollywood, my favorite is the overstuffed satchels of T-shirts, caps, key fobs, conditioner, CDs and other miscellaneous free shit that you get at certain Hollywood hoedowns. It's all pretty much worthless, but seeing as I can't get a single studio to so much as reply to a query letter, I might as well take them for all the goodies I can get.

A little getaway will do me good, I think as I pack my giant suitcase, leaving plenty of room for all the free stuff I'm going to accrue. Last week, Angel came through for me, setting up a meeting with Kevin Love, an independent producer at the company he works for, Magnum Films. Kevin's supposedly "apeshit" about *Deck Games* and wants to make it but has to run it past the president of the company, a man's man kind of guy who won't be back from a hunting trip in Africa until he bags the beast he's after. Which may take weeks.

So I can just as well go to Vegas since there's nothing I can do in L.A. except temp and alternately envision the following worst- and best-case scenarios: Worst, falling down the Magnum Films elevator shaft ten seconds after I sign the contract. Best, the hands-on Gucci tux fitting I'd get by Tom Ford before the Golden Globes during which he'd spend an inordinate amount of time on my inseam. A Vegas bonus is that I'll be able to surprise Dandy when *Grease!* invades the Aladdin Theater for the Performing Arts at the end of the week. And if that weren't enough, I really ought to check out the Debbie Reynolds Museum before one of us dies.

"I knew it would be tacky," I say as Miles and I lunch at the MGM Grand's Oz buffet after he picks me up from the airport, "but I had no idea *how* tacky." The place looks as though the decorator had been told to feature every color in the rainbow at least twice per square foot. "I mean, women in muumuus could walk through here and never be heard from again."

"Believe me, they do," says Miles. "But I've learned to embrace the tackiness. You're in the least hypocritical city on earth, Craig. Enjoy."

Well, there's plenty to embrace at the Sony luncheon, which is the first big event of the week. I stand to the side of a big stage and help keep the commoners from approaching the star area while the likes of Harrison, Julia, Will, Jack and Gwyneth take to the dais to try and get the exhibitors to look kindly on their 1997 films. Not only is it exciting to be in the company of such A-listers, but the complimentary backpacks rock.

Good thing too, for at the Fox extravaganza the next night (an "on ice" version of their Disney-wannabe *Anastasia* held outdoors in a big cold tent), all I walk out with is hypothermia.

"This is endless," gripes Miles, rubbing his goose bumps.

"I know," I say through my chattering teeth. "Ten bucks says we leave here with full beards."

"And I look horrible with facial hair."

The next day is the Warner Bros. luncheon, which goes on so long I wouldn't be surprised to learn that Joel Schumacher snuck out, took a pee, made *Batman 5*, and then returned in time for dessert. But what a haul! T-shirts a go-go, two hats and a useless chewed-up necktie in honor of *Father's Day* that I can't throw away soon enough. The packs it's all loaded into are finished off with a fetching *Batman* key ring hanging from the zipper that I know some poor sap in my income bracket spent all last week installing.

Back in my room on the last afternoon of the convention, I dump all my goodies into the suitcase, then fill the remaining nooks and crannies with the free concession candy they were giving out on the trade show floor. If the big one hits when I return to L.A. and my apartment collapses, I'll be able to survive on Skittles and Junior Mints for at least two weeks, provided Claudia doesn't come crashing down too.

The last night I help Miles out at the star-studded ShoWest Awards, at which Elizabeth Hurley wins the trophy for Best Supporting Actress for the upcoming *Austin Powers*. Though I'm sure she'll be hot in that, I can't help but think that her finest performance to date was as the loyal girlfriend at the *Nine Months* premiere a few years back. When the awards finish, I take a taxi to the Aladdin Hotel, where, according to the desk clerk, the cast of *Grease!* arrived three hours ago. I bump into the actor who plays Kenickie in the lobby and ask him if he's seen Dandy.

"She went back to her room," he says.

"Do you know which room she's in?" I ask.

"Well, I'm in 1210 and she's directly across the hall from me," he says.

I start to go when Kenickie adds, "But she's not alone."

"Not Doody," I say sadly, hoping that Dandy had the decency to throw the poor little fish back.

"No," says Kenickie, "some guy that she met in the bar."

The elevator doors open on the twelfth floor and the first thing I see is my best friend's left butt cheek, peeking out from below a white bathrobe and moving away from me down the hall. She's carrying an ice bucket and riding piggyback on top of some guy who's wearing nothing but boxer shorts and, I'd venture to guess, a grimace.

"Dandy!" I holler, stepping out of the elevator.

The pair turn around and look at me.

"Craig?" says Godfrey.

My face crumbles and all I can see is Dandy's free hand planted squarely across Godfrey's naked chest. This can't be happening. Everything feels like it's draining out of my body through a couple of holes in the backs of my knees.

I look from Godfrey's chest into his eyes. He shakes his head no as Dandy slides off his back and adjusts her robe. I move my eyes to hers and, like his, they're blinking and bloodshot and guilty looking. She swallows hard then opens her mouth to speak but nothing comes out. The whole world falls silent.

Ten minutes later, I'm back at my hotel, having run all the way. The blood is pounding in my ears, and over the deafening thud of my heartbeat, I can hear the echo of Dandy's voice calling out as I fled. Wait, she was saying. She can explain.

I knock on Miles's door, praying that he's there instead of tying one on somewhere. When he fails to answer, I plod to my room and discover my airline ticket for tomorrow and a note.

"Craig, I'm spending the night at Tim and Roger's," it reads. *"Two chorus boys I met at the Hard Rock. I'll be back in the a.m. to take you to the airport. Miles."* Next to his name, he's drawn a little winking smiley face. It's the third face of the night that I'd like to grind into tatters and the only one I do.

I stagger down to the Strip and consider barfing on someone's car à la Elizabeth Berkley in *Showgirls*. That's how she found her best friend, after all. Instead, I happen upon an open Dairy Queen and order the largest Oreo Blizzard they make. Twice.

31

"Well, *there's* a movie moment for you," Claudia says when I call from the DQ pay phone and tell her I saw Dandy with Godfrey. "I'm really sorry, Craig."

"Will you pick me up at the airport tomorrow?" I ask.

"Of course," she says.

I thank her, then hang up and stumble out into the street.

Getting back to my hotel, I loiter in the deserted minimall and come upon the Silver Bells wedding chapel. Feeling my spirits lifting a bit, I decide to take a moment and count my blessings. I may not have a best friend or a career or a warm body to wake up next to, but I think it's fair to say that I have better fashion sense than just about every groom pictured on the chapel's "Wall of Fame." Except perhaps for the guy in the Armani tux.

Holy shit.

Holy matrimony would be more like it though, for there, in a collage of at least fifty happy couples, is Ulysses, coddling his blushing bride, Kathryn. In the corner of the photo is a date, 07/27/96.

They're already *married*? The poster children for abstinence have been married, and therefore genitally intimate, for the last four and a half months? And didn't tell me?

I consider calling them but then decide it's too late in the day. A real breakthrough in assertiveness, I think. My friend for years doesn't have the consideration to tell me he's a married man, yet I'm thoughtful enough not to wake him up with an irate phone call.

The thought that Ulysses may have carried Kathryn over the threshold of my hotel room and proceeded to pound the devil out of her sours my previous idea of returning there. Instead, I hail a cab and ask the driver to take me to that place with the spectacular view of the Strip where Nomi went in *Showgirls* when it all got to be too much. He nods knowingly and takes me right there.

I sit and cry. *Really* cry. I have those convulsions in my chest and do the involuntary bouncing thing. I spend the next three hours having intermittent sniffing and spasming and wondering if I really know my friends at all. Maybe they are just "L.A. friends."

I take inventory and convince myself that Ulysses and Kathryn probably have a good reason for pulling the ruse and that he'll probably be relieved to explain it to me when I get home. Miles, meanwhile, hasn't really done anything to incur my wrath except be his sexually cavalier self. As for Godfrey, well, who cares about Godfrey anyway? Not me, really. Really.

Dandy, on the other hand, is a whole other kettle of fish. I can't bring myself to think about her yet.

As I play over and over in my head what I saw, I find the person I'm most disappointed in is myself. I've always known that Dandy was the kind of person who would do such a thing, but I never thought it would be me she did it to. I've always taken pride in thinking that I bring out the best in her: the kindness, the loyalty, the trust she doesn't always demonstrate to the world at large. When people talk trash about her behind her back, I can always understand why, but at the same time I think that I'm the exception. She's not like that with me. They don't know her like I know her. But now, I'm wondering if I really know her at all.

The sun comes up and I stagger back to the hotel like one of the survivors in the last frame of a disaster movie. Back in my room, I put in another call to Claudia, my one friend who doesn't seem to be leading a double life.

"You're not a Russian spy, are you?" I ask, after giving her my flight details.

"No," she says, unsure of where this is going.

"Or a junkie or a Trekker or a body snatcher or a chick with a dick, by any chance?"

"No."

"Or married?"

"God, no. Why are you asking me this stuff?"

"Tell you later," I say. "Thanks."

I hang up and smile, relieved that my neighbor won't show up at LAX in the Batmobile, then struggle to close my suitcase and go next door to Miles's room.

"Where the hell have you been?" he practically spits.

"Out," I say. "It's a long, awful story. I'll tell you in the car."

"Because I tried calling you late last night," he adds angrily. "I needed you."

"You needed *me,*" I say incredulously. "I thought the cast of *Jubilee!* was taking care of you."

"Fuck you, Craig," he says. "It was a nightmare. I ended up at someplace called Hal's Dungeon which was really just this rec room in some tract house in God knows where. It was so unsavory that I called you repeatedly to come and find me but you weren't there."

"Dandy slept with Godfrey," I say flatly, one-upping Miles's dungeon nightmare.

"Oh my God," he says. "No wonder you look like shit."

We walk down to his rent-a-car in silence save for the groans caused by the two of us trying to maneuver The Suitcase That Ate Las Vegas. Once we're in the car, I explain to him in vivid Vegas Technicolor exactly what went down at Dandy's hotel.

"So you don't know for sure that anything sexual happened?" says Miles when I finish.

"They were half naked," I say.

"Maybe they were just hanging out," he says.

"We're talking about Dandy," I remind him.

"I still think you should give her a chance to explain," he says.

"They could have caught up with me if they had wanted to. I wasn't running that fast."

"I thought you said they were naked," he says.

"Half naked," I say.

The duration of the ride is taken up by Miles recounting what exactly went on in that suburban tract house rec room. "It was really empty and stupid and that damn Sheryl Crow song, 'If it Makes You Happy,' kept going through my head."

"You had the Sheryl Crow epiphany," I offer, as though it's a scientifically proven phenomenon.

"So anyway, it was a nightmare, and you can't ever let me do something like that again," he says. I open the car door to get out and am about to say something supportive when Miles adds, "Of course, I had to come twice."

I shut the door.

"Jesus Christ, Miles!" I bark, finally unloading some of the anger that's been consuming me for the last twelve hours. "You make this big plea to me about how lousy you feel, like you want someone to commiserate with. Fine. I'm there for you. But you have to end it by throwing in what a fucking stud you are. 'Oh, gee, Craig, I wish I could be more like you, I'm just so *virile*. I'm such a *man*. You wouldn't understand.' Well, the next time you decide to play naked Smear the Queer and need someone to report it to, call a chat line, 'cause I'm over it."

"You know what? Go fuck yourself, Craig," Miles yells, punctuating his ire with a pop of the trunk lever.

I slam my car door, then lug my suitcase out of the trunk and storm into the terminal. My eyes start to water.

Some people lose their shirts in Las Vegas, I lose my friends. I plod toward my gate, trying not to make eye contact with another living person for fear of ruining relationships with people I don't even know, when a golf cart zips past.

"Stop, that's him!" shouts a voice.

Dandy hops out of the back of the cart, kisses the driver on the cheek, then stalks toward me like she's in slow motion. I stop where I am, my suitcase and my heart too heavy to move. With every step Dandy takes toward me, a snapshot of some moment we shared flashes in front of me like a slide show.

"I'm so sorry, Craig," she pleads.

Her face is streaked with tears, but these aren't the tears I've repeatedly seen her produce on cue. Maybe these are the ones she tries to keep from being produced at all.

"It's not what you think," she continues.

"How do you know what I think?" I say.

"You think we fucked," she says. "Well, we didn't. I ran into him in the hotel bar, he came up to my room to hang out, and that's where you came in. We both feel terrible."

"Where is he?"

"Shooting some video."

"Would you have if I hadn't shown up?" I ask, dreading the answer. "Be honest."

Dandy clears her throat, looks down at her shoes and says, "Maybe."

I can practically feel the knife that had entered my back last night poke through the front of my chest.

"We were drunk, Craig," she continues. "Tom Snyder was on and he kept calling Patrick Stewart Patrick Swayze. Plus, Godfrey's on this whole kick about needing to straighten up his image. I don't know what my excuse is. Maybe I'm lonely. Maybe these musical theater geeks are getting on my nerves. Maybe I'm the world's shittiest friend. I like to think that I would have stopped before things went too far but I can't honestly say that."

Dandy sits down on a bench while I try to come up with that one perfect zinger that I'm later going to wish I had said.

"Would it have been such a big deal if we had?" she asks. "You're not going out with him anymore. How many times have you told me you're over him? I mean, if you were to sleep with one of my ex-lovers, I wouldn't care."

"That's because you probably didn't care at the time," I say.

There's my zinger and I still feel horrible. A minute or so passes and neither of us says anything.

"Look, Craig, guys for me can come and go," Dandy says, "but I couldn't take it if I didn't have you. You're supposed to meet people in your life that you feel *destined* to be with. I've never had that with any lover, but I have that with you. If I lose you, I'll die."

The most dead silent moment I think I've ever experienced in an airport is finally interrupted by the sound of the intercom beckoning me to my plane.

"I have to go," I say.

"So do I," says Dandy.

"You know what it is, Dandy?" I say, finally realizing why I feel so broken. "I've always held on to the fact that in a world full of secrets, we didn't have to hide anything from each other. The only secrets you and I had were the ones we kept from everybody else. And now, I have this image of you banging Godfrey and not telling me and then sort of smiling off into the distance whenever I talk about him. And I hate that image."

"I hate it too," she says. "I'm sorry."

"I should have just let you fuck Doody," I say, begrudgingly lightening the mood a little.

The look that then appears on Dandy's face tells me that she probably did make Doody in the Jacuzzi and has, for the first time in recorded history, lost the urge to brag about it.

"Craig, I'm going to call you every day, from every shithole town this tour takes me to, and beg your forgiveness."

"You're going to have to," I say, surrendering a smile.

"For what it's worth," Dandy says, tentatively putting her arm around me as I walk to the counter, "Godfrey thinks the world of you. He talked about you nonstop, particularly when he started getting loaded."

"That explains all the phone calls, and letters, and faxes, and e-mails," I sigh. "He's practically stalking me."

"You don't have e-mail," she says.

"I assume you know my number," I say before allowing her to hug me good-bye.

I hobble to the check-in area and get in line behind a frazzled mom with at least six kids under ten, half of whom seem to be crying. As a result, my head is pounding when I finally make it to the counter. There I learn that my bag's fifteen pounds overweight and they're going to charge me for excess baggage. With no cash in my wallet and no room on my Visa, I find a clear spot in the terminal and open up my suitcase.

I'm about to start layering T-shirts over the one I'm wearing—desperate to have *something* good come out of this trip—but it just feels ridiculous.

"Mom, Zachary hit me," cries one of the moppets from the line.

"Well, *he* kept hitting me during the funeral," cries another.

I look up and catch the mother's eye. She gives me a weary smile, then moves the hair off her shoulder as if hoping it will take the weight of the world with it.

"Mom, I'm *bored,*" says the littlest girl.

I get an idea.

"Hey kids!" I call. "How would you like some Batman T-shirts?"

The brood rushes over like locusts, and for the next five minutes, I'm Santa Claus. As my suitcase gets lighter, so do my spirits, like I'm not only ridding myself of Gummi Bears and baseball caps, but a lot of miscellaneous emotional baggage as well.

"Mom, how come *Zachary* gets the Will Smith shirt?" whines one of the kids. "He gets *everything.*"

"Chad, be quiet," scolds the mom halfheartedly.

"It's okay, Chad," I say comfortingly, looking into the relieved mother's eyes. "I have another one just like it a few layers down."

32

I don't think you can truly call yourself a Los Angeleno until you've played nursemaid to someone who's just gotten plastic surgery. A few short hours ago, Miles had approximately two liters of fat sucked out of his midsection by one of Pasadena's finest. As I wheel my heavily medicated and diapered friend from the waiting room to the car, I try to conjure all my caretaking impulses to the fore, as I'd promised to last month when he first scheduled the procedure, but the feeling that he brought this major, and in my opinion, unnecessary, surgery on himself seems to distance me somehow. It's hard to play Florence Nightingale when you can't get the image of a bandaged Florence Henderson out of your head.

The day after he got back from Vegas, we got together over an endless dinner and thrashed out our differences, coming to the conclusion that we have differences because we're different. Hey, what a revelation. We agreed to try not to push each other's buttons particularly when it comes to our wildly varying levels of chastity. It's been about a week since then and though things are better between us, I still wonder if the Stepford Homo mentality he seems to be buying into in ever-increasing denominations won't ultimately do us in.

Dandy, meanwhile, has made good on her promise to call every day. Though I don't doubt the sincerity of her desperate missives, I have come to the conclusion that these calls are most satisfying when answered by the machine.

I guess if anything good has come out of the Vegas fiasco, it's the realization that I can't go on relying on Dandy the way I do, like she's some kind of upper, that cocktail I need to get me onto the dance floor. Repeat after me, Craig, I think as I gingerly position Miles in my front seat then walk around to my door, I am responsible for my own Movie Moments.

"I love you, man," Miles utters before passing out. Apparently, one of the side effects of the drugs he's on is a penchant for making unexpected statements of undying devotion. I should ask him to save a few capsules for future romantic entanglements.

I get him home and into bed, then call to check my messages. Ulysses has been in Kansas meeting Kathryn's family, so I've yet to confront him about the fact that I know that their "abstinence is bliss" song and dance is a country crock. Instead, I leave another message insisting he call me the second they're not in Kansas anymore.

I'm also expecting a call from Magnum Films, the company that's supposedly interested in making *Deck Games*. If the smoke signals they have been blowing can be trusted, everyone at Magnum has read it except for the company president, Mr. Gunderson, who just got back from Africa and could be falling in love with my masterwork as we speak.

"Craig, you don't know me," begins the only message on my machine. "My name is Dick Smart and I'm the stage manager of *Grease!*"

What has she done now, I think.

"Your friend Dandy has disappeared," Dick continues. "Even though we don't have a show until tomorrow night, we're still a bit worried. She's been hanging out with this kind of weird guy. Anyway, we were wondering if you had heard anything . . ."

I call Dick and tell him I haven't, then get on the horn to anyone that I think might have. I'm relieved to learn that she is, in fact, missing in action. Fucked up as it is, I think I'd prefer to think Dandy were lying dead in some gutter—slain by a *Grease!* groupie for twenty-three bucks and a satin show jacket—than calling someone else before me if she were up to something, which she undoubtedly is.

The next morning, the phone rings at seven A.M.

"Where are you?" I grunt, assuming it's Dandy.

"I'm on the toilet," says Miles. "I love you, Craig."

"I love you too, Miles," I mutter.

"My genitals are blue," he says.

"So are mine, buddy," I say. "So are mine."

"No, I mean, literally. They look like Play-Doh."

"Oh, I thought you meant you were just, like, sad down there. Like me."

"They told me this might happen."

"See, you're already more attractive," I offer. "I'm surprised the suitors aren't beating down your door."

"Go ahead, laugh," he says, "but I've already got three dates lined up for when the bruises go away."

"Make that four," I say.

"What do you mean?"

"Kiss my ass," I snarl. "That makes four."

The other line clicks. "Dandy?" I say hopefully.

"Wrong," says Ulysses. "We got back late last night. What's so important that you have to talk to me?"

"It needs to be in person," I say.

"Lunch?"

"Fine."

Ulysses insists on introducing me to Kenny Rogers Roasters, the country singer's fast food chain, which my friend got hooked on when he was visiting Kathryn's kin in Kansas. We mosey past the flaming rotisserie, loaded down with mouth-watering birds, to the counter, where await a glorious array of home-cooked side dishes, each of which I imagine Kenny had to taste-test and later pick out of his beard.

Once we get our food and settle in at a table, Ulysses says, "So what's this important thing you have to tell me about? Did you get laid?"

"No, nothing like that," I say, pulling apart my chicken. "You would have heard about it on CNN." I take a sip of soda then look my friend in the eye. "I happen to know you're married."

Ulysses says nothing, leaving me to cram my face with stuffing and gravy.

"How did you . . ." he starts finally. "I mean, did Kathryn wear the ring when she was cleaning or something?"

"I saw a picture of you guys outside a wedding chapel in Vegas. You were the only couple on the whole board that didn't look drunk or like they'd just come from having sex."

"Actually we had just seen Tom Jones," Ulysses says, stunned.

My single-no-more friend looks down into his plate and starts to explain.

"I wanted to tell you but Kathryn didn't want me to tell anybody," he says.

Ulysses doesn't seem to want to make eye contact while he explains, so I start to look around the room and notice for the first time that the place's walls are covered chockablock with pictures of Kenny Rogers.

"As you know, Kathryn refused to have sex with me if we weren't married and I accepted that . . ." he starts.

Kenny singing with Dolly.

"Well, it got to be too difficult, more for her really, I had sort of resigned myself to it . . ."

Kenny enjoying a bit of fishing.

"So she suggested we go to Vegas and get married . . ."

Kenny golfing with a black man.

"The reason we couldn't tell anybody is that Kathryn promised her mother that she'd wait for her father to get out of prison to get married . . ."

Kenny holding a basketball with a group of men wearing jerseys that say KENNY ROGERS on them.

"He's been locked up for a couple of years for tax evasion . . ."

Kenny getting flowers at a concert.

"He gets out in April so we figured we'd have the ceremony then . . ."

Kenny, in the same shirt he went fishing in, getting a provocative back rub from a young blond man.

"I was hoping you'd be my best man . . ."

"Jesus Christ," I wail, dropping my face into my hands.

"I understand why you're upset, Craig," Ulysses says, trying to calm me down. "Maybe you could just think about it for a while."

"Oh no," I say dizzily before looking across the table and into the eyes of someone *other* than Kenny Rogers, thank God. "I'm not mad at you. I just can't get over all the Kenny."

We escape the unappetizing omnipresence of Kenny before my goatee turns white, and as we walk through the parking lot, I happily agree to Ulysses's offer of best-man-dom.

Back in the safe haven of his car, I attempt to make some sense out of the convoluted family saga my friend just laid on me.

"So why couldn't you guys tell them you're married and then reaffirm your vows when her old man's out of the slammer?"

"They'd never go for it," he explains. "Kathryn's their only daughter so they want everything to be by the book."

"The good book," I say.

"Well, yeah. Plus, she's trying to stay on their good side because they're loaded and probably not long for this earth."

"Now, that's the Christian way to be," I remark. "Go for the money."

"Craig, she may be born-again, but she's not stupid."

Ulysses pulls into his driveway and before we get out of the car I say, "So you guys have been having sex for like six months?"

Ulysses simply nods. Unlike certain people we know, Ulysses has always been sensitive enough to spill the gory details only when asked to.

"Why didn't you at least tell me that?" I ask. "You could have said she cracked or something."

He reaches his arm across the back seat and puts it on my shoulder. "We wanted to make you feel like you weren't the only one."

His tone is too genuine, his face too serious, for me to say anything but thanks. I walk across the street to my apartment hoping to have gotten some word from Dandy. My phone's ringing when I get there, so I rush in and pick it up before the machine can.

"Craig, where have you been?" says a voice I recognize as Angel, the aerobic-teaching drag queen cum Magnum receptionist. "Look, Gunderson is here and wants you to come in and pitch your movie this afternoon. He's going to Spain tomorrow to get chased by the bulls, so it's now or never."

I finish wetting my pants, take down the information, then call Miles to ask him what I should wear.

"I don't know," he says. "But I love you, man."

"Ditto," I say, shamelessly pilfering from the Oscar-nominated *Ghost*.

After changing clothes more times than Vendela during fashion week, I finally settle on a writer-on-the-verge outfit and haul ass to Magnum. Angel gives me a warm welcome and a glass of water, then ushers me into a ground-floor corner office with a *Today* show type view of Wilshire Boulevard. Gunderson's got his back to us and is talking on the phone when we enter.

"He likes people to look him in the eye," Angel whispers before leaving me alone with his boss. Judging by the outdoorsy paraphernalia and photographs in the room, Gunderson's a rugged man's man who probably plays racquetball during his lunch hour. There's something oddly familiar about the man with the malevolent smile in all the room's photos and it isn't until he hangs up and turns around that I realize what it is.

"Craig Clybourn," says the man who, when last I saw his face, at Pool Aid a year and a half ago, was chasing after me with a pool cue and a thirst for blood. I look down at my shoes and try to decide what to do.

I look him in the eye for the first time when he stands to give me a brisk handshake. He shows no sign of recognition so I decide to play it cool.

"You caught that huge fish?" I say gesturing to a framed shot of Gunderson holding a marlin that's longer that he is.

"Nah, that's my twin brother, Norbert," laughs Gunderson, causing a wave of relief to wash over me. "But he didn't catch that fish either. He paid some graphic designer to make it *look* like he did. I busted him on it by paying the guy more. I keep the picture around as a trophy of sorts. In case you couldn't tell, we're a little competitive."

Gunderson plops his feet on the desk, kicking over the photo of his brother and the fish in the process. To tell or not to tell? Tell, Craig. It's the brave new you.

"I've actually met your brother," I say.

"What a pussy, huh?" Gunderson replies.

Gunderson's smile grows wider and wider as the tale unfolds of how I ruined his brother's night. By the time I get to the part where Norbert's chasing me around the pool table and I literally have to climb between Yasmine Bleeth's shapely legs to get away, Gunderson is rocked back in his chair and roaring with laughter.

"You just made my day, man," he says, wiping the tears from his eyes. "Now about this script, I've skimmed it, but I'm too high strung to read the whole thing. I'd rather hear it from the writer's mouth. So, lay it on me."

I'm about to launch into my shpiel, pleased that my Norbert gamble paid off, when out of the corner of my eye, I see a breathtaking silver Porsche screech into a handicapped space about twenty feet from the window. Distracted, I pause for a drink of water. While I guzzle, I glance outside to see a fur-coated Dandy emerging from the Porsche's driver's seat with an obviously medicated Miles sitting shotgun.

"It's set on a luxury cruise ship in the Caribbean . . ." I begin, my water break finished. It's all I can do not to run to the window and scream, "What the hell are you doing here?" and "Whose car is that?" and "Why are you wearing a full-length fur in the middle of Southern California?" but this is my moment and I hold on tight.

Look him in the eye, I remind myself, then I proceed as though I'm Roger Ebert on a full stomach talking about how much I loved *Fargo*. I'm happy to report that my eyes leave Gunderson's only once. Unfortunately, it's just long enough for me to notice Dandy pulling out the waistband of Miles's sweatpants and looking down at something that both disgusts and intrigues her.

"So, who do you see in the lead?" Gunderson says when I finish my plot synopsis. "If you could have anyone." He claps his hands, then opens them up to the ceiling as if to turn the floor back to me.

"Blue Genitals," I say dazedly. "I mean, um, Christian Slater." I start to chuckle desperately, then prattle on. "My girlfriend calls him Blue Genitals. I don't know why. Maybe she knows something we don't. She's kind of, well, she has a bit of a past."

So now not only do I have a girlfriend, but I have a girlfriend who is a slut. I can't seem to stop digging myself into a hole, and everything I come up with to explain what just left my mouth only makes it worse.

Though Gunderson actually appears to be laughing, I'm so frazzled at this point that I barely hear a single word he's saying. We shake hands again and before I can collect my thoughts, I'm outside on the curb being embraced by a woman in a dead animal and a man in a diaper.

While we drive to the Revival Cafe for a reunion gorge, Dandy explains that the Porsche belongs to her new boyfriend.

"He's a prince," Miles says.

"Obviously," I say, rubbing my hand over the leather dash. "What does he do?"

"He's a prince," says Dandy. "He has his own country."

"C'mon," I say skeptically. "Prince isn't even a prince anymore."

"She's serious," says Miles.

My temporary speechlessness leaves Dandy free to go on about her royal relationship and it isn't until we arrive at the Revival that the subject of my pitch meeting comes up.

"So, what'd the guy say?" Miles asks. "From where we were, he looked pretty enthusiastic."

I practically drop my bread stick when it finally dawns on me what Gunderson said during that Blue Genitals–induced mental fog I was in back in his office.

"He said, 'Let's make the puppy,' " I say.

33

If you had told me when I first moved to Hollywood that someone would actually be making my script *Deck Games* into a feature film, I would have turned my gaze instantly skyward to look for the flying pigs. The only thing I can think of that's more preposterous than *Deck Games* getting made is Dandy getting engaged. To a prince, no less. Seems the darkly handsome yet painfully shy Prince Ramon Gahsid of the Kingdom of Bahrain, wherever the hell that is, has been smitten with the fair maiden ever since her eponymous sitcom started playing in his hemisphere six months ago. Upon learning that Dandy was bus-and-trucking it in *Grease!* he jetted over, hitched his limo to the tour and proceeded to seduce her with roses after every performance, love poems written in perfect English, and the promise of palaces, subjects, domiciles and, most importantly, an ongoing public persona. The fact that Dandy had just been canned from the tour to make room for the "more bankable" Mackenzie Phillips made the decision to wed Ramon a virtual no-brainer, which is one of Dandy's specialties, after all.

Dandy will be leaving for Bahrain later this week to finalize the wedding plans and acquaint herself with the huddled masses she'll be lording over once she gets her hands on that crown. Since these are her last days in town for a while, Dandy, who I'm happy to report still feels guilty enough about the Godfrey incident that she almost always allows me to have my way, has suggested we get together for some quality time before she leaves. One last Softcore Saturday for old time's sake.

"What the hell is this?" I say, looking through the videos she brought home from Blockbuster. "*Princess Grace: An Intimate Portrait*? Jaclyn Smith as *Jacqueline Bouvier Kennedy*? Phoebe Cates in *Princess Carabou*? Where's the titties?"

"I wanted to pick up some tips on how to be regal," Dandy explains.

"Well, then, by all means, pop in Phoebe Cates," I say.

Ignoring my obvious disappointment in the sanitization that's befallen our cherished Softcore Saturday, Dandy sticks the Grace Kelly video into the VCR and hits play.

"I still don't understand why you're doing this," I say while Dandy practices waving like Grace. "I mean, going to live in some country you've never heard of away from your friends, putting your career on hold, all for some guy you've known less than a month."

"I'll tell you why I'm doing this," says Dandy, before grabbing the remote and hitting "pause" for effect. "Because they can't cancel a country, Craig."

Well, she's got me there. Before long, Dandy figures she's learned all she can from Grace, so she sticks in Jackie.

"I have to make sure to get a hat like that," Dandy chirps, before hitting "pause" again and snapping a Polaroid of the TV. "Ramon says I can have anything I want, which is another reason that I'm kind of into it."

I shake my head, then turn my attention back to the screen. "Take it off, Jackie!" I shout, "Show us some bush!"

I haven't really let myself ponder the emotional ramifications of Dandy tying the knot, because frankly, I don't think it will come to pass. Yet, as dubious as I am about the ensuing nuptials, I have to say I like Ramon more than any guy Dandy's ever gone out with, and that's a lot of guys. He's bright and sort of dashing, but shy and totally obsessed with all things American. Plus, he treats Dandy like a queen, and, judging by the amount of time he spends talking about his recently deceased mother, he knows from queens.

Truth be told, my fondness for Ramon has more than a little to do with the remarkable amount of interest he's taken in the well-being of my hanger-on ass. The other night, he actually offered to put up the money to produce *The Last Prom,* the script I started after *Deck Games,* claiming he's always wanted to get into the movie business. For someone from across the globe, Ramon knows scads about Hollywood and its denizens. He shows a particular savvy in matters of casting, coming up with the inspired choice of using the chick from *Sabrina the Teenage Witch* for the lead in *Prom,* when I'd been thinking brunette the whole time. Of course, I realize that there are more shrewd ways for a rich royal to get into the Hollywood game than being Craig Clybourn's meal ticket, but I won't tell him if you don't.

The Monday after Softcore Saturday, my middling five-figure paycheck for *Deck Games* arrives in the mail and I immediately call Dandy to discuss it. When Ramon answers, explaining that his betrothed is off having a hat made, I gloat to him instead. Overcome with pride, he insists that we celebrate my triumph over drinks—on him, of course—at his hotel, the ultra-Starck Mondrian.

"I deposit a check and you pick one up," I quip. "Sounds like the perfect evening to me."

"Me too," he says genially. "And bring your friends."

Later that night, six of us, Ulysses, Kathryn, Miles, Claudia, myself, and a fresh-from-Japan Damon Darlington, gather at my place and carpool to the Mondrian to meet Ramon and Dandy.

"Who does the hiring here, Aaron Spelling?" wonders Claudia as we enter the swank lobby and walk past a row of pert and perky bellbabes.

"I feel like I'm going to set off some sort of nerd alarm," frets Ulysses.

"Just be cool," advises Miles, as though he were a Rockefeller breaking in a Clampett.

"Are you sure it's okay that I came, Craig?" worries Kathryn. "I mean, this prince guy has never even met me. I'm just going to have a ginger ale anyway."

"Never met me either, bro," says Damon cockily. "But that don't mean I ain't gonna drink."

Ever since Damon got back from his stint with the G-string brigade everything's dude this and bro that.

"Besides, I'm twenty-one now, dude," he adds.

"Oh, eat me," I say.

"Maybe," he says, improbably.

It's important to note here that I don't, in fact, have any interest in his flirtation. I called Damon solely because I realize that with Dandy about to move away I need to start nursing as many other friendships as possible, and Damon was always fun to be with when he wasn't cock-teasing me into a frenzy. And *now* he's got male stripper stories.

As we approach the door to the Sky Bar, the hotel's painfully exclusive watering hole, I remind myself of my rule of thumb when it comes to infiltrating environments that are known for their attitude, like say, anywhere in France. You get what you give. In other words, if we're pleasant to Sebastian, the burly Sky Bar doorman, then Sebastian, the burly Sky Bar doorman, will be pleasant to us.

Wrong. After an altercation in which the normally shy Ramon had to do everything but threaten to jack up the price of oil, we're finally allowed to proceed onto the patio. Dandy immediately lays claim to what looks like a parked flying carpet, diving headlong onto the object like a child onto a Slip 'N' Slide. The rest of us assume various slumber party type postures atop the candlelit cushion and order our first round, annoying the humorless waitress with our teen sleepover chatter about where babies come from and who's cuter, Scott Baio or Willie Aames.

"How's your show going?" Dandy asks Claudia, with what seems like genuine interest. Perhaps she realizes if she's going to be a princess she's going to have to start caring about the little people.

"Phenomenal," replies Claudia. "There's talk about taking it to New

York and we've had to add an extra night to keep up with demand. In fact, tonight is the only night I'm dark."

Miles and I share a look that expresses both shock and pride that we've lived long enough to hear Claudia use theater lingo. Then Kathryn and Dandy start commiserating about the angst of planning a wedding while Damon stops one of the future soap star waiters and asks him if they're hiring here, explaining that he's just returned from modeling in the Orient and needs a job.

"You'd be perfect, bro," the fellow Cute Club member says after giving him the secret handshake. "Let me give you the number to call."

The waiter accidentally drops his pen and when he bends down to get it, grimaces and says, "Leg day, man."

"Tell me about it, dude," Damon says. "It's arm day for me."

Meanwhile, Ulysses asks Ramon if it would be okay if he visited his room, having read about the decor in *Buzz* magazine. Ramon interrupts the foot massage he's giving Dandy and happily gives him the key. A few minutes later, Kathryn excuses herself to call one of her housecleaning clients. Then I decide it's time to check out the men's room.

When I return, after foolishly mistaking a bowl of round blue chunks of blackboard chalk for oversized breath mints, the gang is deep into a discussion of charity brought on by Ramon's curiosity about Dreamtown, where Damon's headed tomorrow.

"I hope you don't plan to strip for those kids," I say, before plopping back down.

"Only the older ones," says Damon.

"Well, I help out a lot with events because of my work," Miles explains to Ramon. "But it's hard to find the time. Like I wanted to do the AIDS Ride, which is this weeklong bike trip from San Francisco to Los Angeles, but I couldn't get the time off work."

"Since when have you wanted to do the AIDS Ride?" I say.

"Craig, I've wanted to do it for a long time," Miles claims. "My Nazi boss wouldn't give me the time off though."

"You could get time off for liposuction," I point out.

"Maybe you could say that a little louder," Miles snaps. "I don't think they heard you over at the bar." He glares at me then squints his eyes. "You've got some blue stuff on your mouth."

"Is it gone?" I say, wiping. "I went down on a Smurf in the bathroom."

Ramon, whose head has been going back and forth like a Ping-Pong referee's, finally throws it back to laugh.

"You know the Smurfs?" wonders Claudia.

"They're very popular in my country," says Ramon.

"Well, *there's* something to look forward to," I say to Dandy.

"Well, even if I could do the Ride," says Miles, returning the subject to his unfaltering goodwill. "It's too late for me to get sponsors."

By the time the next round arrives, Ramon has offered to not only sponsor him to the tune of $5,000 but buy him a bike as well.

"What about the snazzy little outfits?" chirps Dandy.

"Done," says Ramon.

Though Miles has barely consumed one cosmopolitan, I'm sure that come tomorrow, he'll be claiming to have been too looped to have been serious about his selfless pledge to bike over five hundred miles, not to mention sleep outdoors for a week, for the good of his fellow men.

"Is Ulysses still not back yet?" wonders Kathryn, returning from the phone.

"There he is," says Damon, pointing.

"I'm sorry, but the rooms are lame," reports Ulysses. "They're like the nurse's office when you went to elementary school but without the foxy nurse. I helped myself to some Mondrian Post-it notes, though. Hope you don't mind."

Ramon just smiles, genuinely pleased that he can bring happiness to this gaggle of tragically unfabulous people that he seems so fond of. Ulysses hands the Post-its off to Damon to pass around, then sits down on the futon next to me.

"You and Kathryn did it on Ramon's bed, didn't you?" I say under my breath to him, while the rest of the gang take turns fondling the notes.

"Of course not," he whispers, offended at my presumptuousness, before adding, "In the bathroom. Better mirrors, man."

Claudia produces a Funsaver disposable camera from her purse and asks one of the inebriated agents on the neighboring futon if they'd mind snapping a group shot for us. No sooner does the flash go off than Sebastian, the burly Sky Bar doorman, is upon us. He grabs the camera from the drunk agent and snarls, "You're not allowed to take pictures in here."

"That's ridiculous," scoffs Ulysses.

"Why not?" wonders Claudia.

"Because we get a lot of celebrities in here and we try to respect their privacy," Sebastian explains firmly.

That he doesn't seem to regard Dandy as a celebrity only adds to the tension.

"I'm the only celebrity here," says Dandy with her characteristic delicacy, "and I *want* to be in the picture."

"For your information," he says sarcastically, "there happens to be someone bigger than you sitting right over there."

The eight of us can't turn around fast enough. I can sense our faces contorting in simultaneous puzzlement when we realize that Sebastian hasn't turned us onto a Fonda or a Baldwin or even a Sutherland, but a Saget, as in Bob, host of *America's Funniest Home Videos*.

"Look, it's just a picture of us," I say, before engaging our muscle-bound foe in a testy game of camera tug of war. "I'm sure Bob wouldn't mind. I mean, if it weren't for people like us using cameras, the guy wouldn't *be* a celebrity. I promise you, if you give it back we won't take any more pictures. This is just kind of a special night for me and I'd like to have something to remember it by."

"How 'bout a concussion?" Sebastian says.

"Look!" spouts Claudia, pointing across the patio. "Someone just spilled a martini on Cindy Crawford!"

With Sebastian distracted by the prospect of supermodel spooge, I'm able to wrest the camera away. I fake to Damon, then hand off to Ulysses while Claudia and Kathryn go in to block. In a rare display of athleticism, no doubt connected to all that AIDS Ride big talk, Miles goes long. Realizing that the Cindy sighting is nothing but a cheap ploy, Sebastian heads for Ulysses to get the camera back, but it's too late. My college crony has already passed the Funsaver, perfect-spiral style, to Miles, who for the first time in recorded history actually catches a flying object. Miles does a brief but funky touchdown dance, then takes off through the lobby. Ulysses, Claudia, Kathryn, Damon and I follow, leaving Dandy to apologize for our unhip behavior and Ramon to pick up the check.

The next day, I go to Dandy's to bid farewell and thank Ramon for his hospitality last evening.

"You're not very emotional, Craig," she points out while I help her sit on a suitcase.

"I'm sorry," I say, twirling the house keys, which I'll be in charge of in her absence. "I guess since you've been out on the road in *Grease!* this just feels like more of that."

"But it's a lot different than that," she says.

"What am I supposed to do?" I ask. "Get down on my knees and beg you not to do it? We both know that wouldn't work and it would be embarrassing anyway."

"I think you would be more upset if that whole Godfrey thing hadn't happened," she says.

"But it did," I say, before carrying one of her bags to the door. "You know what it is?" I continue when I return. "I don't think you're going to go through with it. You'll get over there and not like the food or the weather or the man and be back on a plane by pilot season."

"Maybe," she says. "But you're forgetting one thing. I am in love with him."

"Really?" I say seriously. "Like butterflies in the stomach, shoot yourself out of a cannon kind of love?"

"Well, I wouldn't go that far," jokes Dandy. "That was schoolgirl bullshit. This is different. This is better." She looks around the room and lets out a frustrated sigh. "Now, where's my book about tiaras?"

A few hours later, I watch Ramon and his Princess-Elect disappear down the hill in their limo, then jump in my car and head to Thrifty to pick up the pictures from last night for Claudia. When he said goodbye, Ramon presented me with a beautiful wooden frame and suggested I put the shot that got us booted from the Mondrian inside it. It'll look great atop my milk crate wall unit.

I'm standing in the Thrifty parking lot going through the pictures—mostly backstage shots of *Asshole 'N' Me*—when a jet streams loudly past overhead. I look up and say a silent prayer for the safe passage of Bahrain's new royal couple, and the future of Dandy's and my friendship, then look back to the pictures.

When I discover that the once-in-a-lifetime group shot I was most anticipating is actually a picture of Bob Saget in profile, I'm not at all surprised, given the blood alcohol level of the photographer and my usual luck with such things. What is surprising is what a great picture it is. Smoke streams caress Bob's face and the light bounces off his martini glass like the little gleam in toothpaste commercials. But what's most compelling about it is the distant look on Bob's face, one that seems to imply that all the residual checks in the world can't atone for the world's inability to truly understand all that is him. Either that or he's just loaded. Either way, I have a five-by-seven made and insert it into Ramon's frame.

I show it to Miles the next day when I go to help him buy a bike.

"Oh my God," he says. "Bob looks like a fucking *movie star*."

"Tell me about it," I say.

"I want a copy."

34

Miles and I are airborne, halfway between L.A. and Bahrain (or "Dandyland" as it was dubbed by *Extra*), when he wakes me up from a sound slumber to tell me he quit his job.

"Yesterday," he continues. "My beast of a boss, who'd previously told me it was fine, said I couldn't have time off for both Dandy's wedding and the AIDS Ride, even though I had tons of vacation days accrued, so I said, 'I quit.' "

"Wow," I say, still half asleep.

"What was I thinking?" he mutters.

"I think it's a good thing," I say, trying to be encouraging. "That job was consuming you. You'll find something else."

"Yeah, but what?" he says, literally shaking. "While you were asleep I was talking to the flight attendant, who is adorable by the way, and he goes, 'So, tell me about yourself,' and I just looked at him and thought, 'I have no idea what to say.' Am I so defined by that stupid job that without it, I have no identity? What am I supposed to say, 'Um, I used to handle the publicity of the marginally talented, but now I don't really do anything'? Then he asked me if I have any hobbies and you know what I said? I looked him in the eye and said, 'I like working out.' No, I don't, Craig. I don't *like* working out. I do it because I'm gay, I'm single, I live in L.A. and it's the *law*. I mean, who am I? My whole fucking life is up in the air."

It's an impressive speech from Miles, and one that truly moves me to believe the best of my newly unemployed friend. As if to underline his point, the plane skitters through a patch of turbulence and Miles's boyishly handsome flight attendant passes through, advising us to fasten our seat belts.

"You know who you are?" I say caringly when things settle down. "You're a good friend and you're a smart guy and you're a funny guy and you're going to be glad you're going through this because there's probably something better waiting on the other side. *That's* who you are."

"I'm sorry, Craig," Miles says dazedly. "I was watching my boy walk away. What did you say?"

We change planes twice before touching down, a few hundred hours later, in Bahrain. I realize the princess-to-be made good on her promise to send someone to pick us up when I see a swarthy thirtyish Bahrainian in a chauffeur's uniform standing at the bottom of the gate holding a sign that reads BUTT PIRATES OF AMERICA, written in Dandy's hand.

"Hi, we're the Butt Pirates," I say.

"I was thinking so," he says with a blinding smile and a friendly handshake.

The young man introduces himself as Armahd, then leads us to baggage claim. There's an optimistic gait to his step and mischievousness to his smiles, which he issues liberally, as though they're one of the few things there's no shortage of in Bahrain. His congeniality takes a backseat, however, to the dangerous sexuality that drips off him like maple syrup on a short stack.

"The princess is very excited for your coming," he says as he loads our bags into the limo.

"She's not a princess yet," I remind him.

"I think that she is always a princess," Armahd says with a twinkle in his eye. "She was only waiting for a kingdom."

"Here we go," says Miles.

"Remember," I whisper to Miles as we ride, "as far as you know Dandy's koi are as happy and healthy as they've ever been. We don't want her to freak out and call off the wedding."

"Got it," he says.

We arrive at the palace, a gorgeous white mansion that could double as a Parapets Are Us franchise. Armahd honks the horn three times, then Dandy, looking resplendent in a strapless sun dress, sashays out onto the moonlit balcony to give us an *Evita* wave.

"I'd shave the pits if you're going to keep doing that," I say when she greets us inside. "You look like Juliette Lewis."

"Was Robin Leach on your plane?" she asks nervously. "He's covering the wedding for some cable special."

"I don't think so," Miles says. "I think we would have heard him if he were."

"What about the *In Style* people?" she asks.

Miles and I just shrug, too exhausted to speculate on the press credentials of our fellow travelers. Dandy leads us upstairs to our rooms, explaining that Ramon insisted I take the room he slept in until last year—when his beloved mother croaked and he was upgraded—while Miles is granted an equally sumptuous suite down the hall. Then Dandy gives us each a peck good night, promising to show us around in the morning.

I've scarcely sat down on the bed and kicked off my shoes when my right contact lens, worn out from the trip, takes leave of my retina and flies to the carpet. I'm down on all fours feeling about for it when I notice something reflecting the light from underneath the bed. I reach forward and retrieve the object. Even with only one operative contact, I know that I've seen it before.

"The Heather glass?" I gasp, as I fondle the lipstick-stained champagne flute in my hands, the same one I stole from the set of *Melrose*

Place and gave to Miles to auction off for charity. Judging from the crusty, wadded-up piece of Kleenex inside the glass, it looks like Ramon began his relationship with Dandy's mouth long before he realizes. I gingerly put the flute back where I found it, then find my lost contact, thank God, remove the other, and place them both in a case for the night. I expect to be unconscious the second my head hits the pillow, but, alas, the more unsavory ramifications of the Heather glass discovery keep me up for a good ten or fifteen seconds.

With less than forty-eight hours to go before the ceremony, Dandy, Miles, two sumo-sized bodyguards and I spend the next day being driven about by Armahd, running wedding-related errands with the odd sightseeing stop squeezed in.

"Say 'sex'!" the suave chauffeur taunts from behind my camera at one of Bahrain's more picturesque spots. Though I know I'll be happy later to have photographic souvenirs of our trip, I can't help but think that we'd all be better served if Armahd would simply hand the camera back to me and start undressing.

Lunchtime finds us at Bahrain's answer to the American shopping mall, and dammit if there isn't a Sunglass Hut. As we walk—as inconspicuously as one can when being bookended by human houses with guns—through the mall, I notice that the reaction of the common folk to their princess-to-be is worlds different than any fan-type adulation I've seen Dandy encounter back home. The people invariably shrink back in wide-eyed awe, as though they're auditioning to be extras in *Close Encounters of the Third World Kind.*

"Ramon says that once we're married, they'll actually start bowing," Dandy says. Miles and I share an incredulous look. "And they better," Dandy adds before letting out a cackle that can be heard in the next kingdom.

While Miles and I are being fitted for tuxedos in what Dandy claims is the country's nicest shop, the subject of Ramon's mother comes up.

"From what I gather," Dandy says to me through the dressing room curtain, "I think she was quite the royal bitch and she kept Ramon so sheltered that he had never even gone out with a girl until after she died. I was like the third girl he had ever kissed. Before then, he would just attend to her and sort of escape into whatever American movies and TV shows he could get his hands on. He said he knew he was in love with me when I shot myself out of a cannon on *Circus of the Stars*."

"See how things work out?" I say. "If you had been able to get along with that chimp, we might not be standing here now."

"I know," Dandy agrees.

Just then, a head, namely Armahd's, appears from under the partition separating my cubicle from the one next door.

"What are you doing?" I gasp.

He covers his mouth with one finger as if to shush me.

"Going over my list," says Dandy. "I think this is the last thing we have to do, then it's play time."

I grab the tux pants off the floor and cover my underwear area. Armahd laughs silently, winks and then disappears.

We spend the afternoon tooling about the countryside, posing for pictures, stopping for ice cream, and watching people react to Dandy. As we frolic, the Clash's "Rock the Casbah" plays in a continuous loop in my head, which is odd because I'm not entirely sure what a casbah is. I don't even think they have them in Bahrain.

After a lovely dinner in which we meet Ramon's silent but formidable father, King Gahsid, for the first time, I manage to get Dandy alone in her room.

"How do you feel?" I ask.

"Better, now that I know Robin Leach made it," she says. "I was like, 'Give me a heart attack, why don't you?' "

I just sigh.

"I know that's not what you meant," Dandy continues, before plopping onto her gigantic bed. "I feel good, Craig. I feel like this is the right thing to do. You saw what it's like for me here. It's like a fairy tale. And Ramon said I could go back to L.A. and work whenever I'm ready to. And the next time one of the Friends gives me attitude at a store or whatever I can just say, 'Kiss my ass, skinny-bones, I have my own country.' "

"That's a really good reason to get married, Dandy," I scoff.

"I love him, Craig," she says.

"We all love him, Dandy," I say. "But are you ready to be his *wife*?"

"Sure," says Dandy. "Why not? I keep waiting for him to do something wrong or weird but he never does."

I consider telling her I found the Heather glass under his old bed, then decide not to.

"Oh, before I forget," I say, pulling a cassette tape out of my shirt pocket. "Ulysses and Kathryn send their regards. They had no idea what to get a princess so he wrote you guys a Love Theme."

"Oh my God," says Dandy, grabbing the tape and skipping over to the stereo.

"And he wants to know if there's any way he can use Miles's and my tuxes for his wedding next month. They don't have quite the budget you and Ramon do."

"I don't care," Dandy says before hitting play and spinning about the room like a lovesick teenager to the beautiful music she inspired.

"It's nice, huh?" I say, joining her on the floor for a little partner work. "Though it doesn't hold a candle to his earlier work with Rio Grande."

"Rio Grande rocked," says Dandy.

The next day, Dandy convinces Ramon to let her walk down the aisle to Ulysses's theme instead of the Bahrainian folk ditty they'd previously settled on, and when she does so the entire palace lets out a collective gasp at her glorious visage. An hour before the ceremony, I saw her face literally start to glow—I believe it was when the *In Style* photographer shoved his light meter into it—and it's only gotten more luminous since then. When she and Ramon actually say their "I do's" it's all I can do not to cry at the absurd beauty of it all.

After the sumptuous moonlight reception dinner, Miles and I bid farewell to the princess bride and her dashing groom on the steps of the palace, where a limo waits to take them on their month-long honeymoon.

"I still have no idea where we're going," says Dandy.

"No one does," teases Ramon. "It's a surprise."

After hugs all around, Dandy reassures us that Armahd has been instructed to get us safely to the airport in the morning. Then the five of them, Dandy and Ramon, his driver, and two bodyguards, hit the honeymoon highway.

When we get back to the courtyard, the dignified reception area has turned into a full-scale disco inferno. Tuxedo jackets and wraps are left on chairs as revelers of every age succumb to the celebratory backbeat of Madonna's "Holiday." About the only person not on the dance floor is King Gahsid, and that's only because he's opted to shake his sizable groove thang atop the royal table. And why shouldn't he? It's his country.

After about an hour of sweat-soaked cavorting, Miles and I strut over to one of the many bars to knock back some libations.

"Craig!" I hear someone say out of nowhere. "Over here."

I turn around and see a hand poke out from the hedge and beckon me to pass through it.

"Come," the voice says. "It's me, Armahd."

"What's going on?" I ask after crawling through the shrubbery and discovering it's actually a maze, like the one in *The Shining*. "Why aren't you at the party?"

"I'm not allowed," he explains. "But I watched from upstairs. Dandy was the most beautiful."

"Yes, she was the most beautiful," I agree.

"You are sweating," he says before touching my face and kissing me.

"Wait a second," I stammer, fifteen Mississippis later. "This isn't good."

"I know," he says, looking around nervously. "I know somewhere more alone."

I pull my mouth off his and say, "No, Armahd. Wait here. I'll be right back."

I disappear back through the hedge, find Miles and explain in vivid detail exactly why my head is about to explode.

"This is so 'Midnight at the Oasis,' " he says giddily. "What are you waiting for?"

"I don't know," I say my heart pounding in syncopation with Crystal Waters's "100% Pure Love." "He's really hot and all but it's not my style."

"I know you have your rules, Craig," Miles says firmly. "That you want it to be meaningful and all that crap, but the great thing is, those rules don't apply outside of the continental United States. You've been drooling over him since we got here. Now, go for it. It'll give you something to remember the trip by."

"Yeah, Bahrainian crabs," I say.

"Don't knock it," he says. "They're duty free." Miles grabs me by the shoulders and turns serious. "How long has it been, Craig?" he asks.

"Godfrey," I say with a sad shrug. "Over a year."

"Fuck your rules," says Miles. "When in Rome, Craig."

When Crystal fades into "Stupid Girl" by Garbage and I realize that I could be on the other side of that bush mashing like a madman before the first chorus, I decide that the situation is out of my hands now. It must by my destiny to bang Dandy's chauffeur, otherwise the deejay would have played Jewel.

"I have to make out to this song," I say breathlessly. "Look, if I'm not around in the morning, call the American embassy."

Armahd has his shirt off—*has his shirt off*—when I rediscover him in a cranny of the maze and before you know it we're on the ground. After a couple of minutes, he jumps off me and gasps, "I know a place. Come."

He grabs my hand and leads me to an outdoor corridor between two rows of buildings he explains are servant's quarters. With Shirley Manson's sexed-up wail still audible in the background, Armahd shoves me against the wall and starts in on my neck.

Just then we hear footsteps coming from around the corner and abruptly separate. We're playing it cool on opposite walls of the corridor when the source of the footsteps comes around the corner.

"Evening, Mr. Leach," I say casually, trying to act as though this flushed shirtless local and I were just shooting the balmy breeze and that the tent poles in our trousers were caused by that selfsame breeze.

"Hello, Dandy's friend," Robin Leach says in his characteristic shout. "You seen the loo?"

After pointing the *Lifestyles* host toward the little prince's room, Armahd proceeds to repin me to the wall and grind his gorgeous salty body into my own. Weakened by the ferocious assault on my various erogenous zones, I take my hands from his hairy chest and place them behind me on the wall, grabbing a protruding brick in each hand for support.

The left brick gives way just as Armahd turns his attention to my pants and the delicious sound of unzipping is drowned out by a startling creaking coming from behind me. A metal-and-brick door opens up, causing me to lose my footing and fall backwards with a loud clunk.

The first face I see when I open my eyes is not Armahd's, but some slightly familiar-looking blond girl peering down on me from the ceiling where her picture has been plastered. I sit up and discover it's one of at least two hundred likenesses of this same girl. In fact, it appears that this entire secret chamber has been designed as a shrine to this golden-tressed teen. There are life-size cardboard cutouts, collages composed of shots from magazines, and renderings in every medium from oils to pencil to Crayola. There's a big-screen TV with a VCR set up and a stack of videotapes stacked on top of it. It isn't until I notice the ABC logo in the corner of one of the pictures that I realize who she is.

"Sabrina," says Armahd. "The teenager witch."

"Have you been in here before?" I ask.

"No," he says. "I don't know about it. I think it is a secret place."

I look down at the coffee table and notice the ashtray overflowing with Ramon's brand of cigarettes. Then I remember how gung ho he was about suggesting the *Sabrina* girl for *The Last Prom*. Could it be possible that Dandy's new husband, Ramon, is now as obsessed with Melissa Joan Hart, aka TV's Sabrina, as he once was with the star of *That's Just Dandy*? I get my answer when I pick up a framed eight-by-ten from one of the shelves and Melissa's picture slides out, revealing a shot of Dandy underneath. And underneath Dandy? Heather Locklear.

"Let's get out of here before we get to Morgan Fairchild," I say nervously.

Armahd takes my hand and shoots me an amorous look that says he's keen to get back to the nookie. I follow him into the hall, checking to make sure we left everything as we found it. We slide the mystery door back into place and just as it clicks shut an alarm starts to blare.

"Oh no!" Armahd exclaims. "I go."

He kisses me hard and fast, then disappears into the darkness. When the security guard arrives, I put on my best Foster Brooks imitation, and naively claim that in my drunken state I must have tripped the alarm somehow. Sorry.

"That Melissa Joan Hart is such a total cock block," carps Miles when I tell him the whole story on the plane home the next day. "You should have chased after the guy and gone for it."

"I didn't care anymore after that," I admit. "Besides, I think you're missing the bigger point here, which is, do we tell Dandy about the Sabrina room?"

"Do you even know where she is?" Miles asks.

"No, Ramon was keeping it top secret."

"So, let her enjoy her honeymoon."

"Right," I sigh. "I hear it's beautiful in Salem this time of year."

35

Though she's come close to doing it many times, particularly during her touchingly uncanny Natalie Wood turn opposite Keanu Reeves in the "Rush, Rush" video, today is the first time Paula Abdul has actually made me cry. As she chokes her way though the presentation of the "riderless bicycle" at the closing ceremonies of the California AIDS Ride, I have to admit I'm tearing up over the enormity of the goodwill involved.

I spot Miles among the hundreds of cyclists just as Paula wraps up her tribute and turns the podium over to the *Who's the Boss* star cum AIDS rider Judith Light.

"I am so proud of you," I say to Miles, giving him a hug. "You looked so sun-kissed!"

"Sun-fucked is more like it," he grumbles. "Can you believe Judith Light came in ahead of me every day, except those two days I took the bus? Plus, she's about the only person here who I didn't see go to the bathroom outside and the only one I wanted to. I want my money back."

Despite Miles's feigned animosity toward the blond sitcom star, he starts sobbing uncontrollably when Judith says something about not being able to read her speech because it's smeared with PowerBar gunk.

"Honey, I can relate," he blubbers.

After the ceremonies, Miles introduces me to a few of his new friends, not one of whom, he gripes, invited him to affix his sleeping bag to theirs.

"So much for the meat market on wheels," he laments as we load his bike into my trunk. "I literally haven't been engorged in seven days, Craig, not even when I wake up. It's going to be weeks before I regain feeling down there. Oh, I think I found a job though. Somewhere around Santa Cruz, I lent this guy some of my Butt Balm and it turned out that he's one of the head honchos of AIDS Project Los Angeles. Anyway, he wants me to come and work in the communications department. It's PR work like my old job, but instead of feeding actor's egos all day, I'll be feeding, you know, the common good or whatever. Humanity."

"That's awesome," I say. "What's Butt Balm?"

"Butt Balm is my best fucking friend," groans Miles.

When I get home, there's a message on my machine from the Arizona State University Alumni Association. I'm dialing them back, wondering what they could want from me, when I remember that I bragged about my big *Deck Games* break on that "What are you up to?" form they send out every year or so. Perhaps they're wondering if it would be okay if they named a bench or a library wing after me. Or maybe they want to interview me for the alumni newsletter, in which case I'll get Miles to tell them, "He wants a cover or nothing."

"Thanks for calling back so soon, Craig," says the Alumni Association representative, Rhonda Whiting, when I call back. "Do you remember me? We sat next to each other on a plane from Miami to Phoenix a couple years back."

"Oh yeah," I say suddenly, remembering the well-meaning blond housewife with three kids. "How are you?"

"Oh, fine," she says. "The reason I'm calling is that we were very happy to hear about your success and were wondering if you'd be willing to come and speak about your adventures in Hollywood to our students, many of whom are aspiring writers like yourself."

"Wow," I say, flattered that anyone anywhere thinks I could tell a plot point from a ball point. "I don't know. I don't really feel like I've done anything to merit it."

"Did you sell your script?" she asks.

"Well, yeah," I say.

"Did you follow your dream?"

"Well, yeah. One of them."

"Did you give up?"

"No. I guess not."

"Well, that's exactly what these kids need to hear—that it's possible."

"To be honest, Rhonda," I say. "I'm not exactly some big player. I could be working at Taco Bell next month."

"Which is another reason why you should come now," she insists. "We'll pay for all your expenses."

"When is it?"

Later that night, I'm making a list of points to cover in my speech when Dandy calls, for the first time in nearly a month, to say she's home from her honeymoon.

"Thanks for keeping in touch," I say breezily. "So where did you go?"

"Thailand, Singapore, Hong Kong . . ." she says.

"That's incredible," I say.

"Bali, Manila, Sydney . . ."

"Wow. How are you?"

"Fine," she says. "Tired. Did I say Malaysia?"

"No. How's Ramon?"

There's a silence on the other end of the line, then finally, "He's fine."

"Please thank him again for flying us down there and everything," I say, ignoring Dandy's odd tone. "We had a blast."

"What's going on with your movie?"

"Well, they finished shooting in the Mediterranean and tomorrow they start the interiors here in L.A. They're letting me go on the set. I can't wait."

"Sounds fun," Dandy says despondently. "I never have any fun, Craig."

"What about Malaysia?"

"I guess that was fun," she says. "I would have had more fun if you were there."

"Dandy, there's more to life than fun."

"Like what?"

"I have no idea."

"Why don't you move here and we'll appoint you to be Minister of Fun and we can be like we were in L.A.?"

"I can't do that," I say. "Besides, Dandy, all that so-called fun was your doing. I was just sort of along for the ride."

"Yeah, okay, but if you weren't along for the ride, then it wouldn't have been worth doing."

"Are you drunk?"

"No. I just miss you and all the stuff we used to do."

"Dandy, most of that stuff was illegal."

"You inspired me, Craig. And I'm not inspired here."

"Dandy, are you going to start singing "Wind Beneath My Wings"?"

"Maybe."

"Please don't."

"I think Ramon might be gay, Craig."

"What are you talking about?"

"He gets less interested in me as the days go by. Like I wanted to fool around in one of the pyramids . . . did I say Egypt?"

"No."

"Well, we went to Egypt, and he was like, 'I can't, Dandy. I'm not

Superman.' Craig, it'd had been like two days since we did it. And he keeps saying, 'Mel, oh Mel,' in his sleep. The only Mel I can think of is the fat guy on *Alice*."

"Vic Tayback," I say matter-of-factly. "I think he's dead."

"So that rules him out," she sighs. "So then who the fuck is Mel, Craig?"

I take a deep breath and decide to tell.

"Dandy, I'm going to tell you something that I think is the right thing to tell you. Please know that whatever happens, I'm doing this because I care about you."

"What, Craig? You're freaking me out."

"I think I know who Mel is," I confess. "You know that area behind the palace where the servants stay . . ."

After giving an increasingly distraught Dandy directions to the Melissa Joan Hart suite, I hang up and try to sleep, all the while telling myself that spilling the Sabrina beans was the right thing to do.

The next morning, I'm heading out the door on my way to visit the set of what I've taken to referring to as "my movie" when Viola asks me to come in for a moment. She pours me a cup of coffee, then says, "I want to give you something to commemorate your big day."

"You don't have to do anything," I say.

"I know," she says before walking over to a bookshelf, picking up a beautiful weathered leather script cover and placing it in my hands. "This belonged to Ty Walker."

A blank look appears on my face even as I try to look appreciative.

"He was my costar in *Summer Solstice,*" she says. "The man you were so, um, curious about. You young people have no attention span. It's all that MTV nonsense."

"You shouldn't part with this," I say, holding up the script cover. "You should keep it."

"I want you to have it," she says. "Ty gave it to me and then two days later, he was dead." She looks down sadly, then says, "Ty Walker was a very kind and very funny man. You remind me of him."

"It's beautiful," I stammer, rubbing my hand over the smooth old leather.

"So are you excited about your big day?" she asks.

"So excited," I say setting my coffee cup down and leaning back against the *Roseanne* afghan. "I feel like my life is starting."

"I know exactly how you feel," she says, sitting down across from me. "But you know what? Life isn't something that starts when Hollywood starts paying attention to you." She places her hand on my knee and pats it. "Nor is it something that ends when they stop. And they *do* stop." She takes her hand from my knee and rests it on Ty Walker's script as if to say good-bye to it. "Life, my friend, is everything else."

I stare into the cracked face of my Oscar-nominated landlady like she's Yoda bestowing the secrets of the Force on me and it's all I can do not to dissolve into tears. Instead, I look at my watch and announce that I should be going. I give Viola a hug, then disappear out her screen door with Ty Walker's script cover under my arm and a collection of lumps in my throat.

I arrive at the San Pedro dock where the ship interiors are being shot with a half hour to spare. It was easy to find, given the handmade DECK GAMES signs sprinkled along the way. I consider taking one as a souvenir but worry that some best boy will get lost if I do. It's enough that the signs exist.

I pull up to the guard gate and collect my bearings for the usual security skirmish. Then the most remarkable thing happens.

"Good morning, Mr. Clybourn," the guard says cheerfully when I give him my name. "We've been expecting you."

As I zip past unhindered, the "Hallelujah Chorus" plays in my mind and I smile, pleased that my subconscious had the good sense to pick a song in the public domain.

"Excuse me," I say to the first person I see after I park, a gorgeous brunette in floral dress and full makeup. "I'm looking for the set of *Deck Games*."

"Who are you?" she asks guardedly.

"My name is Craig Clybourn," I say, before holding up my new script cover. "I'm the screenwriter."

"Oh, Mr. Clybourn," she says warming. "I'm Sofia Cruccas. I'm playing Miranda."

"Of course," I stammer. "I should have recognized you, but you're much prettier than the picture they sent me. Not that the picture isn't pretty."

My leading lady smiles sweetly, then leads me to the set explaining they're about to shoot the first scene of the movie, in which Miranda and her new husband, Walter, enter their stateroom at the beginning of the cruise, blissful and unaware of all the maritime mayhem that awaits them.

"Your dialogue is *incredible,*" Sofia gushes, adding fuel to my fantasy that once the Hollywood powers-that-be get a load of *Deck Games,* I'll become the Gonzo Gates of overpaid script doctors. That is, when I'm not creating my own award-winning works. "I love Miranda's first line about the stateroom being the size of a closet," Sofia adds, "because that's exactly what I thought the first time I was on a ship."

"Well, you know, I know from closets."

Sofia laughs vivaciously, then introduces me to our intense German director, Karsten Wenner, before dashing off to get a neck massage from her personal trainer.

"I love a woman with an entourage," I say to no one in particular.

"I don't," mutters Wenner.

Wenner's assistant apologizes for his boss's brevity, explaining that they're running behind, then leads me onto the ship to the stateroom where the scene is to be filmed. My mouth drops open when I get my first gander at the meticulously art-directed set. Everything is exactly how I envisioned it, right down to the mints on the pillow.

I know we're close to shooting when Sofia returns to the set accompanied by the square-jawed actor who's playing the pussy-whipped Walter. He, too, looks exactly as I imagined.

"Quiet on the set!" hollers Wenner. "I'm going to try to make up some lost time here, so let's shoot the first one!"

The crew settles. The actors go outside and prepare to make their entrance. My heart stops.

"We have speed," someone says.

"And action!" shouts Wenner.

My eyes dart directly to the doorknob. After a second or two, it starts to turn and Sofia Cruccas enters. Well, actually, Sofia's nowhere to be found, for she has become the woman I created on the page. She saunters in ahead of Walter and peers over her designer sunglasses. A disgruntled look plays across her face when she realizes that this stateroom simply will not do. She lowers her glasses and prepares to utter the first line of dialogue. My dialogue. My "incredible" dialogue.

"L'Armadio va' bene, adesso. Di temi dov'e' la camera?" she says.

"Oh my God!" I shout completely involuntarily.

"Cut!" hollers Wenner before turning on me angrily. "Is there a *problem?"*

"That's not the line," I gasp. "Um, she's . . . she's speaking in tongues."

"Italian, actually," barks Wenner.

"Huh?" I say.

"Italian," he says, the smoke still billowing from his ears. "Just like the rest of the film."

"I can't believe your agent didn't tell you they were translating it into Italian," Sofia Cruccas says to me, an hour or so later in her Starwagon. Sensing my disappointment in this latest turn of events, Sofia invited me to join her for lunch.

"Actually, I don't have an agent," I admit. "I had a publicist friend read over the contract."

"Bet you won't do that again," she says, and we both laugh. Just then, Sofia's nanny ushers in Paulo, Sofia's adorable four-year-old son, who can't wait to show his mommy the ship picture he drew. As he speaks—in Italian, natch—I'm struck by how much his mannerisms and inflections remind me of a child in a movie. As Paulo shows me his picture I come to the realization that the reason that he seems like something out of a movie is that the only time I'm ever around children is when I shell out to see the likes of *One Fine Day*. Paulo promises to make me a picture too.

"Let's go eat," Sofia says, grabbing her son and lifting him into the air. "They have the best food on this shoot. I had them hire my personal chef from Rome. Yet another reason contracts are important."

We arrive at the buffet and as Sofia hands me a plate, I wonder if it would be humanly possible to consume enough food to make up for the fact that no one in my homeland will ever even hear of *Deck Games*. I decide to give it a shot.

"It all looks so good," I say, "Should I go for the chicken or the penne?"

"Both," says Sofia.

Or the greenest eyes I've ever seen?

"Sergio?" I say.

"Craig!" Sergio replies.

"What are you doing here?" we say in stereo.

"You two know each other?" says a befuddled Sofia.

"We used to, um, work together," I explain.

"In the ship," adds Sergio.

With a crew of hungry teamsters riding our asses in the buffet line, my reunion with my long-lost culinary bedfellow will have to wait until after lunch. We finish eating some twenty-odd courses later, and though Sofia invites me to watch more filming, I pass, explaining I'd rather catch up with my old friend than watch a bunch of foreigners say things that I wrote but don't understand.

"I'm sorry I stopped writing," I say to Sergio as I help him clean up the buffet table. "I just got busy."

"I stopped first," he says. "I didn't have anyone to translate."

"Your English is much better now," I say.

"Sofia helps me," he says. "She says if I want to work in America, I must speak in English all the time."

"You want to work in America?"

"Very much," he says. "Sofia's husband has a friend with a restaurant in Beverly Hills who maybe will give me a job when the movie is finished."

"That's great," I say.

I follow him into the kitchen trailer where he starts rinsing out the bowls. The sound of water running drowns out our conversation so I just watch him work. His hands move with a finesse that says not only that he's done this many times before, but that he sort of likes it. I notice a picture of a house that Paulo drew for Sergio on the refrigerator and smile, imagining the moment of presentation. Why does this smile seem so foreign, apart from the whole language fiasco? Has my world become so small and phony that seeing someone wash the dishes or a kid give their mom a picture that he drew himself feels like a journey to another planet? A better planet?

"It's good to see you," Sergio says when he turns off the water. "I almost called you last night, but I thought it was maybe too much time passed."

"No," I insist. "Please call me. I'm going away for the weekend but I'll be back next week."

"You will show me Hollywood, maybe?" he asks.

"I will show you Hollywood," I say.

Sergio gives me a doggie bag and the phone number where he's staying and then walks me to my car.

"See you soon," I say.

"I hope," he says. "Ciao, bello."

"Ciao," I say.

Sergio gives me a longish, sweet kiss, then whispers some sweet nothing in my ear in Italian. Foreign tongue indeed.

36

The day after my visit to the set, I meet Miles for lunch at El Coyote near his new job at APLA. Before I discovered, the hard way, what a bang-up job he'd done advising me on my *Deck Games* contract, I had asked him to read over the short speech I planned to give to the unfettered youth of my alma mater, the speech in which I basically admit that I don't know a three-picture deal from my left butt cheek, and that the only helpful hints I could bestow were not to underestimate the influence of aerobics-teaching drag queens and not to give up.

"I like it," says Miles pulling my speech out of his briefcase. "It's honest and funny and short."

"Good," I say. "I have no idea what to tell these people. I just want to go hang out at some hotel in Scottsdale for a few days. You sure you can't come?"

"I'm helping out with this thing for work," he says. "We're going around talking sex to a bunch of high school kids who get it more than I do." When our food arrives, Miles slides my speech across the table out of salsa's way, then says, "You know, a few months ago I would have given you a ton of notes and said we have to lie and create an image for you and all this bullshit. But now, I sort of don't care about that stuff."

"It's easier to just be honest," I say.

"You're not gonna tell them it's not in English, are you?"

"Hell, no," I say.

"You heard from Dandy?" he asks.

"Not since I told her about the Sabrina shrine," I say, "which she's probably pouring gasoline on as we speak. Claudia called though, from New York. She wanted me to go up to her apartment and send her more head shots because she ran out."

"Is she giving them to casting people or just like dry cleaners and pizza joints?" Miles wonders.

"I'm sure all three," I say. "Did I show you the Playbill she sent me?" I continue before digging in my backpack for the Off-Broadway program to *Asshole 'N' Me* and handing it to Miles.

"Oh my God," he says. "It's got the yellow masthead like a real *Playbill* and everything. Except for instead of it being for *Cats* or something . . ."

"It's for my whacked-out neighbor," I say proudly. "How wild is that?"

With my flight to Arizona only a couple of hours away, I say goodbye to Miles, drop Claudia's pictures off at FedEx and head home to finish packing. I'm on my way out the door to the airport when Dandy calls.

"Where are you?" I say.

"I'm coming home, Craig," she stammers, the humming in the background indicating she's on a plane somewhere. "It all happened so fast I didn't have time to call. Can you pick me up at LAX tonight?"

"I'm going to Arizona," I explain. "My flight's in a couple hours."

"Go tomorrow," she cries. "I'm a wreck, Craig."

"I'm supposed to talk at ASU tomorrow morning about my fabulous screenwriting career. The youth of America needs me."

"*I* need you," she begs.

"I can't not show up," I say.

"Okay, how 'bout this? Blow off your flight and pick me up tonight and we can drive all night to Arizona and I'll tell you the whole saga."

"My car would never make it, Dandy."

"Then we'll rent the most obnoxious car we can get and tell everybody that it's yours. I'll pay."

"You sure you want to go to Arizona?" I ask. "All I'm going to do is hang out by the pool and go to Dairy Queen."

"Sounds like heaven," she says. "Besides, I never go anywhere fun."

I'm writing down Dandy's flight info when a jarring thought pops into my mind.

"If I drive all night, Dandy," I fret, "I'm going to look like shit when I give my speech."

"Which will make you even cooler," she says. "Heroin chic, Craig."

With a few hours to spare before I have to go to the airport, I make a comp tape for the trip and a sign for the airport that reads JUSTINE BATEMAN. Then I pick up a Mercedes convertible from the rent-a-car place, charge it to Dandy, drive to the airport and park next to a van from *Hard Copy*.

"What's going on?" I say when I see a cameraman inside.

"You know that bimbo, Dandy Rio, that married that prince guy?" he asks.

"Not personally," I say.

"Well, I have it on good authority that they're splitsville and she's on this flight," the guy says.

"Who told you that?"

"Some guy who works for the prince called us," he says. "A bodyguard, I think, though I wouldn't be surprised if he were her accountant the way he scammed us for more money."

I realize at this point that it's going to take a hell of a lot more than a Justine Bateman sign to make this homecoming palatable for Dandy. I rush back out to the car and swap the Justine sign for a change of clothes, some sunglasses and a baseball cap. Back inside, I notice an unmarked door in the corner of the terminal. I open it and discover a long hallway that leads to several offices and then, fortuitiously, to the curb outside. I dash back to the nearest ladies room and, using my phone card and a little elbow grease, scrape the "women" sign off the door. Then I run back and affix the sign to my new door with a wad of Juicy Fruit and a prayer. Please let Dandy be one of the first full-bladdered females to come off the plane.

By the time her 737 touches down, two other camera crews have also appeared on the scene. Bad news travels fast.

Dandy's face is streaked with dried tears when she steps through the gate. Her Jackie O hat sits lopsidedly upon her head with a big dent in it. As the flashbulbs pop, she walks numbly into my arms.

"Do you have bags to claim?" I whisper.

"No," she says. "I didn't have time to pack anything."

"Let's pretend you do," I whisper, handing her a Tower Records bag with the change of clothes and the key to the Mercedes. "That ladies' room over there isn't a ladies' room. It leads outside. So go through that door, change in the hall, and sneak out to the car. It's a dark blue Mercedes convertible, parked in 3C, and wait for me. I'm going to try and get these guys to follow me to baggage claim, and then meet you out at the car."

"God, I've missed all this," Dandy says.

The first part of the plan, Dandy changing and sneaking out of the airport unspotted, works perfectly. No one follows me to baggage claim, so I'm able to make an unfettered exit as well. It isn't until I get to the car, where Dandy's hunched down in the passenger seat, that I realize we're still not out of the woods.

"There's still a bunch of camera people waiting at the exit to the parking structure," I say.

"So let's just go through," Dandy says resignedly. "Fuck 'em."

"They'll follow us all the way to Arizona," I lament. "We don't want that."

I get out of the car to check out the gate I came in from: if it's out of the view of the paparazzi and if it promises severe tire damage to those who pass through it the wrong way. It is and it doesn't.

"What are we doing, Craig?" Dandy says as I start the car and head straight toward it.

"Something I've wanted to do since I arrived in this town," I say through gritted teeth. "Stay down."

A split second later, our gorgeous rent-a-car crashes triumphantly through the lone wooden arm of the parking structure gate. In no time, we're on the 405 on our way to the 10 on our way to Arizona.

"Did you buy the insurance when you rented this car?" Dandy asks. "In case we banged it up?"

"No," I say giddily, still riding high on the adrenaline of the crash. "You did."

I pop in the comp tape I made earlier today and as the Indigo Girls serenade us, Dandy tells me all about what went down with her and Ramon. It seems that after she discovered the Sabrina shrine, which Dandy tells me now includes a life-size wax figure of Melissa Joan Hart, Dandy gave Ramon an ultimatum.

"I said, 'It's either me or the witch,' " she recalls, "and he just sort of looked at me and that was it. That he had to actually think about it was all the answer I needed." She takes a breath and continues, "I love Ramon, Craig, I really do. But he's obviously a little bit crazy. So I went straight to his father and told him everything and now it looks like we're getting an annulment."

"Wow," I say.

"It's going to hit me in a couple of days what's happened and I hope I don't lose it."

"Well, I'll be there," I offer.

I drive for a while in silence then try to change the subject.

"Speaking of happy couples," I say, "Ulysses and Kathryn will be so glad you're going to be here for their wedding next weekend."

"Are they still getting it on in weird places?" Dandy wonders.

"No. Not unless you consider the Ripley's Believe It or Not Museum on Hollywood Boulevard in front of the three-headed goat a weird place," I say. "Now, you can't let on that you know that they're already married, okay?"

Dandy doesn't answer.

"Okay?" I stress. "Because he'll be so mad at me. Oh, hey, guess what. He just won a thousand dollars doing that Internet death pool so they're going to Maui for their honeymoon. He was like one of the few players that got Brian Keith."

I look over to the passenger seat and see that Dandy has passed out asleep. She doesn't stir again until we arrive in Barstow a few hours later. We both check our machines and I don't think she can top the fact that I got two flirtatious messages from Sergio in pretty good English, both of which are being saved for future dissection, but she does.

"It's John Waters, Craig," she says, pointing ecstatically at the phone as she listens. "He wants to meet with me for his next movie."

"It's official," I say when she hangs up. "You're camp."

"Thank God," she says.

With my debut as a role model mere hours away, Dandy offers to drive while I catch some beauty sleep.

"So is there going to be a Q-and-A session?" Dandy wonders as we pull back onto the highway.

"I hope not," I groan.

"Mr. Clybourn! Mr. Clybourn!" she chirps, adopting the anxious tone of a wide-eyed co-ed hungry for knowledge. "What advice would you give to someone like me who hopes to make it in Hollywood?"

"Well, get some tits for starters," I growl, before settling into nap position. "Try not to do it by yourself, I guess," I add a few seconds later.

"Mr. Clybourn, is it true this big movie you wrote isn't even in English?"

"No comment."

"Mr. Clybourn, is it true you stole a fish from Tina Louise's backyard?"

"Um, no comment."

"Is it true that you told Alicia Silverstone that her boyfriend has sex with watermelons?"

"My attorney advised me not to discuss that."

Fed up with my comp tape, Dandy turns on the radio and tunes into a station that's playing Casey Kasem's *American Top 40*.

"Coming in at number two . . ." Casey says with more energy than anyone should have at 3:30 in the morning, ". . . kept out of the top spot for the fourth week in a row by Hanson, are the Godmakers with 'Playground.' "

"Shown up by three moppets whose nuts haven't even dropped," says Dandy.

"Serves him right," I say.

"Mr. Clybourn, Mr. Clybourn!" Dandy says a minute or so later.

"Please," I mutter. "Call me Craig."

"Craig, is it true you slept with the lead singer of the Godmakers?"

"Yes, that's true."

As we pass the state line, I tune out Godfrey's grossly overplayed warblings on the radio and lose myself in the luxurious din and aroma of our getaway car and this feeling of rightness that's come over me—odd considering there's a runaway princess behind the wheel who's slept two out of the past forty-eight hours. I hear Dandy open her window a crack, allowing the cool Arizona air to stream into the car, air that seems lighter, less complicated, than the air just a mile back.

I start to close my eyes, hopeful that whatever REM images appear in my subconscious won't require subtitles. I take one last look across the car at Dandy, that infamous mouth pursed in concentration, and sigh, thankful for the return of her blessed inconvenience yet confident that I won't lose myself in its service. Then, as the cool breeze tickles my eyelashes, a smile forms on my face and I drift into dreamland.

ACKNOWLEDGMENTS

To my family, particularly my parents, for their love, humor, faith, and support no matter what wacky undertaking I was involved with. Though we don't see each other much, the foundation and values you've provided me with help me believe that anything is possible.

To Rob Weisbach for receiving my proposal (unsolicited, of course) two years ago and thinking "Why not?" Thank you for taking a chance on me. Your unfaltering positivity, vision and energy are contagious and made me feel that there was no reason I couldn't write this book. I feel honored to be part of your family. What's my sign? Somewhere on the cusp between *honored to know you* and *forever in your debt*.

To David Szanto: Thank you for knowing my book so well and laughing and crying in all the right places. Your commitment to this project went far beyond just doing your job. Knowing you cared so much, I felt like every decision we made was the right one. If *Misadventures in the (213)* is my baby, then you're the best baby-sitter in the world.

To my agent, Bonnie Nadell: Anyone who laughs out loud in a coffeehouse at the watermelon chapter is okay in my book. Thank you for your enthusiasm, dedication, patience, and for suggesting that it might be a good idea for me to learn the difference between *its* and *it's*. You expertly took care of business, but more than that, you helped me write a better book.

To Luis Barajas, Jim Turner and everyone at *Detour*. Thank you for providing me with a wonderful forum in which to spin these ridiculous stories and for giving me time to find my way. Special thanks to Juan Morales, for your unwavering encouragement, patience and gentility.

To Edward Margulies at *Movieline* for giving me my first break. You once remarked that you knew I was a writer before I did. Thank you for pointing it out to me. I will always be grateful.

Thanks to the magazine editors who have trusted their pages to me and the fabulous interview subjects for making my job so enlightening and fun.

Thanks to the following people who have helped nurture this project along: Tony Adams, Katherine Beitner, Mark Brunetz, Joshua Cagan, Eric Kops, Barry Krost, Sam Jones, Matt Mueller, and everyone at Weisbach/Morrow who worked on the book.

Finally, *Misadventures in the (213)* is a book about friendship, and thanks to the following people, I happen to know a little bit about that. Thank you all for your friendship and for allowing me—and in some cases *imploring* me—to pilfer from your lives for fun and profit: Tony Tripoli, Scott Williams, Judy Hopkins, Paul Schneider, Tom Walsh, Jack Plotnick, Robert Abele, Steve A'Dyani, Norman Arnold, David Buik, Clark Carlton, Paul Castellaneta, Jo Champa, Margaret Cho, Norm Christian, Mike Cisneros, Ray Cochran, Bill Condon, Antonio Cruccas, John D'Amico, Duane Dauphine, Alonso Duralde, Jeffrey Epstein, David Fisher, Denise Fraser, Gabriel Goldberg, Kathy Griffin, Derek Hartley, Shane Jacobsen, Dale Jervis, Karsten Kastelan, Alex Kaufman, Shannon Kelley, Evan Koursh, Corey McDaniel, Scott Meckling, Brian Moore, Gina Newton, Alan Oakes, the members of Off-Off-Fairfax, Jose Ortiz, Stephen Pietreface, Felix A. Pire, Gregg Rainwater, Peter Ray, Renee Rosenfeld, Paul Rousseas, Claudio Salvini, Red Savage, Grant Shaffer, Ed Sikov, Scott Silverman, Leslie Smith, Rachel Smith, Jim Tompkins-MacLaine, Gilles Wheeler and Mike Windt.